# ACKNOWLEDGMENTS

•

Many thanks to Chief District Ranger Ron Lewis and Chief District Ranger Barry Nelson, both of the Bureau of Land Management, who took time from their busy schedules to share some hair-raising adventures and to fill me in on how law enforcement for the Bureau of Land Management works. Any errors about procedure, equipment, and policy in this story are mine and not theirs.

I owe a special debt of gratitude to Tony Hillerman for his help, encouragement, and generosity of spirit. And I am especially fortunate in having Cameron McClure for my agent. Her candor and insights made this a better book. Every writer should be so lucky.

My deepest thanks to the late Julian Battaile for creating a place where writers shared ideas in an atmosphere of civilized discourse, warmed by his gracious kindness, his wonderful baking, and his unfailing humor. To all those people who patiently read the many drafts of the emerging manuscript—to Robert D. LaRue, a fellow wordsmith and master of the well-formed sentence, to Kirk Showalter, who hears a clinker from afar, to Marilyn Slagle for her patient reading and rereading, and for lending me the memory of Hobbes, her cat—thank you. I'll be back. And finally, to my wife, Jacque, without whose unflagging support and patience this book wouldn't have found print.

# SHADOW of the RAVEN

*David Sundstrand*

·

# SHADOW

## of the

# RAVEN

THOMAS DUNNE BOOKS

ST. MARTIN'S MINOTAUR

NEW YORK

THOMAS DUNNE BOOKS.
An imprint of St. Martin's Press.

www.thomasdunnebooks.com
www.minotaurbooks.com

Book design by Jonathan Bennett

Library of Congress Cataloging-in-Publication Data

Sundstrand, David.
    Shadow of the raven / David Sundstrand.
      p. cm.
    ISBN-13: 978-0-312-36135-8
    ISBN-10: 0-312-36135-1
    1. Mojave Desert (Calif.)—Fiction.   I. Title.

PS3619.U563S53 2007
813'.6—dc22

               2006050916

First Edition: February 2007

10  9  8  7  6  5  4  3  2  1

For the late Lewis Stokem, who loved the Mojave Desert almost as much as winning a game of snooker. Forever in our memory.

# AUTHOR'S NOTE

•

I spoke with many men and women who work for the Bureau of Land Management. Three things struck me. The rangers work without backup, where cell phones don't reach and rules don't apply. Dangerous stuff. All the people who work for the BLM are caught in the middle of powerful social and political forces that tug them this way and that. They are often the subject of blame, but rarely the subject of praise. Yet despite frequently being targeted for public bashing, these people love their work and the lands they protect. We owe them a debt of thanks.

# SHADOW of the RAVEN

# I

•

Finding another dead body ruined Frank Flynn's day off. He had planned to hike up to the spring, watch the bighorn sheep, maybe take a picture or two. But that was out of the question now. The air stank of rotting flesh.

This was the third corpse in six months, and he knew that he would again be the butt of black humor back at the Bureau of Land Management station in Ridgecrest. He didn't need this. First the guy in the motor home and then the "mummy."

After two months' worth of needling about the mummy, the Boris Karloff stuff had finally tailed off. He'd come across the mummy at the bottom of one of the many abandoned mine shafts that dotted the Mojave Desert. A desiccated corpse, the skin like parchment, dead for more than a year.

But this corpse was swollen, discolored, and putrid. The body lay propped between the canyon wall and a wedge of sharp rock that protruded from the sandy wash like the fin of some huge black shark. The facial features were no longer recognizable, the purplish skin fissured with dark cracks. The torso was shirtless, the legs stretched out in front at a thirty-degree angle. Ravens had been at the eyes, nose, and feet. Bare feet—odd, where were his boots?

Frank scanned the immediate area. A camouflage fatigue cap lay in the sand near the base of the canyon wall. Otherwise, there was nothing except the dead guy. Very dumb, if he had decided to go on a summer walk in the Mojave Desert without shirt or shoes. Frank didn't think he had. He looked at the feet again. Where the ravens had been at them, the toe bones protruded from the swollen flesh like blackened twigs.

He took a kerchief from his pants pocket, moistened it with water from his canteen, and tied it over his nose and mouth, bandit-style. Holding his breath, he bent over the corpse and examined it with care. The splits and cracks in the soles of the feet had apparently happened before death. They were packed with sand and dirt. It must have been difficult and painful to walk on those damaged feet.

He thought about the forced marches in basic training, his feet crammed into the stiff new leather boots. He'd had to soak his feet to get his socks off, glued to his skin with dried blood, but this must have been worse, much worse.

He spotted a remnant of cloth clinging to the top of the right foot. Evidently, the dead man had tried to wrap his feet, probably with the missing shirt, but where were the boots? For that matter, he seemed to be wholly without the barest essentials of survival. No canteen. No pack. No boots. Apparently, he had been coming down the canyon. It was difficult to tell for sure. There were too many tracks, but in Frank's experience, people tended to die facing in the direction they were traveling, incomplete journeys. The dead man's journey had ended here in Surprise Canyon, next to petroglyphs of bighorn sheep and the stick figures of dancing hunters in frozen pursuit.

Flynn unsnapped his cell phone and punched in the number for headquarters. He'd brought the phone along this time despite the fact that it was usually useless in the canyons.

"This is Flynn."

"What's up, Frank? This is supposed to be your day off." She was barely coming in.

"Mmm, Lynn, tell Dave I need to talk with him."

"What's the matter, Frank? You stumble on some Manson left-overs?" It was starting already, even before he'd made his report. The Manson family had come to the Mojave for some private togetherness before their Hollywood fling, and now there were as many stories of encounters with Charlie and company among the desert denizens as there were sightings of Elvis in Las Vegas.

"Lynn, please tell Meecham I need to talk with him."

"Right away, Officer Flynn."

She sounded huffy. Well, now wasn't the time. Frank hiked a few yards up the canyon, away from the corpse. The sun hadn't crested the Panamints yet, but it was beginning to be hot. It would reach the low hundreds down in the Panamint Valley, and in Badwater, at the very bottom of Death Valley, it would approach 120 degrees. Mid-September, it was just beginning to cool off.

"Frank, Dave here. What's up?" Meecham's voice sounded guarded.

"I'm a couple miles up into Surprise Canyon from the end of the jeep track. Umm, Dave, there's a dead guy here. Looks to be gone for quite a while, maybe a week. It's kinda messy, Dave." Flynn paused.

"You kidding around, Frank?"

Flynn sighed. "I wish I were, but I'm not. There's a dead guy here without shirt or shoes, but it looks like he got here under his own power. Give the Sheriff's a call and find out what they want me to do. I think they ought to take a look."

"That's up to them, Frank. They'll have to send someone from the coroner's office to pick up the body, but you'll have to show them where it is. You'd better come on in, so you can be here when they show up."

More than an hour's drive to the Bureau of Land Management headquarters in Ridgecrest. "This is my day off, Dave. Send Sierra or Wilson. The dead guy's not hard to find. Hike up Surprise Canyon until you see him sitting in the sand, wondering why he can't see his toes. If they don't see him, they'll sure as hell smell him. He's wearing eau de fetid flesh. A little dab'll do ya."

"Come again?"

"Couldn't miss him in the dark, Dave. He stinks."

"Sierra and Wilson don't like dead guys. That seems to be your department, Frank." Meecham paused. "The thing is, you know where he is for sure. I don't want the guys from the county wandering around the desert looking for a body we can't find. So it's on you, Flynn. When do you think you can get here?"

No more "Frank," just "Flynn" now. He glanced at his watch:

7:23. He looked up the sandy floor of the canyon, wondering what else was up there by the spring.

"I don't think this is all of it. I'm going to hike on up to the spring. Why don't you have our county law-enforcement brethren bring the body baggers and meet me where the jeep trail joins the power-line road. I'll be waiting for them at about . . ." He stopped to calculate. If he moved fast, two hours to the spring, some time to look around up there, then an hour and a half back to his truck. Another fifteen minutes of driving. "Say around twelve. As long as they don't send up a couple of pudgy puffers, everyone should be out by dark."

Meecham's voice sounded wary. "Sheriff's are not going to like this much, Frank."

Flynn started up the canyon, holding the phone to his ear. "Dave, what if there's another body up there? Something's not right. With all due respect for our brothers in uniform, can you picture a couple of Inyo County's finest hiking up Surprise Canyon to take a look around? Only if we had a complaint about naked hippie girls exposing themselves for passersby and handing out fruit." He waited, no response. "On the other hand, what if some civilian finds another rotting corpse up in the canyon? We'd look pretty damn derelict."

He'd played the "civilian" card. As the district ranger, Meecham hated the idea of civilians making the Bureau of Land Management look inept. He'd been especially sensitive since the *Los Angeles Times* had done an article that suggested that the BLM was a poor steward of public lands, more interested in grazing rights and mining interests than in the ecological health of the millions of acres over which it presided.

Outside criticism was one of Meecham's hot buttons. Nobody liked it much, but knowing the tender spots was damned handy when your superior needed a nudge into taking the initiative, or, to be more accurate, in letting him think he was taking the initiative.

"Okay, but don't screw up. Don't leave the county guys cooking in the sun. Let's get the stiff to the coroner, and let's get it done before dark."

"Thanks, Dave. It'll get done. I'll call when I get back into phone range, which won't be for a few hours."

•

The decapitated remains of a ram lay about twenty feet from the spring. It had been trying for the steep talus slope before being cut down. Near the pool, toppled on its side, lay an older ram with battered horns, the forelegs still partially folded back from where it had knelt to drink. Dried blood caked its right flank.

Frank closed his eyes, the sickening sight of the slaughtered sheep vivid in his mind's eye. Why were the sights of death and destruction so permanently imprinted? Some primitive survival response cataloging scenes of violence for easy access to the memory. *¡Peligro, hombre!* Danger! Look out! *La jornada de la muerte termina aquí.* The journey of death ends here. He felt the hair on the back of his neck lift. Was he alone?

Moving only his eyes first, and then slowly turning his head, he carefully surveyed the small spring-fed meadow that gave Surprise Canyon its name. He looked along the ridge lines of the canyon walls and then above the cliff face where the spring slipped over a rocky shelf in a shower of cool water into the pool below. Only then did he allow himself to approach the spring and return his attention to the detritus of death.

Frank recognized the ram's dark saddle of wool and the broomed horns. His breath came in quick gasps. For a few moments, he was seized by a ragged rage. He had watched this old ram's comings and goings for more than three years. It was one of his old friends, but its huge horns had marked it for death. But why hadn't the hunter taken the head?

The mayhem at the spring provided few answers and raised more questions. Obviously, the dead guy down the canyon had been a poacher. These animals had been butchered. Probably taken down with an automatic rifle. There weren't many hunters left who followed the old codes. This sorry excuse for a sportsman hadn't even made a pretense.

Possibly the dead guy was a headhunter for one of the taxidermists who doctored up heads or sold trophies to instant sportsmen too busy to hunt their own. He'd heard of it, even seen the results: trophy horns taken from an old ram long dead from natural causes, remounted on the head of a ewe killed for her skull and skin. Ready-made trophies were even easier to come by than the sad results of the guaranteed hunts provided by unscrupulous guides. Must be a wonderful sight, hunters blasting away at animals released from pens, so tranquilized that they could hardly walk.

Or maybe the guy was just another jerk who lived by the credo that defied nature: If it moves, shoot it. If it's green, cut it down. If it's brown, burn it. There were enough of those good citizens to last a lifetime. But if the poacher had been taking heads for sale, why had he left the head on the big ram? It was a head that would have made the "book." Frank squatted in front of the head, trying not to breathe the stink of dead flesh. It was bad, but not as bad as the smell of dead *Homo sapiens,* which somehow seemed to evoke a repulsion bordering on the primeval.

The ram's right horn had been "broomed" back about two or three inches where it had curled up, obstructing his vision. Many old rams had broomed tips. The big rams did this themselves, rubbing the points of their horns against the rocks to remove the horn tip blocking their line of sight. They depended almost entirely on their keen vision to elude predators. A ram whose vision was obstructed was a ram with a short lease on life. So nature had developed this way of compensating the dominant rams with huge horns. The broomed tips frustrated the trophy hunters who sought to make the record book and decorate their dens with perfect horns, but there was an easy solution for one-trip hunters—epoxy and fiberglass. If the taxidermist was good, only an expert could detect the fraud.

Frank saw that the left horn had been badly damaged, four or five inches of the tip broken away and part of the central horn mass shattered and split. Not too unusual for these old rams to have scars from mating battles, but this damage was recent. Chunks of horn had been torn away, leaving jagged craters and sharp edges that showed no signs of wear. Most likely, the damage to the horn had been done by the poacher, the horn smashed by rifle fire. The bodies of the downed sheep were too bloated to determine easily how many times they had been hit, but it was obvious that the corpse of the headless ram had been shot to hell.

Frank poked around in the sandy dirt of the rock blind where the poacher had hidden. There was empty brass all over the ground, bright, shiny brass from a .223. Must have let off a thirty-round clip, he thought. It looked as if the poacher had hidden at the far point of the blind and let go when the sheep had come down to drink. Why had he been at the end of the blind, away from the spring? The point had been to kill sheep, so why not be even closer? He walked over to the near end of the blind and examined the ground.

The sandy soil was shaped into a smooth concave depression about two feet from the wall. It would just fit someone's butt if he were sitting facing the spring. A butt print. He wondered how that would play in court. He smiled, the corners of his mouth tugged down as he imagined the scenario. And how do you know, Officer Flynn, that this individual is the perpetrator of this hideous slaughter? We have a positive butt print, Your Honor. It's a forensic technique recently developed by the FBI. It's how we identify the real assholes, Your Honor.

Still, it was definitely a butt print, and it was out of place unless there had been a second guy, a live guy who got away. A second guy might explain a lot. He poked around in the soft sand. Nothing. Then he spotted a glint of metallic reflection coming from the base of a brass casing. He pulled it from a sandy footprint; the boot had probably embedded it in the soil. A .300 Magnum. A bit more than needed for bighorns, but it had stopping power and a flat trajectory. Still, it struck Frank as overkill. The second-guy theory seemed confirmed. Maybe the second man knew what had happened to his partner's foot gear. Then again, maybe the dead guy had simply changed positions. Changed weapons?

Frank looked at his watch. It was 10:18. There wasn't any time left if he was going to meet the county guys on time. He'd already spent almost an hour looking around. Officially, the poaching problem was California Fish and Game's. BLM watched over the land but not the animals; they belonged to the state of California. The dead guy was the county's problem. But when something happened on BLM land, it was more than likely that BLM would be first on the scene. Frank wanted more time to poke around. Something was missing. There was a real possibility the dead guy had not been alone. He was also pretty sure that this was going to be a closed book.

But if there was another sheep killer wandering around the Mojave, Frank was going to do his best to make sure he got the trophy he deserved anyhow—at least a fine and some humiliation. Poachers never seemed to serve any real time. As far as Frank was concerned, nobody could give poachers what they deserved and stay on the right side of the law.

He was going to have to make tracks in order to meet the county guys on time.

●

It had not gone well. Why had they sent people so unused to being out in the desert? The county people hadn't been ready for a long walk in the desert sun. By the time they had reached the body (and that had taken almost two hours longer than Frank had estimated), the guys from the coroner's office had emptied their canteens and were eying his with undisguised desperation. Frank rationed out his water, sharing it with them. Deputy Harris of the Inyo County Sheriff's Department managed on his own, grimly sucking on the pebble that Frank suggested he put in his mouth to stimulate saliva.

By the time they bagged the body, it was past four o'clock, and Frank's plans of talking the deputy into returning to the spring to look around vaporized. "What the hell for, Flynn? If there is a crime scene, it's right here. And I'm not saying there's a crime. If an autopsy shows that there's been foul play, we'll search for a perp." Harris smirked. Frank kept his face blank. It was something he was good at. It caused people to underestimate him, become careless about what they said.

"The point is, Flynn, there's no way in hell I'm hiking around in this heat to go look at dead sheep and butt prints." Frank had shared his suspicions about a second guy, and Harris had said, "Butt print. Jesus, Flynn. What are you, an expert on butt prints? Does BLM have a butt-print file? The dead sheep are for Fish and Game. The dead guy's ours. So your worries are over, Flynn. None of this shit is in your jurisdiction."

Already, Frank wished he hadn't brought it up. Harris kept mumbling about butt prints all the way back to the vehicles. Somehow, Frank knew the word would get back to the BLM station in Ridgecrest. He could see Sierra's grinning face now, imagine him saying, Hey, it's Cisco Flynn, the world's only forensic buttologist. It wasn't the ribbing itself that would bother him but the invasion of his privacy. It was like pointing. His mother's people didn't point. It was considered more than rude, a personal violation. He'd have to learn to keep a lower profile, but the blood of Francis Flynn flowed in his veins, ever the Irish rebel. It was Frank's heritage, although he didn't pursue it as noisily as his father had.

Something about Frank's sense of discomfort made him a target for the wise guys like Sierra. Well, if he got lucky, maybe Deputy Harris would be too tired and thirsty from his hike in the sun to indulge in cop talk. Maybe something else would come along to occupy Sierra's talent for stand-up comedy. Still, he couldn't help wondering about the possibility of a second guy. He'd have to go back and take another look around. He could check out some of the watering holes on his time off and see if there was any talk. The desert was a big place with few people. The word spread magically from bar to bar. Stories of felonious frolics and sexual adventures were the stuff of barroom conversation. He could count on saloon gossip to keep him informed. The booze grapevine was quicker than the wire service.

There were a couple of places he particularly wanted to check out. He'd heard that some odd characters had bought the bar in Red Mountain. He'd seen the sign announcing UNDER NEW MANAGEMENT. GOOD FOOD AND DRINK NOW AVAILABLE. Time to pay a visit and see what kind of crazy person would buy a place named the Joshua Tree

Athletic Club. No surprise there really. The Mojave was full of crazy people. Hell, he was living proof, an Irish mestizo living in a Southern Pacific caboose. No wonder Mary Alice had left him and gone back to L.A.

# 2

•

Roy Miller had been chasing around the desert bars looking for his brother Donnie for three long days. Hickey and Jason weren't ideal traveling companions, a pothead and a loose cannon. He'd started with Donnie's favorite hangouts in Victorville and then began working his way up 395, the north-south highway stretching from the Mexican border to Canada along the east side of the Sierra Nevada and the Cascade mountain ranges. Where the highway spilled into the Mojave Desert and up into the Owens River Valley, it was mostly a two-lane ribbon of blacktop, shimmering in the summer heat, buckling and cracking in the dry cold of winter: Biker Alley.

Roy leaned his Harley into the sweeping exit curve from I-15 onto the old road, keeping an eye out for the speed traps on the downhill slope leading into Adelanto. Tracts of tiny houses huddled against the perpetual wind funneling through the pass. Strings of real estate pennants snapped and fluttered in the sandy gusts, an indication of what life might be like in a wind tunnel. The great sprawl of Southern California crept into the southern Mojave like a skin growth. People made the fifty-plus-mile commute from Victorville over the Cajon Pass into the conglomerate of borderless suburbs of greater Los Angeles in exchange for the promise of home ownership, the American dream marooned on a chunk of desert. Roy despised it. The real desert didn't begin until he passed the truck stops and twenty-four-hour "food marts" clustered around Kramer Corners. Only then did he feel the freedom to do as he damn well pleased—no towns, no cops.

After the federal prison at Boron, there was nothing until Red Mountain. Red Mountain was a leftover from another era, a ghost town wheezing its last gasp of atrophied life in the hot breath of the northern Mojave Desert.

In Roy's hierarchy of useful things, geezers were smelly, full of crap, and broke, not worth his attention, unlike duffers. Duffers were old guys in white poly pants, basket-weave loafers, and shirts with little animals on them. Duffers were full of economic potential. Menacing for money meant mixing business with pleasure, an opportunity crafted for someone like Roy. He smiled to himself, keeping his mouth closed against the wind. Having a biker bodyguard was like having brass balls.

As they approached Red Mountain, Roy eased back on the Harley's throttle and pulled into a dirt lot next to the Joshua Tree Athletic Club, the last bar on Highway 395 in San Bernardino County. It was a false-fronted box with a cute name. He looked at the sign in disgust. He disliked cute names, cute crap in general. He was sick of cheap bars that stank of puke and urinal soap.

Jace and Hickey went zipping by, Jace making a honking sound, Hickey doing a rebel yell, his gray ponytail streaming in the wind: Roy's gang having a good time. Traveling with a doper and a loony definitely had drawbacks. Roy watched as they figured it out. Tufts of ash blond hair protruding from under the front of Roy's leather cap bobbed limply in the dry breeze. Hickey and Jace came zigzagging back down 395, crossing over the double line, still screwing around before bringing their bikes over to the shoulder. Roy removed his Ray•Bans and hung them in the V of his shirt front. People found it difficult to meet Roy's gaze. With eyes of the palest blue, ringed in pink and framed by white skin and wispy, colorless hair, he exuded a tangy smell of suppressed violence and toxic energy.

"When we get inside, I want you to be cool, Jace," Roy said, his voice like dry sand. "We're not going to find out about Donnie if you start in with the weird noises and looks." But staring his brother down was a waste of time. He just grinned back at Roy, bright blue eyes glittering vacantly from a face full of red hair. Getting Jace's attention was like watching a flashlight bobbing around in the dark. Roy nodded until Jason's mop of red hair bobbed along in exaggerated mimicry. "You and Hickey play some pool, or pinball or whatever, but stay away from the other people. Right?" Roy shifted his gaze to Hickey.

"No problem, man." Hickey's slack smile exposed yellow teeth rimmed in green. He took a sideways peek at Jason, who continued to nod, his eyes wandering to a Red Dodge pickup parked near the entrance. Suddenly, Jace sucked his tongue off the roof of his mouth, making a wet popping sound, like a cork being pulled from a bottle. Roy shook his head in disgust. "Shit."

"Not in the bar, Roy." Jace rolled his head from side to side, his grin huge in the thicket of red whiskers. "Not in the bar."

Sometimes he wished his brother had an off switch.

•

Roy paused inside the door of the darkened bar, waiting for his eyes to adjust, taking it in. No music, no women, just the click of pool balls and an occasional dry cackle above the murmur of conversation—a geezer bar. At the far end of the polished bar top stood a heavyset bartender with a gray mustache. The more Roy looked around, the more he decided the place was a bullshit factory, a place for chicken-necked old farts—a bunch of loony tunes.

A man reading a newspaper seated at the bar directed an angular face Roy's way and caught him looking at him. Dark marble eyes met Roy's gaze, then shifted to Jace and Hickey, and then returned to the newspaper. Roy looked at the guy's old-fashioned leather lace-up boots. He was a tall man, taller than Roy, with big bony hands that were cracked and weathered, long fingers, and big knuckles like old knotted branches. After the eyes, look at a man's hands—that was the only useful thing he'd learned from a succession of "uncles" who had taken up temporary residence with their mother, Betts, in the decaying Airstream trailer under the cotton-woods that grew along the Mojave River.

Betts and her three boys had crowded into the trailer in the dry, sharp cold of winter, but in the balmy days of fall and spring and during the heat of summer, they'd escaped the trailer's confinement and slept outside. Sometimes Donnie had cried, afraid of the dark. Roy'd let him sleep in the middle. Family life in Oro Grande.

Roy leaned his sinewy frame against the bar and pointed Jason and Hickey to the high-backed observer chairs along the wall near the pool table.

"What'll it be?" Beer clung to the tips of the bartender's mustache.

"Gimme a long-neck Bud." Roy looked back at Jace and Hickey. "Bud?" he said. They nodded in unison. "Three Buds," Roy said.

"No Bud." The cigar waggled back and forth. "Sierra Nevada on tap or any of those up there." The bartender pointed to a row of beer bottles lined up on top of the backbar. Bits of light winked back from the glass where shafts of sunlight filtered through cracks and holes in the wall above the bar. Roy recognized Corona and Dos Equis. Most of the others he had never heard of—Foster's, Labatt, Bass, Guinness. The bartender's expression said he didn't give a damn one way or another whether Roy had a beer or not. Roy thought the guy lacked manners. "Make it three Coronas," Roy said, turning to face the room, his elbows on the bar.

When the beer came, Jace jumped up, knocking over his chair, and headed for the bar. As he took exaggerated rolling strides, his large, muscular torso appeared about to topple off truncated legs. His body rocked from side to side like some movie villain from an old Western. He grinned back at Hickey, then swept the beer up, grasping a bottle in each hand. By now, everyone was watching his antics. He spun around and strutted back to the table, swigging beer from each bottle. He banged down a half-empty bottle in front of Hickey, belched loudly, and wiped his beard with the back of his hand.

"What's up with your pal there?"

"He likes Westerns."

The bartender nodded. "Mmm."

Behind him, Roy heard a loud guffaw. "You see that asshole?" The beery voice carried into the room, interrupting the ebb and flow of conversation. Roy turned away from the bar, his eyes seeking out the speaker.

"That's not polite, talking like that," Roy said to the three men seated at a table crowded with empty bottles, unsure who had made the remark.

"Hey, you gotta admit that was weird." The speaker grinned at Roy and looked around the room for approval, his eyes overly bright from drink. Tension seeped into darkened air, the easy rhythm of bar sounds broken and subdued. Roy let the time tick away in the gathering quiet. "It's bad manners to make fun of people." He shook his head from side to side. "You trying to make him feel bad?"

It wasn't the reaction they had been expecting. They were in their early twenties, dressed alike in khaki T-shirts and desert camo pants and caps. They shuffled their feet and peered about in the silent gloom. Roy put them down as urban wanna-bes. Most likely, they belonged to the new red Dodge pickup parked near the entrance. He'd noticed the deer rifles in the gun rack on the way in.

Jason began making soft clicking sounds. Roy didn't need to look. He'd heard it before. Something had caught his brother's attention. He hoped it wasn't a woman, but it was. Out of the corner of his eye, he saw a dark-haired woman in a denim shirt and jeans moving across the room to the bar. He held the speaker's gaze for a few more moments, then turned his attention to Jace.

"I've got it, Dad." The woman lifted a hinged section of mahogany, ready to step behind the bar.

"Not for now." The bartender shook his head. "You come on back later."

Her glance shifted quickly around the room, taking in the tension. "Okay, see you in a bit." She paused to push soft dark curls away from her forehead. Her hand patted the arm of the tall man. "How's it going, Bill?" She raised dark eyebrows in inquiry.

"Just fine." But the tall man's eyes were on Roy.

She recrossed the room and disappeared through a swinging door.

Jason made little rhythmic clicking sounds as she walked.

"Something stuck in his throat?" said the one she'd called Bill.

"Yeah, he's got an allergy." Roy turned back to the bartender, raised his empty bottle, and put a twenty on the bar. "You got a minute?"

The bartender pulled his gaze away from Jace and looked at Roy.

"Maybe you can help me out here." Roy flashed what he thought passed for a friendly smile. "I'm looking for a guy, a little guy with dark hair, tattoos on his arms and neck." He paused. "He's a friend of mine." Roy waited, watching the broad face.

"Doubt if he's been in here." Watery blue eyes regarded him through a cloud of cigar smoke.

"Why's that?" Roy sounded curious, interested.

"This isn't a biker bar." The bartender transferred the cigar from one side of his mouth to the other. "Guess you can see that. Not their music. Not their beer." He glanced over at Hickey. "Not their kind of place. Most of 'em find it about as interesting as your two friends." He gestured with his head toward the far wall, where Jace and Hickey sat staring at the pool players. "We don't see many bikers in here." He met Roy's game-show smile with a flat stare.

Roy thought about the surprised look that'd be on his face just before his eyes rolled up into the back of his head. "Hey, well if you do see one of those low-life biker types . . ." He paused, letting a touch of menace creep into his sandy voice. "It could happen, you know. Some nasty biker might come in by accident. I mean, there's no sign outside saying low-life bikers keep out. Right?" He broke into a smile. "Lookee here, it's already happened. There's three of us here now, drinking beer, and being polite. You notice that?"

The bartender listened without expression. "No offense meant."

Roy shrugged. "Maybe you could do me a favor before we move on down the road, okay? No reason to stick around, except we need to find the guy we're looking for. So if you see the person I described to you, small man with tattoos and dark hair"—he fixed his eyes on the bartender's face—"pass this on to him, okay? I'll write it down for you." Roy took a matchbook and a stubby pencil out of his shirt pocket and printed out a note on the inside cover: "Donnie, call home. Roy." He paused, watching the bartender, waiting for a response. He could see the tall guy watching him out of the corner of his eye. Roy pushed the matchbook and the twenty across the bar. "See there, nothing but a little family problem." The bartender nodded imperceptibly and stuck the matchbook cover between the bar's mirror and the wood frame. There were matchbook covers with the same note in seven or eight bars up and down highway 395.

"Keep your money." A stubby hand pushed the twenty back at Roy.

"No problem," Roy said, thinking about what an uptight asshole the bartender was, too good to take his money.

"Anything else?" The bartender sent a cloud of smoke in Roy's general direction.

Roy shook his head. The bartender turned his broad face away without saying anything more and spoke quietly to the hatchet-faced man still looking down at the newspaper.

Roy caught Hickey's eye and nodded toward the door. As he slid off the bar stool, the hatchet-faced man listening to the bartender stood up and shoved his newspaper down the bar. A bony finger tapped a picture of a police sketch on the front page. "This the guy you're looking for?" Roy sucked in his breath. The sketch on the front page of the *InyoKern Courier* accompanied a story about the discovery of a badly decomposed body in the Panamint Mountains, found by an Officer Francisco Flynn of the Bureau of Land Management.

The one-column story reported that the body of a bighorn sheep had been found not far from the unidentified body of a man the authorities presumed to have been a poacher. The sheriff's spokesperson said that the circumstances surrounding the death indicated that the victim had underestimated the dangers of the desert and died of dehydration. The spokesperson went on to make some stale observations about ironic justice and the dangers of the desert in the summertime. The story finished with a recap about the poaching of bighorn sheep in the desert and ended with an appeal from the Inyo County Sheriff's Department for information leading to the identification of the body, which had been taken to the morgue in Independence.

The police artist had made a sketch of a tattoo visible on the victim's neck. There was no missing the crude death's-head tattoo that Roy had scratched into Donnie's skin with a pin and india ink when they had both been kids in Oro Grande. He could feel the bartender and his buddy watching him. They must have noticed the death's-head tattoo on his own neck and guessed at a connection. Well, fuck them. He made an effort to breathe normally.

"Naw, that's not him." Roy looked away from the hawklike face and turned toward the bartender. "The guy I'm looking for rides a Harley. He wouldn't go walking around in the desert like some dummy."

The paper said they hadn't identified Donnie, and they might not, at least not for a while. Donnie had been arrested and printed, but evidently the "badly decomposed body" was too messed up for prints. Roy tried to figure it out. What the hell had happened? Donnie knew his limits, cheating, petty theft, an occasional scam, nothing that involved violence. He just coasted along on the fringes. Nobody paid attention to his bullshit, except Roy, looking out for him, and for Jace, for all of them all the damn time.

He looked up at the lean face, all angles and edges, big nose, sharp and intense. He shut his eyes, memorizing the details. He'd remember him—and the rude bartender.

He gestured at Hickey and Jace, cocking his head at the door. "Time to hit the road." He turned back toward the bar, catching the attention of the camo-clad trio.

"You watch your mouth now. Learn to be polite," he said. His sandy voice cut through the murmur of talk. He lifted his hand in a casual wave.

The thick one with the weight lifter's body and ropy arms decided he couldn't let it pass. Roy had counted on that.

"Hey, fuck you and your soft-brain pal."

"That's it. Take it outside." The bartender glared at the trio. "It's time you guys were moving along, as well." This was directed at Roy.

Roy grinned again. "So long, folks." He gave another casual wave and walked out into the bright, hot air of the Mojave Desert. He stepped immediately to one side of the push-through door and squinted away from the light, letting his eyes adjust. His right hand closed around the roll of nickels he kept in his pocket.

He raised his voice and called into the bar. "Come on, Jace." "Let's go."

Instead, the trio of hunters came bursting through the door into the bright light, blinking in the whiteness. Roy caught the moon-faced thick one in the kidneys with the fisted nickels as he came through the door. The man dropped to his knees and rolled into a fetal position, gasping in silent agony. That's one, Roy thought, feeling the familiar adrenaline rush pumping up his pulse. The man's companions stood looking at their downed leader, eyes full of surprise.

"Hey, wait a minute, man." The one closest to Roy put up his hands.

Roy looked at him, shaking his head in disbelief. Why'd these guys always want to talk? Jason caught him from behind and pinned his arms. Roy stepped forward and drove his fist deep into the softness of his stomach. The man on the ground struggled to all fours. Hickey kicked him in the side of the head and grinned over at the remaining youth, who stood immobile, mouth agape. "What you gonna do there, man, take a picture?" Hickey laughed. Frightened eyes shifted from Hickey to Jason and Roy and back to Hickey. As he stumbled backward toward the door, the bar emptied in a rush, everyone trying to see the action.

Roy raised his hands up, palms out. "Hey, it's all over. The man was rude; now he's polite." He bent down over the ashen face. "You have to be careful how you talk to people, right?" The man nodded. Roy cupped his hand to his ear. "What's that?" Can't hear you."

"Right. That's right." The man's voice was hoarse with pain.

Roy turned away, ignoring the onlookers by the tavern door. The paper that had the news of Donnie's death was stuffed in the back pocket of his white denims. It was all that was left of Donnie— Donnie, the one who remembered when they'd all lived along the river in Oro Grande. Now there was just himself and Jason, and Jace could barely remember what had happened yesterday.

He grabbed Jace by the arm, fingers digging in. "Donnie's dead."

He slapped the newspaper into his face. "That's right, dickbrain, Donnie's dead."

"Come on, man. We gotta go." Hickey pulled Roy toward the bikes. As Roy reached for his brother's arm, Jason jerked away from Roy's grasp, his bright little eyes alive with malice. Roy looked back at the men standing in confusion around the door and raised his hand in a gesture of farewell, his mouth pulled into a flashy smile, exposing the gums made blood red by the whiteness of his skin. "Hope you enjoyed the show, assholes." His voice soft as dry leaves. But they couldn't hear him.

# 3

•

As Frank pulled into the dirt parking lot next to the Joshua Tree Athletic Club, he found himself sucking dust. His beloved '53 Chevy pickup pinged from the gravel thrown up from some motorcycles careening onto 395 in an earsplitting cacophony. He cursed under his breath as he watched them disappear down the highway toward Boron and Kramer Corners. He shook his head.

He wondered if the new owners of the Joshua Tree Athletic Club were turning the old place into a biker bar. He hoped not. The desert didn't need any more macho vacuumheads littering up the landscape. Still, it was none of his concern.

He pulled his truck in well away from the other vehicles scattered about on the weedy, oil-soaked dirt patch that passed for a parking lot. It had taken him more than a year to bring the truck back to life. He liked the way it felt when he drove it, not much speed, but a lot of torque. A five-window pickup with the original chrome grille and bumpers, real bumpers, not five-mile-an-hour aluminum foil. People looked at the truck. "Nice truck," they'd say. It made him feel good.

Mary Alice had accused him of taking better care of his truck than of their "relationship." How did a love affair, a romance, become a relationship? Only with the help of the psychobabblers. She was always reading self-help books and articles about "quality time" and building "self-esteem." Weren't there people who were justified in their self-loathing, when it was just an accurate appraisal? Assholes with insight? He could see her peering intently at a book and then intently at him, cataloging his shortcomings, particularly his "inability to communicate his feelings." Maybe she'd never liked what he said. He shook his head. The seven, ten, twelve steps—twelve steps seemed to be in—to a more fulfilling relationship were always cluttered up with the jargon of confession and failed communication. Was that Bogey's problem in *Casablanca*? Was he thinking about failed opportunities for communication as he put Ingrid Bergman on the plane to Lisbon? That must've been it. If old Bogie had only gone to a few sensitivity sessions, he would've gotten his head right, given up gambling, drinking, and heartbreak, and taken up with a rich widow.

Frank stepped up onto the short, board sidewalk that extended along the front of the bar and pushed past a knot of guys hashing over some sort of bar fight. Inside, it was the same place he remembered, and yet it wasn't. Someone had taken all the crap off from behind the bar; no jars of greasy sausage, no mini racks of stale chips, no neon signs for Bud or Coors. The backbar gleamed, the dark mahogany rubbed with polish, the beveled mirrors reflecting back his curious gaze. Long ago, he had come to terms with his unprepossessing appearance—slight build, the face somewhat enigmatic, laugh lines at the corners of sad hazel eyes set evenly above a prominent nose, the mouth and chin serious.

Behind him, caught in the tavern's permanent half-light, the men went about the timeless business of spinning the tedium of the day's events into the stories where they beat their enemies and won the women. Frank could make out snatches of excited conversation. The rhythm of the beery brotherhood had been disrupted. Maybe the latest gold strike. They were forever waving about little glass flasks of gold flakes caught in water. Bottled hope.

A tall, hawk-nosed man watched him from the far end of the bar. Frank nodded as they made eye contact. That was a big thing with men. In college, he'd read about the way chimps, gorillas, and baboons established dominance by staring one another down. You could see it in any bar.

Frank stood with his arms resting lightly on the polished wood. Perched on a stool your feet lost contact with the ground. It was too easy for the rest of the body to follow. He preferred standing. The bartender ambled down to where Frank leaned against the bar.

"What's been going on?"

"Not much. A couple guys sharing pain." The blue eyes were watchful, looking him over.

"How come?"

The bartender leveled his gaze at Frank. "Who knows why bikers beat on people? What'll it be?"

Off to a bad start. Frank looked at the bottles lined up along the top of the backbar. He smiled to himself at the sight of the ubiquitous jackalope, where it kept watch over the beery brotherhood from above the bar. There used to be one in every desert bar and hotel. A marvel for children, and the taxidermist's triumph—the horns of an antelope protruding from the head of a rabbit. He remembered the one in Simon's Pool Hall in Mojave, the rail town where his dad, Francis Flynn, had been a freight conductor for the Southern Pacific. He could see the sun-wrinkled face of Three-Fourths Larson telling him how he had stalked a jackalope for days and finally lassoed it, caught it by the horns using a rope made from owl feathers. Three-Fourths had explained that it had to be made of owl feathers so it would fly through the air so silently that not even a jackalope could dodge the loop.

"Beer or not?" The bartender lifted a cigar from under the counter, bit off the end, and spit it behind the bar.

"What's on tap?"

"Sierra Nevada."

Frank studied the beer along the bar again. "So much to do and so little time."

A small smile creased the broad face.

Frank gestured toward the bottles along the top of the bar. "There're quite a few up there I've never met, but I see you've got Guinness, Dublin's finest."

The smile widened. "I see you're another lover of God's own gift to thirsty men."

"And women," Frank added. "I'm Frank Flynn." He hesitated for a moment, then offered his hand. "From the Bureau of Land Management."

"Well, Officer Flynn, welcome to the Joshua Tree Athletic Club." The bartender's hand was leathery and dry. "Jack Collins. This is my place. You here on business?"

"Not officially, and make it Frank, okay? I'm off duty. Just dropped by, so to speak. I'd be sorry to make you or your patrons here uneasy, Mr. Collins."

"Just Jack will do. Mr. Collins was my father."

Frank nodded. "Okay, Jack."

Collins's broad face waited impassively for Frank to continue.

"We had a nature trail out by the Hole-in-the-Wall campground, signs identifying the plants and animals. People seemed to enjoy it. So when the BLM got a few extra bucks, we put in some signs in braille." His voice trailed away. Collins leaned forward to catch his words. "Someone came along with a rock or a hammer and pounded the little bumps flat so the blind people couldn't read 'em." He looked calmly up at Collins's round face. "I wish we had caught the guy, but we didn't.

"Then there're folks who kill the animals that live in the desert, for no particular reason other than it's pretty easy. I've found tortoise shells with bullet holes in them." Frank drank half his beer and set the glass down. He looked at it absently and then drank the rest. "It's tough bagging a desert tortoise, especially on the move. But you gotta follow the gun nut's code. 'If it moves, shoot it.'" He looked up into the bartender's face. "I used to save the tortoise shells. Too depressing." He shook his head. "So I boxed up six or seven shot-up shells and sent 'em to the NRA. Made me feel better, even though it was an empty gesture, so to speak." His smile was mirthless. "They probably used them for ashtrays, gave them a laugh."

He leaned forward for emphasis, engaging the large man's gaze. "Now they're back to killing the bighorn sheep." The tall guy at the end of the bar seemed to be listening to him. "It's a lot easier to do now than in the old days, when a hunt meant four or five days of living in camp, stalking, reading sign. Now they come in close by plane or helicopter and wait by the water holes with automatic weapons. Wham, bam, thank you, ram. Gone back home after a tough half day hunting. Of course, if the horns are too small, they leave the animal to rot. If they bag a trophy ram, the so-called guides lug the heads out for them. It's a lotta work lugging a big old ram's head around, but then, the fees are pretty good. Maybe ten grand if the horns make the book."

" 'The book'?"

"Yeah, well, there's a scale, the Boone and Crocket scale, and a record book. If the ram makes the book, you've earned major bragging rights. There's the head up on the wall, where clients and colleagues can see they're in the presence of a big white hunter." Frank looked up at Collins's ruddy skin and graying blond hair, suddenly aware of his own olive complexion. "Sorry." He grinned. "No offense."

"None taken." Collins took a mug from the refrigerator under the bar and opened a Bishops Finger for himself. "Frank Flynn." Collins eyed the uniform. "You the Francisco Flynn in the paper, the one that found the dead guy?"

"Yup, that's me. I found the dead guy up in the Panamints. A story with a happy ending. A poached poacher. Too bad he's not the last of his kind." He eased himself up on a bar stool and leaned forward, his voice barely audible. "I'm trying to get a line on these sports folks." He paused. "Unofficially. Trying to help out Fish and Game, my colleagues in law enforcement. Someone who knows something about the desert has to be taking them in, showing them the places the sheep go."

"So that's what brings you here?"

Frank studied the brown liquid in the bottom of his glass. "Bartenders hear things. I'd like to give the sheep an even break. If you hear about poachers, I'd like to know. Sometimes, they've just got to brag about it." He looked up into Collins's broad face and plunged on. "Just that. Nothing else. Most of the guys in this room, I know they don't give a damn for BLM regulations. Hell, most of them were here before the BLM. They're not my concern." He looked around the room. "Actually, not so. They are my concern. They're an endangered species."

Collins took a clean mug from under the bar. "Try a Bishops Finger. It's a wonderful beer. A balm to sore hearts." Giving Frank a blarney grin, he poured the amber liquid not quite to the rim. "On me. Hang on for a bit. I need to talk with a fellow."

Frank watched as Collins and the tall man at the end of the bar had a quick, quiet exchange. The tall man unfolded himself and crossed the room on long legs. He bent over a man with a gray beard streaked with dark whiskers on either side of his mouth. The bearded man was leaning forward in an observer's chair, watching a game of pool, smoking a pipe. The tall one spoke into the pipe smoker's ear. A pair of sharp eyes fixed on Frank from under a snap-brim fedora. A Bogie hat, thought Frank. The man took the pipe from his mouth and tapped it against the heel of his shoe, a soft leather desert boot. Then he fished a pipe cleaner from his pocket and stuck it in the pipe, and began absently pushing it back and forth, just listening. Now and then, he glanced over at Frank. Finally, he looked up and nodded once, and returned his attention to the pool players. The tall guy returned to the bar and nodded at Collins.

Collins shrugged. He lifted his glass and absently set it back on the bar. "I guess you read the piece in the *InyoKern Courier*, about you finding the body in the Panamints?"

"Yup, didn't do me justice. I didn't see anything about me being brave, clean, and reverent. What about it?"

"Well, this might be something you can use." Collins's expression was matter-of-fact. "The paper had a sketch of the tattoo on the guy's neck."

"Yeah, that's right."

"Well, one of the bikers in here was asking questions, trying to find a friend of his. Just left before you came in."

"Uh-huh," Frank nodded. "What club?"

"Didn't advertise."

"Can you remember what they looked like?" Frank thought of the jerks who had sprayed gravel on his truck.

Collins placed both hands on the bar and squinted up into cigar smoke. "There were three of them. One guy in his forties, gray ponytail, bad teeth, skinny, about six feet tall, maybe a hundred and sixty or so, definitely needed a shower. His partner looked like an orangutan—short legs, big torso, red hair all over."

"You'd have made a good cop."

Collins frowned. "Protecting the rich from the poor is like protecting the English from the Irish."

Frank smiled. "Point taken. Notice anything special about them?"

Collins seemed mollified. "Something was the matter with the redheaded one. You could tell the way he bobbed and jerked his head around that he was short a few cards, not at home, you know what I mean? Knock on the door and maybe you'd get an answer, maybe not."

Frank nodded. "What about the third guy?"

"He'd be hard to forget. I never saw a guy with hair so white and skin to match, and he had strange pale eyes, like doll's eyes painted on porcelain."

"Maybe he was an albino," Frank offered. He remembered that one of the bikers had been wearing a long-sleeved shirt and a kerchief cap. The desert wasn't an ideal environment for the fair of skin.

"Maybe so." Collins went on, "And he had this sort of intense way of talking, as if he were reading from a page in his head. You got the feeling he wasn't really talking to you. That's about it."

"Ought to know 'im if I see 'im."

Collins turned his head slightly away from Frank, looking toward the door of the bar, and brought his hand up as if to shade his eyes from the cracks of bright sunlight. "The redhead made funny noises with his mouth. The white-haired guy, the one who did all the talking, didn't like it. I didn't care much for it myself."

"What did he talk about?"

Collins gave a Celtic shrug, a gesture familiar to generations of British constabulary—shades of Francis Flynn. "He asked me to help him find some biker buddy. I didn't much care for him or his pals, so I wasn't very helpful, but he left a note for me to pass on if I should run into the guy." Collins plucked the matchbook with the note on it from where he had stuck it against the mirror and pushed it across the bar.

Frank read the note: " 'Donnie, call home. Roy.' So how's this connected to the dead man?"

"Bill over there"—Collins pointed with his chin at his tall companion at the end of the bar—"was reading the paper about you finding the body. There was that sketch of the tattoo. The white-haired guy had one like it on the right side of his neck, like the drawing in the paper." Frank looked over at the lean, angular face. The man named Bill gave a slight nod.

"Bill showed it to Mr. White Hair. Asked him if he was looking for the man you found dead in the desert. Well, he stares at the paper, swallows a couple times. Then he looks up and says, naw, it's not him. But he's obviously upset. He gets up, collects his buddies, and they go outside. He had words with some deer hunters passing through, and they followed him outside. By the time the rest of us went out, two of them were on the ground. The white-haired one holds up his hands and says it's all over. And it was. White Hair never batted an eye. Cool and calm. He waved to the boys hanging around the door. Then they got on their bikes and tore on down the highway. That's when you showed up."

Frank picked up the note and looked at the names again— Donnie, Roy. The dead man must've been named Donnie. He looked up at Collins. "Did the white-haired guy mention where home was?"

Collins shook his head. "Nope, I wasn't exactly being conversational. I just wanted him and his pals out of here."

Frank put the matchbook into his pocket. "Thanks, Jack. I really appreciate you telling me about this." He pushed away from the bar and slid off the stool. "I better be getting back home. Come tomorrow, I gotta give Uncle Sam a day's work for a day's pay."

"Stick around for some tamale pie. Today's Wednesday. We serve tamale pie on Wednesdays."

"Man, I really like tamale pie, but I've got miles to go before I sleep."

Collins grinned, "And promises to keep. Listen, on Fridays we have cioppino. Come some Friday and have some cioppino."

•

"So what's your take? Think he suspects anything?" Bill Jerome looked down at the cards caught up in his sinewy hands.

The three of them were seated around the kitchen table. Ben Shaw's pipe rested on the table. He fidgeted in his shirt pocket and produced a pipe tamper. A yellow cone of light thick with smoke illuminated the linoleum tabletop. Collins puffed on his cigar, shaking his head. "Nope, I don't think so. Why would he? Be kinda dumb to question suspects and let them know they were suspects."

"No one ever said cops were smart." Ben Shaw glared back at Collins. "Cops catch criminals because criminals are dumber than dirt, not because cops are smart. He probably thinks he's slicker than hell with his stories about braille trails and heartrending stuff like that." He discarded the queen of spades on Jerome's club lead.

"Shit, thanks a lot." Collins gave Shaw a disgusted look and dropped the jack of clubs on the trick. Shaw grinned. Collins glanced up from his hand. "Seemed like a pretty sincere kid to me. Likes his beer, that's for sure." He set his jaw for the response he was sure would follow.

Shaw shook his head in disgust. "He's a fucking cop, Jack." He turned to Jerome. "Whaddya think, Bill? Cops your pals these days? Nothing like a guy in a uniform telling people what to do." He poured beer into the side of his glass, careful not to raise a head.

"Ben's right, Jack." The sharp edges of Jerome's features divided his face into planes of shade and light. "We played along with him because not to play along would just make him suspicious. I wish he'd just go away."

Jack raised his glass and drank deeply. Beer dripped from his mustache, making small puddles on the table. He wiped his mouth with the back of his sleeve. My God, they never changed. "You guys are the most grudge-holding bastards in the world. He's a kid playing detective. That's all. Why be coming around here looking for us?" He led with the ten of diamonds. Jerome dropped the ten of hearts. Shaw followed with a small heart, giving Collins a wolfish grin. Fifteen and counting. Collins shuffled the cards around in his hand.

"Who the hell knows why he was here," Shaw remarked, "but he was here." He pointed across the table, arm outstretched, four fingers pointing at Collins. "Right here where we live, Jack, where we live." Jerome nodded in agreement.

"Okay, then, we lay off for a while."

"We'll see." Shaw grinned. "Maybe we'll find the need upon us."

"Suit yourself. Someone's got to tend bar, cook meals, and run the business. So I'm out of it for now."

Shaw smiled over at Jerome. "Hear that, Bill? Jack's giving us time off."

Collins laughed. "Hah, how the hell would I tell?" He led with another diamond. Shaw looked down at his cards. "Shit. You're Mr. Slick, Jack."

Collins grinned and laid down the four cards remaining in his hand, all diamonds. "Shot the moon, boys. Looks like old Jack stuck you with twenty-six big ones."

# 4

•

Frank was paying the piper. Why had he agreed to do a guest lecture for Jan Rockford's anthropology class? The sun glinted off the windshield into his eyes, painfully bright. What the hell was he going to talk about? Nobody really knew what rock art was all about. The Pleistocene artists were unavailable for comment, turned to dust for lo these thousands of years. All he had were theories. Well, he had this advantage: He could make it up as he went along. A lack of fact meant a lot of latitude. But this whole lecture bit made him uneasy. He preferred people in less concentrated doses, two or three at a time, not twenty or thirty.

Why had he agreed so readily? What had gotten into him? Oh hell, this was a favor for a nice lady. He'd met Jan Rockford at the dig near Barstow and immediately liked her. Despite his brown skin and shiny badge, she made no assumptions about his interests or intellect. Actually, she'd slyly conducted an oblique interview, listening attentively to his observations, tapping his knowledge of the desert, drawing him out.

She'd asked questions about the terrain. Could he spot the remnants of the shoreline of Lake Manix, the Pleistocene lake that had once filled the now-dry valleys of the central Mojave Desert? Did he know of any promising sites for digs? An actual native of the Mojave! How very interesting! He should have recognized the technique. Frank was a professional listener, but he had succumbed to personal vanity and babbled on about things he rarely voiced.

He spoke of his Mexican/Paiute mother, for the first time since her death. Told Jan about her marriage to Francis Flynn, railroad man, who died of grief, Jameson whiskey, and trying to stay on the catwalks while two sheets to the wind. He plunged between the cars, and they'd had to search more than a mile of track looking for body parts.

Of course, Jan had been plying him steadily with Beck's beer. That was another thing he liked about Jan. She drank good beer and in large quantities, seemingly without dimming her lights, matching him beer for beer without slurring her words. He'd had to nap alongside his truck for a couple hours before venturing back out onto paved roads. Slow learner, here he was again, suffering from a mild hangover. He shouldn't have had a second Bishops Finger. It packed a wallop.

He thought about Jan. Never trust innocent-looking gray-haired ladies who reminded you of your mother, especially if they could down a six-pack and never bat an eyelash. The words had all rushed out of him in a stream of personal revelation. Then again, he hadn't really talked with anyone since Mary Alice had departed the desert for Los Angeles, telling him she couldn't bear the isolation and emptiness.

"Oh Frank, I can't stand it. It's all brown and gray. There're no trees. Just vultures and crows picking at dead animals on the highway," she'd said. He had pointed out that crows didn't live in the desert. The birds she'd seen were ravens, not crows. "Crows gather in flocks called 'murders,' " he'd explained. "Ravens travel in mated pairs." He'd given her a flat stare. "They mate for life."

"Jesus, Frank. What is it with you? 'They're ravens, not crows.' Is that it? Ravens not crows, another wildlife lecture. Did I get it wrong again? Would you try really listening to me? Could you live in Los Angeles or up in Washington, where you told me how all those trees made you feel like you were trapped, closed in? Here in the desert, I feel exposed, like I'm disappearing. It's so damned empty. God, six miles to the highway and twelve miles to the turnoff for Ridgecrest. Frank, there are only six buildings at Olancha, and two of them are boarded up. I can't live in this place. Could you live away from your picture rocks, Joshua trees, and *Artemisia tridentata*—I got it right, *Artemisia tridentata*—and your beloved bighorn sheep, which no one but you ever sees?"

What was there to say? He'd been born in the Mojave. His mother's mother had been a Paiute. The desert had claimed the child, and the man had given himself up to the desert. Emptiness? Vast, uncluttered, rigorously frugal, but never empty. It was full of shapes and colors and the stillness of open spaces, a land of illusions, a place where cloud shadows moved across a dreamscape of empty lakes whose dry beds miraculously filled with water when the desert gods emptied the sky in dark torrents, washing the rocks and filling the canyons with ephemeral rivers of brown water.

The smell of damp creosote bush rising in tendrils of moisture after a thundershower filled him with primeval joy. Its destruction filled him with primeval rage. The gods he sought lived here, and he drank life from the land they had created.

Frank disliked driving through Ridgecrest. The Naval Weapons Test Center had given birth to urban sprawl. There was no there there. At the University of Arizona, in Tucson, he'd witnessed the encroachment of urban sprawl into the fragile Colorado Desert, the inevitable capitulation of the land to development and the accumulation of wealth. The voices of expediency proclaimed a brave new utilitarian world, but the so-called reclamation of "wasteland" was nothing more than smash and grab on a scale unimaginable to the inept thugs who wandered aimlessly in the exercise yards of penal institutions.

It was happening in the Mojave, too, so seemingly endless and barren. To most people, the Mojave was too stark, too apparently devoid of life to attract the average tourist or provide a haven for urban refugees. To the denizens of the speeding cars on Interstate 15, rushing to Las Vegas to part with their money, the Mojave was a land inhabited by rocks turned dark in the sun, where ancient lava flows spilled out of barren hills and lay like black tongues on the desert floor.

Frank looked out the window at the land sliding by, the folded mountains, cinder rock, and creosote bush. Trees were okay, but they blocked the view. Too moist. Cottonwoods by a spring, the spiny

Joshua tree on the flats and slopes, juniper and piñon higher up, just right. Some shade, good fuel, and tasty nuts.

Frank turned his truck into a parking slot reserved for guests at Arroyo Seco Community College. As he stepped out of the truck, the heat rushed up at him from asphalt already made soft by the sun. He thought about that first cold beer, how good it would taste. But first the penance.

He moved quickly into the shade of the covered walkways that sheltered the students against the sun as they passed from one class to another. He followed the walkway to a small central park protected from the heat by sun cloth suspended from plastic piping that supplied water to overhead outlets, discharging a spray so fine that most of it evaporated before reaching the ground, like desert rain. It was a good place to wait and gather his thoughts. The park was an island of damp green, thriving in the softened light and moisture. For a moment, Frank's inner eye flashed on the cascade of water falling from the cliff in Surprise Canyon, a pocket of tender plants surviving in the harshest of climates.

He glanced down at the torn scrap of paper he held in his hand. It said, Social and Behavioral Sciences Building, Room 6. Bring slides. He had them. He took a deep breath. He'd done this before, but facing a group of people—no, an audience—that was the hard part, meeting their expectations. Once he got into it, he knew it wasn't going to be so bad, but the first ten minutes being the designated expert were never that comfortable.

Jan's classroom was windowless, low-ceilinged, and claustrophobic. The student desks had been shoved toward the far wall to make room for additional folding chairs. Those who couldn't find a place to sit stood at the back. Someone had put up posters of Ansel Adams's desert photographs: giant saguaros standing in the moonlight in the Sonoran Desert, far away from the high desert of the Mojave, where no saguaros grew.

Jan Rockford was seated at a long table at the front of the room, talking with a scruffy-looking male in jeans and a T-shirt and an emaciated girl in cutoff shorts, a tank top, and sandals. The male student's bare arms were covered with intricate tattoos. A tiny tulip tattooed on the girl's neck, just under her ear, reminded Frank of the death's-head tattoo on the neck of the dead man in Surprise Canyon. Picture people.

Now the girl was talking to Jan. The guy nodded as she talked. They were obviously a team. Jan looked up at them, smiling. He couldn't hear her, but she seemed to be getting along with them okay. He must have caught her eye, because she smiled and waved him over as she rose to greet him.

Taking Frank by the arm, she led him to the front of the room. "Class, this is Frank Flynn, ranger for the Bureau of Land Management." As the buzz of conversation died, the tinny tune of a cell phone caught Frank's ear. A young woman with pouty lips and spiky blond hair tilted her head into the hand holding a tiny cell phone. Jan had caught it, too, and shot the woman a steely look.

The young woman began shaking her head back and forth, a vertical frown creasing her smooth forehead. "That's bullshit. That's what she always says." She nodded. "Yeah. Well, she can kiss my ass." This last admonition was clearly audible in the descending silence.

She's not even here; we're invisible, Frank thought. He wanted to reach over and take the phone out of her hand. Tell her she couldn't have it back until she learned to be polite. He hated the damn intrusive things.

Jan looked out over the class. Clearly, they were expectantly watching for her reaction. "We'll just have to wait for a bit until Eloise can rejoin us." She smiled. "Something has obviously displeased her." There were titters and guffaws. The students stared at Eloise in amused group cruelty.

"Hey, I've gotta go." This was uttered sotto voce. "Sorry, Ms. Rockford." Eloise looked around the room as if reemerging from another realm. Jan nodded in her direction. "Now that we're together again, may I remind you all to turn off phones, pagers, chiming clocks, and other modern noisemakers, so we can proceed without too much interruption." She smiled in the student's direction. "I know it was just an oversight, Eloise."

She turned to Frank. "Officer Flynn watches over the land, rescues the foolish, and helps to protect the sites of early human activity, which—as you know—are very fragile. I asked him to come to our class and share some of his knowledge of the rock art in the Mojave Desert, and he was kind enough to spare us some time.

"Officer Flynn, this is my Introduction to Anthropology class, and a few guests"—she gave him a sly smile—"who have been waiting in anticipation for your words of knowledge. So now why don't you tell us about what you know about the pictures on the rocks." She turned to Frank. "Here, let me take that, and I'll set it up for you." Jan pulled down a projection screen and seated herself at the back of the room.

The students looked up at him, silent, waiting for him to speak. The thin blond girl with the tulip sat primly at the front, knees pressed together, hands gently grasping the edge of the desk. Her companion sprawled next to her in studied nonchalance, his eyes fixed intently on Frank's face. He was the only male up front. The younger male students clustered toward the back, in a protective knot near the door. There were several older women in the class, older than Frank, at least—more than thirty-four. Serious and intent, ring binders open, they waited expectantly, ready to take down his words of wisdom.

He began nervously. "Um, for most people, the desert is something they drive through going someplace else, and that's okay. But it's hard to see the details of things when you're going too fast, just passing through at seventy miles an hour." There was no place to put his hands. "If you're really going to see the desert, you have to get out of your car and walk around, so that lets a lot of people out."

Frank could hear himself talking. "Snakes, heat, cactus, prickly plants, and rocks blackened by the sun aren't a particularly inviting prospect." Not a sound. He glimpsed a faintly amused face framed by thick dark hair, cut to just below a determined chin. She nodded almost imperceptibly.

He pushed on. "But to tell you the truth, there are a few of us who like the prickly plants. The cacti and the Joshua trees lead an interesting existence, but for me, it's the dark rocks that are the most interesting of all, because some of them have pictures on them made thousands of years ago by the people who lived here before the birth of Christ. When you see them, you can't help but wonder, Why were they made? Why this rock and not another rock? Who made them? The truth of the matter is that nobody knows for sure, but there are some reasonable theories."

The young males clustered near the door carried on a private conversation, talking to one another in inaudible voices, exchanging remarks that, Frank surmised, amused them. At least they weren't loud. He drew a breath. "Art doesn't serve a pragmatic purpose. When you find an ax head or an arrow point, you can say with a degree of certainty that these were used for building, hunting, or warfare. So the question is, Why would the aboriginal inhabitants of the Mojave make pictures on rocks?"

The young man he had seen talking with Jan stuck up his hand. His gangly frame flopped at angles around the too-small student desk, his legs thrust in front of him. Frank wondered how he had managed to fold himself into his seat in the first place.

"Yes." Frank pointed to the raised hand.

"Maybe they were bored. Maybe they had too much time on their hands."

Frank wondered briefly if the kid had done some time. He had some of the earmarks—the tattoos, the edgy cool. He nodded slowly in agreement and seemed to catch the questioner by surprise.

"You know, I think that could've had something to do with it. If you think about some aboriginal hunter, hiding behind some rocks, waiting for a deer or a sheep to come trotting by, you figure it must have been a long wait. So maybe he passed the time by doodling on the rocks. It makes sense, but I think there was more to it than that. Let me show you some pictures."

He threaded his way between the students to the back of the room where a projector rested on a raised stand. Jan dimmed the lights as Frank focused the projector for the first slide. Large, brightly painted figures in varying shades of reds, yellows, and dark browns stretched up the underside of an arched overhang. The figures seemed to be stopped in time, their dance steps caught on the face of the cliff. As the cliff face diminished in height, the figures diminished in size, creating an odd three-dimensional perspective.

"This first slide is from Baja California," Frank began. "It's of a pictograph, not a petroglyph. Because these figures were painted under an overhanging cliff, they have survived weathering. Painted rock figures are pictographs. Most of the surviving pictographs in the United States are in Arizona, Colorado, New Mexico, and Utah, where there are more overhanging cliffs.

"Caves and overhanging cliffs are not a common feature of the Mojave. Weathering is severe in the desert. The Chumash of the California coast made beautiful pictographs, but few have survived. Most have succumbed to weathering and vandalism."

Frank pushed the button to change slides. He liked being just a voice in the dim light, the students looking up at the screen, not at him.

Bighorn sheep with sticklike legs appeared to be running across the bottom face of a rock dark from the sun. "This is one of the petroglyphs found in the Cosos, up in the Naval Weapons Test Range Center, about thirty miles from here. How many of you have relatives working at China Lake?" Frank looked around the classroom and saw several hands in the air. "Well, you'll be happy to know that the navy tries to avoid bombing the petroglyph canyons. The greatest concentration of petroglyphs in North America are right here in the Cosos. You could say Ridgecrest is the petroglyph capital of the world, but on second thought, I'm not sure I'd begin any conversations that way." Frank heard a few appreciative chuckles.

"Now, you can see that these figures have been chipped into the rock itself. These are petroglyphs. The aboriginal artist used a hard, sharp stone and pecked the design into the rock, sort of a reverse tattoo, chipping away the dark surface to reveal the original color of the rock underneath.

"The dark purplish brown surface of the rock is called 'desert varnish.' It happens when moisture and heat work together. The moisture soaks into the rock and then the sun bakes the rock, leaching the moisture out. When this happens, the water leaves mineral deposits on the surface of the rock, desert varnish. How long does it take? Well, that's a problem."

Frank changed the slide. The petroglyphs of the bighorn sheep were in different clusters, two smaller sheep near the top face. These were done with greater attention to detail and proportion. Two small lines protruded from the stick legs, ending in a depiction of cloven hooves. The bodies of the sheep were in relative proportion to the heads. Directly below these were a line of sheep, touching nose to tail, as if they were in a stately parade. The heads of the sheep were tiny, but the horns curved around in large full arcs.

"Now in this slide, there are two groupings of pictures on the same rock face, one much older than the other. How can you tell?" He waited, hoping not to have to answer his own question.

Behind him, a female voice offered, "The figures near the top look like they've faded, started to turn color again. Are those the oldest?"

Frank turned his head in her direction. He could just see the top of the young woman's head. She was seated next to the door, by the boys. He craned his neck and caught the dark eyes framed by the dark hair. Again he noticed her faintly amused smile.

"Right, the older petroglyphs are starting to gain color again, picking up a patina of desert varnish. The bighorn sheep depicted near the top of the rock are the oldest. The sheep in a line at the bottom are the most recent.

"It's not too difficult to tell which petroglyphs are the oldest in a given site. But it's nearly impossible to tell how old the figures are, give or take a thousand years, and that's because we aren't sure how long it takes for desert varnish to accumulate, as there are different rates for different rocks and microclimates. On the whole, you'd have to leave a new rock out in the sun and rain from somewhere between two to five thousand years."

He changed the slide. A human figure grasping what appeared to be a club of some sort stood next to a bighorn sheep in flight, an odd sticklike club protruding from its body.

"But there are other clues. See the figure of the bighorn sheep. Notice how his head and horns are in profile. This configuration is typical of the early period, when bighorns were hunted with the atlatl, or the spear-throwing device. See the stick with the hook at one end and what looks like a grip on the other end? That's the atlatl. It worked like an extension of the arm, giving the hunter greater power and range. The same sort of figure is protruding from the body of the sheep. It's as if the artist meant to represent the atlatl in its entirety, rather than showing its separate parts.

"Any of you use a stick to throw another stick when you were about nine or ten?" Frank looked around the room. "Come on, throwing sticks is the next most important thing for a ten-year-old to throwing rocks." Frank saw some hands come up, a few at first, then more than a dozen.

"Well, you creative stick throwers know that it's an advantage. You can throw farther. You probably controlled a couple of vacant lots and a hill fort, right? Anyhow, the atlatl was an effective hunting tool for thousands of years, but then something important happened about two thousand years ago. The rocks tell the story."

Frank changed slides again, moving fairly quickly through a series depicting bighorn sheep and the figures of ancient hunters pecked into the dark stone surfaces. He stopped on the figure of a sheep surrounded by hunters clutching primitive bows. The sheep's body was penetrated by arrows.

"Things have changed. These hunters are using the bow and arrow. They can shoot the arrows from behind rock blinds, and they don't have to stand up." From the corner of his eye, Frank could see that the cluster of males near the door was sitting up, craning to see the slide. "They can kill sheep at a greater range. Things are looking up"—he paused—"but not for the sheep.

"Over a period of time, the aboriginal ancestors of the Paiute, Shoshone, Ute, and Comanche were probably too successful. They killed off a principal supply of food, emptied the store. At the same time, the last pluvial period was coming to an end, and the Pleistocene lakes were drying up. It was time to move on or starve.

"Look at this slide. The figures of the sheep have become stylized. The head shape is merely representational, still in profile, but the horns are frontal. The body has a straight back and a bow-shaped belly. The artist made no attempt to depict hooves.

"In this slide, there is a shaman figure. He's holding three arrows in one hand and what could be a medicine bag in the other. Are these stylized figures ritual symbols? Were the last inhabitants of the Cosos trying to bring the sheep back? I think so. But it was too late. The damage had been done. As a matter of fact, bighorn sheep have never returned to the Cosos. There are a few in the Panamints and scattered throughout the ranges of the Mojave, but their survival is still questionable.

"All-terrain vehicles make much more of the desert accessible. Increased accessibility puts the sheep into contact with poachers and threatens the habitat. Unfortunately for the sheep, the poacher's high-powered rifle reaches even farther than the bow and arrow. Perhaps we can learn from those who went before us and not repeat their mistakes."

After Jan turned on the lights, Frank offered to take questions. Lots of hands went up.

"Why didn't later Indians make petroglyphs?"

Frank explained how the bow and arrow changed everything. How the atlatl required that the hunter get close to the quarry. The hunt shaman and his special magic had been a necessary part of a successful hunt, he said. With the bow and arrow, the sheep were much easier to kill. Ritual magic wasn't needed for hunting sheep any longer. The shamans probably had other things on their minds.

"Why are there so many petroglyphs in the Coso range?" someone asked. The students were experiencing moments of awakened curiosity, making teaching possible. Perhaps the great clustering of rock art in the petroglyph canyons of the Cosos had been a flowering of desperate incantations for the return of the vanished sheep, Frank suggested. He saw that the class period was nearly over.

"In any case, about a thousand years ago, the Shoshonean-speaking peoples began their diaspora. Those tribes that continued to live within the bighorn range carried the rock art with them, but the greatest concentration of petroglyphs is in the Cosos, Panamints, and Death Valley.

"Yes." He pointed to an intense-looking girl wearing a single feather earring.

"Then you think the original people weren't living in harmony with their environment. They were no better than we are?"

"Well, probably not." Frank thought for a moment. "What happened to them might not be much different from what's happening to us. If you think about it, the development of the bow and arrow was a technological change. It extended their power. They were able to kill lots of sheep, and perhaps they didn't value them in the same way. Certainly the nature of the hunt changed. They were just people living on the land and making mistakes."

"Following that logic, if they had had guns, they would have killed everything off and starved to death," she said, and turned her head slightly, trying to see how the class would react to her comment.

Frank pushed on. "Probably not. However, technological change usually requires cultural adjustment. I like the thought of the Pilgrims armed with bows and arrows and Squanto and his pals armed with flintlocks. The westward expansion might've ended at Plymouth Rock."

There were a few chuckles. The girl gave him a dark scowl, so he searched the room for someone with a friendly face who had raised a hand.

"Is the poaching of bighorn sheep still a problem in the Panamints, inside Death Valley National Park itself?" The question came from the same dark-haired young woman by the door, more businesslike now, her face turned serious.

Frank sensed a logical intelligence at work. "Despite the fact that hunting the desert bighorn has been illegal in California since 1876, there are still poachers."

"Why? Why would someone want to kill desert bighorn sheep?"

Frank could see that she was taking notes. "The desert bighorn is hunted as a trophy. Despite the invention of firearms, hunting the bighorn on foot requires stalking skills and marksmanship. There are four major varieties of bighorn sheep in North America, from Alaska to the desert. The Holy Grail of big-game hunting in North America is the grand slam, the taking of the four major species of bighorn sheep."

" 'Taking'?" Her tone was quietly challenging. The room was very quiet. Frank realized his credibility was on the line.

"Okay, killing. The favored term among hunting advocates is

harvesting. It implies a food supply, so people tend to go along with the 'harvesting' of game animals. But the bighorns are no longer hunted for their meat, so I chose a more neutral term, a word hunters used before everyone started choosing up sides."

Her look was direct, curious; Frank could feel her mind at work. "Well, if hunting the desert bighorn has been illegal since 1876, then how does someone become an accepted member of the club, make a grand slam?"

"The answer is simple: They hunt illegally. They hunt in Baja California, or they get lucky with the lottery. The state of California has a lottery for a few spots, maybe ten or twenty at most, so Desert bighorns can be hunted legally with these special permits. Of these, the state may auction off two or three to the highest bidder. The money goes to fund the study of the desert bighorn and to support habitat programs. The bidding has gone as high as a hundred thousand dollars for the chance, just the chance, to take a trophy. So you can see that the motive for illegal hunting can be very strong."

Frank saw a tattooed arm raised in studied nonchalance. It was the slender blond man seated up front. He was not as young as most of them. Frank could see that now.

"Are you the BLM ranger who discovered the dead poacher in Surprise Canyon?" He looked at Frank as if experiencing some sort of personal communion.

Jan Rockford got to her feet. "I'm afraid we're out of time. I want to thank Officer Flynn for coming to our class and for the interesting and informed discussion of rock art. Perhaps he will come back another time and share some more of his knowledge and insights." The applause was more than halfhearted. Frank was surprised and pleased. He hoped it was because the students found the subject interesting and not because he'd finally finished.

Students for the next class began filing into the classroom. Jan reached for Frank's hand with both of hers. "Frank, thank you so much. They loved it. I could tell. Please, come back soon. Unfortunately, I have another class. But if you have time, I'd like to take you to lunch. There's someone I want you to meet, and I know a place where the food's good and the beer's cold."

He nodded. "Sure, sounds great. I'll wander around campus and meet you back here in an hour."

The classroom was nearly full again with incoming students. As Frank slipped out the door, he waved good-bye and stepped into the covered walkway. The young couple with the tattoos was waiting for him just outside the door. The man stuck out his hand. "Hey, man, that was really interesting. Sometimes you see things without really looking at them."

Frank shook his hand. "Frank Flynn."

"Uh, yeah, Mitch Cooper." He shuffled from one foot to the other. There was obviously something else on his mind. Frank waited. "I read about the dead guy in the desert. You the guy who found him?"

Frank nodded. He caught the girl's watery blue eyes looking at him, and then she quickly looked away, her eyes cast down at grimy feet. "Yes, that's right." He paused. "I'm the guy."

Cooper's whole body seemed to fidget. Finally, he met Frank's eyes, tossing his stringy shoulder-length hair back with a defiant flip. "Well, I might know him. I mean, who he was. But I got another class, and then I have to go to work."

Frank spoke to Cooper in his best matter-of-fact voice. "Look, Mitch, why don't you give me a call." He took a card from his wallet and carefully printed his cell phone number on the back. "Give me a call, and we'll meet someplace." Frank wished he'd worn civvies. Outside in the sunlight, his uniform obviously made Mitch skittish. Frank smiled reassuringly. "I'd really appreciate anything you can tell me that would help to identify the body." This one would be easy to scare away, and Frank didn't want to do that. Not now, when he was considerably closer to finding out who the second man was. He might still be around. Maybe he was a poacher of men as well as of sheep.

# 5

•

Frank followed Jan's beat-up Gremlin up the road toward Ridge-crest. The car was a little like Jan, wide-bodied, unusual, and, according to Jan, dependable. Cars told the tale. Fat cats in fat cars. Poor folks in junkers, leaking oil in sad little puddles wherever they stopped on their journey to the junkyard, or, more likely, to the last stop in some desert gully. The desert was dotted with rusting shells, the final remnants of disposable dreams, from gleaming showroom to desert detritus.

He was living in a glass house again. His '53 Chevy pickup marked him a latent Luddite with a streak of vanity—no air conditioning, no power this or power that, just a carburetor and distributor, mechanical fuel pump, stuff he could work on. It had all been carefully restored—shiny and bright, neat and clean, like his faded khakis, which were always ironed, with just a touch of a crease.

The truck was his time capsule, insulating him from the frantic present. After a couple of beers, sitting in the cab of his truck at night, he could hear the distant echos of the past, a steam train working its way up the grade to Keeler, the yellow light from the caboose flickering across the tops of the creosote bushes. He shook his head, thinking that perhaps he ought to buy a new four-wheel-drive truck. If nothing else, it would save a lot of digging, but he knew he wouldn't.

Jan was zipping along at seventy, faster than Frank usually drove. He pressed on the throttle and listened to the even ripple of the tappets, a little bit noisy—time to adjust the valves.

He followed Jan onto Highway 178. Where was she going? They had almost run out of town. Then she turned into an abandoned gas station, the service island a deserted strip of cement, the asphalt cracked and weedy. Jan pulled under the shade of a tattered canopy. At the far corner of the commercial lot, a squat cube of white-washed cement block had been recently erected. It stood there, glaringly bright in the afternoon sun. A hand-painted sign ran along three edges of the roof, announcing Ralph's Burritos. Ralph's Burritos? He'd withhold judgment on Ralph, but anything could happen. Recently, on one of his infrequent trips he'd eaten a great *chile relleno* made by a Korean, but that was in L.A., the mecca of ethnic food.

He pulled up next to Jan's Gremlin, where she stood waiting with a younger woman, the dark-haired woman from the class. He hadn't been expecting this, but he should have. For some reason or other, he seemed to awaken a maternal response in older women. Maybe it was his size or his shyness, but it made him apprehensive and irritated. He could do without the well-meaning matchmaking that seemed to plague his life.

Jan took his arm and propelled him toward her companion. "Frank, I want you to meet Linda Reyes. She's with the *InyoKern Courier*." The name was familiar. He had declined to be interviewed about finding the body in the Panamints. He was glad to leave that stuff up to Dave Meecham, who preferred to deal with the press. What was Jan up to?

He took Linda's outstretched hand. The grip was firm and dry. "Pleased to meet you." For some reason, he grinned, feeling a bit foolish, as if he'd been caught at something he shouldn't have been doing. Damn Jan Rockford.

They took stools on the side of the whitewashed stand that was somewhat protected from the sun. Jan suggested he try Ralph's special burrito, which was okay with Frank. The smells of chili, cumin, and cilantro wafting up from the stainless-steel pots reminded Frank how hungry he was.

Ralph, who looked more like Pancho Villa than a Ralph, wrapped beans, rice, and *pico de gallo* in a huge steamed tortilla, frowning at his customers as he worked.

"Wet or dry?"

Frank opted for dry and was immediately sorry when Ralph ladled a rich onion and tomatillo salsa over Jan and Linda's burritos. He pushed his paper plate back toward the scowling Ralph.

"Make mine wet, too."

Ralph's scowl deepened. Evidently, he didn't like weak-minded costumers. He eyed Frank.

"*Picante?*"

This had to be some sort of challenge. Eat this *salsa picante*, which I also sell as drain cleaner, and I'll know you to be a man, *muy macho*. He smiled at the surly Ralph, shaking his head in mock dismay. "No thanks, just the *salsa verde*." He flattened the vowels, giving them a nice midwestern "I learned my Spanish in school" sound.

Ralph nodded, his face closed off. Frank knew Ralph now regarded him as an ersatz Mexican. Tough. Frank reclaimed his plate, the burrito swimming in green sauce. He was very, very hungry. Before anyone could speak, he had forked a bite dripping with sauce into his mouth. God, it was delicious. He closed his eyes for a moment.

"Really good, Jan. Really, really good."

Ralph's frown softened.

Linda eyed Frank curiously. He suddenly felt much better. Jan suggested that they adjourn to a dilapidated wooden picnic table huddled under the sporadic shade of some tamarisk trees. Linda and Frank sat in uneasy silence while Jan trundled off to her car.

Actually, it was Frank who felt uneasy. Linda seemed perfectly relaxed watching Jan's progress across the asphalt. She leaned forward, her arms resting lightly on the table. She was dressed for the desert in tan chinos and a long-sleeved blue shirt, her face shaded by a straw hat, eyes hidden by oversize sunglasses. She had to be aware that he was looking at her, yet she seemed remarkably comfortable despite his scrutiny.

It was the high heat of early afternoon, and Frank longed for a beer. That first beer of the day was becoming increasingly important. He'd have to cut back, but not right now. As Jan approached the table, Frank could see she carried a small Playmate cooler. His spirits rose. She plunked the cooler on the table and produced three Coronas, ice still clinging to the glass bottles.

"Thought we could use a beer to wash down the burritos. Damn, forgot the church key."

"That's okay. Use mine." Linda produced a Swiss army knife from the side pocket of a large canvas and leather purse resting beside her on the bench.

Frank tipped his up. There was nothing like that first swallow of cold beer after an evening of a bit too much. Right now, it seemed like it had been wrung from the hand of God. He sighed with satisfaction. He felt his whole being begin to relax. He was suddenly aware that he, too, was being observed. There was that slight smile of amusement on Linda's face.

"Tastes good, huh? Especially the morning after." Linda grinned.

Was she mocking him? Probably. Well that was okay, too.

Jan pushed a wispy end of gray hair away from her face. "Linda's interested in Desert bighorns, Frank, and nobody knows more about them than you do. So I'm afraid I trapped you. She told me that you hadn't returned her calls, that she had been referred to your supervisor. So I told her I'd try to set up an introduction. I'm afraid it was my idea, not Linda's. So anyway, here we are."

Frank took a swallow of his beer, then turned to Linda. He waited, making his face blank, uninterested. He wasn't going to be the first to talk.

"Maybe this wasn't such a good idea." Linda met his gaze. "This feels like an imposition." She started to rise. "I'll call you at your office."

This wasn't the way he wanted it to go. "Wait a minute." He gestured toward the table. "You haven't finished your beer." He gave her his best Flynn grin. She stopped and peered at him from over the top of her sunglasses, her dark eyes probing him.

He scrambled to recover. "Look, I admit I don't particularly like talking to reporters. What's more important, the district ranger, Dave Meecham, prefers to handle the press, but we're here now." He waited for a response. She stood by the table, her dark eyes searching his face. Frank liked the way she watched him without embarrassment or hostility. She took off the hat and pushed her hair, damp with perspiration, away from her face, tucking it behind her ears.

"Okay." Linda sat back down, the hat pushed to the back of her head. "First of all, I'm not here as a reporter for the *Courier*. The dead body you found in the Panamints is yesterday's news. I'm writing an article about Desert bighorns for *Western Living*. They do vacation stuff—where to stay, what to see, where to eat, that sort of thing. They also have a feature called *Outback*. It takes a look at the rare and unusual, things most people will probably never see, or will probably never want to see. But it's one of their most popular features. Lots of letters.

"I've read all sorts of stuff about bighorns, but to tell you the truth, I've never seen one. I didn't know about all this poaching and petroglyph stuff until the corpse you found made news. I covered the story for the *Courier*." Linda smiled at Jan. "When I talked with Jan about what I was doing, she said I ought to talk to you." She sighed. "Is there another beer in there?" She nodded at the cooler. When Jan handed her a beer, Linda took the icy bottle and rubbed it across her forehead.

"Well, I figured trying to contact you was probably a dead end, unless I tackled you in the parking lot over at BLM," she said. "So, Jan told me about you coming to her class. Now you know what I want to know and why I want to know it." She gave him a slight smile. "There's no hidden agenda. I just want to know about the sheep."

"Yeah, well, I guess I get to acting like the sheep are my personal responsibility. They're not, though. But they're wonderful animals. I hate to see them harmed."

Linda's face was very serious. "I know. I could tell from your lecture. I liked the way you tied what we do now to the people who lived here first, especially about how they were like us, just trying to live but making mistakes in the process. I'd never felt connected to any of that before. It was a really good lecture."

He smiled, and fished out the last beer and opened it for Jan. She was beaming good-naturedly, evidently pleased that the tension had dissipated.

"I guess you know that the BLM watches over the land, not the animals. The sheep belong to the state of California, so wildlife management is the responsibility of Fish and Game. But they're understaffed, just like we are, so we help each other out." He felt like he was doing one of his talks to tourists by the campfire. "Do you need to know all this stuff?"

Linda looked up from the notebook she had taken out of her canvas purse. "Actually, I've looked up most of what you've been telling me, but it's good to know how you feel about it, how it works in practice."

"Well, we work together as much as possible. Of course, it's personal. Some agents and some agencies work well together, some not. But on the whole, we cooperate." He watched her writing in her notebook. He was glad she wasn't using a tape recorder. Recorded conversations had a way of reminding him he was dispensing words.

"Do the dominant rams lead the flock?" she asked.

Frank shook his head. "Nope, usually it's the oldest female with the largest number of descendants. The rams hang out together until fall—mating season. Then they snort and cough, run around stiff-legged, and butt heads."

Linda pushed her sunglasses back on her nose. She was smiling.

"Yeah." Frank grinned. "I know, it sounds familiar. Only the sheep get to take a break, since rutting season comes only once a year." He felt his face flush. He was grateful for his dark skin. Where the hell had that come from? Just the image he wanted to convey, a macho cop with a perpetual woody. He lifted his sunglasses from their resting place in his shirt and put them on.

"How many desert bighorns are left?"

"Altogether, or here in the Mojave?" He was glad they were on safer ground now. He wasn't used to feeling flustered.

"When you say 'altogether,' where do you mean?"

"North America, which means the United States and Mexico. The sheep live in the deserts of the Southwest."

"Okay." She turned to a fresh page in her notebook. "How many in North America?"

"I wish I could give you a solid number, but I can't. They're hard to count, and they live over a wide range, thousands of square miles. Maybe a total population of eighteen to twenty thousand."

"How many in Mexico?"

He looked at his hands resting on the weathered wood. "Six to eight thousand, but they're on their way out."

"Why's that?" Her shirt had developed wet patches of sweat under her arms. He watched as perspiration beaded on her face and made little rivulets of moisture down her cheeks.

"In Mexico, they don't do too well at managing animal populations. The fees for acting as an illegal guide, the *mordida* for officials to look the other way, it's too much temptation. Now that Baja is more accessible, you can probably kiss the sheep there good-bye. In another ten years at most, finding bighorns in Baja will be a rare occurrence."

"And in the States?"

"There might be ten to twelve thousand, scattered throughout the deserts, mainly in Arizona, California, and Nevada."

"And in the Mojave Desert?"

"That depends on whose Mojave Desert. If you define the desert by flora and fauna, it lies in California, Nevada, and Arizona. But some of the sheep live in the Colorado and Sonoran deserts, which stretch into California from Mexico. If you're near Joshua trees, you're in the Mojave Desert. That's a good rule of thumb."

"So how many sheep are in the Mojave?"

"The census figures are by state, so we'll do a guesstimate. If we leave Arizona and Nevada out of it, there might be three thousand sheep in about a hundred thousand square miles of desert, including Death Valley and the Panamints."

"That's one sheep for every thirty-three square miles."

Frank nodded. "Or one sheep for every twenty-one thousand or so acres."

Linda frowned. "No wonder I've never seen one."

Jan gave a short laugh. "I think Frank makes it all up just to have an excuse to go hiking. Bill Pearson's the only other person who claims to have close encounters of the third kind, and he's a biologist, so that makes him suspect."

"Come on, Jan, give me a break. Pearson knows when and where to look. I'll be damned if I could tell a hand ax from a rock with a sharp edge until you showed me what to look for." Jan looked somewhat mollified. "Besides, after you've watched bighorns for a while, you get to know where and when they're going to show up. They have favorite spots."

Linda fiddled with her pencil. "I suppose you know where they hang out, don't you?"

This was going a little better. Somewhere, he had reasserted himself. "Yeah, the flock in the Panamints are on the west side of Telescope Peak, coming down to the springs in Wildrose and Surprise canyons."

Linda reached into her pants pocket and produced a red kerchief. She set her sunglasses on the table and wiped the perspiration from her face and neck. "How would you like to take me up there and show me some bighorns firsthand?" Her smile was both challenging and disconcerting.

Somehow, Frank felt he had been sandbagged, that the whole conversation had been leading up to this. He glanced over at Jan, who seemed to be studying Ralph's whitewashed cubicle with unwarranted interest. He regarded Linda with care. Actually, he knew he wanted to show this woman the things that lifted his heart. She seemed physically fit, but that could be deceiving. He hesitated for a moment and then found himself nodding.

"Okay, I was planning on going into the Panamints this week. How about Friday? I've got some time off."

Her face lit up. "Great. That'd be just great. I was really afraid you'd say no."

Jan grinned. "Now we'll find out if Frank has been sitting around in his caboose chewing the sacred datura or he's actually been among the bighorn sheep."

"You live in a caboose?" Linda asked.

"Yeah, well, that's another story. We'll need an early start. Say about four-thirty."

"Four-thirty in the morning!" A frown creased her forehead.

"That's the way to beat the heat. Tell me how to get to your place and I'll pick you up."

"It's too far out of the way. Why don't we meet in the college parking lot?"

He was disappointed. "Okay, suit yourself. I just thought it would be, uh, easier."

"I live in Red Mountain. Do you know where the Joshua Tree Athletic Club is?" Frank nodded. "Well, that's my dad's place. I'll meet you out front at five with coffee and sandwiches. How's that sound?"

Jack Collins was her dad? Things were getting off to a tangled start. "Great." He caught Jan in an unguarded smirk. "Is this okay with you, Jan? I don't want to spoil your plans."

"No, no, you can invite me over to that caboose of yours, and we'll have a beer, okay?"

She glanced at her watch, suddenly aware of the time. "I've got to get back. Strategic Planning Committee. Sounds like we should be meeting with the brass at China Lake, but it's part of the drill. We churn out a five-year plan every year." Jan and Linda rose. As Linda moved off toward the car, Jan turned and winked at Frank. He didn't know whether to laugh or be annoyed.

# 6

•

Mitch Cooper had called Frank and said to meet him at 4:00 P.M., but Frank had come early so that he could look the place over and find somewhere to sit that had a degree of privacy. The privacy turned out to be a nonconsideration. The afternoon temperature was still over a hundred, and the few customers lounging about weren't there for the food. They sat around the tiny dance floor, resting in the air-conditioned darkness and waited for the cloaking din of music to mask the poverty of conversation and usher in the rituals of the one-night stand. Frank felt jaded. They were just people out to meet one another, after all. His exclusion from the premating activities had been his choice.

He especially didn't like ersatz Mexican restaurants with cute names like Maria's Casita, or the bland food swimming in tasteless sauce served up by chirpy waitresses. These unfortunates were fitted out in short skirts and low-cut peasant blouses trimmed with matching ribbon. Many people seemed to love the insincere familiarity of such places, but Frank was put off by the frothy margaritas, the colorful plates of tasteless food, the commercial glimpses of fleshy bosoms, and, most especially, the dead warmth of purchased perkiness.

He shook his head. He had no business making judgments, casting the first stone, as his mother would've reminded him. But he preferred getting to know people gradually. Courtships required time. He liked the idea of courtship, of the sweet tension of pursuit. The image of a mischievous grin and hazel eyes briefly formed in his mind's eye. He smiled back, letting himself picture the easy way Linda Reyes had teased him. He had found it annoying that she seemed to sense his discomfort, yet he had agreed to help her with her story about sheep poaching, even agreed to take her into Surprise Canyon, surprising himself in the process.

A young Mexican girl, her thin body poking out from a billowing blouse and skirt, interrupted his reverie. She launched unenthusiastically into a canned spiel.

"Hi, my name is Lupe, and I'm going to be your server this evening."

As she paused for breath, Frank interrupted. "*Hola, Lupe. Me llamo Francisco y quisiera cerveza solamente.* And Lupe, I will be here for a while. I am waiting for a friend, a tall man with brown hair, probably tied back. Show him out here if you see him, okay? And while I'm waiting, make that beer a Corona, *por favor.*"

She smiled shyly. "*Sí. ¿Nada más?*" she asked, making sure there was nothing more he wanted.

"*Nada más, gracias.*" Frank watched her retreat across the tiled patio, carried away on legs made sticklike by the ridiculous costume. He wanted to tell her to find another place to work. When he got the beer, it was cold, but the glass was warm, another message from indifferent management. Frank muttered a soft "*Gracias*" and drank from the bottle, his thoughts on Mitch Cooper.

If Cooper could help him identify the corpse, he would be much closer to discovering what had happened in Surprise Canyon. More than ever he was convinced that there had been a second person at the scene of the sheep killing by the spring. And if that were the case, it was very likely that the dead man had been deliberately abandoned, left without shoes or sufficient water to die of dehydration, a rapid process in the intense heat of the Mojave. A deliberate and thoughtful sort of murder.

Frank looked and saw Mitch Cooper and the blond girl, whom Mitch had introduced as Shawna, standing by the entrance to the patio. Lupe was pointing over to the table where Frank sat. He rose to greet them. They were holding hands, as if for reassurance. It made him remember his copness, the weight of the uniform.

"Mitch. Shawna." Frank smiled and thrust out his hand. "Good to see you again. How about something to drink? Beer, margarita?"

"Beer for me." Mitch glanced over at Shawna.

"Ice tea, please." She smiled a sort of dreamy, beatific smile.

He ordered the beer and iced tea, then waited until they were served to begin asking questions. In the meantime, Mitch asked Frank if it was hot enough for him. Probably the most frequently asked question in the Mojave. Frank replied that the heat didn't bother him much. In fact, he liked the heat, enjoyed the hot, dry stillness of the day, followed by the cool night, when the living things of the desert came out to hunt and make love. The desert had nightlife.

There was a lull in the conversation as the small talk petered out. When the drinks came, Frank said, "So, Mitch, what can you tell me about the man who died in the desert?" He kept his voice matter-of-fact, his expression neutral.

Mitch and Shawna exchanged glances.

"Well, before I changed—let the Lord into my life—I used to run with this motorcycle club, the Sidewinders." Mitch looked from Frank back to Shawna. She nodded encouragement.

"The Sidewinders? That's a club I've never heard of."

"It's a small club. There were never more than ten or twelve of us, guys who went on the rides and stuff." He took a deep breath. "Well, we all had tattoos like the guy you found." He laid his forearm on the table, revealing a crudely done death's head, the lines of ink uneven, thick, and blurred. The figure of the skull itself was disproportionate, the mouth too large for the eyeless sockets. Its uniqueness lay in the crudity of its rendering—a true primitive, a totem meant to ward off, to frighten.

"You say you all had them?"

"Yeah, that's right, but only two of the guys had them on their necks. The Millers, Roy and Donnie. The dead guy's gotta be one of them, because they were the only ones who had it on their necks."

The note on the matchbook from the Joshua Tree Athletic Club said, "Donnie, call home. Roy." He resisted taking it out of his pocket and looking at it. Looks like it had to have been Donnie who died in Surprise Canyon, Frank thought. Was Roy the second person? Perhaps. But they were brothers. Maybe Cain and Abel.

Mitch went on explaining about the tattoos.

"See, the tattoos were part of the initiation. When a new guy came into the club, we had a ceremony. Roy ran it. He'd tell about where the different races came from. He was always reading stuff about history and how the white race started civilization and how it had been copied and corrupted by the other races. Anyhow, we swore to uphold the purity of the white race." Mitch looked at Frank's olive skin. "No offense, man. I didn't believe any of that shit, but at the time, I went along, you know."

Frank did know, and for a brief moment he had the urge to tell Mitch about reaping what you sow, reaping the whirlwind, but he needed to hear what Mitch had to say. "Yeah, well, we all make mistakes, Mitch. You're not there now. You've started a different life. That's the point. So, the initiation?"

"Yeah, that's true." Mitch leaned back in the plastic patio chair and peered into his beer. "After the stuff about being Aryan, Roy explained about the snake. How it had been a part of an earlier American flag that said 'Don't tread on me.' Roy said that was our motto. Out here in the Mojave Desert, we could do whatever we wanted, and if somebody screwed us over, then it was like stepping on a rattler—they were going to get bit. After that, Donnie got out this cork with needles sticking out of it. They were all bunched together in the center. He dipped the needles in india ink and etched the tattoo on the new guy's skin. Some guys wanted it on their back or arm, some on the shoulder. But the neck, that was just for Roy and Donnie."

Mitch paused. Most people had a need to fill the silence, but Frank waited, saying nothing. Mitch raised his eyebrows, then nodded, as if answering an unasked question. "Oh, yeah. There was another brother, Jason; he had it on the palm of his hand. He'd hold up his hand and make the eyes wink by wrinkling the lines on his palm. Like this." Mitch held his hand up toward Frank and bent the index finger and then the little finger, creasing the skin around the lines. "Roy said when Jason made death wink with both eyes, it was

'*Adiós*, motherfucker.' " He turned to Shawna. "Excuse me, honey, but that's what he said."

Shawna gazed up at Mitch, the beatific smile radiating martyr-dom. Some victims worked hard at it, perfected the vulnerability until it cried out for injury. Frank had to look away.

"Tell me about the brothers. What was Donnie like?"

Mitch sneered. "He was okay most of the time, when his brothers weren't around. We sorta hung out together."

"What did he look like? Was he a big guy?"

"Naw, he was about five eight, skinny, maybe a hundred and thirty-five pounds. He had curly brown hair." Mitch paused, trying to remember.

"Anything special about him? Scars, other tattoos?"

"Oh yeah, he had a bunch of tattoos on his arms, mostly girls' initials. He said he was going to put the initials of all the girls he boffed on his arms, but he had to give up, because he would've had to be an octopus to fit them all. He was always bragging, trying to be tough like his brothers. He tried to act like a real badass. He was always walking around with a gun, shooting at something.

"One time, he sees this lizard on a rock, so he shoots at it from only about twenty feet away. The bullet ricochets off the rock and hits Jace in the leg. Jace grabs Donnie and starts pounding on him. Roy's there, and he just watches until Donnie starts calling out for him to come and stop Jace from beating the shit out of him. After awhile, Roy comes over and lifts Jace off Donnie by the hair. He's got both hands in Jace's hair, the skin on his face all pulled up away from his eyes. He just hung there, looking up at Roy, his eyes look-ing like they could've rolled out of his face. It was weird. Donnie was crying." Mitch shook his heard, as if clearing away a bad dream.

"They were always pounding on each other. But touch one of them, and you had Roy on your butt. So Donnie got away with a lotta stuff, 'cause of his brothers." Mitch gulped down the rest of his beer and wiped his mouth with the back of his hand. "But mostly, Donnie was full of crap. Always coming up with some dopey scheme to make the big score. Nobody listened much, because it was all talk, except for the porno tape. The tape was Donnie's big idea." Mitch stole a glance at Shawna.

"Tape?" Frank felt like he was doing echo therapy.

"Yeah, they made a porno tape. Donnie said there was real money in porno flicks." Mitch leaned forward, becoming animated, his sinewy arms resting on the table, white skin peeping out of the sleeveless Levi's jacket around the ropy muscles of his shoulders. "So he talked his girl, Vicki, into making a tape. They were always doing it in front of somebody anyhow, so she didn't give a shit who watched or not."

From the corner of his eye, Frank detected a ripple of emotion disturb the placid calm of Shawna's perpetual contact with a higher power. He wondered if she had had her fifteen minutes of fame in front of a cheap video camera.

Mitch's tale gained momentum. "Donnie told Vicki that a lot of big-time actresses started out in pornos, so she got all excited about being in movies. Donnie gives her a porno name, 'Moana Spasm.'" Mitch grinned conspiratorially at Frank. "Man, the Moana part turned out to be right. Donnie was really hyped. He wrote this script, and Vicki starts talking about production values, how she needs the right costumes and lighting. Right away, Vicki gets huffy when Donnie tells her she doesn't need a special costume, 'cause it's tits and ass."

Frank could see that Mitch was waiting for him to appreciate the witticism. He mustered up a grin and nodded knowingly. Real *compadres*. During this recitation, Shawna fixed her tranquil smile on Mitch, avoiding eye contact with Frank. Mitch was getting into it, a regular raconteur.

"Anyhow, in the tape, Vicki's supposed to be this nymphomaniac, can't stop herself when she sees the big red. She read some book on acting that says you have to live the part. So she starts to moan, and, man oh man, she really moaned. She moaned through the whole tape. When we played it for a bunch a guys at the Pit Stop in Victorville, the guys at the bar started laughing. I mean, man it was loud. She was howling like a dog. Pretty soon, we were all cracking up. I mean it was pretty funny, but there wasn't a woody in the room."

Mitch laughed, shaking his head, remembering the good old days.

"Donnie tried to be pissed off, but he started laughing, too. Said Vicki needed some more acting lessons. Vicki left in a big huff. So no one made any money, and Vicki ran off with one of the guys she met at the bar. That's pure Donnie. Without his brothers, just a sad-ass punk, but he was always a laugh." He nodded, chuckling softly.

Frank decided there was a side to Mitch that hadn't been born again. He caught glimpses of the old Mitch, the laid-back biker, with just enough mean in him to make it in tough company.

"How did Roy take all this?" Frank asked.

"He just watched, not saying a thing, not laughing. Roy never really goofed around much. He said the guys in the bar wouldn't have thought it was so funny if Jace had cut Vicki up. That kind of shut things down. He said after listening to all that moaning, they would've probably paid double just to watch her finally shut up."

Mitch's mouth puckered, the good humor gone. He had the look of a trapped rodent. "Roy didn't like Vicki. I'm glad she ran off and didn't come back. Bad things happened to the people Roy didn't like. And Jace, he liked to hurt things. Animals, people, it didn't make any difference. Sometimes he set things on fire." Mitch took a deep breath and shook his head again, trying to empty it of bad memories. He went on in a quiet voice.

"Once he burned up this guy's dog 'cause it barked at him when he rode by. It'd run along the fence, chasing after the bike. The first time it happened, Jace stopped, swung his bike around, and cruised back and forth, the dog barking and going crazy and Jace staring back. After that, Jace went out of his way to ride by the dog, both of them hating each other.

"Then one time, Jace noticed there were no cars around the guy's place and that extra food and water had been set out. So he goes back that night. It was only a couple hundred yards up the river from the trailer, so he walked. He was carrying a gas can. Pretty soon, we hear the dog howling, and Jace was howling with the dog.

When the dog would scream, Jason would scream along. Man, it was the worst thing I ever heard."

Frank's scalp tingled and his stomach knotted.

"Where was Roy when this was going on?"

Mitch's face was taut with the sort of concentration that comes from fear. "He was sitting there with this little smile on his face. All you could hear was Jace and the dog screaming in the night, and he just grinned at us. He said Jace was doing karaoke, having a sing-along with the neighbors."

"What about the police? Didn't one of the neighbors call the police, or the dog's owner when he got back?" Frank thought he knew the answer.

Mitch reached over for Shawna's hand. "Nobody fucked with the Miller brothers, man, they'da had to have bodyguards for the rest of their lives. Naw, the guy moved out the day after he got back." Mitch touched a scar on his eyebrow. "This is from Roy." He tapped his front teeth. "These aren't mine. I pissed Roy off when I called Jace a freak. He beat the hell out of me. Man, I've been beat before, but this was bad. After I was down and I thought it was over, I tried to move. He came over and kicked me. He was sitting in this folding chair, drinking a beer. Every time I tried to move, he'd get up and walk over and kick me, not saying anything, just kick me in the face, in the ribs, in the back.

"When I started spitting blood, Donnie took the party wagon and dropped me off at the emergency hospital. I had a rib in one of my lungs. That's where I met Shawna—she was a volunteer. I never went back, not even for my bike."

"Ever see any of them again?"

"I ran into Donnie a couple times after that. He told me I was smart not to come around. He said Roy and Jace were hiring out as bodyguards, beating up people for money. I got the impression that Donnie'd moved in with some woman, but he was being cagey about where he was livin'. But that was okay, because I was, too. By that time, I had the job at the mine. Shawna and I live up on Red Mountain, caretaking the old Ophir mine."

Lupe came over to ask if anyone wanted anything more. Frank forced a smile. "*No mas, gracias.*"

Mitch searched Frank's face. "Now maybe you can tell me something. Who died out there in the desert? Was it Donnie or Roy? Man, guess I don't have to tell you I'm really hoping it was Roy."

Mitch and Shawna were leaning into each other, Mitch looking more like a frightened kid than a biker. The pair had reasons to be afraid of the Miller brothers, especially Mitch, who no doubt had seen enough to be a threat, a loose end. Frank thought about telling Mitch the identity of the corpse was police business, but he decided against it. Officially, it wasn't BLM business. It was only a matter of time before the identity of the dead man would be official. He wanted to know more, though.

"To be absolutely sure, Mitch, I need to have a better picture of what Roy and Jason Miller looked like."

"Jace? Jace's got nothing to do with it." Mitch's voice was tight. He leaned forward. "Jace is built like an ape, a redheaded ape. He doesn't look anything like the others. Roy's got white skin, white hair, real white, but nobody called him Whitey. Donnie told me never to call him that. He hated it."

Frank drew small wet circles on the tabletop, waiting for Mitch to go on.

"He has weird eyes, pale blue, with pink rims. He's no taller than me, and I'm six one. But he weighs more—about one eighty, no fat, works out all the time." He looked at Frank expectantly.

An early-evening breeze gusted across the patio, flapping the umbrellas. The sudden coolness of the air raised goose bumps on Frank's arms. "It looks like the dead guy was Donnie Miller. The corpse was that of a small man with curly dark hair. If your description is accurate, there's no way it could have been Roy. Of course, we won't know for sure until after a positive identification." But Frank could see from the tight look on Mitch's face that they both knew Roy Miller was still somewhere out there in the desert.

# 7

•

Frank switched off the truck's lights. "On a bright night like this, you can see better without the glare."

As they emerged from Salt Wash Canyon, the land lay bathed in moonlight. Searles Dry Lake stretched before them like a vast silver sea. The stark bareness of the Slate Range rose up from the east side of the valley floor, the moonlit ridges bright against the dark shadows of the canyons.

"More coffee?" Linda had to raise her voice to make herself heard over the tappet clatter of Frank's truck. She held the thermos up, and Frank passed her his cup. He inhaled the aroma of the coffee and the faint smell of shampoo from her hair, still damp. He couldn't see Linda's face clearly. The soft light touched only her left cheek and the edge of an ear where it poked through dark hair.

"Dad buys Costa Rican beans and grinds them fresh every morning. He's a fanatic about coffee, and now he's ruined me for the regular stuff."

"Lucky you, to have your own personal Juan Valdez in the morning." Frank thought she was smiling, but he couldn't tell.

"He doesn't sleep the way he used to. Most of the time, he's up early. I usually see his light on when I come home late. He reads everything in sight, then leaves little stacks of books on my porch with his own brief reviews. 'Another Matthew Scudder, good read.' Or 'If you like Hiaasen, you'll like Shames.' 'This one's funny, great villain.' Stuff like that. He's been picking out books for me for years."

Frank noticed her deliberate way of responding. Pauses in conversation didn't seem to bother her. She turned to face him, a bit of her ear catching the light. "But yes, you're right," she told him. "It is nice to have someone to do things for you, have coffee for you in the morning. Can you make a decent cup of coffee, Frank, or do you settle for instant like most people who live alone?"

Somehow, the question was unsettling. He shifted around in his seat. "My coffee's okay, but it's not like this." He imagined Linda wrapped in one of his old shirts, seated in one of his rickety folding chairs, drinking his coffee, her feet on the iron railing that rimmed the rear of the caboose. He swung the truck under the huge rolling mill that spanned the Trona road. They had reached what was called the West End Facility, part of the huge borax-processing operation that the Kerr-Magee Corporation had built on the edge of the dry lake bed.

The plant was the single reason for the existence of Trona. Frank loved the desert, but Trona was a place unto itself, a company town perched on the edge of Searles Dry Lake, an alkaline depression so inhospitable that it was nearly without life. The dry lake bed yielded up riches greater than the elusive gold and silver for which the prospectors wandered the desert. But not in rich pockets of quartz laced with spiderwebs of gold. Nothing all that exciting, just millions of dollars' worth of borax spread across the lifeless bottom of an ancient lake bed, precious in the vastness of its quantity.

Frank explained the operation to Linda, telling her about the history of borax mining in the desert and the famous twenty-mule teams that had hauled the great wagons from below sea level up and over Wingate Pass to the railroad junction at Mojave. The mules were long gone, but the old road was still there. Marks on the land lasted a long time in the desert.

As they rounded the curve toward the scattered lights of Trona, Frank pointed out the skeletal structure of a mine head, the tailings scattered down the slope of the hill in conical piles. "The Mojave has its share of scars. There are mines and tailings scattered all across the desert. It seems that people either come here to dig the desert up or get across it. Have you been up near Tecopa?" Frank turned the lights back on as they approached Trona.

Linda nodded. "Yes, Dad and I camped out near Dumont Dunes. He liked it out there until it became a popular place for dune buggies. The noise spoiled it." She sipped coffee from the thermos cup, holding it with both hands.

"Well, from right there, where the Amargosa River turns to empty into Death Valley, to the next available water at Bitter Springs, it's more than fifty miles. No big deal by car, but very tough on foot or by horseback." Frank had this compulsion to tell her about the desert. It was like the guys in the army always talking about their hometown.

"Where the water reaches the surface along the Amargosa River, it's so saline that it makes animals and people sick. Same story at Bitter Springs. The Spaniards ran pack trains from Santa Fe to Los Angeles. They called that stretch the Jornada de la Muerte."

"The journey of death," she murmured softly.

Frank stole a glance. She had a way of wrinkling her forehead and pursing out her lower lip when she was thinking about something. "That's been the story. Not many people have come here to live. If it hadn't been for mining, people would've just passed on through."

Linda half-turned in her seat. "Dad came here to live. He used to kid around about coming out to live in the desert in an Airstream trailer with flat tires. It turned out he wasn't kidding. When he told me he'd bought a bar and restaurant in the Mojave Desert, I couldn't believe it. I almost stayed where we were living in Pasadena."

"Why didn't you?"

Linda stared out the window, watching the town of Trona go by. "Oh, I don't know. I knew Dad would need help, especially with his drinking buddies for partners. Living in Red Mountain was a bit much."

"Who are his drinking buddies?"

Turning toward Frank, she lifted her chin. "Ben and Bill. They've all been friends for more than thirty years. They quarrel and make plans, mostly plans that don't happen, but they're inseparable. I know it sounds funny and old-fashioned, but they're closer than blood relatives."

He looked over at a wrecking yard north of town, where the rusting hulks of cars lay strewn across the desert floor. The Mojave Desert, graveyard of dead machines, their engines finally falling silent, ashes to ashes, rust to dust. Maybe her dad and his buddies were like that. Maybe they'd come to the desert to die. Frank liked the way she stuck up for them. She made no apologies for their peculiarities.

Linda breathed deeply and looked out at the desert. "Did you know the Joshua Tree Athletic Club was what the miners liked to call a 'pleasure palace'?"

"Yeah, so I've heard. Some of the old-timers still talk about it." He grinned. "With fond memories, I might add. To hear them tell it, the girls were all beautiful, warmhearted, and never took a dime from the guy telling the story."

"Yeah, sometimes I hear Ben and Bill talking about Janey's place over in Nevada. They make it sound like a social club. Maybe it is. Did you know about the tunnels leading from the bar to the crib houses where the girls worked?"

Frank downshifted as they approached a low pass. "I've heard about them."

"Well, they're real. When my dad and his buddies fixed up the old crib house where I live, they cleaned out the tunnel leading from the bar to the house. They even strung lights. I hardly ever use it, though. It's full of spiderwebs, but it's sort of fun to think of the girls leading their men through the tunnels to escape being caught by the sheriff." Linda sighed, staring into the darkness of the hills sloping down to the steeply cut bank on her right.

"I love being with Dad, and I've known Bill and Ben since I was born. But when I first came to Red Mountain, I was kind of going crazy. Working at the bar, reading everything in sight, and playing hearts with Dad and his pals just wasn't enough." She turned to face Frank, giving him a soft smile. "You know how it is. You plan on doing this or that thing, just for a little while, and then the next thing you know, you've settled in."

Frank nodded. "Um-hmm. Yeah." He knew exactly how it was. "If you let it, life makes the decisions for you, and the next thing you know, you're just sort of following along."

They rounded a corner, and he could see her face in the moonlight, a frown creasing her forehead, her lip sticking out, ready to be nibbled. He needed to get a grip on this. She was doing a story. He was showing her where the bighorns were. This isn't a social outing, he told himself.

"The job opened up at the *Courier*. That's been great. I really like being a reporter, especially for a small paper." She laughed quietly. "Hey, if it happens, I get to cover it, from bake sales to crime."

They came to the top of the rise, and Frank slowed the truck. He stole a glance at Linda, who was sitting there in her khaki shorts and hiking boots, her hair blowing around from the open window. "You ever regret living out here? It's sure not L.A."

"Oh, now and then. Like when I want to go to a good restaurant that's not a steak house, or see a play or go to a concert. But it's so"— she paused, searching for the right word—"primeval here. It reminds me of the beginning of the world."

Her response made him feel momentarily empty. She seemed to see the beginnings of things, where he saw life leaking out of everything. The cancer had come to his mother without warning and took away everything but her quiet patience. His foolish, drunken, loving father—God, how he missed the fun! As he wept by his mother's bedside, she had blessed him, resting her brown hand on his head, slowly moving her fingers in his hair. She knew he had no belief in God, but she blessed him because she believed that she had enough faith for the three of them. Grief squatted in Frank's stomach like a living weight, cutting him off from life. He used his love of solitude as a means of keeping passion at a safe distance. Dry as the desert.

The first hint of gray light softened the sharp lines of the land, washing away the stark contrast between canyon darkness and moonlit slope, blurring the distinction between ridge line and sky. Frank pulled the jeep into a dirt turnaround at the crest of the hill. Linda gave him a questioning look.

"This is a good spot."

Frank got out of the truck and walked to the edge of the dirt, where the land sloped sharply away into the darkness of early morning.

"From here, you can see up Panamint Valley and, back there, Searles Dry Lake." He pointed up at the mountains bathed in silver light and shadow. "That's Telescope Peak. It's the highest point in Death Valley, over eleven thousand feet. Pretty soon, we'll be directly below it, but you can't see it from down in the canyon." They walked back to the truck in silence. Frank went to the right side of the vehicle to open the door, suddenly feeling awkward. Standing close to Linda he smelled her soap and shampoo again. There was a constriction in his chest. He opened the door and stepped back quickly, beating a clumsy retreat from his feelings. He couldn't tell if she'd noticed his awkwardness or not.

She spoke without turning her head. "Sometimes, when I'm up early, working on something I've put off, I watch the sunrise on Red Mountain." She turned to Frank, smiling now. "It always seems to put things in perspective."

Frank winced at the irony. Right now, moonlight in the desert wasn't doing much for his sense of perspective. If anything, the dry perfume of sage and creosote seemed to be fused with the smell of Linda's shampoo. He concentrated on the pale edges of her ears. The rush of sensation wasn't unfamiliar. Alone in the desert, he'd let himself merge with the surroundings, the land and sky seeping into him, but there had never been a woman in these moments.

The Panamint Road lay before them in a straight line that bisected the valley floor. Frank concentrated on driving now. He was pleased to find that neither of them found it necessary to fill the silence with the comfort of small talk. He needed the time to regain his composure. It had been almost three months since Mary Alice had departed for Los Angeles. This hermit thing had been going on too long, despite bruised egos and broken hearts. He liked women in his life. He was pretty sure he'd like this particular woman in his life. She hadn't inquired into the incongruity of the Irish name and the brown skin. He smiled to himself. He had been wondering about the Reyes name and the oh-so-white skin.

"What are you grinning about?"

"Nothing at all, Linda Reyes. Just thinking the thoughts of an Irish cop."

"Well, when you want to share, let me know."

●

They bounced their way up the last three miles of the dirt track leading to Surprise Canyon, their stuff shifting around in the back of the truck. The glove compartment flew open, spilling maps and pencils on the floor and causing Frank to curse. Linda just grinned and held on to the wind-wing bar. Two things particularly set Frank's teeth on edge, wind blowing everything every which way and being bounced around in the cab of a vehicle. By the time he pulled off the track, he was in a state of irritation.

Linda had brought a soft half-gallon canteen, good for hiking, and an aluminum camera case. She wore sturdy lightweight ankle boots, a light long-sleeve shirt, and a straw hat with a strap. He wondered about the advisability of shorts when they'd have to scramble up some of the steep slopes. He hoped she was in shape for the tough climbing ahead. He thought about her pale white legs catching the faint light.

"It's about five miles from here to the end of Surprise Canyon. It's a steady climb, and some of it's damn steep. We have about nine hours to make the round-trip, which means we've gotta make pretty good time." Frank looked at Linda inquiringly, giving her a chance to back out. Now that they were here, he wasn't completely sure this was such a good idea. He'd made this hike many times, but walking was part of his life. It was part of his job, part of his Paiute heritage. Vehicles were a means of getting to a place where he had to go on foot. They were meant to be left behind. If a place could be reached by car, there would be people, cans, papers, trash. Walk a mile away from the road, it was a different world. Walk a couple miles into the desert, you could hear the silence.

Frank watched Linda, her foot resting on the bumper of the truck as she concentrated on tightening up the laces of her boots. She seemed to know what she was doing. She had put a small first-aid kit in her day pack, along with the lunch stuff that she had brought for both of them. Frank strapped on two half-gallon soft canteens, shouldered his pack, and started up the trail that led toward the spring. In a couple of miles, he'd know whether she was up to doing this or not.

# 8

•

Jason shuffled along the buckled sidewalk, simian-gaited, his thick torso rocking on bandy legs. On the other side of the chain-link fence, the dogs kept pace in watchful silence. Now and then, he stopped to stare at the muscular black bodies of the rottweilers, which were casually alert, their tongues lolling in the thick heat. His head bobbed up and down in an eerie pantomime of primate behavior, the rottweilers' huge heads mimicking the motion. Roy got out of the van to stand in the partial shade of its squat profile. His brother and the dogs continued their silent parade down the bright new fence. From time to time, Jason reached out a furry red hand and jiggled the fence, enticing one of the dogs to jump at his flattened palm in frustrated fury. Bits of sunlight glittered from the razor wire topping the fence.

Roy found a familiar reassurance in his brother's oddities. He watched Jason come around the corner of the property, a location momentarily screened from the building by a eucalyptus tree, its slender gray-green leaves dusty and motionless in the humid valley heat. Jason reached into his pants pocket and produced a package wrapped in butcher paper. He opened the package and leaned forward, sniffing the contents with care—ground meat laced with chloral hydrate, a canine Mickey Finn. He hunched over, his large head shifting from side to side as if to ward off detection. Then he lurched near the fence, shoving gobs of meat through the wire squares, high up, out of reach of the crushing teeth.

The larger of the two dogs gulped the meat down without

hesitation. The smaller one, the female, sniffed suspiciously, eyeing Jason. He crouched forward and pushed another gob of meat through the fence and backed away. This time, the dog took the meat into her mouth.

"Sleepy time, dogs. Oh yes, sleepy time, dogs." Roy hummed to himself and moved toward the gate. As he drew near, the dogs broke away from Jason and trotted to a security gate complete with electronic locking mechanism and two-way speakers. The smaller of the dogs bared her teeth, a barely audible rumble coming from deep within her throat. Roy looked on them with a sort of approval. They were creatures of menace, trained not to bark, more threatening in their silent watchfulness than slavering junkyard dogs. Passersby hurried their steps or crossed the street to avoid the dogs' attention.

Roy pushed the buzzer next to the gate and waited.

A half acre of asphalt surrounded a large single-story corrugated-iron building topped by a small cupola. The clerestory windows of the cupola were painted black, with the unpainted exception facing Holt Boulevard and the gated entrance into the compound. Above the streetside door, a new, professionally done sign in foot-high black lettering against a Caltrans yellow background proclaimed GOLDEN STATE FIREARMS. The coils of razor wire topping the bright, new eight-foot-high chain-link fence suggested a sort of recent prosperity. It was a safe haven, an untouchable retreat. Roy nodded to himself. A place with something soft at its center.

Jason padded after the dogs, grinning in anticipation, happy again to be back in Roy's good graces. A suggestion of movement in the unpainted window confirmed Roy's suspicion that they were being watched. "Hey look me over . . ." Roy hummed. He had dressed for the occasion in soft chamois leather pants, matching shirt, lizard-skin boots—eight-hundred-dollar threads, topped off with a low-crowned, wide-brimmed 10x Stetson. A rich dude, flush customer. Even Jason passed muster in clean, pressed Wrangler pants and shirt, hired help.

The dogs' ears pricked up in unison, probably responding to a silent whistle. They turned as one and trotted toward the building, disappearing through the corrugated door, which was partially open, allowing them to pass.

"Identify yourself, please." The voice coming from the speaker sounded tinny and slightly garbled.

"It's Mr. Hauptman, Eric Hauptman—we spoke on the phone—and Mr. Rojas, my associate." Roy smiled at his little linguistic joke.

"When you hear the buzzer, push the gate."

The sound was familiar—that of institutional lockdown, doors controlled from a bulletproof booth. Roy gave the gate a shove. They were in. A visit from the Miller boys.

A smallish pear-shaped man stood back from the door, well behind the phalanx of dogs. "The dogs are okay. Just don't touch anything."

It was the same soft, indistinct voice Roy had had trouble hearing on the phone. The pear man was all dressed up like an urban storm trooper—khaki T-shirt, camo pants, and brightly polished jump boots, sort of a combat Pillsbury Doughboy. Hickey would be cracking up, wanting to know if he got his clothes at Banana Republic. The guy's stomach ballooned over a tooled belt and threatened to swallow up the butt of a 9-mm Glock semiautomatic pistol. The Glock rested in a clip-on holster, easy to reach, a point of consideration.

Roy slipped into persona, smiling confidently. "I'm Eric Hauptman. This is my driver and assistant, Jesus Rojas." He gave the name Jesus the Spanish pronunciation, *hay—zoos*. Roy gestured toward Jason, who bobbed his head, his tiny blue eyes bright with concentration.

"You're Calvin Bates?"

"Yeah, that's right."

Bates bent down, squinting into the open action of a large-bore sporting rifle resting in a padded cradle. The bolt lay next to a small padded vise on the bench.

"As I said on the phone, I'd like you to custom a thousand-yard rifle for me. I've seen your work. It's the best." Roy delivered his slow personal smile, his teeth pale yellow against white skin and red gums.

"Where'd you see my work?" Bates blew some invisible debris from the open bolt action.

Roy spoke with enthusiasm. "Pomona Gun Show. Some Japanese guy was selling a very nice three seventy-five Weatherby Magnum. He said he'd had it customized by Golden State Firearms. That's you, right?"

"Yeah, I know the little yeller feller." Bates nodded without looking up. "A dentist who can't talk English and who can't hit shit." He fished a large cigar from the cargo pocket on his fatigue pants. He bit off the end and spit the severed tip in the direction of a trash bin. "Ol' Doc Jap took it to the range to sight it in. What a fucking joke. He said it kicked too hard, asked would I fix it." Bates looked up at Roy. "I told him it would knock his Asian butt on the ground." He shook his head in disgust. "He shoulda bought a twenty-two and stuck to tin cans."

Roy nodded his head in shared disgust. It was easy to empathize. Roy liked "yeller fellers" even less than Bates.

Bates shifted his gaze from Roy back to the rifle he was working on. "You know, that was a really nice piece I made for him. So how come you didn't buy it when you had the chance?"

"Like you said," Roy replied, "a three seventy-five's too much, unless you're hunting really big stuff. Besides, it's not for reaching out, is it? And the stock was too short, made for little Jap arms." Roy grinned in conspiratorial fellowship.

Bates took a wooden match from his shirt pocket and struck with his thumbnail. He applied the match to the end of the cigar, puffing carefully until it was evenly lit. Clouds of smoke hung in the still air.

"If you think a three seventy-five's too much, you ought to try this baby, a four fifty-eight, the most powerful shoulder weapon made. Want to stop a car, this fucker'll do it. Purdy's makes them in doubles, but I like the Weatherby bolt action, the strongest—five shots, three more for insurance."

He waved his hand absently at the cloud of smoke.

"So what you're thinking of—I mean, if you want the thousand-yard shot—is maybe a two twenty or a two seventy. The two seventy's got the flat trajectory, and it's steady, groups tight. The two twenty's fast, but not much stopping power, and to tell you the truth the loads are critical. They have to be just right or the thing shoots all over the map. The two seventy does more work."

Roy looked past Bates to the stock blanks neatly resting from Peg-Board pins against the wall behind the workbench. "Mind if I look over the stocks?"

The dogs sat panting heavily. The male, especially laboring for breath, half-slid into an outstretched position. Bates squatted down on one knee next to the dog. "Hey, boy, what's up?" He rubbed behind the dog's ears, talking softly. "Hey, Nero, come on, boy."

Roy stepped swiftly past the long workbench and the dogs and kneed Bates in the face. The male dog was too stupefied to respond, but the female struggled to her feet and staggered at Roy, a growl rumbling in her throat. Jason kicked into her side hard enough to crack ribs. Her rear end collapsed in shaky spasms. She sank to the ground with a soft whimper, feet splayed awkwardly against the floor.

Roy grasped Bates by the throat with one hand and grabbed the Glock with the other, pushing him down next to the prostrate dogs. He smiled affably.

"Surprise, Mr. Bates, you've got company."

Bates sat up, a small, soft hand unconsciously rubbing his throat. His eyes shifted quickly about and came to rest on Roy, sizing things up. Too calm by half, Roy thought. He'd been fucked over before.

Roy leaned forward. "Hey, don't you want to know why we're here?"

Bates nodded in stupefied acquiescence.

"See, it's like this, Cal—vin. . . ." He drew out the name in singsong fashion, with a hint of a musical rise on the last syllable. "There's a family matter involved here. We're here to talk about a guy we think you know, a guy we've got business with. Little guy with dark hair and a lot of tattoos, named Donnie. Ring a bell, does it?"

Bates's face wrinkled in perplexity.

"That's okay, Cal—vin. We'll give your memory a jog."

Roy glanced around the shop, his head swiveling owl-like, the muscular cords flexing on the pale stem of his neck, the white Stetson tracking the room. His gaze stopped on a large plastic reel of heavy-gauge electrical wire. "Jace, cut off about fifteen feet of that wire there on the orange spool." They waited in the heat, watching as Jason pulled wire from the spool and coiled it around his shoulder and arm. "Yeah, that'll do. Now bring it on over here, and we'll play Isaac Parker, just like when you were a kid."

Roy turned to Bates. "You know who Isaac Parker was, Bates? He was the hanging judge at Fort Smith, Arkansas. He strung 'em up four and five at a time, an honest-to-goodness law-and-order judge. A real American."

Bates shifted around to a position where he could face Roy more directly. "Jesus, I'd tell you if I knew about this Donnie guy, but I don't know what you're talking about."

Roy looked over at Jason and rolled his eyes.

"Come on, man, I didn't do anything. You want money?" Bates's eyes shifted back and forth between Roy and Jace. "Money's no problem. I'll make you any kind of gun you want. For Christ's sake, tell me what you want, you've got it. You don't have to hurt me, man."

Roy shook his head in mock disapproval.

"Jeez, Cal—vin, what kind of guys do you think we are? We're family guys. You a family guy, Calvin? I mean, are you married—wife, kids, that sort of thing?"

Bates shook his head.

"No? That's sort of what I thought. Well hell, I'm not married, either. A studly type, such as yourself, does better prowlin' on his own. Right?"

Bates looked over at Jace's face, which was eager with anticipation, and then up at Roy. The shock and fear were beginning to register. "Yeah, I suppose so." His attempt at a grin sort of slid down his face.

"Like I said, we're family-oriented." Roy turned solemn. "That's the point here, maintaining family values. See, a member of our family was hurt, so we've been thinking tit for tat, an eye for an eye, like in the Bible. Now it sorta looks like your family's gone to the dogs, Cal—vin. Little joke there."

Roy pointed his forefinger up toward the iron slope of the ceiling and made a twirling motion. "Okay now. Here we go. Judge Jesus will string up the criminals, the little one first. She's still sort of lively." Roy laughed. "You don't know whether to be relieved or sad, do you, Calvin? Thought we might be stringing you up. Gee whiz, not a nice thought, but the point is, this dog's first." He put his forefinger alongside his nose and gave a knowing wink.

Bates's body sagged. His face seemed to hang, the flesh pulled downward by gravity and fear. "Hey look, ask me anything. I'll tell you anything you want to know. What did this Donnie look like? I don't know anybody named Donnie."

Roy nodded at Jason, who deftly looped the wire around the smaller dog and tossed the remaining wire over the steel I beam that supported the lights and a small hoist.

"Wait a minute, Jace. Slide the hoist down here. Let's do this right."

Jace's head twisted back, eyes glittering. "I'm hanging the dog, Roy. This is the bad one. It tried to bite me, and now I'm hanging it."

"I never said different, dickbrain. Just go on down and slide the hoist back. Then tie the wire around the hook. See, it'll be easier."

Roy shrugged elaborately. "What can I do, Bates? The guy's got a mind of his own. Now this guy, Donnie, says he knows you. Truth is, we found your phone number on the wall next to a note, 'Call for a good time.' Naw, just kidding. Anyway, Donnie did some work for you. Now my guess, it wasn't a completely legal deal."

"I do stuff for a lot of guys. I don't remember any Donnie."

"Okay, Jesus, take 'er up."

"Aw shit, come on, please."

The rottweiler's feet waved frantically in the air. Roy and Jace watched intently. Gasps of guttural wheezing filled the hot stillness of the shop. A cascade of urine streamed from the swinging dog and splashed on the cement floor. Roy stepped quickly back to keep his outfit from being splattered. Jason Miller's hands tensed on the hoist's chain, his gaze fixed on the strangling dog. The dog's paws flipped in the air in spasmodic jerks.

Bates moaned a sort of distracted prayer. "Oh my God, Jesus, oh my God. You bastards."

"Now, now, Cal—vin, don't be downhearted. You've still got old Nero here." Roy paused. "Nero, right?"

Bates nodded numbly.

"Yeah, well, now listen up. Nero's not out of the woods yet. Jesus here doesn't much care for Nero, either. Do you, Jesus?" Roy leaned back against the workbench. Jason's gaze remained fixed on the dead rottweiler swinging gently from the hoist. "So what about Donnie Miller, Cal? Mind if I call you Cal? I figured it would be okay, 'cause we've been involved in an intimate emotional experience, witnessing the death of a loved one, right?" Roy's face wrinkled in concerned inquiry.

"Anyhow, Donnie Miller, a little guy with tattoos. Oh yeah, and he used a lot of bad language, but a good guy underneath. Heart of gold, like Jesus here, except, of course, he was a liar, a cheat, and full of bullshit, but otherwise a nice guy." He chuckled to himself, shaking his head back and forth. "Yup, outside of that, he was a prince."

Roy figured breaking a guy down was just a matter of timing, and it was going just about right. Bates was coming around in a nice predictable sequence: Oh my, what's happening here? Then: How can you do that? You have no right! Finally, it dawned on the dumb dickheads that they were fucking helpless and that they were looking at a couple a guys who just didn't give a shit. That's when they rolled, just like Calvin here.

"So now that we're all acquainted, and such, Cal—vin, when did you talk to Donnie?"

"A little guy, you said, with a lot of tattoos, right?" Bates looked up at Roy for confirmation.

"That's my man Donnie. I knew you'd turn out to be a good listener."

Bates nodded in eager camaraderie. "I set a guy like that up with one of my clients a few weeks back, around the middle of August. Only he called himself Miller McDonald, not Donnie Miller." Bates kept nodding his head vigorously. "Shit, yeah, I remember him." He glanced back at Roy. Some life had oozed back into his face, the ever-present Judas of hope tracing itself in his expression. "Mind if I have a smoke?"

"Naw, go ahead." Roy smiled. "But just bring a cigar out of that pocket, okay, Cal? No little surprises."

Bates fished out another cigar and went through the ritual of lighting up. Clouds of blue smoke twisted in wraithlike shapes in the column of sunlight streaming in from the clerestory window.

"So what about this Miller?" Roy sounded interested, conversational, empathetic. He shifted easily from one pathology to another.

Bates frowned in concentration. "Well, he came around here talking about being a hunting guide. Said he could hook up hunters with Desert bighorns. Said he knew the desert like the back of his hand. I figured he was full of shit, but then one of my customers tells me he wants to complete the grand slam."

"Grand slam?"

"Yeah, the big four, the four kinds of bighorn sheep in North America. It's a big deal with some hunters, a very big deal, since the desert bighorn is mostly illegal to hunt and hard to find.

"Well anyhow, this Miller guy starts in telling me he'll take the guy out on a guaranteed hunt. No sheep, no pay. So I went for it and lined up Miller as a guide with this doctor. Guy's a big deal. Has a special clinic for infertility."

The dead rottweiler swung gently from the wire. The shadow of the forelegs played across Bates's chest and face. He squinted up his eyes each time the sunlight hit his face. "Guy forked over cash for expenses and agreed to pay a big bonus for a sheep that would make the book, the Boone and Crockett record book."

"How big a bonus?"

"Ten thousand."

"How much for Miller?"

"I told him a thousand. He went for it big-time. That's when I knew he didn't know shit about poaching bighorns."

"Why's that?"

"The dumb fuck didn't know the price of a ticket."

"So when did you see him last?"

"Right here, near the end of August. He came by to show off his

AR-fifteen and get me to make it full automatic. I said, 'What for?' He sort of grinned and said he had more going on than taking dudes into the desert, like he was some sort of bad man."

Roy frowned. "So what happened to the big-ticket doctor? Did he get his big horny sheep, Cal—vin?"

"Naw, he called me sometime in early September, all pissed off. Said the guide didn't know jack about hunting. So I lined him up with another guy I know about."

"Yeah, what guy was that?"

Bates puffed on the cigar, blew a smoke ring. He looked up at Roy. "I don't want to get anyone in trouble. This guy could get in big trouble for poaching."

"Not as much trouble as you're in, Cal—vin." Roy looked thoughtful. "You want to be able to find your dick when you take a leak, right, Cal?"

Bates's hand moved inadvertently to his crotch. "This guy's like one of us, right?" Roy's expression remained neutral. Bates tried again. "You know, a hunter. He calls himself 'Redhawk,' but he's in the Bishop phone book as Eddie Laguna. That's it. I don't know another fucking thing. Just that this Miller guy was full of shit. Wish to God I'd never seen him, man."

"Yeah, Calvin, he was full of shit, but here's the funny part. I hope you're paying attention here. You see, he was our brother, Calvin. We're the Miller brothers, Roy, Jesus here, and Donnie. And guess what? Donnie's dead. Some shithead left him out in the desert to die, maybe this fucking doctor, maybe this Redhawk." Roy looked sad. "So things didn't work out for brother Donnie, did they?" Bates's eyes widened with fear. "And here you are, speaking ill of the dead. No bonus from the doc for Donnie, just dying of thirst in the desert. Sort of an ugly way to go, don'tcha think?" Bates nodded slowly, unable to take his eyes away from Roy's face. "And Calvin, there are lots of ways to go that are ugly." He paused, smiling down at Bates. "So you can see we're anxious to talk with the doc and this Redhawk and see if we can clear up a few details."

Roy felt the first edge of rage flickering at the edges of his eyes.

"Yeah, definitely need to talk to the doc. So who is he, Cal? What's his name? How do I get ahold of him for a little chat?"

"I leave messages with his exchange. I only called him a couple of times. The other times, he called me when he wanted something."

"So what's the number at the exchange?'

"It's in the address book next to the phone there." He pointed over toward the far wall. "The brown metal one."

Roy looked over at Jace, who was still humming to himself and swinging the dead rottweiler back and forth on the hoist.

"Jace, keep an eye on Calvin here. Okay, Jace?"

"Umm-hmmm, okay, Roy," he hummed.

Roy threaded his way between the prostrate male rottweiler and Bates to the rough-sawn plywood desk, which was strewn with gun catalogs and advertising pamphlets singing the praises of various firearms, reloading equipment, and sighting devices. He found an old dime-store metal address book, the kind that flipped open to different letters by moving the slide up or down the side of the cover.

"What name, Calvin?"

"Sorensen, Dr. Michael Sorensen."

Roy slid the key up to the *S* and pushed the metal tab at the bottom of the tin cover. "Just a phone number. No fucking address, Calvin."

"I told you—I call and leave messages, or he calls me."

Roy stepped back to where Bates leaned against the workbench. "That's talking back, Calvin. Talking back is rude." Roy's backhand snapped Bates's head back. Blood leaked from his nose.

"What kind of doctor?"

"A gynecologist."

"Hear that, Jace, a pussy doctor. Old Doc Sorensen is a pussy doctor."

Jason exposed his teeth, nodding at Roy.

"What town's he live in?"

"Pasadena, I think."

"You think? Why do you think Pasadena, Calvin?"

"He mentioned it a couple of times. Complained about all the gooks moving in." Bates grinned up at Roy, trying for Aryan brotherhood.

"Now that's helpful, Calvin." Roy stood looking down at the pathetic grin. The blood had dried on Bates's upper lip and had crusted around his nostrils. Another bag of pain. "Well, we got to be going, Cal—vin. We've got a busy social calendar."

Bates slowly nodded his head, sighing with relief.

Roy slipped the Glock quickly from his belt and pointed it down at Bates.

"No. No. Please, no." Bates held up his hands, as if somehow he could ward off death.

" 'No. No. Please, no.' " The red creature's mouth mocked Bates's words in eerie imitation.

"Put down your fucking hands, Cal—vin. Can't you take a joke?" Roy flashed a smile. "You know, I'll bet you're sorry to see us go, Cal—vin."

Bates nodded his head and shifted his eyes from the Glock to peer up at Roy. Here it was again, the pathetic face of hope. "But you know how it is, Calvin. When you gotta go, you gotta go."

The first shot caught Bates in the chest, knocking him backward onto the floor, cheating Roy of the look of surprise. He stepped quickly forward and looked down. Bates's eyes had already begun to lose their luster.

"Shit!"

He stepped back to avoid the splatter and put a second shot into the dead man's head. He looked up at his brother, really smiling now. " 'When a job's worth doing, it's worth doing right.' Words to live by, brother Jason." Roy took the .458 Magnum from the cradle and slipped the bolt into the pocket of his jacket.

"Never know when we might have to kill a car. Right?"

Jason scrabbled forward and began tugging at the drugged Nero.

"We don't have time, Jace. Here, take the gun."

Roy handed the Glock over to his brother.

"You get three shots, just three. And don't get blood all over yourself. After that, you can start a little fire. Then we gotta talk to Redhawk and the doctor."

# 9

•

Frank stopped in the sandy wash. A jumble of car-size boulders lay across the canyon, blocking their path. He could hear Linda's even breathing in the morning stillness.

"We're almost there. Once we've climbed the rocks, the canyon opens up into a small meadow. It's the surprise in Surprise Canyon."

"How do we get up?" Linda's voice was tight.

"We work our way up the left side."

Frank gestured with his arm. Boulders spilled out of the dark mouth of the canyon. They seemed caught in a frozen avalanche, waiting to tumble out of the shadows and come crashing down the narrow wash to the valley floor. "We cross over to the middle. There's a gap there. Then we're home free."

She turned and walked back about twenty feet and looked up at the rocks. Frank tried to sound reassuring. "It looks nasty from here, but it's not so bad if you know the way." He casually waved her on and headed for a house-size rock tucked up against the canyon wall. Her footsteps crunched in the sand behind him.

"We don't climb this one." Frank slipped through a wedge-shaped gap between the rock and the canyon wall and scrambled from rock to rock, pausing now and then to observe Linda's progress. She had hardly drawn a short breath coming up the steep climb from the valley floor, but now she seemed tentative. "How ya doin'?" he asked.

She stepped across a narrow crevice, teetering awkwardly before regaining her balance. "Okay, but I'm not used to hiking around in the dark."

They climbed up an uneven stairway of huge boulders that were sharp-edged and angular, then emerged on the flattened surface of a two-story basaltic dome. Frank felt momentarily relieved. She'd made it this far, but the tough part lay ahead. The traverse across the rocks would require a jump of four or five feet between the tops of two upright monoliths. Frank and Linda stood near the edge of the drop.

They seemed to be standing on silvery sheets suspended in the soft light. Frank carefully scanned the other side. Linda peered into the void between the rocks. The gap dropped away into the bottomlessness of pitch-dark. The top of the far rock appeared to be floating above the dark of the canyon, its surface softened by deceptive undulations interspersed with patches of narrow shadow.

"We take a little jump—from here to over there." His attempt at reassurance sounded hollow. It was no more than five feet. He had done it many times, but now, in the darkness of false dawn, the other side seemed far away, the blackness of the pit palpable.

Linda continued to stare down into the darkness. "How far is it to the other side?"

"Four, maybe five feet, and where we are is quite a bit higher than the other side. That makes it easier." Silence. "Jumping downhill." He knew that if she thought about it too long, she'd lose her nerve, work up some real fear. It wasn't really that far. He hoped it was a matter of just doing it.

"Watch when I jump. I'm going to land on that flat spot right there." He pointed toward the other rock. "Take a small run; then give it your best. You'll clear it with no problem."

Frank stepped back, poised for the jump. "When you take off, keep your eye on the flat spot, where you're going to land." He ran forward and leaped easily to the other side.

Linda stood motionless in the moonlight, still staring down into the black space between the rocks.

"Take off your pack and toss it over."

"It's got my camera case in it."

"Not to worry. I was first-string shortstop for the Lone Pine Warriors."

She shrugged off the pack and stood with it hanging indifferently from her right hand. Frank waited. Then she stepped to the edge. "Here it comes." She swung it back and forth underhanded and then tossed it in a high arc. It was all Frank could do to keep it from going over his head.

"Hey, some arm. You can pitch on my team anytime." He laid the pack down, being careful not to bang it. "There, that should help your balance when you land."

He waited. He hadn't figured on this. She'd seemed so assured, so fit, and now she was freezing up. It would be more than difficult to leap back. It was uphill. If he tried it, he'd be taking a hell of a chance of falling. It would take at least half an hour to get back to her by taking the long way around, following the trail that skirted the slide by going around the shoulder of the canyon. He very much didn't want her to be hurt. "If you don't think you can make it, Linda, don't do it. We'll wait for light. There's another way. It just takes longer."

"There's another way? That's just great." Her voice was tight with anger.

She walked back about twenty feet to the middle of the rock, then turned and sprinted for the edge. Frank watched as she sprang into the air, almost two feet from the edge, too far back. He stepped forward as she hurtled through the air, just in time to be knocked sprawling as she drove her knee into his stomach. He fought for breath as Linda scrambled to her feet. He tried to ask if she was all right, but all that came out were indecipherable wheezy sounds.

Her face was invisible in the dark, but her shoulders were shaking. He wondered if she was sobbing with relief. No, she was making gurgling sounds, not sobs of relief. She was laughing.

He tried to say, Thanks a lot. But all that came out were more wheezy grunts and squeaks. Her spluttering giggles exploded into a raucous belly laugh that echoed eerily in the canyon, a dissonant chorus against the vast silence of the place.

Frank felt a flash of humiliation and anger, and then, as he replayed the scene in his mind, it struck him as funny, too. He hadn't sufficiently regained his breath to laugh normally, so he made chuffing sounds interspersed with gasps for air.

Linda reached out her hand and helped him to his feet. "There's another way. Now you tell me. Thanks, Frank. I thought I was going to die. I'm very nearsighted. I have practically no depth perception, and you've got me leaping the Grand Canyon in the dark. No way am I coming back this way."

He felt like an idiot. "We can't come back this way anyhow—the jump back is uphill." He studied her face in the rising light. "Why didn't you tell me you're nearsighted? You're not wearing glasses or anything."

"Contacts, Frank. I'm wearing contact lenses. They make them in the big cities, because 'Men seldom make passes at . . .' "

" 'Girls who wear glasses,' " he finished

"How come you're familiar with Dorothy Parker?"

"Indians read books, too." He felt better.

●

Puffs of cool, damp air carried the smells of plant life into the dry desert air. A tiny waterfall spilled from the rocks above them at the head of the canyon, watering a small meadow where the sheep came to drink and graze in the cool of the morning. They had arrived in time. He turned, pointing, directing her gaze back toward the Sierras. "Look." As he spoke, the high tips of the range turned yellow-white in the first rays of morning light, melting the shadows in the valley below. Color seeped into the land, pastel browns brightening into brilliant yellows, the timeless transformation from night to day, unspoiled by urban light.

They moved almost noiselessly along the right side of the canyon, heading toward a low wall of rocks that extended from the canyon wall and butted up against a dark outcropping jutting out from the cliff's face. The wall and outcropping formed a rough semicircle close to twenty feet in length and six or seven feet wide at the broadest point. He watched as Linda placed her hand on the top of the wall and vaulted easily over the barrier. She could jump, no doubt about it. Frank led her toward the point of the enclosure nearest the spring.

"We wait here," he said, his voice almost a whisper. "If we're lucky, they'll come. The adults don't need to drink every day. But the lambs need water more frequently."

"How long can they go without water?"

"The old rams can go six or seven days. They're pretty amazing. They can drink a quarter of their body weight at one time."

They waited in the morning chill of the rock blind. Now there was enough light to reveal the petroglyphs along the face of the cliff—stick figures of fat-bellied sheep and ancient hunters caught in a ritual dance of death on the rock surface. Linda looked at the prehistoric pictures, touching them gently with her fingertips. "Actually seeing these up close, where you can touch them, is different from seeing them in a book or on slides. They seem oddly alive"— she paused—"and so strange. It's like the past is still right here."

"In a way, it is. Hunters have waited for the sheep to come here for thousands of years. My mother's people, and now . . ." He paused, not wanting to offend her.

"And now the white people."

"Yeah, the only difference is we're not waiting to kill them."

"Who built the rock walls—the people who made the petroglyphs?"

He nodded. "We're sitting in a blind, a place for hunters to hide. They would wait for the sheep to come and drink, then raise up with their atlatls, hurling spears into the sides of the sheep. They had to be close. The atlatl probably wasn't very effective much over fifty feet. I made one once, copied it from one found in a cave burial in Arizona. The best I could do with any accuracy was more like thirty or forty feet. But then, I hadn't been practicing with it all my life, either."

He made a small sweeping gesture, confining the motion behind the low wall. "The rocks in these walls were probably piled up more than three thousand years ago."

"How can you tell?"

"The petroglyphs depict atlatls—that means the pictures were made before the bow and arrow. So by inference, the guys who were sitting around pecking at the rock face, waiting for sheep or trying to make magic, were the same guys who built the blind."

He could see her wrinkling her forehead, mulling it over.

"Of course, I could be wrong. The New Age people think all these pictures were made by aliens from space. Maybe that's where my ancestors came from. Maybe that's why I can become a raven or a coyote and wander the earth, unseen by human eyes."

"Wrong. I can see you being a smart-ass right now, even though you're sitting back there in the shadows."

She brushed the hair away from her face. "Where will the sheep come from, if they come?"

"From up above. They always approach things from above and run uphill if something frightens them. Nothing can catch them when they're running uphill. If they come, they'll be cautious. Here, take these." He held out his 10 x 50 navy spotting binoculars. "I've got a pair of pocket binoculars in my fanny pack." He pointed to the opposite canyon wall, a talus slide that dropped for almost a thousand feet down into the canyon. "Search the slopes, but don't move around much. You won't have to worry about sunlight reflecting from the lens, because we're on the shady side for a while, but stay down. Sheep have an especially sharp sense of movement."

Frank scanned the slopes and ridges. He thought he saw something about halfway up the east slope. He fished into his fanny pack for the pocket binoculars. Sure enough, an old ewe stepped easily down the steep slope, pausing now and then, sniffing the air. She was followed by two younger ewes, probably yearlings.

"Linda, be very still. See where the piñons are clustered above that dark outcropping?"

She shaded her eyes from the bright sunlight striking the opposite canyon wall.

"Use the binoculars."

She lifted the binoculars, focusing on the grove of twisted pines that clutched the rock. "I don't see anything," she whispered in a voice husky with anticipation.

"Okay, now come down from there a bit."

"Oh, yes, I see them. Three of them. I don't see any males, just females. Where're the guys, Frank, off doing guylike things?"

"Could be. Rams will be rams. Actually, the rams usually travel separately. Sometimes they don't come at all. If they do, they'll wait until the ewes and lambs have had their fill."

The old ewe came first, leading the rest of the ewes and lambs down to the spring. She stood patiently as the others knelt by the water, folding their forelegs under them to drink from the spring.

"Frank, why isn't that one sheep drinking?"

"She's watching out. Usually, the flock is led by the oldest ewe. She acts as lookout while the others drink."

Linda smiled. "These are very smart animals, aren't they? Maybe I can get a couple of articles out of this. One for *Ms.* magazine. Let's see—maybe 'Ewe are a Born Leader. The Genetics of Group Process.'"

"Yeah, well, keep your eyes open. They won't be here long. If one of the old boys shows up, I think you'll be impressed."

As the last of the lambs rose from the pool, the old ewe knelt and drank deeply from the spring, the others watching patiently for her to finish. As she led them back up the talus slope to the cluster of pines, a mature ram stepped into the sunlight, his huge horns spiraled into a full curl.

"Linda, do you see him? There're a couple of rams in this area buttin' heads." He grinned. "Literally buttin' heads over the ewes." The smile disappeared. "Well, no, not anymore. Now there's only one."

She let out a small gasp. "Wow, he's really something."

They watched as two more rams moved out of the piñons into the increasingly bright sunlight. They were much younger, their horns not yet reaching into a half curl.

"What's the matter with the big one's horns?" she asked. "They're all broken on the ends."

"He's been rubbing them against the rocks. He has to do that to see. Otherwise, the horns would curl around and block his side vision. It's called 'brooming.'"

Linda set aside the binoculars, taking an aluminum camera

case from her backpack. She attached a telephoto lens to the camera, fiddled with the setting, and squinted into the viewfinder. Frank watched in consternation as the camera whirred and clicked, capturing images of the ram as it made its progress down the slope.

"Linda," he said, "I hope you won't use those pictures in your article."

"Why not? God, this is what I came for. There're some great shots here."

"Linda, this old guy is a trophy ram, one for the record book. If you publish his picture, it'll be his death warrant. There'll be guys out here in helicopters hunting him down."

"Aren't you exaggerating a bit?" She clicked away.

"Last year, one of the desert bighorn permits went for over a hundred thousand dollars at a government auction—a hundred thousand just for the chance to hunt one."

She looked up from the camera to face him.

"How would they know where to look?"

"They'd start with the paper. Read your article and then track your sources. The rest would be a matter of deduction and paying people to scout around. Believe me, they'd find him."

They watched as the rams approached the spring. They seemed especially cautious. She squinted into the camera but didn't click the shutter.

"If you look closely at his horns, you can see where they're battered and cracked from combat. See how they flare out at the tips? He's worked hard to wear them down. He's maybe seven or eight years old. Probably only has a couple more years as top ram, at best. Then he'll be solo. But right now, he's the king of the mountain. I'd like to see him around when I come up here, or at least know his head isn't on some wall as a conversation piece, providing bragging rights for some urban white hunter." He'd done it again. He couldn't seem to stop commenting on white skin. Just great, he thought. They watched the ram's unhurried progress as he made his way down the steep slope, moving with easy grace.

"I would, too."

"Would what?"

"Would like to see him around here when we come up the mountain again." She smiled, and Frank recognized the familiar stirring that drew him into the life of a woman. It passed between them, an elemental linking, far older than the dancing figures on the face of the cliff.

"Good, that's good." He knew he was grinning foolishly, but he didn't care. He turned his attention back to the sheep. Now they were both watching the old ram, sharing a sort of spiritual communion. His chest ached with the pleasure of life.

The ram had stopped to sniff the morning air, puffs of condensation disappearing into the brittle dryness of the desert. Then all three rams stood motionless, poised for flight. Frank had seen them sniff like that, give a guttural cough of alarm, and bound away into the rocks. For the briefest moment, he felt the old ram staring at him where he and Linda lay in the place of ancient ambush.

Then the old ram seemed to stagger sideways, falling to the earth, its slender legs kicking into the air. The crack of a high-powered rifle boomed and echoed in the canyon. Linda gasped, her "Oh my God" swallowed by the reverberation of a second shot. The two younger rams lunged up the steep slope, one of them falling behind, bright blood spraying from its nostrils. Linda stood up, as if about to run toward the fallen ram. Frank reached up and pulled her roughly to the ground.

"Stay down. We probably haven't been seen yet. If we have, we're in serious trouble." He looked at his watch. "We've got to move. The sun won't reach into the canyon until midmorning. So we still have time."

# 10

•

The echo of the last shot faded into silence, leaving the canyon devoid of sound.

"What're we going to do?"

It was a good question. Get the hell out of here, to start with, he thought. But it wasn't going to be easy to do without being seen. If some poacher was running around with a scoped rifle, being invisible meant staying alive, especially if this was the same hunter whom Frank suspected of murder.

"If we stay here, we're trapped." His hoarse whispering seemed unnaturally loud. "They'll be coming to take the head."

Linda stared out at the spring where the dead ram lay, her face hard with anger. "Let's wait, and when they get close enough, I'll take their pictures with the dead sheep. You'll have proof positive."

"And end up just as dead as the sheep?"

"They're not going to kill a cop."

"I wouldn't bet my life on it, or yours, either." He scanned the far side of the canyon wall. "In the first place, how're they going to know I'm a cop? No uniform, no gun. Not that they'd let me get close enough to use a handgun, even if I had one. Second, we're witnesses to a crime that could carry prison time and a heavy fine. The rich think staying out of jail is very, very important. There's no one here but us. No one watching. No rules to follow. They can do whatever the hell they want to. No, we've got to get back to the truck and the cell phone, get Fish and Game on it, get the bastards with the evidence in their possession."

He continued to look at the canyon walls, all rock and shadow, a million places for someone to remain unseen. He watched for movement, light reflected from any bright surface, lenses, a watch, anything that would betray the shooter's location. Nothing, as far as he could see.

"Come on. We've got to get going. If we hug the canyon wall, we should be okay. From the way the ram fell, they're probably on the slope above us. They'll be working their way to the head of the canyon. That'll give us time to reach the rocks. We'll have to go back the way we came."

"The way we came? I thought you said it was impossible."

"Not impossible, just dangerous."

Frank stood up, feeling exposed and vulnerable. He'd seen the results of high-velocity soft-nose hunting rounds and knew a tiny entrance wound wouldn't begin to reveal the internal damage. Bullets expanded and tumbled in an erratic path of destruction, ripping through flesh and bone, tearing into vital organs and severing nerves and arteries. Sometimes an exit wound could be the size of a fist; more frequently, though, the round lodged itself in some unlikely resting spot far from the point of entry, its energy spent in the destruction of living tissue. Most things didn't die easily. His skin crawled.

"Come on," he urged. "Stay as close to the cliff as possible."

They worked their way along the base of the canyon wall toward the cascade of boulders over which they had ascended to the hidden meadow. They'd be okay up to that point, but then they would have to come out into the open. The split in the rock was below the lip of the meadow, invisible from the spring, but in plain sight from the top of the slide.

He gestured to her to halt.

"What?" She still clutched the camera in front of her.

"Listen, if we try and run across the rock to make the jump back, one of us is sure to be hurt. There won't be any time to set up. We'd just have to sprint and jump, not take the chance of being seen."

She nodded, waiting for him to go on.

"There's a sort of passageway between two of the boulders on this side of the slide. It'll save us a half hour over the long way around. Only it's very narrow and steep. Once you're in, you're in." Just the thought of being trapped shortened his breath, constricting his throat and tightening his chest.

"What's the matter? You okay?" she asked.

"Oh yeah, just fine." He forced a smile. "Here we are, in danger of being hunted down by a couple of good ol' American sportsmen. One way out, we fall to our deaths; the other, we're stuck tight and die of thirst. I'd say we're between a rock and a hard place."

She wrinkled her face in disbelief. " 'Between a rock and a hard place'?"

"It's a joke. You know, ironic humor." He gave what he hoped was a devil-may-care smile, not the rictus grin he suspected was pasted on his face. Maybe his clumsy attempt at humor would convince her that the panic she'd seen in his face wasn't really there.

She grinned back. "Well, now that you put it like that, I realize that I've been terribly insensitive." She shook her head again. "Let's go for the slide. Anything's better than jumping around like mountain goats."

Frank knew there were worse things, like being stuck in nasty tight places, places where you couldn't move your arms, places that suffocated the life out of you.

•

Linda leaned forward, peering down the narrow chute. "You're right. It's pretty tight. Where's it come out?"

"You drop out onto a sandy spot. From there, you go to the right, where you come to the floor of the ravine. After that, you're back at the place where we climbed up."

"You? You mean 'we,' right?"

Frank shook his head. "Nope, I don't fit."

"What do you mean? You're not staying up here while I slide off to safety. No way."

"Why would I stay here? I'm not doing the heroic bit. It's just that I'm going to go a different way. Okay?"

"What way is that? You said we'd be sure to get hurt."

"No, I said, 'One of us is sure to be hurt.'" He held up his hand as she was about to protest. "Wait. I'm not going to try to jump back. I'm going to drop down the crevice to the sand. It's only about fifteen feet. No problem."

She gave him a doubtful look. "You could be killed or break bones."

"I can't—I can't be in tight places. That's it," he snapped. He struggled to sound matter-of-fact. "I wait here for you to clear the chute, then slide the packs down to you and head for the jump. Only I won't jump. I'll hang and drop off the edge. I'll be a couple hundred feet from where you'll come out."

She squinted her eyes, trying to read his expression, then shrugged her shoulders and scrunched up her face in acquiescence. "Okay, but you're going first. I can slide the packs myself."

Frank eyed the camera resting against her stomach. It sure wasn't in the nice safe aluminum case. Instead, she had secured it with a waist strap to keep it from banging around. "Don't fool around trying to take pictures. If you're spotted, you've had it."

She stared past his shoulder at some invisible spot.

"Jesus, Linda, don't take any chances. These guys could be very dangerous."

"Don't worry about me. You're the one who's doing the bungee jump without the bungee." This time, she raised her hand to silence him. "Frank, it's the only way I'm going to do it. We're wasting time."

"Okay, I'll go first, but as soon as I'm out of sight, you move, right?" She nodded her head just a little bit, as if to say, I hear you. But she wasn't giving any definite response—not very reassuring.

"Good. That's worked out," he said, sounding brisk and businesslike. Who was he fooling? "When you start down the chute, you'll get to a point where you have to slide. Don't try to stop yourself. You could get stuck, and you don't want that." He heard the tightness in his voice. "Keep your legs straight and put your arms over your head. You'll be landing in sand feet first, so you'll be okay. Bend your knees."

"I'll be careful. You be careful, too." Her face was serious, her eyes fixed on his.

He shrugged off his backpack and unsnapped the fanny pack and water bottles.

She put a hand on his arm. "Don't kill yourself. I'm not sure I know the way out."

He grinned. "Piece o' cake."

●

He was running much too fast on the uneven surface, flying over the face of the rock. Here and there he felt loose gravel and sand slip under his boots. Skidding to a stop dangerously close to the edge, he flopped down on the rock, skinning his hands and knees. The edge, round and smooth from erosion, provided nothing to hang on to. There was no way to lower himself over the side and drop, and no time to work it out. It was either jump or run back and try the chute. Not a real choice. Scrambling to his feet, he picked the widest point and jumped into the void.

Frank tried to roll, but the sand grabbed at his feet as he plunged forward, arms stretched out. Pain shot through his shoulder, and he lay gasping for breath for the second time in less than eight hours.

He let himself go, unclenching his hands, the world falling away on all sides. The breeze whispered ancient secrets among the rocks. High above him, turkey vultures drifted in lazy arcs across a jagged strip of blue sky, searching for the dead. He fought to sit up, pain shooting through the injured shoulder. His right arm felt next to useless. Steadying himself against the smooth granite, he regained his footing and tottered off toward the point where the chute emptied out into the canyon. He hoped his memory was correct and Linda would land in a sandy patch.

He'd only dropped through the chute once, more than twenty years ago, when he and Jimmy Tecopa had come here to play hunter, hide in the blind, and watch the sheep come down to drink at the spring. Jimmy had slipped down the chute, shouting with glee, but somehow Frank's leg had folded back under him, and he'd been stuck, held fast between unyielding granite walls.

Jimmy had climbed back up the rocks, cut one of the springy willows growing by the spring, and attached his belt to it. Bracing himself between the rocks, Jimmy had managed to lower the belt loop down so that Frank could grasp it, and Jimmy had pulled him up far enough to free his leg. Finally, he'd dropped onto the sand, his leg numb but uninjured. In Frank's mind, Jimmy had saved his life and his sanity. Nevertheless, the hour spent trapped between the rocks had left him with a permanent fear of confined places.

He rounded the corner where the narrow defile opened out onto the boulder-strewn slide. There were the packs and water bottles, but no Linda.

The crack and boom of a gunshot ruptured the morning stillness. Heart thumping, Frank ran toward the mouth of the chute, where the packs and water bottles lay scattered on the sand. Linda's body slipped out of the narrow opening in a crumpled heap. She gave him a small, twisted smile, her eyes unnaturally bright. "You're right. There's a point where you can't stop. You just start sliding."

"What the hell were they shooting at?"

"I'm not sure."

"Damn, they know we're here."

Drawing up her legs, she sat up. She gingerly flexed her arms, rotating them back and forth as if she were turning on a faucet.

"I stayed for pictures. I've got them both, right in here." She flashed a look of defiance and tapped her backpack, which held the aluminum camera case.

"For Christ's sake, what happened?"

She drew in a breath. "I watched you run across the rocks and nearly fall into the ravine, which probably would have been just as good as stepping off into thin air. Some careful approach. I thought you were going to hang and drop. What happened?"

He shook his head in irritation. "Never mind about that. Then what?"

"Well, after you went over the edge, I heard noises from above me, in the canyon. So I crawled up a ways and took a look. There were two guys making their way down the talus slope to the right of the falls. You were right. They were above us."

"Yeah, but why did they shoot at you? They must've seen you."

"I'm coming to that." She paused for a moment to complete an examination of an extended leg. Blood oozed and beaded from a scrape along the outside of her knee. She poked at it carefully, smearing the blood along her calf. "I'm not sure they saw me."

Frank leaned carefully forward and looked back up the chute. Nothing but good old blue sky.

"We better get out of here. Go back to the ravine, where we're less exposed." They picked up the packs, canteen, and water bottles and slipped into the protection of the crevice, temporarily safe from discovery in the alcove that extended along the base of the lower monolith. They sat in the sand, which was still damp from the last runoff. "Now, what happened up there? Why did they shoot at you?"

She unscrewed the top of her canteen and raised it to her mouth. It blocked her face from view and exposed the pale skin of her throat, which pulsed evenly and damn near endlessly, the quiet gurgle of her swallowing filling him with irritation.

He couldn't stop himself. "Well?"

"Well, I got their pictures."

"Got their pictures?"

"Frank, I took their pictures. They're right here, in my camera." She grinned. "Like I was saying, I heard these noises. Then I saw them come down the slope." She paused, waiting for him to interrupt.

He waited—silent, ready to explode.

"The little guy came first. He came down the slope sure-footed as a sheep."

Frank nodded encouragement.

"The big guy followed, knocking rocks loose and starting small slides at every step. It must've been him I heard. I'd already dropped your pack and the water down the chute. I wanted to watch what happened to them before I sent my pack down with the camera, so I still had it. Being a photojournalist as well as a damn good reporter, I snapped on the telephoto and took their pictures." She smiled triumphantly.

"What did they look like?"

"The big guy was maybe in his early forties, but it was hard to tell through the lens. He had the sort of looks that don't age all that much. You know—groomed, well cared for. He was blond, rugged, picture-perfect. Wore all the right clothes. He was the one with the rifle.

"The little guy was very dark-skinned. His face was weathered. I couldn't get a fix on his age—older than thirty and younger than fifty. Definitely not from Brentwood or San Marino. He wore jeans, a scruffy khaki shirt, and a beat-up straw hat. He was carrying a pack and two canteens. He didn't have a gun."

Frank felt a sinking feeling. The money for illegal guiding was too tempting. He'd heard rumors that some of the people from the Paiute and Shoshone communities had taken illegal hunters into the desert for sheep.

"What was the shooting about?"

"Actually, I'm not sure. After I took the pictures, I let my pack go down the chute. It was then I heard the shot. It scared me a lot, so when I started down the chute, I didn't do a very good job of slowing down. I just sort of fell and slid, but I'm okay."

Frank frowned in thought. "It was the second sheep. It was still alive. They must have been finishing it off. I thought for sure they'd spotted you and that you were a goner." He breathed heavily. "God, I thought I'd brought you up here to get killed." His chest clenched with the beginnings of rage. "Jesus, I'd like to get those bastards."

"We've got 'em." Linda tapped her pack again.

He nodded. "Yeah, maybe we do. Now all we have to do is get back to the truck."

•

Frank stopped to catch his breath where the canyon narrowed between a rounded shoulder on the left and a gray basaltic cliff some ten or twelve feet high. A dark blade of rock rose out of the sandy wash about a third of the way in from the cliff face.

Nine days earlier, Frank, Deputy Harris from the Inyo County Sheriff's Department, and the unhappy guys from the coroner's office had bagged the corpse and lugged it down to the county truck; now there was nothing. The thunderstorms that had swept across the desert the last few afternoons had washed away the last traces of Donnie Miller's life.

Linda reached into the cargo pockets of her hiking shorts and drew out a red paisley kerchief. The midmorning heat made the air quiver. Mopping her face and neck, she looked inquiringly at Frank. "Can't take it, huh?" She grinned at him.

She sure as hell had been keeping up. She was in shape, very good shape. He looked back at the place were Miller had lain in the sun, food for worms.

"This is where you found the dead man, isn't it?" She regarded Frank more closely—the reporter look. She seemed unconcerned in the face of danger. Did she feel she was in good hands, or was she one of those individuals who maintained "grace under pressure"?

"He was next to the cliff there." Frank gestured toward the rock face. He hadn't told her yet that he knew who the dead guy was. For now, it was a closed book.

"Hey, those are petroglyphs." Linda crossed over to the rock face and squatted down to examine the pictures of the bighorn sheep pecked into the rock. "Why are these so far down? Were these very, very short people, or what?" She looked up at Frank, wisps of hair clinging to her neck.

"Actually, that's probably as high as they could reach. They were little guys, but not that little—maybe five one or two on the average. The canyon floor was probably five or six feet lower when these were made. Making these might have been a stretch."

"How did you get the body out of here?"

He gave her a crooked grin. "Carried him. It's a very adventurous job. You get to carry rotting guys on hot days. Builds character."

"*Muy macho, Señor Francisco.*"

"Actually, that's my name." He began moving down the canyon.

"Actually, I knew that. I'm a reporter."

## 11

•

The afternoon breeze drifted in small swirls, coating a stagnant back eddy of the Mojave River with a film of fine dust. The corners of Roy's thin mouth turned up in a private smile as he watched his brother playing near the edge of the water.

Home sweet home. It had been a long time coming.

When Betts and Cass moved them to Los Angeles, away from the desert, everything went to hell. They were all trapped in a two-room apartment with Betts and "Uncle" Cass. No place to get away, no place to hide, except for the cellar—not as good as under the trailer, but better than being inside. The old Victorian house in south Los Angeles had been cut up into four units. Cass, Betts, and the three boys were in the smaller of the two downstairs apartments at the back of the house, where it opened up on a tiny patch of bare dirt next to the Harbor Freeway.

Before Cass came along, the succession of "uncles" had been short-time live-ins with a taste for liquor, pot, television, and occasional rutting with Betts. The boys had been left to their own devices, which had been okay with Roy. He'd found things to do, some of them unpleasant but largely unnoticed. But Cass was different from the other uncles, to whom they had been all but invisible. Cass decided to "take a hand" with the boys, "teach 'em good manners" and the importance of obedience.

Cass's instructional technique had been to smack them whenever he decided they were "out of line." Being out of line meant not minding their own "beeswax." Mostly, it meant being in the same room with him. Roy was quick and kept out of reach, but Jace never ran. When Cass reached for him, he froze, closed his eyes, and waited. Donnie began to whimper as soon as Cass looked at him. The whimpering whipped Cass into a regular fury. He rained down blows on the silent Jace and the screaming Donnie, sometimes not knowing which of them to hit. When he could catch Roy, he hit him a good one with a closed fist to make up for lost opportunity. Roy never cried. He was only twelve, but even then Cass found the odd eyes and reptilian stare disturbing. The boys spent more and more time in the cellar—out of sight, out of mind.

Roy hadn't let these transgressions against his person and his brothers pass unanswered. He broke things that belonged to Cass and left them for him to discover. Cass always exploded into a paroxysm of rage, screaming curses and threats. It was very gratifying, and, to Roy's surprise, a sure thing, easy to strike back. He stole Cass's porno magazines and videotapes. They were of special interest to Jason, despite his being only eleven. In some areas, Jason was ahead of his older brother. Roy hid the magazines in the cellar and gummed up the tapes with cooking oil before returning them to a cardboard carton in the closet.

When he discovered a videotape of Cass and Betts doing it, he squeezed glue into the VCR. Cass nearly came apart, screaming how he was gonna turn them over to the court as "fucking incorrigibles." Betts never interfered, not even when Cass hit Jace again and again, trying to get a reaction, or pounded on Donnie for pissing his pants with fear. Cass had some sort of pension, and Betts figured she'd finally hit pay dirt. She was living the good life of sweet wine and funny smokes.

When Roy talked Jason into shitting in Cass's shoes, Cass went white with rage. He locked them in the cellar and promised they'd stay there until the guilty party confessed to doing such a "filthy thing." Cass had come to know his boys, so he turned on the weakest link. He told Donnie that there were poisonous snakes under the house and that the snakes would come out at night and get them, unless, of course, they told who'd put shit in his shoes. Donnie couldn't stop crying. Jace wouldn't open his eyes or move. Roy told them it was a lie, that Cass was just trying to scare them, but it was dark in the cellar and Cass took the lightbulb when he left. The cellar door closed on three upturned faces, leaving them in darkness. They heard him turn the hasp against the latch plate. Then they heard things scrabbling around under the house. Jace and Donnie were too scared to move.

On the second day, Cass called down through the closed door, "You ready to tell who did the filthy thing?"

"Yes," said Roy, who still had a boy's voice.

"What's that? I can't hear you." Cass was always saying that, real loud in a big voice—"I can't hear you"—like soldiers in war movies.

"Yes. I'm ready to tell. It was me." Roy's voice was flat. He was experiencing flashes of red at the corners of his vision, like lightning in a dark tunnel.

"What about the others?"

"They didn't do anything."

"Yeah, just laughing and thinking what hot shit you are." He let them wait for a few beats, but they were silent. "Okay." He lifted the cellar door. It was mounted at an angle, made of pine, heavy with layers of paint and moisture. "Come on up and take your medicine."

"Help me with Jace. He can't move," Roy pleaded.

"You mean he won't move. Shit." Cass came down the cement steps into the half-light of the cellar.

Roy hit Cass in the left temple with a ball-peen hammer. Cass slumped down, but the blow hadn't been hard enough. He was moving his arms and legs, scraping at the cement like an injured insect. Roy hit him again on the top of his head, driving the round end into Cass's skull. This time, he heard a crunching sound. Cass's body twitched some more, but Roy knew he was dead. He turned to Jace and offered him the hammer. "Here, you do it." Jace sat staring at the fallen Cass. "Go ahead. It feels good. Do it, Jace. Do it."

Jace got to his feet and shuffled over to the body of the man who had beaten him with such relish. He gave a tentative blow and then jumped back. The body remained motionless.

"It's okay. He can't do anything now."

Jason hit Cass's head again, then again, and then he began smashing the hammer into the back of Cass's head, moaning softly to himself. Roy watched as Jace hit the dead man's head with rhythmic regularity, keeping time with tuneless moaning. Donnie started to cry. They heard Betts yell from upstairs, from another world.

"What's going on down there?" Then: "Cass? Cass?"

The boys waited for their mother to come down into cellar, to come and get them. Betts came tentatively down the steps. When she saw Jason with the hammer, his face and shirt spattered with Cass's blood, she made a quick sucking sound. "Jesus, oh my Jesus. You've killed him. Oh my God." She backed slowly up the stairs, murmuring, "Oh my God! Oh my God!" as if the words could exorcise the sight of the dead man and the upturned faces of her children in the pale light. When she reached the top step, she darted into the daylight, slamming the cellar door behind her. "Wicked boys. Wicked! Wicked! Wicked boys." They heard the scrape of the hasp.

Roy kept an eye on Cass to see if there was any movement. He knew Cass was dead, but he was afraid he might move anyway. He had entered his own horror movie, and he wasn't sure how it would turn out. He watched Cass for three days and nights, clutching the hammer, just in case. Then Cass began to smell, which Roy found reassuring. Cass was rotting. Dead was dead.

It was surprising how nobody missed them, but the other residents weren't exactly neighbors. When the cellar door finally swung open and a young policeman with a flashlight peered down at them, Roy was disappointed it wasn't Betts coming down the stairs. He still had the hammer. The last time he saw her was in juvenile court, when she told them how he was incorrigible—a word she had learned from Cass—how he was a defiant boy, nothing but trouble, how he had broken her heart. Roy had wanted to break other things then—things that would crunch.

After his release from the California Youth Authority, where he had been a model resident, acquiring all sorts of useful extracurricular knowledge, he set about to reassemble his family. Donnie had been the easiest to find. He was a constant runaway. When he skipped out with Roy from his fourth and last foster home, the family was relieved to be rid of an unpleasant fourteen-year-old who stole anything that wasn't nailed down and refused to shower. Nobody made a real effort to find him after that. Jace had been harder to locate. He'd been institutionalized since the day they had been brought out of the cellar. When Roy finally found him, he'd been so medicated, he didn't recognize Roy when he approached him in the recreation area. Of course, it had been almost seven years, and Jason had never tracked things well. But the drugs made him docile, and he went with Roy without knowing where he was going. Now and then, when he became too agitated, Roy would put him back on his meds for a week or so, but he wasn't the same. The light faded from the bright little eyes into a soft confusion. Roy preferred Jace active, always doing something. Roy had a special reunion planned for Betts. So far, he hadn't been able to locate her, but he was patient. They'd taught him to be patient. It was a virtue, one of seven. The others seemed less important.

•

Jason tossed a stick in a pool of brown water and peered intently as the filmy surface broke into tiny islands. Roy and Hickey sat in dilapidated lawn chairs under the huge cottonwoods that followed the course of the Mojave out into the desert.

Hickey took a swallow from a tall Budweiser tucked into a Styrofoam holder. The foam ran down the sides of his face and into his graying beard. "So you think this doctor dude left Donnie out there to die, or killed him, or something, that right?"

At the mention of Donnie's name, Roy's smile faded into blankness. "Yeah, that's what I think." His sandy voice was like dry leaves scuttling on pavement. "Probably figured he could do whatever he wanted to someone like Donnie. Nobody'd give a fuck." He turned to fix his gaze on Hickey. "But he didn't get it right, didn't think about what might happen next. Now he gets a trip to the boneyard. Gets to join up with Cass and good old Calvin and his doggy pals."

Roy leaned forward to yell something at Jason, then thought better of it and settled back into the chair. He fished a small foil-wrapped packet from his pocket and took out three joints rolled in brown cigarette paper. He leaned back and touched a match to the twisted tip of a tightly rolled joint, and quickly brought it to his lips, sucked the smoke deep into his lungs, and held his breath. He waited calmly for almost a minute, then slowly exhaled. He took in another deep lungful and passed the joint over to Hickey without looking away from where Jason waded barefoot in the water.

Roy exhaled the thin smoke in a long, slow sigh. "He lives in Pasadena, near the Rose Bowl." He shook his head. "We'd be in town about fifteen minutes before the cops would be asking us questions." He frowned, giving it some thought. "So what I want to have happen is for him to come to us."

Hickey was making little wheezing sounds. A trickle of smoke slipped out from the corner of his mouth. His pent-up breath exploded in a strangled cough. "Yeah, how're we going to do that?"

"Don't know the answer to that yet, my man. But we got a few people to contact. That candy-ass Mitch was still hanging around Donnie. He might know something. He knows something about us." Roy looked thoughtful.

Hickey took another big drag. Where his face wasn't layered with grime, the effort of holding his breath was turning his skin red. A big whoosh of nearly transparent smoke rushed out of Hickey in a shuddery exhalation. "Whooeee, that touched base." He reached into a Styrofoam chest that divided the space between them, grabbed another Budweiser, popped it open, and swallowed half the can in long gulps, the beer running down the sides of his face in little muddy rivulets.

Hickey nodded. "Yeah, I'd like to talk to old Mitch again. See how he is since he's got religion. That skinny blond girlfriend, Shawna, 'member her? She useta be a real space case before she got God and old Mitch's wang to guide her through life." Hickey grinned and winked at Roy, calling over to where Jason Miller waded in the water. "Hey, Jace. How'd you'd like to make another movie? Whatta ya think, Jace? A little push-push sound good?"

Jason stopped splashing around in the water and stood spraddle-legged. He leered back at Hickey, cupping his hand around an invisible penis, stroking it up and down. His mouth hung partly open, making a sort of *uunh, uunh, uunh* noise.

Hickey laughed. "I guess that's a big affirmative."

Roy turned an unsmiling face on Hickey, his voice low and hard. "Don't get him excited. How many times do I hafta tell you. He'll be asking about it all the time now. If you say something, he expects it to happen. So don't say it, goddamn it."

"Hey, just kidding around."

Jace's eyes followed the conversation, flicking back and forth between the speakers, straining to catch the drift. Roy leaned back in his chair, eyes half-closed.

Hickey twisted around to face him. "So who do we see besides Mitch?"

Roy motioned for Hickey to pass him a beer. He tipped the beer up to his lips. His Adam's apple worked steadily under the white skin, the death's-head tattoo at the side of his neck wriggling with each swallow in a lifeless pantomime.

Roy tossed the empty on the sand.

"There's the newspaper lady who wrote up the story. She'll know more than was in the paper. We'll want to talk to her. And there's the BLM cop who found Donnie. I want to know how it looked to him, what he saw." He frowned in thought. "That might be tougher. We'll start with the reporter. And the bars. Hit the bars and ask around." The wind lifted his soft white hair in a wispy halo. "And I've got that number we took off Bates for the Indian who calls himself Redhawk. Before old Calvin cashed in his chips, he mentioned that this Eddie Laguna, Redhawk's regular name, was a big-time guide, some sort of mountain man and Indian badass. He set the doctor up with this guy when things didn't pan out for Donnie."

Roy spit into the dirt. "Old Calvin was a real pus bag. He'da given up Jesus for a few more minutes of living. I hate that kind of coward." He shook his head in disgust. "So we're going back up the highway and chat with these folks. Have a little dialogue." He grinned, his red gums dark in the shadow of the cottonwoods. He pointed over at Jace. "You've gone and gotten him all excited; so now we have to take him on an adventure. Right?"

Jace jumped up howling, holding his foot. Blood was streaming from under his arch.

"Ow! Ow! Ow!"

He hopped toward Roy on one foot.

"Ow! Ow! Ow!"

He sat down heavily on the ground, holding his foot, the blood dripping down into the dirt.

"Here, let me take a look."

Jason lifted the injured foot to Roy's lap. Roy wiped the dirt and mud away with the sleeve of his shirt. "It's okay, Jace. It's just a cut. We'll wash it off and put a Band-Aid on it. And keep your foot out of the dirt."

Roy shook his head. "Jesus, I shoulda told him not to wade in there barefoot. Hickey, go on back to the trailer and bring some peroxide and a Band-Aid."

Tears welled up in Jason's eyes, only to be swallowed in the red whiskers that sprouted out high on his cheekbones. "Jesus, it hurts, Roy."

"Now maybe you'll listen to me when I tell you there's glass in there. You've thrown glass in there yourself, you dumb fuck."

"It hurts. My foot's bleeding." Jason pulled the foot up to his chest and rocked in the shade of the cottonwoods. The wind ruffled his thick red hair as if it were being tousled by an invisible hand.

# 12

•

As Dr. Michael Sorensen hung up the phone, he wondered how he had become involved with another mental defective. First that mindless piece of tattooed filth that ruined the head. Actually, first it had been Bates, then the McDonald person and his endless chatter—well, not quite endless; more like a tree falling in the forest and no one to hear it. A trace of a smile crossed the handsome face. Now he had to deal with this self-styled Indian guide, Redhawk. Considering his fear of being caught by the invisible presence of Fish and Game, Yellowback seemed more appropriate than Redhawk. His encounters with these sorts of people had been confined to emergency rooms during his bondage as an intern, but he never purposely engaged them in conversation. A litany of endless complaint issued from their illiterate mouths. When this business of completing the grand slam was over, he'd put the pathetic camoclad gun freaks and ersatz medicine men far behind him.

He leaned back in his special trophy-room chair, a pastiche of deer antlers from dozens of kills, arranged in an intricate interlocking pattern to form the shape of a high-backed throne. The seat, back, and arms were fitted out with leather panels in such a way as to be reasonably comfortable, despite the fact that it looked as if its occupant would be repeatedly impaled.

The chair flanked one side of the huge fieldstone fireplace in Sorensen's favorite room, the trophy room. Over the years, the Sorensens' place in Pasadena had appeared in various home and garden publications. Originally designed by Greene and Greene, it was one of their finest examples of the California bungalow and the Craftsman Style.

The grounds sloped gently toward the bluff overlooking the Arroyo Seco and the green parkway that stretched from Devil's Gate Dam to the Colorado Street Bridge. The Sorensens hosted summer cocktail parties in their garden and on the patio, where his guests could exclaim over the view of the Rose Bowl, golf greens, and the fashionable houses decorating the hillside of the Linda Vista district across the canyon. Definitely a showplace. It never failed to impress his guests and business associates. It pleased his wife, Denise, and it pleased him.

But for Michael Sorensen, the heart of the home was the trophy room. It reflected money, masculinity, and power. In it were the mute witnesses to his skill as a hunter. The walls were crowded with the mounted heads of game that had succumbed to his marksmanship. The wall opposite the fireplace was the African wall, its centerpiece the head of an African bull elephant, the huge tusks protruding out into the room, the ears mounted in a forward position, giving the animal a look of perpetual inquiry. It was flanked by the heads of lion and leopard, mouths frozen in silent snarls. The lesser creatures of prey—gazelle, eland, springbok, ubiquitous wildebeest, the tiny pygmy deer—were gathered around the predators in fixed surprise.

It was all artfully arranged, as was the adjoining wall, where the animals of Asia gathered about the Bengal tiger and its Siberian cousin. Sorensen regretted never having had the chance to take a snow leopard, but they had become so scarce that it was doubtful they would be anywhere but in zoos. All in all, his hunting in Asia had been good, especially the Siberian tiger; the Russians had been eager to exchange their services for American cash.

But nothing gave him quite the same satisfaction as the representative mounts from North America, from the head of an American bison on the left of the fireplace to the jaguar, taken in Mexico's Sierra Madre Occidental. The illegal hunt had been easy to arrange— *mordida* here, *mordida* there, and presto, Mexicans more than willing to help the gringo in his quest. However, the kill had been a bit too easy. The jaguar had been resting under a tree. Twice it had tried to gain its feet at his approach, only to stumble and lie on its side, panting deeply. Sorensen suspected that it had been tranquilized, but no matter, it was one of the big ten, one of the rarest of the big ten, and it had provided an excellent mount.

The antlers of the Rocky Mountain elk, mule deer, and white-tail deer were all in the Boone and Crockett record book, as were the heads of the Dall sheep, Stone's sheep, and Rocky Mountain bighorn above the fireplace.

This room was the perfect place to conduct business. Here, he could be the genial host, cordial and understated. The room spoke for him, reminding friend and foe of his presence, a testament to a successful life. Things went his way in this room. He looked about him with rising satisfaction, his gaze caressing special triumphs—the bison, the grizzly rug on the hearth, the Rocky Mountain bighorn.

A remembered voice intruded into Sorensen's self-congratulatory thoughts, causing a slight frown to crease his tanned and rugged face and darken his blue eyes, as if a cloud had passed across a blue sky: "A very impressive room, Michael. We've been hunting partners in various corners of the world and haven't known it." Sorensen had experienced an unguarded moment, the pleasure of flattery momentarily sweeping away his habitual caution.

In conducting his life, Michael Sorensen normally remained relatively immune to the opinions of others. However, he did require the approval of a very few individuals whom he admired for their wealth and power, especially those who seemed to wear privilege as casually as good clothes. For him, position had been hard won. He had accumulated wealth and influence through the unceasing exercise of a clever mind and a willingness to treat human relationships with detached expediency. On the other hand, his wife's perfect twin brother, Dennis, Michael's intellectual and physical equal, was to the manner born.

Sorensen had acquired an unwavering confidence in himself due to his triumphs over his counterparts in sport, business, and seduction. But Dennis Winthrop had been born with a confidence that required no affirmation. He used people like paper cups, dispensing with them casually and carelessly whenever he found them no longer useful. In the past, he had rarely taken the time to speak with Michael on his infrequent visits from Texas, but now, here in the trophy room, he had extended the hand of friendship—well, not friendship exactly, but at least of recognition.

Sorensen had been more than pleased. "Hunting partners in various corners of the world" had been an acknowledgment of Brahmin equality. The small triumph of acceptance had been quite brief, just enough for a taste, for the flush of pleasure to show in Michael's face.

They had been looking up at the sheep over the fireplace, Dennis's arm casually thrown across Michael's shoulders. "Let me give you the name of a really good guide when I get back to Forth Worth. I'm sure he can bring you within range of a Desert bighorn. He led me to a head in Baja that was a hundred and eighty, Boone and Crockett. You'll complete the grand slam one of these days. Just takes a bit of walking about and a well-placed shot," Dennis had said. Sorensen could still see the condescending smile, the amusement over his having been taken in by the oblique offer of fellowship.

Now he had what he was sure was a record head. Redhawk had proved as good as his word and brought him within range of a trophy head. But then someone else had been in the canyon, perhaps a witness to the killing of the sheep. A hiker? Another hunter? Caution had dictated that they leave the head in an abandoned mine, where it was vulnerable to rot and decay. Now the ridiculous guide refused to go back to retrieve it. Sorensen was sure the Indian's reluctance to return to the canyon was exaggerated. He would have to up the ante. It was only a matter of retrieving the head and his Weatherby from the mine and packing them out, but he'd need the Indian's help to do this. They'd have to come in from the top, the way he had hiked out. From there, they could carry the head and his rifle down the canyon to a waiting vehicle—not an overwhelming task.

When they had seen the reflective flash from someone's equipment—binoculars? scope? camera? (he hoped not a camera)— he'd immediately set off up the canyon, leaving the guide to worry about hiding the head and rifle. He had climbed out by going around

Telescope Peak and picking up the trail that led back to the road's end. He had been fortunate enough to find a young couple at Mahogany Flat Campground who were only too glad to interrupt their weekend and give him a ride back to the airstrip at Trona for a couple of hundred dollars. Evidently, the Redhawk person hadn't encountered any troubles going down the canyon. Nevertheless, better safe than sorry, better the Indian than him. What could someone like an Indian with bad teeth and worse breath have to lose besides the fee he hoped to collect? While he, Sorensen, had put his whole career at risk.

He was sure he could figure out a way to get down the canyon from the top, especially since he would be unencumbered by equipment. Picking up the head and his rifle at the mine and getting them down would be a hell of an effort, although worth it, since this was a record head. Of that, he was absolutely certain. More than 190 points, he guessed. He would definitely have the head on the wall before Dennis Winthrop came to California to visit his perfect sister for the holidays. But he couldn't do it alone. He needed the Indian's help.

# 13

•

"So this is the famous caboose." Jan climbed onto the front platform, ignoring Frank's outstretched hand. He had noticed before that she was surprisingly agile for a woman of her age and build, stocky now, "full-figured" in her heyday. Sad to say, fashion dictated that the voluptuous be displaced by the malnourished. Linda's figure missed the fashionable mark as well, lithe but sturdy, the muscles flexing under the tan skin as she followed Jan onto the platform.

"Not exactly a dance floor." Frank hesitated, shifting to one side to let them pass. "Step inside." The front and rear platforms of the caboose were essentially identical. Steps led up to a small platform from both sides, a platform meant to provide room for one, two at most, of the train crew to pass signals or wrestle with the brake wheel. The door leading into the interior was flanked on the right by a large low window. An iron railing ran along the outer perimeter, the brake wheel opposite the window on the left; a ladder on the right led up to the roof. The door from the front platform opened into what had been the crew's quarters; originally, padded benches had run down the sides, one long, one shortened to accommodate the stove. Now, it had become Frank's combination kitchen/bedroom/living room.

"Well, this is it"—he gestured awkwardly with his hand—"but it serves the purpose."

Linda stepped through the larger of the rooms to the narrow passageway flanked by ladders leading up to what appeared to be a small attic with windows. "What's this for?"

"That's the cupola. It's where the brakemen sat to watch the train for hotboxes."

Linda raised her eyebrows.

"On the old trains, all the way into the sixties, the wheels ran on journal bearings, metal on metal, not modern roller bearings. Oiled bundles of cloth lubricated the journals. If a piece of this packing slipped in between the surfaces, it wiped off the oil and the journal would heat up. Eventually, the axle could melt off from the heat. So the brakemen would watch for the smoke and the smell.

"It's not necessary now." Frank's smile was rueful. "You hardly ever see a caboose anymore. Most of the work brakemen used to do is automated." He shrugged, accepting the inevitable. "This was my dad's last caboose when he crewed for the Southern Pacific."

"How on earth did your dad get it up here on Sage Flat?" Jan gestured down the long slope that led to Highway 395 in the distance.

"It wasn't as bad as it looks. There was a spur track that paralleled the main track, the high line. It serviced the ranches along this side of the valley. They ran old ten eighty-seven up here and shoved it past the end stop and onto the ground. Dad called in a few favors, so they had a big old truck and winch up here. They were pretty well oiled up, so this is as far as they got—a couple hundred yards from the track onto Dad's property. They figured that was good enough. Then the SP abandoned the Owens Valley and the track was torn up. So here she sits."

"Why did he want to live here, Frank? As a matter of fact, why do you?"

"Oh, that's another story." He looked out the window for a moment. "It's pretty hot in here. Why don't we go sit around the pool?"

"The pool? Oh come on." Jan chuckled.

"Nope. Really." He led the way through the rear of the caboose, the area that served as the bathroom. Linda took in the small room, complete with claw-foot tub and shower surround. "I like this big old tub, Frank. Do you ever use it, or do you mostly shower?"

Frank felt slightly uncomfortable discussing his bathing habits. He showered in the morning. But sometimes he'd sit in the tub with a good book and a glass of Jameson, or just the Jameson and memories of riding the high line with his dad and the crew. "Mostly shower," he replied. "But it's good for soaking out the ache of a hard day, when I have one, which isn't too often. The hard day, that is."

He stepped onto the rear platform and down the stairs to a narrow path that sloped off into the sage. Huge boulders lay scattered about the landscape, remnants of upheaval when the back wall of the Sierras lifted up, up, and up to part the sky from the land with serrated teeth, several over fourteen thousand feet high. He waited for Jan and Linda to follow and then moved off toward an outcropping of rock a few hundred yards away.

"Seems like when I'm with you, I'm always scrambling around rocks," Linda remarked. She and Jan were following Frank through a narrow defile that twisted and turned among the boulders. Frank made no reply. He stepped softly onto a sandy shelf, followed by Linda and Jan. The tiny beach bordered a broad pool of water formed by a natural dam of boulders and driftwood, which had blocked the narrow channel between the rocks. The far side of the pool, where the water deepened, was lined by cottonwoods, the leaves perpetually stirring in the gentlest of breezes. A small waterfall at the head of the pool lay hidden by a tangle of stream willows, not the fisherman's friend. The sound of the trickling water was only discernible in the periods of stillness when the leaves ceased their whispering.

They stood in silence, taking in the place, an oasis in the desert, fed by one of the myriad snowmelt streams that flowed into the Owens River. The river itself ran dry below Lone Pine. It had been captured by the city of Los Angeles and fed into a huge pipeline. Now Owens Lake lay dry where once two small steamers had transported charcoal from the rock ovens shaped like beehives along the west shore to the smelters at Keeler. The parched lake bed was a plaything for the wind, which swept alkaline dust into corrosive clouds.

On this day, the air was clear and the late-afternoon sunlight slanted into the cottonwood trees, the light flickering gold and green through the leaves and onto the pool's surface. Trout lay along the bottom in liquid formations invisible in the play of water and light.

Only if they were startled did they momentarily reveal their presence in a flicker of movement.

Frank squatted in the sand, his back to the women. "So, how do you like my pool? All the amenities of a trailer park in Ridgecrest and no rent."

"Do you own the land?" Jan inquired.

"It's all Dad had when he died, twenty acres of abandoned railroad land. A caboose without tracks, and twenty acres of desert to run it on—my Irish patrimony."

"Oh Frank, you know you love it. You have to. It's beautiful. Just look at this place." Linda turned to Frank, the sun making a halo in her hair. At that moment, Frank knew that he wanted to be with Linda Reyes. He had never known a woman who shared his love of the land and the creatures in it in such an easy, unstudied, and unsentimental way. He determined to find the words, to speak in ways in which he had never been at ease. This time, the words would come.

●

Frank lifted the lid off the Dutch oven and tipped the coals off to one side. The aroma of tamale pie filled the evening air. Ever since Linda's father, Jack Collins, had mentioned tamale pie, he'd had a craving for it. It was something he used to help his mother make. A little different each time, but basically the same. Ground meat sautéed in onions and peppers, some jalapeños if guests liked it hot, the way he did. Jan and Linda were no problem on that score, so he had cut up a couple of jalapeños along with the dried, dark, and dusty-red pasilla chiles that had been soaking in Corona beer.

He added three or four tablespoons of powdered cumin, measured in the cup of his hand, and a can of chopped tomatoes; then he simmered the mixture for an hour on the woodstove in the caboose. The stove had come with the caboose, and it served for heat as well as for cooking, just as it had when the caboose rumbled along the high line.

He cooked up cornmeal into a sticky paste and lined the bottom and sides of the well-oiled Dutch oven with it. He added the meat mixture, a can of corn kernels, a can of pitted ripe olives, and some white cheddar. He topped the mixture off with more corn mush and cheese. He set the Dutch oven over medium coals, and covered the lid with hot coals to cook it from the top. An hour later, tamale pie, oh my.

"Mmm. Smells good." Jan rolled her eyes in appreciation. Linda sniffed the air expectantly. At Ralph's Burritos, both Linda and Jan had demonstrated that they could tuck it away. Maybe there would be enough leftovers for breakfast, maybe not. Frank spooned the tamale pie into bowls and passed them around. Linda and Jan had set the old wooden table in the combined shade of a piñon pine and the caboose. The ice chest had been supplied with Dos Equis and Coronas. Tortillas wrapped in foil lay on the upturned lid of the Dutch oven to keep warm.

"What could be better?" Jan smiled. "Good food. Good company, *otra vez*. Here's to us." She raised her beer and they clinked bottles.

They concentrated on the food. Two ravens circled about on the updrafts, riding the wind, fooling about in aerial displays. Frank unconsciously fingered the raven fetish Mrs. Funmaker had placed around his neck for protection. He didn't believe in fetishes any more than he believed in St. Christopher's protection from mishap. His mother had given him the saint's medallion that still hung from the rearview mirror of his truck. Maybe he was hedging his bets.

There was a scrabbling sound by the fire. Frank looked up in time to see the furry shape of a fox dart off into the underbrush. He rose from the table and spoke softly. "Be right back." He disappeared into the trailer and returned with a piece of bread. He had dipped it in the grease he had drained from the meat. He set it on the lip of the Dutch oven's lid, still warm but not hot, and, returning to his seat, put his finger to his lips in a gesture of silence.

"Wait," he whispered. "She'll be back."

They waited, unconsciously taking shallow breaths. As they watched, a tiny gray form materialized from the shadows and slipped across the open ground toward the lid, where it rested about a foot and a half above the ground on a flat rock. She momentarily disappeared in the dusky light, and then a small fox face rose above the rock. For a moment, the fox stared at the three humans sitting motionless and silent, and then she darted her head forward, grabbing the bread, and slipped quickly back into the brush.

"She's been coming around for about a week now. I think she's got kits. It makes her brave about getting the food, so I give her scraps now and then. Soon they'll be out of the den, and I'll stop feeding her. But for now, I'm Frank the food-stamp man." His smile betrayed a trace of embarrassment.

"I didn't think a good-looking young fellow like you could live completely alone out here, and I was right." Jan grinned at Frank. "He's got company, female company at that." Jan leaned back from the table and produced a satisfied belch. "Well, let's clean up and take a look at those pictures Linda's been so excited about."

•

They adjourned to the inside, and Frank fired up the generator, explaining that he preferred the kerosene lamps but that they might need brighter light to get a good look at the pictures.

Linda spread six photos on the table. The first had obviously been taken in haste: the figures of two men, one standing, holding a rifle, the other bent over something on the ground. The figures of the men, too small to be of much use in identification, were centered near the spring. The talus slope on the left formed the backdrop against which the figures could be discerned. For the remaining photos, Linda had used the telephoto lens. The figures had shifted slightly, the smaller man squatting on the ground apparently having turned to address the standing figure. Unfortunately, the taller figure's head had been cut off. Linda had focused on the man on the ground, whose features could be plainly seen, but the standing figure was missing from the chest up. A rifle slanted casually toward the ground from the crook of the headless figure's right arm. The third photo revealed an aristocratic profile of a man in his middle forties. The straw hat shaded his eyes; the sharp Nordic features, straight nose and strong chin, were thrust forward in casual assertiveness, bespeaking one of the ruling class. Only the top of his companion's head—or, to be more accurate, the crown and part of the brim of a straw hat—was visible.

The fourth photo framed them both, the standing man still a figure of casual repose, glancing down at the smaller man, who squatted beside what was clearly the body of a downed ram. There it was, the right picture. In the fifth photo, the two men seemed to be looking directly at the camera. In the sixth photo, the ram's head was turned to face the camera, the full curl of the huge horns caught in morning light. The ram seemed watchfully alert, although somehow calm, a careful king of its domain. Not careful enough, Frank thought.

He picked up the picture of the ram. "Can I have a copy of this one? Damn them all to hell." He stared intently at the picture and reluctantly set it on the table. He touched the photo of the men, who seemed to be staring at the photographer. "I thought you said they didn't see you."

Linda's chin lifted in response. "I said I wasn't sure. I don't see a problem. We're here with their pictures, and they're wherever they are, maybe a bit worried if they think they were seen." She pointed to the photos. "Usually, I do a better job than this, but you'll have to admit there was a bit of pressure."

Frank didn't seem to hear her. He was staring at the second photo. He picked it up and held it to the light. "Damn."

"What?" Linda inquired. Frank shook his head slowly. "Well, what, Frank? What do you see?"

He turned toward Linda and Jan, who were seated at the small table folded down from the wall. "I know this guy, Eddie something. We were in school together. He was Shoshone, Timbasi Shoshone. They're the people who've been trying to claim land from the government inside the park."

Frank sat down in the single straight-backed chair and sighed. "He was an angry guy at school. This stuff about losing their land, I guess he'd be mad about that, too. Didn't know him well, but I always felt like we were in the same boat in a way. At school, there were mostly Paiute; the Shoshone were sort of out of it. Guys named Flynn didn't have a tribe.

"Eddie . . ." Frank paused, rummaging around in his brain. "Eddie

Laguna, that's his last name, Laguna. Anyhow, Eddie was always talking about how white people had cheated everyone. I seem to remember something about him becoming a medicine man, or at least calling himself one."

Jan had been looking at the photos. "What about this man? Anybody recognize him?"

Linda and Frank both shook their heads from side to side.

"Well, yes and no," Linda said. "He's a type. I've met him before, lots of times. He's got the winner look. 'I'm okay, and I'm not interested in much else.'"

"Me, too," said Jan. "He's the PE department chair."

Frank and Linda laughed.

"No, I don't think so. Couldn't afford the duds," Linda said, looking more closely at the picture. "He's dressed for the press."

"Or the rifle." Frank picked up the photo again and held it under the light. "I can't really tell from the picture, but it looks like a customized sporting rifle with an expensive scope. Cost a bundle." He squinted closely, adjusting the photo to the light. "I'll bet it's a Weatherby three hundred Magnum. I wish I had a chance to match it to the shell casings I found the blind. There were two twenty-threes all over the place, but I found a couple three hundred Magnum rounds."

"How could anyone get a match?" Linda inquired. "There's no bullet for a ballistics comparison."

"You're right, lady reporter, but the federal Fish and Wildlife in Ashland, Oregon, has the equipment to match the indentation in the primer to the firing pin in the weapon. What I need is the weapon. What I really need is to know who the guy is." He fell silent, thinking about it.

"What're you going to do about Eddie Laguna?" Linda studied the photo that Frank had returned to the table. "This is one of the photos I submitted for my story about the poaching." She gestured at the photo of the two men near the fallen ram. The features of both men were recognizable.

"Yeah, I know, but for now he won't be recognized, at least by anyone who would talk to cops. The first thing is to talk to him. So that means talking to Jimmy Tecopa. He's head of security at the

Paiute Palace," Frank said, not mentioning that Jimmy had been the one who'd pulled him from the crevice all those years ago.

"Why him?" Linda asked.

"He knows everyone in the valley, or almost everyone, at least all the Paiute and Shoshone, and all the guys who lose too much at the Paiute Palace, drink too much and land in the drunk tank, and especially those who leave their women unattended." He looked abashed. "Jimmy's sort of a ladies' man."

He stood up to light the kerosene lamp hanging over the table. "Scuse me for a minute. I'm going to cut the generator."

The stars had begun to emerge in the evening sky. The Sierras stood in jagged relief against the waning of the light. Across the valley, the Inyos melted into a deep blue haze. It seemed strange to Frank that amid all this beauty there were creatures who destroyed things for the sake of destruction itself. He understood the nature of violence, even the blood lust of rage. He raised his face to the night sky, to the cold clarity of light and the absence of things human. "I would rather be a worm in a wild apple than a son of man." It was a line from a poem he had read in college, by Robinson Jeffers, a poet who loved nature and loathed mankind, a true misanthrope. Jeffers's loathing of humanity was rooted in disgust. Sometimes Frank was dangerously close to embracing it himself.

"Hey, what's keeping you? Communing with your foxy girl-friend?" Jan called out.

He wished she would let it go. "Just stargazing," he replied, walking back to the table.

"This has been nice, Frank. You're a cook and a host par excellence." Jan put her hand on Frank's, almost covering it. "The situation with this Eddie person must be difficult for you."

Frank nodded. "Yeah, it's the sort of thing that keeps me separated. But then again, I work for the BLM." He looked up at them both, his eyes deep in shadow. "And you know they pay me to take care of the land. For me, that's what's called 'a fit.'" He turned toward Linda. "But that's not all of it. I'm sort of worried, too."

"What about?"

"You, me, anyone who's caught alone at the right time by the wrong people, but mostly for you, maybe your dad."

"My dad? What's my dad got to do with anything?" Linda's hand moved unconsciously to her throat.

"If the rifle is a three hundred Magnum, then our Mr. Winner here is probably a murderer."

Frank held up his hand as Linda started to speak. "You're right. Your dad's not in any danger from this person. But if this is the man who left his accomplice to die up in the Panamints, then there's real danger. There's some very bad people looking for him. The dead man, Donnie Miller, had two brothers. I'm pretty sure they were the guys who came by your dad's place, the ones who had the fight."

"Why would dad be in danger?"

"I'm not sure, but I think they could be pretty close to genuine evil." He remembered the look of perplexed fear on Mitch's face when he'd told about the burning of the dog and the hinted at snuff films. "I think these guys are without—" He searched for the right word. *Soul* was as close as he could come, but he had long ago abandoned the teachings he'd picked up from sporadic visits to church—"I think these people are empty inside. You could be in danger because they know your name, and you're a link to their dead brother. You wrote the story. So I guess I want you to be very careful."

"I think we have to go home," Jan said, rising to her feet. "Work tomorrow." She turned, taking Frank's hand in hers. "Thanks again." And then more softly, she said, "You be careful, as well, Frank Flynn. What you say applies to you, and more so. Well, back to Ridgecrest. Town life has its advantages, Frank, but this place is really something."

Linda reached her arms around him, more than a hug goodbye. She kissed him softly on the cheek. "Jan's right, you know, about being careful. Call me and let me know what your friend says." A second kiss good-bye, on the lips, lingering long enough to set Frank's heart racing.

Then Jan and Linda disappeared into the dark.

The air was perfumed with the dry scent of sage. The nocturnal sounds of the desert surrounded the caboose. Frank climbed into the cupola and watched the lights from Jan's car as it moved down the slope to the valley floor and turned onto Highway 395.

# 14

•

"Now lemme see if I've got this right. You and the Reyes woman were up in Surprise Canyon to look at bighorns?" Meecham paused, waiting for Frank to nod or grunt, give some sort of affirmative sign.

Frank didn't. It was all there in the report on Meecham's desk.

"So you're watching the sheep drink at the spring, and then bang, the big ram topples over." Meecham softened his tone. "Sorry about the ram, Frank. I know he was an old pal." He sighed. "Christ, I'm sick of the sight of slaughtered animals."

"Yeah, I'd been watching him awhile." Frank pulled at the tip of his nose, as if to shield the lower part of his face from scrutiny. "In a way, I'm sorrier about the younger one. At least the old guy had a history. The other one was just getting started."

Meecham leaned forward to catch Frank's words, his face shadowed with concern. "Well, maybe Fish and Game will get them next time. Maybe they'll get careless."

Frank remained silent. Meecham had all the information Frank felt bound to give. He knew what had happened, and he knew that Linda's story was going to appear in Saturday's *Courier*. There was no reason for Meecham to know that he had seen Linda's photographs. As soon as the story appeared, Frank would call Fish and Game and identify Eddie Laguna. That gave him just short of forty-eight hours to locate Eddie and talk to him before Fish and Game had him under lock and key. He needed to catch Jimmy Tecopa at the Paiute Palace before he disappeared with one of his many lady friends.

"So that's about it, Dave." At least Frank hoped that was about it. Meecham seemed satisfied that no shadow had been cast on the BLM. In fact, Frank's presence at the scene, followed by a call from his truck on Linda's cell phone, had initiated a manhunt. A helicopter and a plane had been sent out. The perpetrators had been pursued, but to no avail. It was too late, as they were long gone. Nevertheless, the authorities had been interviewed by the local television anchorman Tom Cocheran. Cocheran's square head moved in ponderous cadence to the rumbling baritone of his voice, a voice that seemed to lend significance to the process of self-identification. "Hello out there. I'm Tom Cocheran, and this is KNV News, where local news is first." As long as the teleprompter kept the words flowing from Tom's mouth, his interviews were as predictable as sunshine in the Mojave. The who, what, when, and where inevitably followed by a "How do you personally feel about that?" The unctuous sincerity of the questioner suggested a degree of personal intimacy as inappropriate as the question.

Frank had escaped more than one interview with "Tommy Cockroach," the voice from space. But the chief ranger for the BLM, Dave Meecham, had another fifteen minutes of fame—actually, more like fifteen seconds. He'd looked good in his crisp khaki uniform, and, much more important to Meecham, the BLM had looked good, too, Ranger Francisco Flynn doing his duty even on his day off. So he now hoped Meecham wasn't in a mood to probe.

As Frank rose from the folding chair in front of Meecham's battered desk, Meecham's voice interrupted his progress. "Frank, I want you to let this alone now. I'm not sure exactly why you and the Reyes woman . . ."

Frank gave his superior a bland look. "Linda Reyes or Ms. Reyes seems less demeaning, Chief. I don't think of myself as the Flynn man, or you as the Meecham man." He grinned a bit. "Although Meecham man has a sort of ring to it."

Meecham leaned back in his chair, studying his fellow officer. Frank knew Meecham considered him an equal. They had hired on at about the same time. Both of them had college degrees, Frank's in American studies, Meecham's in police science. But Frank knew he was a puzzlement to his colleagues. He lacked ambition, at least as far as moving up the chain of command was concerned. Meecham and the other rangers thought of him as a bit peculiar—not exactly a loner, but not an easy fit, either. "Guess I march to the beat of a different tom-tom," Frank had told him once. He regarded his boss patiently, his face impassive.

"Okay, Frank. Ms. Reyes. No offense meant."

"None taken, Dave," Frank replied, relieved that the moment had passed.

"But back to the point—this poaching business. You know as well as I do that it's up to Fish and Game."

"And the way Donnie Miller died?"

Meecham sighed. "Frank, the Miller kid died from dumbness. I'm with the Sheriff's Department on this."

"What happened to his boots?"

"Who the hell knows what happened to his boots. Maybe he took them off when his mind started to go. People dying of dehydration do strange things. In any event, it's not our case. And don't start up about the butt prints."

Frank sat back in his chair. "For the record, Dave: Donnie Miller, our dead man, has two brothers. These guys are definitely unpleasant people. They showed up at the Joshua Tree Athletic Club, looking for their missing brother. The new owner, Jack Collins, says they're motorcycle-gang types, and that they were definitely menacing."

"Who'd they menace?"

"It wasn't specific, Dave. Bad language, hostile presence."

" 'Hostile presence.' Jesus, Frank, that's half of the bar patrons in Kern County."

"They got into a fight."

"Yeah, who'd they fight with?"

"Some deer hunters. Okay, forget it." He caught Meecham's eyes. "But don't forget it, either. I think these guys are more than head-busting bikers. The Sheriff's Department trusts you. Tell 'em we're uneasy about these guys. Far as I know, they haven't even talked to the owner of the club."

"That dump." Meecham shook his head. "Frank, you're uneasy. I can't tell them we're uneasy, because I'm not uneasy. Same old stuff, drunks punching one another. Besides, Collins's place is in San Bernardino County." He held up his hand. "But you being uneasy tends to make me uneasy, so I'm alerted." A small wry smile creased his square face. "Now we're all uneasy, for all the good it'll do. It's a cinch that the Sheriff's Department is satisfied that no further investigation into the death of Donald Miller is warranted. But I'm listening, okay? Good enough?"

"Yeah, it'll have to be." Meecham had extended himself. It needed acknowledging. "And I appreciate the hearing." Frank got to his feet.

"One more thing, Frank."

It was like being a kid again, trying to get out of the house without some sort of admonition: Put on your coat. Drive carefully. Remember your gloves. He breathed deeply to relieve the tension.

"This one is definitely our business, Frank. Some screwball or screwballs have decided that they're unhappy with the multiple-use policy."

Frank grinned. "You mean someone besides me?"

Meecham frowned. "This could cause trouble for us, and people could get hurt. These guys are after the all-terrain RVers. They must have spread hundreds of those four-way spike things that always have a point up."

"Caltrops."

"Right, caltrops. Anyhow they're all over the off-road area in Jawbone Canyon. There were maybe twenty, twenty-five flats. ATVs stranded up and down the canyon. The Auto Club garages didn't have enough trucks or people to respond. Some of the RVers were stuck there through the weekend."

Frank tried to remain expressionless. The notion of ATVs with flat tires was far from unappealing, but he could see it wasn't the time to be a smart-ass. He just wished he'd been there to see it.

Meecham leaned forward, his face full of frustration. "They were madder than hell, Frank. Mad at us. They wanted to know who was protecting their rights?"

"Yeah, I know, Dave. And they're right. Someone could've been hurt. I'll see what I can find out."

Meecham looked at something over Frank's right shoulder. "This is related to the other stuff, those dumb signs you seem to find so funny, the ones about Ghost Raven watching them, and the Jackalope Preserve. Jeez, what crap. Jackalope Preserve, for Christ's sake. Probably have reporters out here from L.A. asking about jackalope sightings. Wondering how long we've been protecting jackalope."

Frank smiled at his boss. "Maybe we should start a captive breeding program. I know a couple of guys who claim to have talked with them after smoking the funny stuff." Meecham's face closed, not friendly. Frank couldn't seem to help himself. His mouth moved against his will. "You hafta appreciate the message. 'Ghost Raven eats the eyes of those who destroy the land—especially kids who ride off the trails.'" In the crude handmade poster, Ghost Raven looked more like a horror-cartoon vulture than a raven. Frank gave a short laugh. "Kept those mini road warriors on the trails for at least a week."

Meecham didn't return the grin. "They're doing damage. Vandalizing private property. I don't find it funny. What they are is a pain in the ass, maybe a dangerous pain in the ass. What if a kid broke his neck falling off his ATV?" Meecham glared down a pointed index finger. "Don't say it, Frank. It's our job to put a stop to it. It's up to us to make the desert safe for everyone, not just the people we think are okay."

Frank did his best to look abashed. "Yeah, I know you're right. It's just that I remember places like Jawbone Canyon before it became a playground for the ATVs." It was times like this he appreciated not being a chief, just an Indian, in more ways than one. "I'll look into it, boss." But not right away, he thought. Got to talk to Jimmy Tecopa first. Find Eddie Laguna. Have another talk with Mitch Cooper. When he had enough to interest the Sheriff's Department, he'd leave it alone, but for now, he couldn't turn his back on it.

•

The Paiute Palace had the biggest, brightest, gaudiest electric sign in Bishop, probably the whole length of Highway 395, not counting the stretch through Reno. You wouldn't be able to see it in Las Vegas, swallowed up in a sea of light, but here along the highway, it signaled nightlife. The garish lights had an allure, perfuming the darkness with false promise. There was no denying it; he found himself fascinated by the sight of people staring intently at the electronic slots, the intensity of the blackjack players, the staccato bursts of laughter from the winners and the heartfelt curses of the losers. It was as if here in the casino the gods of chance were more manageable, the face of uncertainty made manifest. In the casino, you knew the odds were stacked, but there were rules to the capriciousness. The dangerous unpredictability of life itself had no rules. The Paiute Palace offered a sort of haven, a place where the smashups had limits. It was a place where hope met despair.

But the Paiute Palace was okay. Indian-run. Jobs. No booze. It was amazing. Gamblers cared more about gambling than drinking. For him, there was no contest. He'd take a cold beer and conversation over the slots every time. But then again, he knew the odds couldn't be beat inside the casino; maybe they were even tougher out in the desert, but in the desert there was beauty.

"Hiya, Frank." Susan Funmaker's shy smile peered out from rounded folds of fat. "How ya been?" She cast her eyes down, the long black lashes brushing her round cheeks.

"Fine, Susan. It's good to see you. How's the family?" He leaned against the countertop separating the customers from the cashier's cage.

"Good, Frank. Everyone's good."

Frank knew that Susan was the main source of income for her family. Susan's older brother had gone to Los Angeles. Her younger brother had been killed in an automobile accident on 395, along with her father. Both had been drinking. Her mother was an invalid, limbs swollen from dropsy, bad heart, diabetes, but she had been a wonderful second mother to Frank, full of fun, and a great cook. When he and Susan had been in school, Susan's mother had told Paiute stories to Frank, some of the old legends and some true stories about people who had lived in the Owens Valley, stories still in people's memories. She had been the principal source of his cultural heritage, at least his Paiute cultural heritage.

Susan had persisted in school. Math came easily to her. Her dark eyes gleamed with intelligence. She had helped the others with their homework. Mostly, they copied hers. It was okay, though. She had always been fat, but being smart made up for it. Frank was pretty sure she still had a crush on him. She had gone to Arroyo Seco Community College for two years and learned bookkeeping and accounting. Now she had a good job in the casino, head cashier. Frank was always glad to see Susan.

"I'll bet you're looking for Jimmy, right?"

"Yeah, is he around, Susan? We haven't talked for a while."

"He said the same thing." She smiled. "He said you've been licking your wounds."

"That sounds like him. I'm okay, Susan. Not to worry." A bit of brightness went out of her expression. "But we'll get together soon and have a good talk, and you can laugh at my misadventures. You women are hard to figure out." He gave what he thought was a rueful grin.

"Jimmy's talking to someone out in the parking lot." Susan looked embarrassed. "He'll be back pretty soon." She glanced over toward the side entrance to the parking lot. "Here he comes now." She seemed relieved not to have to explain about Jimmy's amours.

As Jimmy came across the casino floor, he exchanged greetings with the folks perched in front of the slots, flirted with the elderly ladies, and joshed with the men clustered around the blackjack table. People were always glad to see Jimmy, share a few words. He looked up and waved at Frank, flashing a big smile that exposed his perfect white teeth, the kind of teeth actors pay thousands of dollars for.

"Here's brother Frank come out of the caboose to spread gloom among the natives." Mischief animated the small man's face. "Must need white woman and strong drink." Frank squirmed. Jimmy hadn't bothered to lower his voice, and Frank felt as if he were the center of unwanted attention. In truth, only a couple of people at the slots looked up, but there was Susan.

"Jimmy, I'm kinda here on business. Could we talk in your office, maybe with the door shut and without hollering?"

"Sure, Frank." He lowered his voice. Susan buzzed the door lock, and Frank followed Jimmy into his office and pushed the door quietly closed.

"So Frank, my man. Why the long face?" Jimmy was leaning back in his chair, hands folded behind his head. "I hear you're keeping company with the good-looking lady reporter from the *Courier*."

"That's kind of amazing, Jimmy, since I hardly know that myself." Frank felt the old familiar sense of irritation at the invasion of his privacy. "How's this been getting around?"

Jimmy leaned forward, his small dark brown hands resting lightly on the desk. "Come on, Frank. Nothing happens around here but that people talk about it. It relieves the routine. You're an important guy, Frank Flynn, lawman for the BLM. Inquiring minds want to know. So do I." Jimmy smiled and held up both hands. "But I won't ask, 'cause you'll get all cranky, and I haven't seen you in awhile."

Jimmy's charm always managed to deflect Frank's irritation. Besides, it really was good to see him. "Well, yeah, I'm kinda seeing Linda Reyes, but neither one of us seems to know it."

"Well?"

"That's about it. Except that she's smart, likes to hike, likes beer, and, oh yeah, carries a Swiss army knife." Frank fidgeted about, tapping his fingers quietly on the arms of the battered captain's chair drawn up alongside the big old oak desk.

Jimmy pulled a long face, which hardly disguised his delight in Frank's discomfort. "I've been missing out. I know quite a few women who carry knives, but mostly I try to stay out of their way. Is there something special here, or are you getting into bedroom rough stuff?"

Frank glared across the desk.

"Okay, okay." Jimmy put up a hand as if to ward off an invisible blow. "It's just that I heard she was pretty. Nice figure, good legs, common stuff like that. Didn't hear about no knife, though."

Frank relented with a laugh. "Yeah, she's pretty, and that's the last word on the subject. I really am here on work, sorta."

"Sorta?"

"You know about the poaching up in the Panamints?"

Jimmy nodded. "Sure, saw your boss bragging on TV about you working on your day off."

"Well, one of the guys was Eddie Laguna."

Jimmy frowned. "Doesn't surprise me. I'd heard talk that Eddie was doing a bit of illegal guiding, among other things." Jimmy paused, his face wrinkled in thought. No smile now. "Can't blame him too much, Frank. There's big money there, a lot of temptation for a guy like Eddie. How do you know it was him?"

"Hell, I know it's tempting, more money than someone like Eddie—or me, for that matter—is ever likely to see at one time. But the thing is, his picture and the picture of the other guy are going to be on the front page of the *Courier*. I was there. That's how I know. Eddie's going to be caught, no ifs, ands, or buts. But the guy I'd really like to see caught is the poacher, the moneyman. He's the one needs catching, not some sorry sad sack like Eddie. I think Eddie could lead us to the poacher, but I don't think he'll talk after he's arrested. So I want to talk to him before Fish and Game, off the record."

"What're you up to, Frank?"

"It's just about sure Eddie won't say anything to Fish and Game if they come and get him. He'll play the part. What's more, he probably doesn't even know his client's real name. Can you imagine the guy giving his name?"

Jimmy shook his head.

"That's right, not unless he's dumber than dirt. But Eddie might know more than he thinks. So I want to talk to him before he decides he's not talking to anybody. Starts to think of himself as some sort of an Indian outlaw. I'm talking to you 'cause I don't know where to find him and I bet you do."

# 15

•

Eddie Laguna's trailer had come to permanent rest under some large cottonwoods. Someone had erected a sort of lean-to shelter meant to protect it from the weather, but to no avail. Now both trailer and lean-to had succumbed to the ravages of time. Bilious green paint flaked away in small sheets from the trailer's corrugated skin. Rot and termites had consumed the base of the wooden columns supporting the shelter, so the roofline now formed a shallow inverted V. Eddie's place wouldn't make *Better Homes and Gardens,* maybe *Indian Dumps and Hovels.* Frank was ashamed of Eddie's poverty because Eddie was an Indian, and this realization deepened his shame. They lived in separate worlds.

A hand-lettered sign proclaimed that Eddie Laguna was a taxidermist. Frank wondered if he was any good or if he was another one of those home-schooled taxidermists who made fish look like plastic and cobbled together various snarling beasts—snarling bobcats, snarling mountain lions, snarling jackalope. Maybe he could throw some government work Eddie's way—that is, if he had the skills. Who was he trying to help? Well, he couldn't sit in the car looking at Eddie's place all afternoon.

The trailer was set well back from the road, which afforded Frank a short stroll under the cottonwoods, leaves rustling in an early-afternoon breeze coming off the Sierras. A large black-and-white cat sat on the roof of Eddie's battered Ford pickup, watching his progress. Frank knocked on the door several times and was about to leave, but then it opened partway. He could see an emaciated brown body clad in yellowed Jockey shorts through the tattered screen.

"You're Eddie Laguna, right?"

"Yeah." The small man nodded, his quick dark eyes taking in Frank's uniform.

"Sign says you're a taxidermist. That right?"

Eddie squinted at Frank through the cigarette smoke curling into his right eye. "Yeah, that's right. What've you got?"

"Nothing right now. Just wanted to ask a couple of questions." Eddie stepped back from the door, getting ready to close it. "But maybe I could put you in the way of quite a bit of work, if you're good." He waited. "Do you have any of your work handy?"

"Wait a minute." The door closed, and Frank looked over at the cat, which was still keeping an eye on him from the top of the truck.

Eddie stepped down from the trailer, barefoot. He'd pulled on a T-shirt and a pair of faded Levi's.

"Come on out back."

Evidently, Eddie was pretty handy when he wanted to be. Someone—Frank presumed it was Eddie—had built a fair-size shop building. The materials were mostly scrap and discards, but they had been trimmed and fitted carefully together. Paint of differing hues covered the outer walls, reminding Frank of Joseph's coat of many colors or of motley, a multicolored jest, bright in its newness.

Inside the shop, three of the walls had been insulated and paneled with drywall, but the studs were bare on the end wall by the door. Frank assumed the owner hadn't come across the right building site yet. A woodstove stood in the corner. Double-walled chimney pipe exited the ceiling through a metal surround. Done right.

The far wall was covered with Eddie's work, mostly fish. The Owens River yielded big browns. Frank knew that doing fish right was a difficult task, and these fish looked good, lifelike, not like plastic toys. He spotted a sage hen on the workbench, its feathers ruffled up in mating posture. Laguna was good. His work captured animals in the way a good photograph catches the life of its subject.

"This is really good. How about the big stuff? Elk? Bighorns?"

Eddie Laguna lit a fresh cigarette from the one caught in his tobacco-stained fingers. He tossed the butt on the dirt floor and ground it out with his bare heel. "I do it all." He squinted at Frank again. "You're Frank Flynn, aren't ya?"

"Yeah, that's right, Eddie. I'm surprised you remember me. Long time no see. How ya been doin'?"

"Sure I remember you. You're a BLM cop now, right?" Frank nodded. "You're not here about my work, are you?"

So much for easing into it. "Well, I could be, Eddie, but you're right. It's not about this work." Frank considered his options. Lying never seemed to work out, and he wasn't good at it. He could withhold information with the best of them, but lying convincingly wasn't one of his accomplishments.

"You've been taking people up-country to hunt bighorn sheep. It's illegal." Eddie opened his mouth to protest, but Frank held up his hand. "Don't say anything yet, Eddie. Hear me out. I'm not here to arrest you, or turn you in. It's too late for that. You're going to be talking to Fish and Game, and your picture will be in Saturday's newspaper. You've already been caught."

"Yeah, well, I don't remember being caught." Eddie let the cigarette dangle from the corner of his mouth. It wiggled up and down as he talked around it. It was obvious to Frank he was striking a pose, the tough guy, hard con, although as far as Frank knew, Eddie had never been in jail other than for the kind of minor offenses that kids commit.

"I was there, Eddie, up in Surprise Canyon, and so was a reporter from the *Courier*. She took your picture, yours and the guy you were working for. When that picture shows up on the front page, people are going to recognize you, just like I did. Then Fish and Game is going to know who you are."

"Is that right? Then how come they don't know now, Mr. Indian cop? You're still an apple, Frank. If you know, they know."

Frank felt the old sense of confusion, Eddie's taunt reminding him that he didn't really belong, "red on the outside and white on the inside," but that would have to wait. "They don't know because I haven't told them, Eddie. The story comes out on Saturday. Come

Saturday, I'll know one of the guys in the picture, but I haven't seen Saturday's newspaper, have I?"

Eddie's wizened face became shrewd. He regarded Frank with cautious curiosity. "So why're you here?"

"I want the other guy, Eddie, the guy who paid you, the guy who shot the sheep and left them there to rot." His chest was tightening with anger. It welled up like a red cloud. "I want the son of a bitch who thinks he can do whatever the hell he wants, treat the land like butt wipe and people like outhouse attendants. That's you, Eddie, wiping up his dirt. Guys like that are dead inside, so they bring death to things to feel alive. It's not hunting. It's ownership. Does that prick own the land?" Frank breathed deeply, regaining control. He was sounding like his da now, Irish to the core. Eddie probably thought he sounded like an Indian, like him. But underclass was underclass. Maybe someday they'd all figure it out, then look out Mr. Big Shot.

"I want to see Mr. Big Shot in jail. Mostly, I want to see him caught, his picture in the paper. Then he loses face, big man made small in the eyes of his tribe. Think about that, Eddie. A little humiliation for the big man. And maybe some white man's justice. Pays a big fine, does a little time. What do you think, Eddie?" The door creaked open as the cat squeezed into the shop and calmly regarded master and guest. They stood there looking at the cat, the silence broken by the sound of trucks gearing up for the grade to Tom's Place at the crest of the pass.

"That's Prowler, like a cop car, black and white."

"Knows his job. He's been keeping an eye on me since I arrived."

Smoke swirled in the sunlight from the shop window above the bench. Eddie's cigarette joined the myriad butts on the dirt floor. "I could see you didn't like the smoke." Eddie waved his hand around, swirling the smoke about. "Prowler hates it." Frank waited. His gift, waiting. "I don't know much, Frank. Don't know his name."

"How'd you come across him?"

Eddie shrugged. "There's this guy, Bates. He brought me work from L.A. He's a gunsmith, specializes in sporting rifles, expensive custom stuff, fancy stocks—you know, the kind of rifle needs a special case. Not like the old thirty-thirty or a Springfield." Eddie smirked knowingly at Frank, on the same side now, almost, brown guys and white guys, cowboys and Indians. "Anyhow, he tells me that he's got people willing to pay a guide five thousand for a hunt and ten thousand for a good head. So I figure, Why not? The permit money goes to the state. Our people never see any of it, so I thought, Yeah, I'll take some."

Frank shook his head. "Eddie, the auction money goes to the bighorn sheep program. It's a way the state pays for it. I know it seems like it's for rich white guys, but the money goes to the sheep program."

"It's all the same shit. The government takes, and we get nothing. Fuck the program." Eddie's voice was thick with anger. It was easy to touch Eddie's anger, easy for Frank, even easier for Eddie. He'd been stupid to start preaching; now wasn't the time for a lesson in civics.

"So what about this guy Bates?"

"He was the middleman, that's all. Set things up."

"Come on, Eddie. How did he set you up with the guy at Surprise Canyon, the big straw-haired guy with the fancy rifle?"

"A three hundred Weatherby Magnum."

That's a fit, Frank thought. Bits and pieces. He was getting closer. "So how'd you hook up?"

"Like I said, Bates set it up. I met this guy, called himself Smith, at the Trona Airport. That's what Bates said to call him, Smith, but it wasn't his real name."

"So we'll call him Smith. What kind of plane was he flying?"

"How would I know? By the time I got there, he was waiting by the hut with his stuff. Threw his pack in the back, put the gun case behind the seat, and climbed in."

"What'd he say?"

"Nothing much. 'You Redhawk?' I told Bates to have him call me Redhawk. People think you're the real thing if you have an animal name. Genuine Native American guide."

"So what then?"

"So nothing. I took him up to the spring."

"I know that. Didn't you talk about anything?"

"Just about having to park the truck out in the brush. Didn't see it, did ya?" Eddie looked like a triumphant kid.

Frank hadn't seen it, but then again, he hadn't been looking for it. He was chagrined, though. He should have noticed, should have been more alert. "Nope, didn't see it. Where was it?"

"Down in a parallel sand wash, alongside a cutbank about fifty feet from the jeep trail."

"Well, you did a good job of hiding it, Redhawk." Frank grinned encouragement. "So then what? How did Smith handle himself? Was he in shape? Handle the rifle okay? Say anything else?"

Eddie's expression opened up. An easy face to read, like a kid's. "To tell you the truth, I was surprised how good a shape he was in. Kept right up, never breathing hard. He could shoot, too. The old ram, the one he had me take the head of, an easy shot. It was kneeling down, taking a drink. But the one running, that was a good shot. Smooth and quick."

"What happened to the head?"

Eddie grinned. "That's the good part. When you showed up, or when we knew someone else was in the canyon, Smith got worried."

"How'd you know we were there?"

"Light reflection. I thought it was from binoculars, but I guess it was from the camera lens."

"So then what?"

"Like I said, Smith was worried he'd get caught, but he didn't want to leave the head behind. So I told him to stash the head and his precious rifle in one of the tunnels from the old Silver Queen mine and hike on out over the top to Mahogany Flat Campground. I figured he could do it in good time if he left the head, pack, and rifle behind. I followed you down the canyon. Didn't know it was you though, just that there was someone else. I stayed way back. When I saw the truck pull out, I took my truck and drove up to the campground, but Smith wasn't there, so I came home."

"Pretty slick. Guess you didn't count on having your picture taken."

Eddie looked deflated. He stroked Prowler's back. The cat had jumped up on the workbench. "Nope, didn't figure on that. Bad damn luck."

"Maybe not all bad. Listen, Eddie, as soon as the paper comes out, turn yourself in. It'll go better for you, especially if you're willing to testify against Smith."

Eddie shook his head. "No way, Frank. I'm not going to be a chickenshit stool pigeon for the government."

Stool pigeon? Eddie had seen too many movies. He looked at life like a teenager. Things divided up into being chickenshit and whatever was the opposite of that—tough, hard-bitten, a stand-up guy, a man with sand, anything but chickenshit. Eddie was living in a make-believe world where things were supposed to be fair.

"Look, Eddie, this guy used you, and he gets away. Is that right?" Eddie was silent, glaring at Frank. "Is it fair? Come on, Eddie. Mr. Big Shot hires a 'genuine Native American guide,' and the guide is so smart, he winds up doing time, while the big shot gets off and goes bragging about his trophy. That story's so old, it doesn't have a beginning. You gonna be the dummy who does time for a rich white guy? Eddie the sucker, taken by the smart guy, the guy with the money. Is that you, Eddie the sucker?" The Eddies of this world dreaded being suckers, looking dumb; for that matter, so did the Frank Flynns. Victims were usually pathetic, not their fault always, but still pathetic, something to be pitied.

"Remember when we were in junior high? The kids would get Doug Funmaker to throw rocks at stuff—streetlights, windows, cars—and he always got caught. Everyone hiding in the ditch or the bushes, laughing. Poor fucking dumb Doug. Hey, Eddie, that's what people thought. It's what you thought. And he's dead now. Dumb Doug is dead. Is that it, dumb Eddie wants to go to jail for the big white hunter?"

"Fuck you, Frank, fuck you." Eddie's voice was choked with rage and frustration. He took a deep breath and let it out. His eyes wandered away from Frank and came to rest on his cat. "Christ, I don't know what to do." Eddie looked like a tired little guy who needed a shower. He began absently stroking the big black-and-white cat, gently rubbing behind its ears. "Who the hell will feed Prowler?"

Frank exhaled in silent relief. "I will, Eddie. I'll come every day. Take him to the vet. Whatever he needs. I'm not just saying it. I like cats." Prowler butted his head up against Eddie's arm. Smart cat, good cat, Frank thought. "I can't make any sort of promises about what happens, but if you turn yourself in, you'll be better off. My guess is, you'll probably get a suspended sentence."

Eddie sagged. The defiance had seeped out, leaving a small brown body and a face made haggard by smoke, booze, and anger. Frank put a hand on Eddie's shoulder. For a moment, he was consumed with compassion. The ghost of his mother whispered in his mind, There but for the grace of God . . . "I'll put in a good word. You can count on it."

Eddie shook his head in resignation. "Shit, there goes the ten thousand dollars. He was going to pay me ten thousand dollars, Frank. Man, I could've done a lot with ten thousand dollars."

"You see any of the money yet?"

"Nope, but he was bringing it with him. He was going to give it to me after we got the head."

"After you get the head?" Frank's pulse quickened. "Let me get this straight. Smith's coming back?"

Eddie stroked the cat's back, and Prowler arched and turned with pleasure. "Yeah, he called and wanted me to go with him and help him get the head. I told him that wasn't part of the deal. Told him that I didn't know who else was in the canyon, but that Fish and Game would know about the dead sheep soon enough and that going back up in the canyon was a good way to get caught. Then he says there's nothing to be afraid of and that if I don't help him, no money. No head, no money. Then he offered me another five thousand just to help out. Take it or forget it. It was going to be fifteen thousand or nothing, so I told him I'd do it."

"When was all this going to take place?"

"Don't know. He was going to call me this afternoon." Eddie mimicked Smith. " 'At exactly four o'clock. Be sure you're there, because my schedule is tight.' I tell you what's tight. His asshole, that's what's tight." He lowered his voice, sounding thoughtful, looking at Frank. "But you can bet he'll call. He wants that head. I can see why. It's the biggest set of horns I've ever seen."

Frank felt his compassion harden. "I know that, Eddie. I've been watching that ram for a couple of years. Now his head is rotting in an abandoned mine, and the other ram, killed for no good reason, left to rot on the ground. Not a good day's work."

The small man looked down at his dusty feet. All the bravado gone, just a guy in his shop with his cat on a hot September afternoon. All that was missing was the cold beer. Frank sighed. He wished there were a way to get Eddie out of it, but there wasn't. This was the best he could do. He could feel the warm sunlight on his arm and the side of his face. Prowler closed his eyes in contentment. Frank pulled at the tip of his nose. If Eddie helped, Smith could be caught red-handed. After he turned himself in, Fish and Game would be all over him about Smith, and they'd be out of luck, unless something could be set up, catch Smith with the goods—head, rifle—enough to make it airtight.

"Eddie, I've got an idea. You'll be here to take Smith's call. He'll want to set up some sort of meeting. Go for it."

"What's the point if I'm going to be in jail?"

"Maybe yes, maybe no. Here's the deal. If we could catch him with the head and the rifle, catch him when he comes back to the mine, then he's the dummy, Eddie. He'll do time." Frank thought about Donnie Miller's sunbaked corpse. "Maybe a lot of time."

"Who's going to take him back to the canyon?"

"Maybe you, maybe me." He was thinking out loud. "Maybe you could have sprained your back, hurt yourself somehow, and your cousin from the reservation is filling in."

Eddie shook his head. "I don't think so, Frank. He's a very suspicious guy. When we started up the canyon in the truck, he asked me about how many times I had done this. Wanted to know if I'd ever been caught or been in jail. He kept looking around all the time. And like I told you, as soon as he knew someone else was in the canyon, man he was nervous, but not scared; cool, you know, moving fast but cool.

"He says, 'What's the best way out?' So I told him about hiking out by Telescope Peak. Then he says, 'What about the head?' So I told him to stash it. Then he looks at me and says, 'Don't get caught. It's better if you don't get caught.' He had mean eyes when he said that. Like if I get caught, I get more trouble from him." He looked at Frank and shook his head again. "Naw, I don't think he'll go for it."

Probably not, Frank thought. Then what? The two of them stood there in the afternoon sun, thinking about what to do. Frank felt the pressure of time. He had to go take a look at the mischief in Jawbone Canyon and see if he could get a handle on it. And he wanted to run down Mitch Cooper, see what else he knew about the Miller brothers and company. The thought of them produced a knot of anxiety. It was the look on Mitch's face. There had been real fear there, almost shock, and Mitch didn't seem like the kind of guy who was squeamish.

"Tell you what, Eddie. I'll wait here until you take the call. Just go along with him. Don't say anything to make him suspicious. Then we'll work something out." He looked at his watch: 1:45. "You had lunch yet?"

Eddie brightened. "You want, I'll make some sandwiches."

"Sounds good. Got any cold ones?" It was out of his mouth before he really thought about it.

Eddie shook his head. "Naw, drank the last one this morning to chase away the headache."

"Okay, you fix sandwiches, and I'll get the beer."

•

Bologna on white bread. Frank wasn't at all sure about the mayonnaise, but Eddie served them up on paper plates, along with some stale Pringles. Frank had used Pringles to start fires with—straight grease. His stomach roiled. A couple of Coronas helped wash it down. He hoped it would stay down. Eddie was happy as a kid, delighted to be entertaining company, really into outsmarting Smith. The sandwiches—Eddie had eaten three—apparently had no effect on his stomach. He rattled on, his voice becoming background noise. Frank felt like nodding off, but his stomach said no. He hovered in the twilight zone. No dinner tonight. Stomach wouldn't take it, and he didn't need it. It had been 3:30 by the time they finished up, and he had a long way to drive, at least a couple hours in his truck, holding it at sixty. His chosen chariot was sure, but definitely not speedy. He glanced at his watch: almost four o'clock. His lids felt heavy.

He awoke with Eddie poking his shoulder. The phone was ringing. Frank cleared his head. He pointed at the phone, motioning for Eddie to answer it. "Let him do most of the talking."

Eddie picked up the phone. "Yeah, hello." He nodded. "Yeah, sure." He looked over at Frank and winked, nodding his head. "Um-hm. Sure. That sounds okay." There was a long pause while Frank watched Eddie's head bob up and down. "Yeah, that should work good. No problem."

Frank handed him a piece of paper and a blunt pencil he'd picked up from the floor near the phone. Eddie shook his head and looked away. "What'd you say?" His back was to Frank, shoulders taut with concentration. "Yeah, I got it, about six o'clock." He turned back to face Frank, still nodding his head. Frank briefly wondered why people nodded or shook their heads when talking on the phone. Who could see?

"Right." Eddie had put on the street-smart voice. He was even standing with a swagger. "It's a done deal. See you at six."

Eddie hung up the phone. Frank retrieved the paper and pencil and waited for Eddie to speak.

"So I'm supposed to meet him at Ballarat Sunday morning. He's driving a car this time. Let's see, he wants me to bring canteens and a packboard."

"Uh-huh. How's he want to do it, get the head out?"

"He wants to leave his car at the mouth of the canyon. He liked the way I hid the truck." Eddie looked pleased with himself. "So we're going to hide the car same way I did my truck. Then I'm supposed to take him up to Mahogany Flat, and he's hiking down the canyon, picking up the head on the way down, no uphill hiking."

"How'd you traverse the rocks when you went up?"

"With all the gear, we took the long way. The trail up around the left of the slide."

Frank gave it some thought. "Yeah, and that's the way he'll come down." He smiled at Eddie. "Guess you fooled Mr. Big Shot, right? He's going to be caught. Fish and Game's bound to consider this when the time comes to press charges. First thing Saturday, go on over to the AM/PM for the morning paper. When you see your picture, call Fish and Game."

Eddie picked at his ear, not saying anything. Frank waited. "You won't forget about Prowler?"

"Nope. You show me where his stuff is."

"I'm shutting him in the shop. Someone hit him with a pellet gun awhile back." Eddie ran his hand along the cat's shoulder and upper forearm. "He's okay now, but I don't want anything to happen to him. Maybe you could come on Saturday, check his water and stuff. Make sure he doesn't find a way out. He gets pissed when I leave him alone too long."

"He'll be okay. That's a promise." The cat would be okay. He just hoped that things didn't get too tough for Eddie. Seemed like the law landed harder on the little guys than the big ones.

"Oh, and Eddie, leave the keys to your truck. I might have to borrow it for a bit. Okay?"

Eddie grinned, bad teeth exposed in unconscious pleasure. "You're going to be the surprise up in Surprise Canyon, huh, Frank?"

"We'll see. Probably won't be me, be some agent from Fish and Game."

"Uh-huh," Eddie said, still grinning like a kid, but with really bad teeth.

# 16

•

Frank pulled off Highway 14 where the Jawbone Canyon Road tailed away into the Tehachapi Mountains, well below Walker Pass and the junction with 395. The Los Angeles Aqueduct, a euphemism for the Owens River in a pipe, snaked across the mountains and desert until the river reemerged in a spectacular cascade in the San Fernando Valley, where Interstate 5 rose into the foothills of the San Gabriel Mountains. The diverted water filled the swimming pools and watered the lawns of the endless suburbs that comprised Southern California, leaving the Owens Valley more or less closed to agriculture and development, although things were changing.

Frank considered the theft of the valley's water a blessing in disguise. He could imagine what the floor of the Owens Valley would be like if the city of Los Angeles hadn't acquired the water rights: wall-to-wall burbs.

Rainfall was negligible in Jawbone and vegetation sparse; mostly creosote bush, rabbit bush, burro bush, and brittlebush, not enough rain for Joshua trees—dry, dry, country. When the rain came, it brought flowers in profusion, carpets of lupine and poppies. The brittlebush became bright with crowns of yellow blooms and the great bouquet perfumed the canyon air. All gone in a week or two; ephemeral was an apt tag for these fleeting moments of color. But they were achingly beautiful, maybe made more so by their brief duration, like the butterflies that appeared from nowhere to tend the blossoms.

Farther up the canyon, the road turned into an ever-widening track, encroaching on the sandy floor. In places, the road grew to be more than fifty yards across, six or seven inches deep in sand and dust, the result of thousands of knobby tires chewing up the dirt on the weekends. A couple of fifty-gallon drums overflowed with trash in a vain attempt to contain the accumulated mess of weekend recreation. The canyon floor was littered with bits of paper and plastic blowing about in the wind. Frank felt a sense of helplessness. The canyon was being defaced. Everywhere, the ATVs and motorcycles had cut trails into the hills, scars on the land.

It wasn't yet nine, but he was thinking about breakfast. Some huevos rancheros and a couple of Dos Equis would really hit the spot. Take off the rough edges and push back the sadness. He was rescued from the shadows of introspection by the sight of a boxcar-size motor home stopped crosswise in the wash. He could make out the figure of a woman waving at him with something white in her hand. It looked like the driver had attempted to cross over the wash and pick up the road that led to Dove Springs and eventually to Walker Pass, a long haul. The sight of the motor home bogged down in the sand produced a sense of nasty satisfaction and then irritation. He'd have to help.

A woman in a pale blue print dress and a navy blue windbreaker stood near the door of the motor home, waving frantically, the wind blowing her dress immodestly up elderly legs. He followed the track across the wash, staying away from the chewed-up sand in the center, trying for the harder-packed stuff, which was not yet part of the giant ATV sandbox. He stopped his truck about fifty feet from the motor home; no four-wheel drive meant he had to be careful not to get stuck himself.

The woman didn't stop waving until he got out of the truck. He could see her mouth moving as she tried to talk into the wind. He trudged across the wash and lifted his hand in greeting. The wind whipped at his back, pushing him on. He raised his voice to a shout. "Hello there. Looks like you've got some trouble." He made himself smile. Clearly the woman was frightened. He wondered where the male contingent was. She tried to reply, her voice swallowed by the wind. He shouted to be heard. "I'm from the Bureau of Land Management. Everything okay here?"

"Oh, I'm so glad you're here." He bent forward to hear her. "No, everything's a mess. Please come inside and look at my husband. I think he's overdone it."

Frank pulled the door and followed the woman back into the bedroom. A man in his mid- to late seventies lay on a queen-size bed. Everything seemed to be pink: the bedspread, the curtains, the man's face. His T-shirt was damp from sweat and caked with dust.

"Howard, this man is a forest ranger. He's here to help us."

Howard began struggling to get up. Frank help up his hand. "No, sir, please stay where you are. No need to get up." Howard flopped back on the bed, breathing heavily.

"Actually, I'm from the Bureau of Land Management." The man and woman seemed puzzled. He gave up. "I'm a government ranger. What's the problem here? What can I do to help?"

The man closed his eyes and sighed with relief, exhaustion, probably a combination of both. "We were going to meet some people up on the tableland near Dove Springs. Crossing over this wash here, we started bogging down. When I got out to check, both front tires were flat. I put on the spare, and while I was taking one of the dual tires off for the front, I got dizzy, so I came in to lie down for a moment."

"That was more than two hours ago." The woman's face was pinched with concern.

"Well, you just stay where you are. I'll finish the job up for you. You Auto Club, by any chance?"

"Yep, but we can't reach 'em. The cell phone doesn't work right down here in the canyon."

"Well, don't worry about it. Just take it easy. Ma'am, maybe you could show me where the tools and stuff are." Frank looked at his watch. After nine o'clock, damn it.

•

Frank watched the motor home lumber down the packed dirt road with a sense of relief. It had taken him almost two hours to change the tires and extricate the motor home from the sand. It was no wonder the man was exhausted. Each wheel and tire weighed more than a hundred pounds. Frank was thankful he carried a piece of steel plate to keep the jack from burying itself, as well as sand ramps for traction, or he would've had to go for help. They'd be okay. They both looked fine by the time he pulled the rig back on the hard pack.

Time to get on with it. He'd try to get a lead on the caltrops he'd removed from the tires, but the effort would probably be useless. You could buy them in catalogs. Hell, you could buy almost anything from catalogs, or on the Net.

He parked his truck on the solid road above the cutbank near the turnoff for Dove Springs. Signs had been spaced down the turnoff at intervals along the side of the road, like the old Burma-Shave signs. THIS DESERT'S NOT A PLACE TO ROAM / ESPECIALLY IN A MOTOR HOME / GO BACK NOW! / IT'S NOT TOO LATE / KEEP ON COMING / MEET YOUR FATE! The last sign bore a crude drawing of a raven smoking a pipe. Where had he seen it before? A childhood memory flashed into his mind, the crows from *Dumbo*. That was it. "I seen a horsefly / I seen a dragonfly / I seen a needle that winked its eye . . ." He couldn't remember the rest. The crows sang with the voices of the Ink Spots. He grinned. The old Burma-Shave signs were better, but someone, or several someones, had gone to a lot of trouble to warn people off.

Up the side of a hill, another sign stuck up from the center of a rock pile: KEEP OUT. LAND OF THE JACKALOPE. Underneath the words was the figure of the pipe-smoking raven.

The jackalope thing tickled something in his memory. He gunned the truck and picked up speed for the run across the sand wash. If he didn't slow down, he could shoot right on across. He was about halfway when the truck began slewing to the right. He shifted down and corrected, but it was useless. The sand grabbed at the wheels. He was stuck. Well, it wouldn't be a big deal. He had the sand ramps. He grabbed the entrenching tool from behind the seat and began clearing away the sandy soil from the right front wheel, and there it was, stuck in his tire, another damn caltrops. Damn! Damn! Damn! Jackalope be damned. Jackasses, that's what. Somebody could die of thirst out here, Frank thought, or have a heart attack, or be late for his own funeral! He threw down the entrenching tool in a fit of rage and muttered, "Shit!"

Then he caught a picture of himself stuck in the wash, jumping around like Rumpelstiltskin. It was like an out-of-body experience. He was looking down at his tiny figure in the canyon, watching it dancing about in frustration. He started to laugh. He knew Linda would laugh, that his dad was probably laughing right now, looking down from that pool hall in the sky, and that's what did it. He saw the jackalope above the bar in the Joshua Tree Athletic Club looking down at him in lugubrious solemnity, the glass eyes winking in the light. There was Jack Collins's Irish face winking around at everyone. Have some tamale pie. Come on over on Fridays for some fish stew. Who looked dumb now? Who was the sucker now, the fall guy? Eddie had company. He clenched his teeth, the jaw muscles working under the brown skin. Those old boys were going to get a solid piece of his mind. He didn't have the evidence, but he could connect the dots. If he hurried, he'd just have time to pay Mitch and Shawna a visit. He thought Mitch might be holding back a few things, things that might lead to the Miller brothers. Then he was going to have a personal chat with Jack Collins and Co.

# 17

•

Linda busied herself dusting. She did the bar top, then the glasses, then the backbar and the bottles of hard liquor lining the shelves. It wasn't for show. Everything was coated with a fine alkaline grit. The wind had been blowing for most of the day, sweeping off the mountains, pushing clouds of dust across the desert floor. It found its way into all the nooks and crannies of the Joshua Tree Athletic Club, a structure so drafty that coats and jackets were a part of normal winter attire despite the blazing fire in the large stone fireplace, which only managed to scorch those sitting nearest the flames.

Apart from the fireplace and the oversize kitchen, not that much remained of the original boxlike structure, which had been hastily thrown up during the gold boom of the 1880s and 1890s. When the desert wind kicked up, the building leaked like a sieve. At best, it was no more than a sorry windbreak made rickety by time and shoddy construction. The skeletal remnants of the original building were perforated by various-caliber bullet holes, souvenirs of the gun-toting crowd passing along the desert highway in the dark of night. The pockmarks of vandalism had been transformed by the club's denizens into the stuff of legend, each bullet hole a scar from desperate duels played out on the stage of imagination, a place where outlaws and lawmen, miners and claim jumpers, and pimps and prostitutes distributed the ingredients of death and destruction. It was all broken hearts, broken heads, and derring-do. The colorful inhabitants of fictional memory marched on cracked voices from whiskered mouths into a reality more vibrant than the sad ghosts of forgotten faces.

Linda knew that, seen from one angle, the regulars of the Joshua Tree Athletic Club were odd ducks, like her dad and his pals, a bunch of aging misfits, refugees from smog city, freeways, and pavement. Eccentricities united the "Red Mountain boys" in an undeclared fellowship.

She smiled at the thought of the "boys," as they referred to themselves. No, they were definitely not boys, much too geezerlike. More important, they'd lived the lives of men, old wolves in sheep's clothing. They liked to say they'd seen the elephant. Despite their flinty exteriors, she thought of them fondly as mischievous, although she knew they wouldn't welcome the observation. She tended to be drawn toward the ones who were a bit offbeat. Men like Frank, she thought.

That had been her mistake with Joaquin José Guzman y Reyes. So beautiful, so humorless, so self-absorbed. She should have known on that day she'd teased him about his name that something was missing. "Joaquin José—that's sort of southern, like Billy Joe." She'd grinned. He'd frowned. The dark brows had gathered themselves into lines of displeasure. 'No, not really. It is nothing like that. I am named for Joaquin Guzman, whose family held a patent of land from the king of Spain. The name of José is from my mother's family. I have a cousin who was married to a Figueroa." She'd let it pass, but it was a warning shot, and she had ignored it.

She suspected he'd been relieved to see her go. As an appendage, she'd missed the mark. She lacked compliance, which might have been regarded as an understatement by Joaquin. Fortunately, there were no children, which had been another point of contention. He'd been determined to produce another of his name or names, even if the lands and titles had gone with the wind, perhaps gone with the orange groves, although that didn't have the same ring. She smiled grimly to herself. There's a movie in this somewhere. She had no regrets—well, no material regrets. There were lots of eligible geezers in Red Mountain, if geezers could be considered eligible, and there was Frank Flynn, a puzzlement.

Now she had two jobs, half the pay, no pressure, and a wonderful sense of freedom. The freedom seemed to go with the desert. Despite the fact the Joshua Tree Athletic Club appeared on the verge of collapse, it made enough money to keep the doors open and pay the bills, with some cash left over.

Lately, business had taken an upturn. There was enough money to pay her for her time and provide the boys with sufficient pocket change to get them in trouble. Maybe because the old place looked like a ramshackle saloon from a Western, the club was a regular stop-off point for curious tourists coming up 395 on the way to the skiing or fishing in the Sierras. It seemed like a bit of the Old West caught in a pocket of time. All pretty weird and interesting, but she knew her life was on hold.

The wind increased in ferocity. Linda realized she was fighting a losing battle, but she was determined to keep the backbar clean at least. The dust swirled under the bottom and between the rubber lips of the swinging doors. Her efforts spared her from having to make conversation with the two couples at the bar. The men had sought to impress her with loud talk of desert hangouts and tales of barroom brawls, mostly borrowed from the movies. Whenever she bent down to reach something under the bar, she could feel their eyes on her backside. Lots of the patrons flirted with her, and sometimes she flirted back. But these two were phonies, decked out like Hollywood bad boys, their behavior mimicking celluloid villainy.

The huge baby-faced man with a puffy body was wearing a T-shirt too small to cover four inches of hairy gut adequately, but he was less offensive than his companion, who took an inordinate interest in his own tanned and muscular body, the result of hours in the gym and tanning salon. His eyes were fixed on his flexing biceps in the mirror back of the bar. That is, when he wasn't staring at her bottom. The heavyset one wore an expensive gold wristwatch; his muscular companion sported a thick gold chain against a tan neck and a black Grateful Dead T-shirt—the accoutrement of bucks, not bikers.

The women were less pretentious. Both wore close-fitting leather outfits, dusty but unscuffed. Their faces bore none of the ravages of biker life, such as the flat eyes, hard mouths, and leathery skin. Their complexions were soft and smooth, crow's-feet moistened carefully away. Linda thought she should look so good. Despite the loud talk of the men, the women's laughter was softened by the culture of money, no braying or raucous hoots of approval. The group had ridden up on motorcycles of some sort, but not Harleys, at least not street hogs. Their machines were too quiet, no rumbling punctuated by the staccato of backfires. She watched as one of the men placed a couple of twenties on the bar, crisp from an ATM. Definitely ersatz bikers.

The man with the toned body raised his voice against the steady roar of the wind when it suddenly stilled, and he found himself almost shouting into a hushed void. They paused in the sudden silence. Linda, towel in hand, stood motionless; the others turned toward the entrance as if waiting for the wind to resume. In that moment, the doors swung inward and a short, ugly red-haired man seemed to be propelled through the entrance on a violent blast of wind. He was immediately followed by a stringy companion in a cutoff denim jacket and denim jeans, his clothes embedded with the dun color of the desert. His graying hair had been pulled back into a ponytail, revealing an angular profile that resembled nothing so much as a hood ornament, pointy and hard. Then a third man sauntered lazily in behind them, his hair and skin so white that he seemed almost iridescent in the half-light of the bar. Linda drew in her breath at the third figure. She could only see the pupils of his eyes, which gave him an oddly mechanical appearance. She'd seen them before. The three newcomers stood framed at the entrance for a moment, and then the white-haired one gestured the others to a table and approached the bar.

"Man, that's what I call windy." His smile exposed even white teeth against gums that appeared dark red in the dim light. "Could use three beers to wash away the dust."

He gave off a faintly acrid, metallic odor. Linda's heart was pounding. It was them, the ones who'd beaten up the hunters the last time they'd come in. A miasma of evil clung to them like dirty garments. For the first time in her life, she felt terrified.

"Three Sierra Nevadas on tap." He drummed his fingers on the bar. "Okay, lady? Hey there, we're kinda thirsty here, what with being out in all that dust."

She looked up at the pale face. "Oh, yeah, sure." Linda filled the glasses, glad to have something to do while she tried to think, and keep from looking at the shotgun under the bar, just below the cash register. She set the beers on the bar.

"Six dollars."

"Pay as you go, huh? Well, no offense taken. We're not regulars in here—yet." He gave her a soft grin, then added, "Are we?" A pale, sinewy hand put a wrinkled ten-dollar bill on the bar. "Keep the rest. Kind of a tip in advance." The pallid right eye winked. As he carried the three beers over to the others, she saw that the redheaded one was staring intently, and she turned quickly away to the comfort of the people at the bar, now so seemingly pleasant and normal, she wanted to hug them. She heard a wet clicking sound. From the corner of her eye, she watched in mesmerized fascination as the redheaded dwarfish one pivoted his head about in small jerky motions, as if it were on a ratchet. Each movement of his head was accompanied by a wet clicking sound. A troll from her Arthur Rackham–illustrated *Grimm's Fairy Tales*, all thick and hairy, eyes bright with malice. She had to think, to remain calm.

"Click, click, click." He swiveled his head toward the bar, his gaze resting on the couples seated on the chrome and leather stools. "Click, click." His eyes traveled the length of the bar and back; then the woolly head ceased to move, arrested by the motion of a Loony Bird next to the cash register. It was the kind that tipped and dipped its beak into a water glass, popped upright, rocked back and forth, moving ever closer and closer to the water, then dipped and tipped and rocked back, over and over in endless repetition. He made a loud slurping, sucking sound as the bird's beak touched the water. "Slurrrp." The wet sucking sound was followed by a burst of rapid clicks that paced the frantic bobbing of the bird, then slowed as the dipping head came ever more slowly and surely to dip back into the water. "Cslick . . . csslick . . . cssslick . . . slurrrrp." He grinned over at the people at the bar, who had been watching him in silent fascination.

"Quit it, Jace." The pale one's voice was sandy and matter-of-fact.

"Click, click, click." Jace ratcheted his head around to peer at his companion from under bushy red eyebrows.

"You speaking to me, pilgrim?" It was an eerily accurate imitation of John Wayne's voice.

"Can it, I said." Pale, colorless eyes met the other's bright glare, which glittered like bits of blue glass.

"Click, click, click." The redhead's voice raised in defiance. "Click, fucking click, fucking click." Each syllable was sharp and distinct, the voice increasing in volume. Then catching sight of the jackalope above the bar, he fell silent, his tiny blue eyes bright with curiosity. The lifeless eyes of the jackalope regarded him with glassy calm. It was as if these aberrant entities were transfixed by a sensed kinship, mutants in a moment of mutual recognition.

He turned abruptly toward the people at the bar, a furry red arm extended in their direction. "Who're you?" The big man closest to the one called Jace leaned back, exposing four or five inches of hairy gut. His tattooless fat arms were white and covered with black hair, especially at the back, thick enough to comb. New motorcycle boots rested on the brass foot railing.

"Who wants to know?"

Jace's wiry companion leaned toward the pale one and stage-whispered, "Salty fucker, ain't he?"

Linda recognized the pattern: the beginnings of trouble. Again, she struggled not to look at the shotgun. What good would it be? Her dad said it was for emergencies, but she'd never fired it. It was a heavy thing, a ten-gauge double barrel, with old-fashioned side hammers. Her dad had cut the barrels so it was less unwieldy. He called it Stop and Think, because one look at the size of the barrels made a person do just that. She'd been raised around firearms, but mostly .22s. Plinking with her dad. Hunting Campbell's tomato soup cans, going on tin-can safaris. She'd fired her dad's twelve-gauge at clay pigeons a few times, but she hadn't liked it. Too noisy, and it hurt her shoulder. She imagined what the ten-gauge must be like.

"Hey, what's your name, man?" The pale one asked. "How can we talk until we know each other's names?" The one called Jace bobbed his head in a rhythmic pattern. The heavyset man looked over at his partner, pointed his finger at his head, and made a twirling motion.

Jace's pale companion stood up and strolled toward the bar, his face tight, slender frame and ropy muscles moving under a long-sleeved white T-shirt tucked neatly into dusty white denims. "Hey man, we're just being friendly here." His sandy voice permeated the room with covert menace. "My name's Roy. This here noisy one is Jace. Some folks call him 'Loco Roco.' That what you meant by this?" Roy twirled his finger at the side of his head. "Loco? 'Cause if it is, he's sensitive about it." Jace made another slurping sound as the bird dipped its beak in the water.

"Didn't really mean anything by it." With Roy standing so close, regarding him with those strange eyes, the big man's bravado had disappeared.

Roy shrugged. "And that's my partner there, Wild Bill Hickey." He gestured with his arm, pointing in the general direction of the table but never taking his eyes off the men. "So, who're you guys and these lovely ladies here? Howdy there. I'm Roy." He flashed a smile made ghastly by the red gums.

The woman seated next to the muscular man in the Grateful Dead T-shirt smiled and offered her hand. "I'm Barbara, and this is my friend Joann." She smiled. "Do you and your friends live out here?"

"Yes, ma'am. All around in this desert is our home."

"I'm Fred Nietzsche." A muscular arm extended from the Grateful Dead shirt. "This is my business partner," he added, gesturing at his portly companion, "Art Schopenhauer." He smirked over at the women, his little joke. Barbara and Joann exchanged amused glances. The man dubbed Fred took Roy's hand, squeezing it hard, letting Roy know he was outclassed in the muscle department.

Roy removed his hand, shaking it in front of him. "Man that's some powerful grip you got there. You're some strong mother-fucker. Oops, scuse me, ladies." He turned to Jace and Hickey at the table. "Hey there, say hello to Fred and Art here."

"How ya doin'?" Hickey waved a languid arm.

Jace lifted his right hand, exposing the palm with the crude death's-head tattoo. He slowly bent the little finger forward, causing the image of the empty eye socket to close. "Hi, Fred." Then he repeated the process with the index finger. "Hi, Art." He made a loud explosive sound, halfway between a bark and laugh. "Yeah man, the Grateful Dead," he said, grinning at them with matched rows of perfect little teeth.

"Those big bikes out front belong to you guys, those Gold Wings?" Roy gestured vaguely in the direction of the entrance.

"Um-hmm." Art nodded, sounding uninterested.

Roy gave his companions a look of disbelief. "Man oh man." He began shaking his head. "Never heard of Pearl Harbor, these guys. Drivin' rice cookers." He let his face go blank. "Man, aren't you guys Americans?" he asked, shaking his head again. "You don't want to get caught out here by real bikers, Hells Angels, Mongols, or the Sidewinders, especially the Sidewinders. They're bad folk. Folk you up real good." Laughter on cue from the table. "Isn't that right, brothers?" The redhead nodded vigorously, clicking furiously with each movement. Wild Bill Hickey just gave a dreamy smile.

Fred looked sour. Somehow these rubes seemed to be mocking them, not the other way around. "For your information, fella, we used to ride with the Hells Angels."

"No shit." Roy widened his eyes in mock surprise. "Hear that?" Roy turned to his companions at the table, rolling his eyes. "These guys were with the Hells Angels." Roy gave Art a questioning look. The big man seemed boyish and pudgy. He sat with rounded shoulders, his belly pooching forward. Sweat trickled down the side of his face and neck and disappeared into his T-shirt. "What chapter, man? Victorville, San Bernardino, Fontana?"

Fred puffed himself up, on the defensive now. "Up in northern California. Out of Watsonville."

Roy regarded him expectantly, encouraging him to go on. "Yeah?"

"Some years back." For a moment, he held Roy's gaze, then turned away.

Roy turned back to his buddies at the table. "Whadda ya think, brother Hickey? We should let bygones be bygones, especially since they're from up north?"

Hickey nodded in affirmation. "Why not, man. There's a lot of pus buckets in the Angels." But the furry red one, Jace, shook his head back and forth, clicking furiously.

Art glanced sideways at his companion, then back to Roy. He looked trapped and pitiful. Linda wanted to save him, but she felt equally helpless.

"Hey, it's okay, man." Roy tossed an arm casually over Art's flabby shoulders. "See, we're with the Sidewinders. Bikers, like you guys." He nodded in communion. "Only, only"—he grinned back at his companions, then at Art—"only we kick the shit out of the Angels." He felt the soft shoulders sag. He glanced over at Fred and back to Art again. "You heard of us right, the Sidewinders?" Fred and Art were mute. They shifted their eyes away from their pale interrogator. Something had slipped away.

Roy rolled his eyes in open disbelief. "Sidewinders, like rattlesnakes. You know, like the flag. 'Don't tread on me.'" Roy looked earnestly from one to the other. "Man, like the early American flag, the one we shoulda kept, the one with the rattlesnake. You guys gotta go back to school, find out about our country. I bet Barbara and Joann here know all about snakes." He winked and leered.

"Hey look, pal." Fred's face flushed with red blotches of anger. "I don't need any fucking history lessons from you."

Linda's voice cut in. "I think you and your friends ought to leave, right now, before I call the police." Her remark deflected the focus of Roy's attention. Now it was directed at her. For a moment, no one spoke. Roy turned slowly to face her, pink-rimmed eyes peering into hers over a rictus smile.

He spoke over his shoulder, his eyes never leaving Linda's face. "You want to go, Jace?" The oversize head swiveled back and forth in rhythm with the soft clicking. "How about you, Wild Bill, whadda ya say? Want to leave?"

"Why the fuck would I want to go, Roy? I love it here, watching Jace and the bird, the good-looking squack at the bar, and especially talking to badass Fred and Art here. This place is a home away from home." The slack, humorless smile revealed a greenish gum line at the base of yellowing teeth.

"My boys like it here"—he paused a beat—"Ms. Reyes." Watching as it dawned on her. "Why should they have to leave? Maybe Fatman and Robin big mouth ought to be the ones to take a hike. So there you have it, Linda. You don't mind being called Linda, do you?" He shrugged. "Anyhow, what we have here is a problem of social interaction."

A tight lump of dread knotted up in her stomach. How did they know her name, know who she was? An image of a motorcycle in her rearview mirror flashed through her mind, the gray-ponytailed rider following her down 395. She couldn't remember when she had noticed him. Both men were grinning at her now in open amusement, enjoying her shock, her fear, as if to say, We're here for you, honey. She felt a flush of rage. If only she could get to the shotgun without them getting to her.

Roy spoke to her quietly, in confidence. She had to strain to hear him above the steady moaning of the wind. "See, we wanted to have a little news conference with you about the dead guy in the canyon. Talk to you about it, 'cause we think he was family."

"You know, I think the lady's right, fella." Fred had regrouped, taken courage from Linda's defiance, the talk of police. "You ought to just move on. Move on down the road and leave us alone."

"Is that right?" Roy paused to regard the four people at the bar, then nodded slowly. "Good idea, Fred, soon as we're done."

Art's eyes traveled nervously from speaker to speaker. He seemed unable to comprehend what was going on. Fred glared at Roy, emboldened by what he took for capitulation. He sneered over at his partner. "These guys are hicks. Wanna-be badasses, but hicks nevertheless." Then turning to Roy, he said, "You don't even know who we are." He sneered, his voice filled with contempt.

"Hey, there's where you're wrong, Fred." Roy looked almost mournful. "I know just who you are." His voice was soft and serious. "You're an important man, a German philosopher. I've read some of your books." As he spoke, he moved in close, invading Fred's space. "You wrote one of my favorites, *The Birth of Tragedy*." The last four words dropped with careful precision. Fred drew away, leaning backward against the bar, perplexed by the turn of events. Roy stepped closer yet, pale eyes locked on his face; then Roy's right hand shot into Fred's exposed solar plexus. Fred bent forward, eyes filled with shock. The first blow was followed quickly by a second to the kidneys, a never-fail shot. His eyes rolled up in agony. He dropped to the floor, small grunting sounds emitting from his mouth.

"Man, that must've hurt." Roy dropped a roll of nickels on the bar. "He could be pissing blood for a week." Fred continued making short gasping sounds. Roy bent down, frowning with concern. "What's that you say? Can't hear you too good." He bent even closer, his face inches from the fallen man. "Speak right up. I can hear you real good now." Ray bent down, listening to Fred's strangled efforts to breathe, nodding his head in agreement with his stifled gasps. "Oh yeah, now you're using the old noggin." He stood up casually and regarded Art, who seemed inert, sitting with his mouth open, unable to stop staring at Roy. "He says you ought to get the fuck oughta here, fat boy, before Ms. Reyes here calls the cops on you for disturbing the peace. You ladies, too." He looked over at Hickey and raised his hand to the side of his face, the little finger extended toward his mouth and the thumb pointing at his ear, the telephone sign. Again he bent over the prostrate Fred, speaking into his face. "Fred's not your real name, is it? But don't tell me, 'cause I already know. It's Butt Wipe. I. M. Butt Wipe. I knew it as soon as I looked at your candy-ass bikes out front. Now we both know your real name, Butt Wipe," he said, drawing it out. He spit casually in the fallen man's face. "You sorry sack of shit."

Linda ducked down and came up with the shotgun, pointing it at Hickey, who had risen from the table and was approaching the bar.

"Whoa there, lady." He thrust his arms forward, hands palms out.

"You better sit back down," Linda said. He stopped but made no move to sit. For now, that would have to do. Roy's body reappeared above the bar. She swung the shotgun over, pointing it at him. He regarded her with deliberate calm, sizing things up. Then she noticed the gun wasn't cocked; the side hammers were resting in the forward position. She pulled the heavy shotgun tightly to her shoulder and quickly reached over with her left hand and pulled back both hammers. The muzzle dropped dangerously forward. She jerked the gun back, pointing it at Roy. Her eyes shot over to the standing Hickey and back again to Roy. She stepped back as far as she could, grateful for the fact the bar separated them. They were too close.

"Don't use the old shotgun all that much, do ya?" Roy grinned. "Feels kinda unfamiliar. I know what that's like, things feeling unfamiliar." Hickey had eased a step closer. Her eyes darted back and forth between Hickey and Roy. She had to do something. One or both were going to come over the bar.

"No point in getting upset." Roy put up his hands. "See, hands up. Now what? Seems to me you got a problem here. Two barrels, three guys. And you not even knowing how to use that big ol' shoulder cannon. Probably knock you on your cute little ass."

Hickey chuckled at Roy's joke.

She gritted her teeth. "That's probably true, but you won't see it, 'cause the first one's for you." She trained the gun on Roy, her resolve steadying her hands.

"I don't know, sweet cheeks. I'm not sure you could hit shit."

"Let's find out." She swung the shotgun between Roy and Hickey and pulled the trigger. The noise was stunning. Barbara screamed. Each person remained riveted in position by the blast, except for Linda, who had been driven into the backbar by the recoil, knocking bottles from the shelves. The shock of the sound had given her time to regain her balance, and she leveled the gun back at Roy.

"Now there's only one left, and it's all yours, mister." The adrenaline rush had deadened any pain she might have felt. She was truly angry, angry as she had never been. Who were these people to come uninvited into her life, bringing violence and terror? "You want some of that?" She gestured with the shotgun at the ragged four-inch hole in the woodwork of the far wall. "'Cause, mister, I don't like you very much."

Roy stepped slowly away from the bar. He gestured to the door with his head. The one called Hickey called over to Jace. "Come on, Jace, we're going now." Jace's bright little eyes flashed back and a forth in apparent confusion.

Roy nodded in Jace's direction. "Go on out with Hickey. It's time to go, Jace." Jace stepped away from his chair and followed Hickey out the door in a simian shuffle. At the door, he turned back, smiling hugely. "I'll be bock." It was pure Schwarzenegger. Then he disappeared into the wind. The first fat drops of rain racketed on the tin, each pop and crack distinct in the charged air.

Roy backed toward the door, Linda tracking him with the shotgun.

He smiled. "Know where you work, know where you live. So you take care, Ms. Reyes. Bad things happen to good people. It's a puzzle, isn't it?" His last words were almost drowned out by the roar of the rain on the roof.

# 18

•

The first fat drops of rain kicked little puffs of dust from the powdered dirt that covered the Jawbone Canyon track. It splattered on the grimy windshield, transforming the dirt into rivulets of mud. Soon the entire road would be a sump. Frank stepped on the gas, driving faster than was his custom, faster than was safe. He needed to hit the pavement before he became mired in muck. He could barely see through the muddy windshield. The wipers were still vintage 1953, strictly vacuum, not very efficient at optimum condition, and they weren't at optimum, the blades hardened and rough from baking in the sun. If he could just make the pavement, he'd be all right. If not, he'd be stuck in the mud up to the running boards. Sand ramps would be next to useless. The truck careened to the left, and Frank steered into the skid, gently bringing it back on line, only to have to repeat the process on the right.

He took off his sunglasses and leaned out the window. The rain immediately plastered his hair to his forehead. He squinted against the rush of water and air. He could just make out the pipeline ahead, maybe no more than a quarter of a mile away. He grimly held on to the wheel, guiding the careening truck through the mud. Stopping meant staying. He wasn't stopping. He plowed on, the truck's progress becoming more labored every minute. He felt a thud as the truck steadied. He'd made it onto the asphalt. He still couldn't see much, but the windshield wipers were mercifully more efficient now that he could back off on the gas. He pulled the truck to a stop under the trees at the pumping station and switched off the ignition.

The rain roared off the pipeline and danced off the road, splattering up almost a foot. A short wall of water covered the pavement. On the desert surface, it was different. The rain disappeared, soaking through the porous layer into the ground. If enough rain fell, it would puddle and run off, but the uneroded surface of the desert soaked up the water like a sponge.

Frank stepped out of his truck into the shelter of the trees. Despite the morning's heat, the air was surprisingly cool. He had the urge to build a campfire, heat some coffee, maybe lace it with a bit of Jameson. He thought of Linda. Rain in the trees, rain on the roof, romantic musings. The wind paused. Now there was only the sound of the rain, and already it was lessening. Take your drink and be quick about it. You may not get another for some time.

In the distance, lightning flashed on the horizon. He counted to twenty and gave up. Then he heard a faint rumbling. It must be over toward Red Mountain, he thought. The rain stopped as suddenly as it had begun. Great puffs of cloud parted and shafts of sunlight struck the floor of the canyon. Wisps of vapor rose up from the water-drenched surface, which was still warm from the sun. The smell of creosote bush filled the air, tangy, pungent, and clean.

A patch of sunlight opened on the opposite hillside, changing shape as it moved across the canyon floor. A shadow slipped momentarily across the sunlit hillside, and then another. He looked up. Vultures. They were circling high up toward the mouth of the canyon, cutting the shaft of light in their westward arc. Probably something alive had ventured onto the highway where it had become dead. He experienced a moment of foreboding and unease. He glanced up at the hoarse call of a raven and found it perched on the canyon wall. They were his favorite desert companions, curious, intelligent, and resourceful. They often followed his path, wheedling for food, which he rarely gave them. But they followed along anyhow, observing him as he observed them. It called again. Its mate wheeled above, the wedge-shaped tail correcting the path of flight. It twisted its head to look down at Frank. His unease turned to unspoken dread.

He returned quickly to his truck and brought it to life. He needed to find Linda. Mitch and Shawna could wait. The sound of the engine cut him off from the sounds of the desert. He wanted to get away from there, go to the Joshua Tree Athletic Club and confront Collins about those signs and the caltrops.

•

It was less than an hour from Jawbone Canyon to Red Mountain, but it seemed to be taking forever. His truck pulled up the steep grades and clattered down the hills at a steady sixty miles an hour. It was pointless to push it. What's more, he told himself, his misgivings were irrational, based on seeing vultures and communing with a raven. Big deal. But he couldn't erase the sense of dread. He tried to think about it analytically. Maybe it had to do with what he'd said to Dave Meecham, his insistence that the wandering Miller brothers were to be taken seriously, even if they hadn't been heard from. People like that didn't just go away. That was probably it. He had convinced himself, heard his own argument and believed it. If that was the case, the misgivings were real enough. Just the timing seemed peculiar. Why now, in such a rush? Because he had been pushing it under, wanting it to go away, wanting the Millers to go away. He had a poacher to catch. He had a woman to court. He didn't have time for uglies like the Millers and their grimy buddy. Now he had his pickup doing sixty-eight down the grade. The clatter of the tappets brought him back to the road. Soon he'd be passing through Johannesburg and then he'd be in Red Mountain.

His chest constricted as he rounded the curve and came upon the scattered ramshackle buildings that comprised what was left of Red Mountain. The blue and red lights flashing from an ambulance and two San Bernardino Sheriff's Department cars parked at crazy angles in front of the Joshua Tree Athletic Club winked spasmodically in the midafternoon light. It felt as if he were watching a movie that he was in. He could see himself pull into the dirt parking lot. He remembered not to block the exit, and then he got out of the truck and watched himself walk toward the ambulance. A couple of paramedics struggled through the swinging doors of the saloon with a gurney. He couldn't see who was on it. He hurried forward.

"Stand back, please." A young San Bernardino deputy sheriff blocked Frank's way.

"I'm with Bureau of Land Management."

The deputy eyed Frank's uniform. "Okay," he said dismissively.

"Look, I know the owner and his family. I'd like to know what's going on." Frank struggled to remain calm.

"There's been an altercation, sir. Right now, we have an injured person who needs attention, so please step back."

Frank craned around the deputy, trying to see the gurney before it disappeared into the emergency vehicle. One of the paramedics stepped back for a moment, and he could see that it was a man on the gurney, not Linda, thank God. He breathed a sigh of temporary relief. He hoped it wasn't Jack Collins, or one of his cranky cronies, and not just for Linda's sake. He liked the Joshua Tree Athletic Club and the unyielding way these stubborn old men refused to bend to the times. As his da would have said, "They flew the flag."

The emergency vehicle pulled out onto the blacktop and headed down Highway 395 to the hospital in Adelanto, a long ride. The young deputy crunched his way across the dirt and gravel to a California Highway Patrol cruiser that had pulled off the road to find out what was going on. Cop chitchat. For some of his law-enforcement brothers, he wasn't a real cop. But he was used to it, interagency pride, all that stuff. The LAPD thought the Sheriff's Department guys were hicks. The Sheriff's Department personnel looked down on small-town local police. There was a pecking order, and now and then he was at the bottom. He took advantage of the deputy's absence and slipped through the doors into the bar.

Linda sat at one of the tables, her back to him. Opposite her was a deputy taking notes. He wore a weary expression under a graying buzz cut. Linda sat upright, her back and shoulders rigid. Frank wanted to go to her, but he waited, knowing not to interrupt and thus piss off the deputy.

Another deputy, a heavyset Hispanic, was talking to two women seated at the bar. His shirt was sweat-stained under the arms and down the back. Rivulets of perspiration ran down the sides of his face. The women seemed cool, sort of excited at being questioned by the police, an adventure. They were taking turns talking, nodding to each other. Every so often, the deputy would ask a question, and then he'd write something down in a spiral notebook. The women were wearing expensive leather outfits. One wore her dark hair in a stylish wedge. The other had thick brown hair wound in a French braid. A big heavy man in a tight black T-shirt sat slumped at a table, staring into space. He looked disoriented. Obviously, something bad had happened to him. Frank waited. He could just make out the conversation between Linda and the older deputy.

"So none of them had weapons?" The deputy's tone was neutral.

"Not that I could see, no," Linda said in a taut voice.

"Then what made you go for the gun?"

"I told you. They hurt that man, and I knew I'd be next."

The deputy wrote in his notebook. It seemed like he was writing for a long time. Linda watched him. Then he looked up quickly from his notebook, catching Linda's expression. "What made you think you were in danger?"

"He knew my name. He said he wanted to have a news conference. They came to see me."

"Now why is that?"

"I told you. I'm a reporter for the *InyoKern Courier*. I wrote a story about a man found dead in the Panamints. Apparently, two of these men were his brothers." Frank could hear the edge of anger in her voice.

"It doesn't seem unusual for someone to want to know more about the circumstances of a relative's death. I mean, isn't wanting to talk to you about it natural?"

Linda shook her head in frustration. "These men are dangerous. Look what they did to that man—for nothing. It was vicious. One of them hit him with a roll of nickels, then spit in his face."

The deputy nodded his head. His voice was matter-of-fact. "Okay, there was a fight. Let's call it an assault." He paused for a moment and then changed tack. "Ms. Reyes, you work in a bar. You're familiar with the term barroom brawl, right? What I'm suggesting is that these types of people hang out in bars and hurt one another when they drink too much."

"Not in this bar. Dad doesn't allow it."

The deputy raised his eyebrows. "Um-hm."

"The people who come in here aren't like that."

The deputy looked over his shoulder at the large, hairy, fat man in the tight T-shirt. "Um-hm." The chair creaked as the deputy shifted positions. "Did any of these men threaten you?"

"One of them was going to cut the phone line. I told them I was going to call the police. That's when the one with the ponytail started for the phone. It's behind the bar."

"What made you think he was going to cut the phone? Did he say so? Did someone tell him to cut the phone?"

"Yes. Well, not exactly. The leader, the one with the white hair, made the phone signal." The deputy raised his eyebrows. Linda extended her thumb and little finger and put it to her face. "Like this." The deputy looked at her for a moment, then wrote some more in his notebook. Linda waited. He was taking a long time again. He closed his notebook and tucked it in his shirt pocket.

"Ms. Reyes, I can understand that you were upset about the fight, especially since someone was hurt, although I don't think he's hurt seriously. I think he's just going to be very sore for a while." He paused, looking at Linda, closing his eyes for a moment. "The point is that no threats were made."

"What about—"

The deputy held up his hand. "Let me finish. No threats were made that can be substantiated. These individuals were bikers, violent types, tough and scary, but not nearly as tough and scary as a blast from a ten-gauge shotgun. Someone could've been killed. It's fortunate that no one was injured."

He stood up. "You finished up there, Martinez?"

The other deputy nodded and shoved his notebook in his rear pocket. "Thank you for the information, ladies. I appreciate your taking the time." He flashed a wide grin, going from cop to Latin lover. The dark-haired woman dropped her lashes, and the taller brunette returned the smile. The deputy reached into his shirt pocket and gave each of them a card. "If you have any questions, don't hesitate to call." He hitched up his equipment harness and swaggered toward the door. Frank could hear Raphael Mendez's trumpet playing "Blood of the Brave Bull." The brave bullshit, he thought.

The deputy in charge looked down at Linda, who sat rigid with anger and exasperation. "Next time, if you feel threatened, make the phone call. That's what we're here for." He placed his card on the table.

Linda met his look. "This is Red Mountain. How long did it take you to get here?" The deputy's jaw tightened. "It took you twenty-four minutes," she said. "Where were you when you got the call?" She waited. No response. "Probably somewhere on the road, or it might have taken more than a half an hour."

"We do the best we can, Ms. Reyes. There's a lot of San Bernardino County." His tone was flat. Frank knew, as far as the deputy was concerned, she'd become part of the problem.

"I'm sure you do. But I didn't have the time. These men are dangerous, whether you choose to believe it or not."

"That may be, but until they do something—"

"Until?"

"We'll be on the lookout for them, ma'am." He held up his hand again. "Leave the shotgun under the bar. Better yet, leave it at home."

Linda turned as the deputies were leaving and caught sight of Frank standing just inside the door. She jumped to her feet. "Frank, oh my God, am I glad to see you. They were here, the brothers. They're really horrible. They injured a man for nothing. They know where I work, and they're coming back." The words came spilling out of her in a rush. Frank went to her, giving her a hug made awkward by the chair that stood between them. He reached down and jerked it impatiently aside, flinging it on the floor. They stood there in the silence of the afternoon. Then Linda looked up, a small smile on her face.

"That's the first time I've seen you lose your cool."

Frank looked puzzled. "How'd I lose my cool?"

Linda smiled. "The chair."

Frank looked at the chair lying on its side on the floor. "Oh," he said, and rocked her gently back and forth.

•

Jack Collins sat at the table in the back room. The last of the sunlight cast a glow on his round face, which had hardened into a grim mask. Bill Jerome stood in motionless concentration, for all the world like a stork about to spear a small fish, his sharp features made more angular by the slanting light. Ben Shaw puffed carefully on his pipe, now and then lifting eyes bright with fury.

Linda had finished recounting the afternoon's events. They had listened almost without interruption. When she told about cocking the shotgun and then blasting a hole in the wall, Collins's mouth had turned down in a sardonic smile. Shaw had made only one remark: "You should have taken out the one with the pink eyes." He'd said it so casually that Linda realized that despite the fact that she had known this man for years, there was a great deal she didn't know about him.

Frank stood against the wall, watching in silence.

"So he knows where we live, does he?" Collins looked thoughtful.

Bill Jerome cut in. "Tonight, I'll be on the roof of Linda's place with the two seventy. If they come back, it would be too easy to set fire to the club. They'll be thinking about someone on guard inside, not someone with a night scope." Jerome looked at his companions and then at Linda. "I'll have a shotgun, as well."

Jack smiled at Jerome. "Let's think it through, Bill. We don't want to shoot the hell out of one another."

"I like Bill's way. Wait for 'em and end it." Shaw gave them a nasty smile. "I'm in fear for my life already. Those dead boys were terrorizing us old farts. Didn't have a choice." His face was momentarily lost in a cloud of pipe smoke.

Collins shook his head. "I don't want Linda in harm's way. You know what happens to plans when things start to move."

"Wait a minute, gentlemen." Linda eyed her father. "I'm right here in this room, thank you. I'd like a voice in what's going to happen next, since it seems to concern me. So just hang on a minute."

Frank grinned. He'd been wondering how long Linda was going to let someone else decide her fate.

Jerome looked crestfallen. "You know, I was just . . . I figured that you . . ."

"I know, Bill, and I appreciate it. I'm not so sure I want to know more of what you're planning, Ben." Shaw tamped his pipe. "But I do think you're right about one thing. They're evil people, and someone, not you or Bill or Dad, needs to stop them before they hurt someone." Jerome looked uncomfortable. Frank could see that Collins regarded his daughter with a degree of surprise.

Linda looked at each of them in turn. "Those men are the police's business." Collins opened his mouth to speak. She held up both hands. "Wait a minute, Dad. The deputy was right. They'll be on the lookout for them now, even if they acted like it was nothing but a barroom brawl. I don't want to have to worry about you, Bill, and Ben winding up in jail or something worse on my account. They won't be back. They know the police have been alerted."

Shaw said softly, "Know where you work. Know where you live."

The light had turned from gold to a deep orange tinged with red. It filled the silence of the room with the colors of day's end and turned their faces into masks of dark bronze.

"Shit." Collins stood up, looking down at his daughter. "Honey, I don't want you here. I want you to go back to Los Angeles and stay with one of your friends."

"I can't do that, Dad."

Frank heard himself saying, "She can stay at my place." They all turned toward him, his presence in the room remembered now. "She'll be safe there. No address, hard to find, but mostly no address. I have a PO box. So she'll be safe."

Collins wheeled on Frank. "Right, Mr. Ranger. Where were you when those bastards were beating the shit out of people and threatening Linda?"

Frank met Collins's glare, his face thoughtful. "Up in Jawbone Canyon, changing a flat tire." He paused, his brow furrowed in concentration. "Somebody left a bunch of those funny little spike things lying around. One of 'em punctured my tire. I think they're called caltrops." He held Collins's gaze. "So where were you when the Millers showed up, out putting up signs to scare kids or scattering spikes to cut them up?" He turned his attention to Bill Jerome, who managed to look guilty and angry at the same time. Then he shifted his gaze to Ben Shaw, who was leaning back from the table, puffing on the ever-present pipe. Shaw looked up at Frank and grinned. "They work pretty good, don't they?"

# 19

•

"You were kind of hard on Dad." Linda's face was in darkness. Frank wished he could see her, read her expression. He'd have to settle for the words.

"Yeah, I guess I was." Noncommittal was best. He wondered how much she knew of her dad's activities.

"Seeing the canyon torn up makes them angry."

"They're not alone."

The Sierras rose up on their left, dark and jagged silhouettes against a moonless sky.

"You passed the turnoff, didn't you?" Linda glanced back through the truck's rear window, not quite sure of where she was.

"Yup, just in case someone decided to follow along. We'll turn up the Cottonwood Creek road. There's a long straight stretch going up the hill. If someone's following, it'd be hard to miss, even if they killed their lights."

"Oh." Her reply was barely audible. She seemed subdued by the thought that they could be followed, that the danger was still present, that the Millers were somewhere out there in the vastness of the Mojave. Her brows knit, invisible to Frank. "You could've cut him—them—some slack. At least they were doing something about it."

He drove on in silence, thinking about what she said. "I did."

"Did?"

"I cut them some slack. I wasn't talking to them as law enforcement." He downshifted as the grade grew steeper. "I just wish to hell they had been at the club instead of fooling around, trying to roll back time."

"You don't know that. You don't know where they were. Neither do I."

He paused, searching for the right way to put it. "I wish it hadn't happened." He let out a sigh. "I wish to hell I'd been there." His voice was barely audible above the engine noise. "I was scared thinking about it—you know, feeling helpless." Frank rested his hand on hers. "Something bad could've happened, and I wasn't there. And your dad and his pals weren't there, and you were alone, so I was angry for not being there and angry at them for the same reason."

He felt her shudder. The back of her hand felt soft and dry to his touch, making him conscious of his nicked and roughened palms. "It's very unlikely Miller and his buddies will be stirring around tonight. I think you gave them enough to think about for one day." He gave a dry chuckle, shaking his head at the thought of the blast from a ten-gauge shotgun. "Probably still trying to get their hearing back."

"I can believe that." She nodded in response. "I didn't know it was going to be so loud. It seemed like everything was frozen. I mean right afterward. It was like there wasn't any more sound. At first, I had trouble making out what people were saying. She hunched into herself. "I hope it was worse for them. I hope it scared the hell out of them."

He pulled the truck onto the shoulder of road. They were downslope of a small rise. They walked to the crest of the hill, overlooking the road where it climbed up from Highway 395. She held on to the crook of his arm, standing close, so close that he could feel the warmth of her body through his shirt. He concentrated on scanning the road. The narrow pavement stretched away into the darkness. The lights from the distant cars on 395 gave the highway an oddly corporeal quality, as if it were an artery of light pulsing across the desert floor. Little capillaries branched away from it here and there and petered out in the distance.

"Looks like we're all by ourselves." He turned toward the dark shape of the truck.

Linda turned with him, keeping hold of his arm. "You're full of surprises, Mr. Flynn." Her voice sounded thoughtful. "How'd you know I'd accept your offer to come stay in your caboose?"

"I didn't." He trudged along, his boots crunching on loose dirt. "But it seemed like a good idea." He knew he'd better make that clearer. "You'd be safe." That was the point to make, the main reason. "Well, safer anyway. There's no guarantees as long as they're around." The dark profile of his face seemed expressionless, his long, slender nose poking out from under his hat into the faint light. He turned toward Linda. "We'll have to be very, very careful."

She nodded in agreement. "Yes, you're right. We will."

"So, let me show you the secret way to my place. Come on. You'll like this, another walk in the dark," Frank said, guiding her back to the truck.

"See that berm." They had stopped in the middle of the road, where it crossed the old right-of-way. "It's the old roadbed for the high line." Linda peered into the night shadows, which were only distinguishable by their degrees of darkness. "About a quarter mile back that way"—he pointed in a southerly direction—"is La Casa del Flynn. When we cross Cottonwood Creek—the same creek that runs by my place—there'll be a turnoff to a campground."

The truck thumped across the bridge, and they turned to the right and dropped down onto the sandy bottomland, where huge old cottonwoods hugged the creek. The Bureau of Land Management had developed campsites under the trees that sheltered the creek from the heat of the sun. The sign at the campground entrance informed campers that there was a host on duty.

"We'll leave the truck here." Frank pulled the truck into an empty campsite, where it disappeared under the cottonwoods in the shade of night. "This is a BLM campground. I know the host here, a retired teacher. He'll recognize the truck and keep an eye on it. Now all we have to do is follow the creek for about a half mile back to the caboose."

Linda reached for the soft flight bag that contained her overnight stuff. Pulling the strap over her shoulder, she followed Frank, who had already started moving along the stream. They followed a path that had been made by generations of trout fishermen seeking the perfect fishing hole. The water was deep and cool, a home to flashing brookies and voracious browns. Where there was a stream, you could be sure fishermen had beaten their way through the brush to find the undiscovered spot.

"Well, at least this time I don't have to leap around on the face of a cliff. Good thing, too, 'cause I can't see a thing." She placed her feet down tentatively, taking care not to go sprawling in the dark.

"Nope, no cliffs, but watch out for the snakes." He paused. "Especially the Owens Valley adder."

"Not a problem. I'm familiar with all kinds of snakes. I'll keep an eye out for the caboose viper, as well." Her eyes probed the darkness. "Are you serious about the snakes?"

"Yup. But I'll probably scare 'em up first. By the time you get to them, they'll be really pissed off."

"Oh great. Dating you is such an adventure."

"Is this a date? Guess I'll have to comb my hair."

Frank had taken a side trail that led up the cutbank to a rocky and uneven surface. It was easier to see now that they were out of the shadowed darkness of the streambed, but still dark enough to require slow going. The moon lay hidden behind the upthrust escarpment of the Sierras. They made their way by the light of the stars, which were bright in the rain-washed sky.

Frank stopped and pointed up at the night sky. "See that? That's the Big Dipper."

"I know that one."

"Use those last two stars that make up the cup as a pointer, and you'll find the North Star." He moved his arm in a small arc. "See?"

"Is that it?" Linda pointed up at the canopy of stars.

Frank tried to gauge the direction of her outstretched arm. "I think you've got it. Now think of the North Star as the last star in the handle of another dipper, smaller and not as bright. Can you see it?"

"Yes, only the handle's the other way around. So that's the Little Dipper. I've never seen it before, or at least never recognized it."

"You've probably never seen it, at least not all of it. In cities, the light pollution is so bad that only the brightest stars and constellations are visible." He reached for her hand, giving it a gentle squeeze. "Now that you know how to find the North Star, you'll never be lost in the desert."

She turned toward him, standing so close that he caught a faint whiff of shampoo mixed in with the tangy smells of creosote and sage made fresh by the recent rain. The starlight revealed only the reflection of her eyes and the top of her head. He touched her face, lifting it up, pulling her gently closer, and kissed her, her face cupped in his hands.

He could feel the warm flesh of her cheeks pull into a smile. "Guess I'll just have to stay in the desert so I don't get lost again."

"That's a good idea. Being lost is no fun."

•

They sat on camp chairs on the end of the caboose, feet propped up against the railing. Frank hadn't lit any lamps. Light would make them visible for miles. At night, the desert seemed more populated than by day. The lights from scattered dwellings winked in the darkness, mirroring the stars in the sky above. Linda sipped Jameson over ice from a jelly glass. Frank drank his neat, holding back, careful not to get boozy. He didn't want to fumble his feelings, cloud up his judgment with drink, be like his foolish da.

"Tomorrow, I've got to go up to Bishop." He let the remark drop in a matter-of-fact way. Linda remained silent. She was good at listening, too, but he could sense the question in her mind. "To feed a guy's cat."

"I have a cat, Hobbes."

"Hobbes?"

"As in Calvin and Hobbes. Of course, Hobbes was named for—"

"A gloomy philosopher. I miss that comic strip. Is your cat a gloomy philosopher?"

"Hardly. He's a clever clown. But why are you feeding someone else's cat when you could be feeding Hobbes?"

"It's a long story, but I think I've got a very good chance of catching the poacher with the goods." He smiled to himself. "A very good chance."

He told Linda all about Eddie Laguna and Prowler. "He's a funny guy." He frowned to himself. "I'm not sure you'd like him much, but in his own way, he's okay. I mean, here he is about to be arrested, and what does he worry about? His cat. I liked that."

"Me, too. That's what I'd worry about, Hobbes." She sipped her whiskey and gave an involuntary shudder. "You going to put him in jail?"

"That's not up to me, but I'm going to put in a good word for him. He's not the one I want."

"How come? Without him, the sheep would still be alive."

Frank shook his head, the gesture all but lost in the darkness. "Maybe, for now, but sooner or later, the poacher would've come back. The man who hired Eddie would've hired someone else." He shifted around to look at her. "I think the poacher, the man with the money, killed the first guide, Donnie Miller. Besides, the money's too much for a guy like Eddie to turn down." He nodded to himself. "He's remarkable in his way. Makes it on his own, a damn good taxidermist, self-taught, like everything else he does. Guys like Eddie usually come to a sad end, but he's got . . ." He paused, searching for the right word.

"Pluck?"

"Okay, it sounds corny, but yeah. Maybe grit is a better word."

"Pluck's for girls, huh?"

"Girls with ten-gauge shotguns." He laughed. "Besides, he's going to lead me to the man with the rifle."

When he came to the part about Eddie setting up another meeting with the poacher, the anonymous Smith, he felt excitement welling up at the prospect of catching the guy who'd killed the sheep, the guy who he was sure had left Donnie Miller to die of exposure.

Somehow, Miller's death didn't seem as bad to him as killing the sheep. He'd felt compassion for the unnamed dead man, but now that he knew his identity, he didn't care as much. Maybe it would be better if they were all dead.

These were not good thoughts. He thought about dying of thirst.

Not a good way to go. He didn't want to give in to evil thoughts, become ugly in his heart. "Evil thoughts lead to evil deeds," his mother had reminded him many times.

"So tomorrow, I'll take you into Ridgecrest, check in with my boss, then go on up to Bishop to feed Prowler." I'll be back for you at five. How's that work out?"

"I'd like to get my car. I'm stuck without it. I can get a ride into Red Mountain, pick up my car, and then meet you back here."

It caught him off guard. A sense of foreboding began to gather in the pit of his stomach. "To tell you the truth, I wish you wouldn't. Right now, everything feels pretty safe." He could feel himself becoming too earnest, but she had to understand the danger she was in. "But if you pick up your car, it would be easy to follow you, find out where you're staying." He spoke into the night, not looking in her direction. Linda didn't say anything. "They think you might know more than what the paper said. That's why they wanted to talk to you. They think this Smith left their brother in the desert to die. I think they're right, and I think it's the same man I'm trying to catch for poaching. And to tell you the truth, I think Mr. Smith will be very lucky if I find him before they do."

"That's it, isn't it, the North Star?" Linda extended her arm upward at about a forty-five-degree angle, pointing north.

"Yes, that's it. The Owens Valley runs north-south. You're pointing up the valley at the North Star."

"Okay." She sighed. "It makes sense to wait awhile, but I hate to feel . . ." Her voice trailed off.

"Dependent. But you're not. We're just sharing resources."

"Oh, a wordsmith. Maybe you should think about changing careers, get into PR. You're wasting your talent." She paused, letting the silence take up the space between them. "Frank, it's got nothing to do with you. I'm just used to taking care of myself. You don't have to convince me that these are evil people." She turned and spoke to him directly. "But you're right. It would be too easy to follow someone out here—especially in the daytime. So pick me up. I'll call and get Dad to take care of Hobbes. He'll probably take him to the bar. Hobbes loves that. He is very social."

She thrust her arm at him, poking him in the side. "Only don't be late picking me up. I hate waiting around, especially in the afternoon with the heat bouncing off the pavement."

Frank sighed audibly. "Good. I can't tell you how much better that makes me feel." He stopped himself. Time for a change of subject. "You know, if we catch this guy—and it looks like we might—you've got an exclusive with the cop and/or cops on the job. Should make a good story."

"That's for sure. Probably good enough to be picked up by the *Los Angeles Times*—that is, if we catch him."

"What do you mean, 'we,' white woman?" He was smiling broadly.

She laughed, letting the tension out. "Hey, you better quit flashing your teeth in the dark. They catch the light. Somebody might see us. Besides, all that grinning makes you look like a *bandito*." She really could see his teeth, the smile shining out of the dark. "You know, you're a lucky man, Mr. Flynn. Every great detective needs a Watson. I'm your Watson, Franklock. Your brave deeds and steel-trap mind will go down in history."

"Sounds right to me. Guess I *am* a lucky man."

"Luckier than you know, Mr. Flynn." She leaned over and kissed him ever so softly on the mouth.

He felt his face flush and heard a humming in his ears. For a moment, he wondered if he was going to be able to make it inside.

# 20

•

Linda awoke in the soft gray of false dawn to Frank's humming. She didn't hum in the mornings. She showered, drank coffee, spoke to no one until she hit work. She pulled the covers over her shoulders against the morning chill. He was stirring about near the stove. Linda could smell coffee. She made an exception. "Mmm. Smells good. How about some of that coffee?"

"Ask the Flynn and the Flynn delivers." He poured coffee into a thick brown china mug and took it over to her. As she sat up to take the coffee, the blankets fell away, reminding them both of her nakedness. She reached for the covers with one hand and the coffee with the other.

"Hungry?"

She was. In fact, she was ravenous. "Yeah, you bet."

"How about a breakfast burrito? Beans, eggs, and cheese, and some of Flynn's special store-bought salsa, or, if you've got the stomach for it, some Swab's High Sierra Chileno Indian-style peppers?"

"You're kidding, Swab's Indian-style peppers?"

"Nope, I'm not kidding, and yup, you can have some. They're really good, too. Made right here in the valley. They're not really that hot, just a bit of a bite."

"Why not. Let's have 'em."

Frank turned back to the stove. Linda watched him as he went about warming the tortillas and beans, scrambling up the eggs and then deftly folding eggs, cheese, beans, peppers, and salsa into perfect burritos, ends tucked nicely in, no drips or leaks. Definitely a morning person. He was still humming.

"Hey, you're good. You could give old Ralph a run for his money."

Frank smiled. "Nope. I'm an amateur; Ralph's a pro. Twenty minutes a burrito doesn't cut it. It's still fun for me. Besides, I could never match that black scowl." He handed her a burrito on a warm plate. Wisps of vapor rose from the food into the cool air of the morning, filling the caboose with a spicy fragrance.

"It gets cold up here next to the mountain, doesn't it?" Linda took a bite of burrito. The flavor of the Chileno peppers was delicious, like no other pepper she'd ever eaten, warm and not too hot. It tasted of the desert air after a rain, pungent and just short of sweet. "Mmmm. These peppers are really great."

"Grown on the slopes of the Sierras, right here in the Owens Valley," he intoned in a radio voice. "They *are* good, aren't they? And yeah, it gets cold here. We're at almost at forty-five hundred feet."

"Mm, mm, mmmm," she replied, her mouth full of burrito. Her morning mood was softening. Breakfast in bed. A breakfast of real food.

Frank sat on one of the cloth camping chairs he'd brought inside. They ate in silence as the valley filled with light. Though they had shared the same bed and passion in the dark, Linda felt awkwardly modest about her nakedness, especially in the intimate closeness of the caboose. Reyes had been the last man with whom she had shared a bed. That was just over a year now. Reyes. She wondered how much baggage Frank was lugging around.

Frank interrupted the domestic stillness. "Listen, I have to get an early start." The seriousness in his voice pulled Linda abruptly away from her thoughts and into the affairs of the day.

"Weekends, we rotate duties when we can. I've got a 'walk and talk' over at the charcoal kilns near the dry lake this afternoon." He leaned forward, an earnest expression on his face. She recognized the look from the classroom lecture, serious and intent. "Did you know that there used to be steamships on Owens Lake? Before Los Angeles took the water. And there's a story about a steamer sinking with a cargo of silver bars."

Her thoughts drifted back to the previous night. Their love-making had been both tender and passionate. She had let herself be naked with this man, exposed, vulnerable, and yet perfectly safe. It was something new to her.

He saw that she was smiling at him and changed course. "Anyhow, Meecham will probably have a few things for my plate besides burritos, and I have to get up to Bishop and look in on Eddie Laguna's cat. I'll pick up a BLM vehicle on the way back, so don't look for my truck."

She caught Frank's hand. "I want to know all about the steamships and the lost silver. You're a treasure of information. That's what you are, my treasure chest of information." She pulled him toward her and kissed him on the mouth. He set his plate on the bed, and she could tell that affection had shifted into desire.

She put her hands against his shoulders. "Me, too." She nodded, smiling up at him. "But I have to be at work. The story's coming out today, with the pictures of the poacher and Eddie. Be sure and buy a paper. You and the BLM show up as heroes, not to mention this intrepid reporter." She was still thinking about having to get out of bed naked. Being with Frank was still so new, and there was stuff to get done.

"Thanks. The boss loves good publicity, and the truth is, we need it." He noticed her hand clutching at the bedclothes. "I hung your clothes up in the bathroom; here's my ratty bathrobe." He reached behind the door and laid it on the end of the bed. "I'm going to put a few scraps out for my other foxy girlfriend. Back in a minute."

She watched him go out the door, her heart swelling inside her. It was good that he liked cats. She shifted gears. So let's get on with it, she thought. She wolfed down the rest of her burrito, put her plate on the table, and dashed into the bathroom, taking the robe with her.

•

The desert stretched before them in the morning light, but Linda's mind was already at the paper. She had several projects going besides bighorn sheep. There was the story on the railroad museum at

Laws. Frank had given her the idea. She had found a man in Bishop who used to be an engineer on the old narrow-gauge railroad. He was full of stories; some of them might even be true. Then there was the ghost town of Beverage, so hard to get to that it hadn't been looted, or so one old boy had told her. She'd have to ask Frank if he'd ever been there.

But the project on the front burner was the research she was doing on the new open-pit gold mining operation near Ballarat. The Indians were very unhappy, and they had reason to be, but they were only a scattering of brown voices in the wilderness. They might just as well be coyotes howling in the night, she thought. Maybe she could focus some attention on it. Too late to do anything about this one, but perhaps public awareness might serve in the future. She tried not to get discouraged. Policy and politics seemed such a quagmire. Her job was to write about it—"just the facts, ma'am." She envied Frank, actually doing something out there in the desert, protecting the land. But then again, she knew he chafed under the BLM's policies, which shifted with changes in politics.

"It's not easy, is it?"

He lifted his eyebrows and shot her an inquiring look.

"Sorry, just voicing my own thoughts. I was thinking it must be hard for you. Taking care of the Winnebago crowd, I mean."

"Sometimes, but not as much as you might think. They come out here because they're drawn to the desert. Maybe it's just about getting away from the city, the sense of freedom. Do what you want in the wide-open spaces. Howl around on ATVs, have barbecues and drink too much beer. Some of them even come for the beauty of it. They might not put it that way, but that's what it gets down to. Whatever it is, they come. So it's our job to make it safe *for* them and the land safe *from* them. Dropping by the campgrounds, making sure everything is okay, gives me and the BLM a chance to do a little educating. I really like doing the campfire talks and leading people on nature walks." He glanced over at her, grinning. "Rangers don't have to give talks. I'm a volunteer. Besides, I used to give a lot of them before I shifted to the enforcement side of things. Sometimes people just open up. When you hear things like 'Isn't that beautiful?'

or 'Hey, that's neat,' and see people talking about the things they've just heard, you know you've made a difference, helped take care of the land, because these people go home with a different outlook."

She looked skeptical. "The new and improved citizen, huh?"

"Hardly that. God knows, some of them would make a maggot puke." A frown passed over his face like a cloud shadow on the landscape. "But that's the exception, a nasty exception. Most people are okay. It's important to remember that. And attitudes change over time. Hell, even the pillage and grab crowd pays lip service to the environment. In my dad's time, people thought of the desert as a big wasteland, except for a few characters like Joseph Wood Krutch and Mary Austin. They were the start."

"How about Edward Abbey?"

"Your dad and his pals, huh? The Grumpy Wrench Gang."

"Are you pissed off about that?"

"Getting a flat, naw. At least not anymore. But at the time, I had a few choice things to say." He rested his hand on hers. "My priorities kinda shifted when I saw the cop cars at your dad's place."

She considered this man, a quiet, thoughtful optimist. An optimist, an endangered species. It gave her heart a lift. "So what about Abbey?"

"How can you not love his work, especially *Desert Solitaire*? I remember when I first read it. I thought, I know this guy. He's me. I'm him, even the anger, especially the anger. It was like I had someone to share it with. It wasn't just me, so I could let some of it out. I was just a kid, maybe twenty, twenty-one. But at the time, all I could see was the place where I lived being trashed by a bunch of rich white people from the city. I had some ugly fantasies."

"So you became a cop?"

"Just about perfect, isn't it? I'm being paid to protect my home. How can you beat that?" He grinned into the morning sun.

●

Linda stood by the truck, resting her hands on the window. She raised her voice over the sound of the traffic. "Five o'clock, right here, okay? Remember that I hate to be kept waiting when it's hot.

You never met *moi* when I'm pissed off. So be on time. I don't want to ruin a good thing."

"Hey, you don't have to tell me twice. You left that ten-gauge job at home, right?" He grinned. "Not to worry. I'll be here, or if I'm late, I'll just keep on rolling as a matter of survival."

She waved as he pulled out, then watched as the truck was swallowed up in the traffic, his arm waving back out the window. She felt a pang at his departure. How could she start missing him already? It was ridiculous, but then again, it wasn't. Obviously, she was in love. She laughed to herself. In love, in love with love. No, in love with this strange, enigmatic man, who laughed at things, especially himself. She felt her heart quicken. Get a grip on yourself, Linda, she thought.

•

"The Kern County Sheriff's Department has something going on near some mine in Randsburg. The radio chat sounds like arson, maybe ecovandals." Marston pulled at his splashy purple tie; its swirling white blossoms intertwining with the stylized Art Deco vines complemented his brown-and-white basket-weave shoes. It must have cost him fifty dollars, she figured.

"Reyes?"

"Um-hm. I'm listening." She hoped it wasn't ecovandals. It would be bad timing, and she hoped especially that it wasn't the Grumpy Wrench Gang. Dad and Co. could get out of hand. The hijinks with the caltrops was serious business, and the last thing she wanted was a confrontation between her dad and the BLM, especially Frank. That could really gum things up.

George Marston, the retro dweeb, squinted at her through non-existent cigarette smoke. "Say there, Reyes, why don't you call your buddy over in Tehachapi and see what's up." With him, it was always "Reyes." He'd seen Bogart in *Deadline—U.S.A.* and taken it to heart. He thought of himself as a tough, street-smart city editor. She thought of him as a bright Clark Kent, except for the pocket protector. How could he try and sound like a cynical, world-weary newspaper man and wear a pocket protector?

"What buddy?"

"The one who's always calling here. 'Is Ms. Reyes there?'" he mimicked in a deep baritone. "Voice all aquiver when he says 'Ms. Reyes.' The tall, blond, muscular, oh-my-what-cute-buns Kern County deputy sheriff, Officer Eugene Bohannon. That buddy."

Damn, Linda thought, sorry she'd asked. The dweeb kept his finger on the pulse of gossip, which was just local news, wasn't it? God, how often did the goofy kid call up? She hated to call him, but a source was a source.

She went to her desk and dialed the Tehachapi station of the Kern County Sheriff's Department. She counted the rings. They always picked up by the third ring. She liked them for that. Kern County's finest knew something about serving the public.

"Yes, this is Linda Reyes for Officer Eugene Bohannon." She doodled a daisy flower on a scrap of paper. "I'm returning his call." God, she hated explaining things twelve times. The "returning his call" gambit cut through traffic.

"Hi, Gene. It's Linda Reyes here."

"Linda! How're you doin'?"

"Fine. How about you?"

Now he was telling her. What was the matter with the man? Didn't he know a rhetorical question when he heard one?

"Say, listen, Eugene. What's up over in Randsburg? Heard something about a fire. Is it worth the drive? . . . Okay, I can wait." She doodled another daisy, then started counting the petals. Loves me? Loves me not? Loves me? Loves me not? Loves me not, it came out. Too bad about that. She drew another petal. It's my daisy, she thought.

"Yeah, I'm still here. Um-hm. Yeah. So nothing on who set the fire. The Ophir mine—isn't that part of the Rand District? I'm less than an hour away. I'll go have a look. Say, can you let them know I'll be on the scene? Thanks, Gene. I really appreciate it."

Uh-oh, here it comes, she thought. Couldn't he figure out she was at least ten years older than he was? "Can't this weekend, Eugene. Working my other job. It's a long story. Listen, I gotta get goin'." She nodded. "Sure, anytime. I'll buy you a beer. Thanks again, Eugene."

She felt like a hypocrite. He had a schoolboy crush, and she was using it. Then she remembered she'd been banished from her dad's club. A feeling of dread came creeping back.

Marston was sitting on the edge of his desk, adjusting the margins on his old Smith-Corona. He claimed he wrote better stuff on the typewriter than on the computer, but she'd never seen him type anything on it but notes and memos. He avoided office E-mail. Too impersonal, he said. He'd be dead meat on a big paper, but he was okay. She liked the typed memos. The stuff of *Deadline—U.S.A.*

"Marston," she said, making her voice crack with a cynical lack of interest.

"Yeah, what's up?" He twisted in his chair. The cameras were rolling.

"Need the news wagon. Car's at home."

He frowned. "I was planning to go over to the base."

She knew he liked the official car with the paper's seal on the side when he rolled through the gates at the China Lake Naval Ordnance Test Station. The official car provided presence. The news wagon gave him the right gravitas.

"So borrow Lucky's MG."

Lucky Rogers had seen *Deadline—U.S.A.*, too. Norman Rogers thought of himself as the plucky kid—the kid who'd make the big scoop. He and George Marston inhabited the same movie. She briefly wondered if Marston's mother had the Ethel Barrymore role, plucky grande dame. After all, she did own part of the paper.

Lucky Rogers had a fire engine red 1953 MG TD, restored to its original quirky beauty. It was classy in a way that new cars never seemed to be. What a place, she thought. Small-town newspapers were the last refuge for the weird, and Lord knows, she fit right in.

Marston twisted farther around in his chair, facing Norman Rogers as he kicked one foot up on a partially opened drawer. "Hey, that'd work out, and you could come along, keep your eyes open. Whatta ya say, kid?"

"Sure thing, Mr. Marston. Glad to help out."

How could he stand being called "kid"? Linda wanted to add, Gee whiz, that's swell. Well, it was swell for her. She had a car to use, Marston would have presence, and Norman was on a mission with the boss to the China Lake test center.

•

Actually, Linda hated driving the damn news wagon. It was an eight-year-old Dodge minivan with over 150,000 miles on it, and the suspension was shot. With growing regret, she jounced over the washboard road leading up to the mine. She kept telling herself she'd come this far, might just as well go on. She remembered how cranky Frank had been bouncing around in the truck on the drive up to Surprise Canyon and how he'd frowned at her laughter when the glove compartment had flown open. Well, there was something else they had in common. She hated being tossed around in the cab of a vehicle like laundry in a washing machine.

Finally, up ahead she saw a Kern County police car and an elderly fire truck, probably from the Rand Volunteer Fire Department. The police car had been pulled around across the road so as to control access to the site. The fire truck was farther up, near the blackened shell of a single-wide mobile home. The scorched body of the trailer rested on cement blocks, a good two feet off the ground at the high end. The aluminum poles of what had been the awning stuck out from the top of the trailer in a pointless rectangle, bits of burned cloth draping the metal in dismal shreds. She pulled up, careful not to block access. Never start by being a problem— rule number two. Get there first was rule number one, but rule number two kept the doors from closing.

The smell of burned plastic and the acrid odor of chemicals and ashes filled her nostrils. The trailer had been completely gutted by the fire. Here and there, the remains of pink and gray paint showed through the accumulated grime at what must have been the bedroom end. Someone—probably the firefighters—had pried the burned door open. It hung there in macabre invitation to the smoke-blackened interior. She couldn't see much. A couple of grim-faced deputies stood talking with two unhappy-looking volunteer firemen. Their conversation lapsed into silence at her approach. No barbershop quartet here. She wondered what was up.

"Hi, I'm Linda Reyes, with the *InyoKern Courier*. Did Officer Bohannon contact you yet?"

The older deputy, gray-haired and paunchy, gave a small smile. "He did, and you live right up to his description." He offered his hand. "Cotton DeLacey."

She smiled back as she took DeLacey's hand. "Well, I try not to disappoint."

"This is Pete Fisher." DeLacey gestured to a tall, husky red-headed deputy. Like most denizens of the desert, he wore dark sunglasses. Bits of skin flecked off his nose. It was tough being fair-skinned in the Mojave. He gestured toward the firefighters. "Hillyard and Sandstrom." The two firemen made soft howdy sounds. They shuffled their feet, looking uncomfortable. They seemed to have come in the same box.

She waited. She was used to stoic cops but not to silent ones. As a reporter, she had learned not to fill in the voids of conversation, so she said nothing. Apparently, it was the end of the small talk. The mood was definitely somber. She took out pad and pencil. "So what's up?" she finally asked.

"It was more than a just a fire, Ms. Reyes. There were two people in that trailer. Someone, or several someones, blocked them in. Then they dragged all the wood they could find and stuffed it under the trailer. By the looks of it, most of it by the door. Then they set it on fire and roasted those people alive." DeLacey spit, as if to get the taste out of his mouth.

"Do you know who they are—were?"

"Not for sure. But Hillyard and Sandstrom here tell me there was a young couple living here as caretakers. All this property and the mining rights belong to the Ophir Mining Corporation. My guess is that's who they were, the caretakers, but there's no way of knowing for sure until—"

"Until you've got a positive identification. I know." She was writing quickly even as she spoke. "When did this happen?"

"Rand Fire Department got an anonymous call this morning.

The man didn't want to leave his name. Said he didn't want to wind up having to wait around. Besides, all he claimed to have seen was smoke coming from what was left of the trailer about eight this morning. That right, Bob?" The taller of the two firemen, the one who had been identified as Hillyard, nodded in affirmation. "So that's about it. You've got what we've got."

Both firemen looked uncomfortable.

"Why didn't they try to force their way out, break a window, do something?" Linda directed her question to include the firemen.

" 'Cause, ma'am, they couldn't." She saw two tiny images of herself in the curve of the redheaded deputy's glasses. "See, they'd been tied up." The muscles on his jaw worked in and out.

It struck her with the force of a blow. It was them. Why hadn't she known sooner? Frank had told her about the couple he'd talked to after the lecture, Mitch and Shawna. They'd been in the class, holding hands and talking about Jesus, and now they were gone. My God, it could've been me, she thought, or anyone who got in their way. Then she thought about Frank on his way to take care of Eddie's cat. He was in the valley, so she should be able to reach his cell phone. She punched the autodial and waited. He wasn't picking up, or he'd left it at home again. Damn. The phone buzzed against her ear.

## 21

Frank pulled in under the cottonwoods near Eddie's trailer. There was no sign of Eddie's rust-bucket Ford pickup, a '48 flathead. Too bad, Frank thought, truck like that needed restoring. Not likely Eddie would fix it up. He'd just drive it until it quit and leave it to decay into a sad heap. He supposed that Eddie had forgotten his request about leaving the keys and had driven over to the Sheriff's office in Independence. Now Eddie'd have impound fees, which he couldn't pay, and now he, Frank, would have to figure on using his own truck when he assumed the role of Redhawk, Native American guide. He was looking forward to meeting up with Smith. Provide a surprise for the smug SOB. With any luck, Smith was going to have his hand in the cookie jar up to his armpit. Frank couldn't help grinning to himself, going undercover just like the cops in L.A. Now that Eddie had disappeared with his truck, his own truck would need to go undercover, too. He'd have to go through the cab and get rid of anything that could tie him to law enforcement. From what Eddie had said, Smith was a smart cookie.

He opened the glove compartment and found maps, a pencil with a broken tip, pen, a couple of screwdrivers, pliers, a crescent wrench, matchbooks. He checked the backs of the matchbooks—a couple from bars, one blank book he'd got in a market. All okay. One Colt .45 model 1911A with military parkerized finish. Not okay. It wasn't BLM-issue, but it wasn't the sort of weapon a guy like Eddie would have in his glove compartment. The BLM had turned to the 9-mm, like most of law enforcement, but the .45 ACP was his weapon of choice if he needed one, which so far he hadn't. Law enforcement with the BLM mostly meant dealing with miscreant citizens, rarely crooks. On the other hand, there was no backup. You were out there by yourself, with no one watching. He'd had his moments.

He took the gun from its soft leather holster. It slipped easily into his hand, familiar as a worn glove. The Sig-Sauer, with its fat grip to accommodate the staggered clip, was too thick for his hand, but the .45 just fit. He'd learned to shoot it in the army—when he'd been on the base pistol team, the .45 had become an extension of his hand. He'd point at something and, bingo, he'd hit it. Mostly, it sat in the glove compartment—that is, when he remembered to bring it.

He'd lost interest in guns after he got out of the service. Guns were for killing things. He had an obsolete skill. Still, it could be fun. He rarely missed; people were impressed. It was hard to leave something behind if you were good at it.

He rummaged under the seat. Uh-oh. Some pamphlets about the petroglyphs north of Bishop from one of his walk and talks. He stuffed them in a paper sack he'd found on the floor, along with other unwanted debris that could give him away. The gun was still a problem. He stuck it and the clip-on holster inside his belt, but he could see the bulge from the butt under his T-shirt. He pulled the holster and gun free from his belt and stuffed them under the seat, covering them with an old rag. That would have to do.

It was just past 10:00 A.M. when he pushed open the door to Eddie's trailer. Dirty dishes covered with bits of food and black ants filled the sink. Their busy highway led out the grimy louvered window above the counter. He looked around for Prowler's food bowl, then remembered that Eddie said Prowler used the shop. Probably liked it better than the trailer. Cats were usually fastidious. It looked as if Eddie had left and planned to come back later.

Frank began to have second thoughts about the plan. He hoped Eddie hadn't just taken off. He was pretty sure he could get Eddie a break if he turned himself in, but if he made a run for it, he was in trouble, and so was Frank's job with the BLM. He was definitely having qualms about his brilliant plan. Expecting the Eddies of this world to do what they'd promised was more than mildly optimistic.

He shook his head, wondering what had possessed him. But he knew: a chance to catch the poacher who'd killed his bighorns, which was not BLM business, as Meecham had pointed out to him in no uncertain terms.

He made his way out to the shop. Things looked a little better there. Some food was still in Prowler's dish, and the water was reasonably clean. Keeping house wasn't Eddie's strong suit. Maybe Eddie was filling in the local law enforcement right now. He found a sack of dry cat food on the workbench, where Eddie'd said he'd leave it, and poured some pellets into Prowler's dish. The cat came bounding in the window at the sound of food rattling against the plastic bowl. He stopped at the sight of Frank, tail fluffed out, ready to run. Frank called softly, "Come on, Prowler. Come on there, boy. Chow time." He gently stirred the dry pellets in the bowl. The cat approached cautiously, then began contentedly munching cat fodder. Eddie's pal. Guys like Eddie needed pals.

Time to get going and check in at the station. As his hand touched the door, someone banged on the metal screen on the other side. Couldn't be Eddie, had to be someone looking for Eddie. He pulled the cheap door toward him and peered through the screen at the two men standing on the small wooden platform that served as a porch. The one in front was tall and wiry, graying hair pulled back into a ponytail. Oddly pink-rimmed eyes peered at him from a pale face over the first man's shoulder. Wisps of white-blond hair poked out from under a blue kerchief. The pale face under the kerchief wore a fixed smile, white teeth surrounded by very red gums.

Frank's heart thundered in his chest. This wasn't part of the plan. How the hell had they found Eddie? Fear clouded thought, and he especially needed a clear head.

"Yeah, whaddya want?" Frank tried to sound like Eddie, ersatz tough guy.

"You Redhawk?" Ponytail asked.

"Some people call me that."

"We met a guy who called you Redhawk. Said you were 'heap good guide.' Isn't that right, Roy?" Ponytail winked back at his companion.

The pale one nodded slowly. "That's right. He told us all about you." The soft sandy voice triggered a chill in Frank's stomach. Had they already found Eddie? Were they toying with him? He'd have to bluff it till he figured out what was happening. Get a grip and bluff it.

"So, whaddya want?" He slouched in the doorway.

"Hey, aren't you going to invite us in? It's not too polite to keep company standing around outside. Makes a person feel unwelcome. You don't want us to feel unwelcome, do you?" The pale face was earnest, addressing matters of etiquette.

"Come on in." Frank turned away and plopped himself on the brown Naugahyde couch liberally decorated with duct tape and put his feet up on the bricks and plywood that served as a coffee table. He hoped he looked casual, at ease, nonchalant, or at least not the way he felt—tense, hesitant, and confused. Somehow they'd tracked Eddie down.

Ponytail sat down in one of the two plastic patio chairs that completed the *House Beautiful* decor. While he fished into his pocket and lit up a hand-rolled cigarette, the one called Roy stepped carefully into the room, looking around, sizing up the place, alert. He moved easily, almost languorously, which belied the quick way he seemed to take in the place. He looked into the kitchen, then turned back and leaned against the doorjamb dividing the kitchen from the living room.

"Nice place you got here." Roy exposed the red gums and white teeth. "Real homey." He nodded to himself. "Just like home." His voice was almost inaudible. He gave Frank a slight smile. "So, Mr. Hawk, or do I call you Red?"

"The name's Eddie, wiseass."

Ponytail shook his head in mock disbelief. "Jesus, can't believe it. Everywhere you go, somebody has to be a salty fucker." He lifted his head to stare at Frank. The acrid smell of pot filled the room.

Frank looked from Ponytail's empty eyes back to Roy's now-unsmiling face. "Hell, call me Red, call me Eddie, just don't call me late for dinner." He forced a short laugh. Maybe he was overdoing the Eddie bit. "Shit, I don't care what you call me. What the hell do you want?" He waited. "Come on, guys, I haven't got a clue." He figured Eddie would sound plaintive by now, and the truth was, it came pretty easily.

"Relax, man. We're hunters, just looking for a guide. Isn't that so?" Ponytail looked over at the one called Roy. "Maybe we can throw a little business your way."

Frank had said close to the same thing to Eddie two days ago. Seemed like everyone was in business. "Yeah, what kind of business?"

"Hey, that's better, Mr. Hawk. Right down to brass tacks." The sandy voice trickled into the noon stillness. "See, we're looking for a guy, a guy we know you know. A white hunter, heap big bucks, Red."

Ponytail sucked on the joint, making little gasping sounds.

Roy went on. "You know, I like the name Red better than Eddie. Eddie sounds kind of chickenshit." He paused. "No offense, Red. But don't you think Red sounds more manly than Eddie?"

"I don't give a shit how it sounds."

Ponytail reached across and casually slapped Frank across the face. "Jeez, there you go again with that salty crap. Just listen up. Be polite."

For a moment, Frank felt nothing but fury. He wanted to drive the heel of his hand into the base of Ponytail's nose and watch him go down. Then he was calm, his senses sharp and alert, his surrounding etched with special clarity, the colors vivid, the sounds distinct. The gray threads of the duct tape traced a tangled pattern against the mud brown Naugahyde. He held the pink-rimmed pale eyes of the one standing, the very dangerous one, in photographic detail. The sounds of the leaves stirring in the cottonwoods reached him as clearly as the raspy breathing coming from Ponytail's broken nose.

"Look," Ponytail went on, "what we want here is some information about the guy you took up in the mountains for bighorn sheep about a week ago."

The pale one picked it up. They were a team. "We want to know all about the good Dr. Sorensen." He spoke distinctly, placing the words in the room one at a time. "Little things, like what he looks like. What kind of a car he drove? In fact, everything he said and did. That's pretty clear, isn't it, Ed—die?" They waited, the sound of the trucks on 395 rumbling in the stillness. "What's the matter, Eddie, cat got your tongue?" He regarded Frank with detached contempt. "Come to think of it, Eddie fits a little brown fella like you. Come to think of it, you definitely look like an Ed—die. Whaddya think, Hickey?"

Ponytail nodded. "Yup, a little old Eddie."

It was almost rehearsed, this pas de deux, a dance of intimidation. Frank wasn't sure where it was leading, but he had a hunch it had a grim ending.

"Yeah, I know the guy you mean, the one you're looking for, only he called himself Smith, a big blond guy. Bates said to call him Smith."

Roy gave a soft chuckle, shaking his head. "Man, that Bates, too clever for his own good. So, what was he driving?"

"I picked him up at the airport in Trona."

"Yeah, so then what?"

"Then I took him up the mountain, and he killed a bighorn sheep."

"Did he do a lot of hunting, Eddie? Did he say anything about hunting up there before with another guide?"

Frank knew he had to handle this carefully. His life probably depended on it. When they found out what they needed, he wouldn't be around for another haircut.

"Yeah, he said something about it. Why you want to know?"

Hickey reached out and slapped Frank again, but this time Frank saw it coming and turned his head with the blow.

"We ask the questions. You give the answers. Simple."

Frank measured out his answer, watching the one he was sure was Roy Miller. The man was moving easily about the small room, examining Eddie's things, checking everything out. Frank's innards roiled. There could be stuff that would give him away. He glanced at the shelf running above the header dividing the kitchen from the living room/bedroom. There were some old postcards, a calendar with a partially clad Indian maid lying on some furs, and a photo of three figures in a homemade frame. He couldn't make it out, but it had to be of Eddie. There was an older couple in traditional dress, and the one in the middle had to be Eddie. He needed to get Miller's attention before he looked up from the taxidermists' catalog.

"So you stuff animals, that right, Redhawk?" He thumbed through the catalog.

"He said his last guide was a cretin."

Miller's eyes narrowed. "What'd you say?"

"Said he was so dumb, he couldn't find his boots." Frank paused, looking somewhat puzzled. "He thought that was really funny."

The pale face went blank, eyes fixed on Frank.

Frank looked over at Hickey. "Laughed about it. Said he couldn't find his boots, couldn't find his dick with both hands." He looked over at Miller and back to Hickey, his face full of puzzlement. "He told me I needed to be an improvement. He was a strange dude, man."

Roy Miller's pale eyes seemed to emit a blue light.

Frank held Miller's gaze, his heart pounding. "You want to talk to him so bad, stick around. I'm supposed to meet him up in the mountains around five o'clock this afternoon." He looked over at Hickey. "Going to bring out the ram's head. We had to leave it in an abandoned mine when the law showed up."

"You're meeting Sorensen today?" The sandy voice was tight and controlled.

"That's it, man. We're going back to get it, the bighorn head."

A slow smile creased Roy Miller's thin mouth, pale lips lifting away from the red gums. "What about that, Hickey? We're going to have a face-to-face meet with the good doctor sooner than we thought. See if he can find his dick with both hands."

"Bet he can't." Ponytail grinned.

A popping sound came from the other side of the screen door. "There's a cat out here," someone said.

Miller shook his head in disgust. "I told you to wait in the van."

"There's a cat out here."

"Okay, there's a cat out there."

"I can't catch 'im."

Roy nodded at Hickey. "Shit, go on out and keep him occupied." Hickey blinked thoughtfully, his head wreathed in a cloud of pot smoke. Moving with great deliberation, he got to his feet and pushed out the screen door past a short redheaded man with a thick torso and tiny, startled bright blue eyes.

"Okay, Redhawk. You're going to take me and my friends here to your meeting with the good doctor up in the mountains. Go on a little hike. Have a picnic. How's that sound, my man?" Roy's ghastly smile reflected genuine pleasure.

# 22

•

Frank kept thinking about the gun under his seat. Could he get to it? Would there be an opportunity? Should he get to it? He glanced up at the rearview mirror. The tan van was still there. The sun reflecting off the windshield made it impossible for him to make out Hickey or the other Miller, the one short a few cards, but he knew they were there riding along in the van like a couple of normal psychopaths. With Roy Miller as his faithful copilot, it wasn't likely he'd have the opportunity to get to the .45. Maybe if they stopped for gas, but he didn't need gas. Maybe if Miller needed to take a leak, had some sort of reason to leave him alone in the truck for a moment.

"Hey, man, how about we stop for some beer in Lone Pine?" Frank gave Miller a hopeful look.

Miller looked over and shook his head. "In all this heat, beer dries you out. That's not being a smart guide, Eddie, drying folks out in the desert." He gave Frank what passed for a familiar smile. "I'm gonna have to cut into your business here, Redhawk, take people up into the mountains for a real adventure. We could call it White Man's World. You know, stuff for rich white folks led by a really white man."

Frank looked away from the pale face.

"Hey there, my little brown friend, I like being white, really white." Roy nodded in affirmation. "Maybe I'm ahead of my time. You know what I mean, one of the first, the early ones. Maybe white genes will spread, become dominant. You know about genetics, Eddie?"

"Naw, not much. I mean there's bloodlines in horses and cattle and stuff, but that's about it." He had to be careful to hit it about right, know the stuff Eddie'd know—not too little, not too much.

"Well, there's what's called genetic dominance, see. Some things we inherit always show up, like brown eyes. See, brown eyes are dominant. But it's not that simple. Brown eyes can make blue eyes, but blue eyes always make blue eyes. Blue eyes are pure. Now think about this, Eddie." His smile suggested they were fellow conspirators. "What if being white, really white like me, was dominant? No mixed-up stuff, only pure. After awhile, there'd just be white guys, right?"

Frank looked at Miller and nodded. "Yeah, I guess so." There was something a bit haywire in Roy's logic, to say nothing of his understanding of genetics, but he didn't think now was a good time to straighten him out. Say, Oh, by the way, Roy, you don't know your ass from a hole in the ground. For a moment, he tried to imagine a world full of pale white psychopaths. Not a pretty picture, especially if you tended to be brown and reasonably sane.

"Come on, Eddie, let's show a little more enthusiasm here. We'd have white Indians." Roy paused. "Now there's a thought, white red men. Sorta like the way Indians described niggers, black white men." He exposed his red gums. "There'd be lotsa interesting things, white spics, even white niggers. Hell, I've seen redheaded niggers. It could happen, Eddie. You'd have to change your guide name to Whitehawk." Air escaped rhythmically from his throat in a silent laugh. "Say I met a really fine white woman, white like me, and our kids were just like us, pure and white. A beginning, right?"

"I've never seen anything like you, man." It was out before he thought about it. It had been a special curse, his thoughts rushing out of his mouth "like a fart from an old man's ass," as his da used to say. He looked over at Miller's suddenly alert face. "No offense meant."

Roy looked at Frank, his pale face intent, curious, and oddly lifeless in the midday light. Then he turned away, fixing his eyes on the highway. "Explaining this stuff to you is a waste of time, Eddie. Somehow I don't think we're on the same page, you know what I mean?" He gave a slight smile, which seemed to suggest that Frank was a man without a future.

"Hey, whatever, man. So how about we stop for Cokes?"

Miller shook his head in disbelief. "Forget it, Eddie. We gas up and refill the canteens in Olancha. That's it." His mood seemed to darken, as if he'd found their conversation tiring. It was exhausting for Frank, having to watch every word. Being Eddie Laguna required all his concentration. The fewer words that passed between them, the less likely Miller would become suspicious. Another tiny deviation from Eddie's persona could give him away. He knew this much: Miller possessed an agile mind. He had a probing energy, malevolent and alert. Frank wished he could stretch out on the sand by his pond and let the cottonwoods whisper him to sleep. The steady rhythm of the engine and road noise temporarily cocooned him from his surroundings, shut out the evil next to him, the person directing his path. He hummed tunelessly. It seemed familiar to him from long ago, something Susan Funmaker's mother had taught to him. Something about ravens.

They rode wrapped in their own thoughts. God only knew what went on in the dark places of Miller's mind. Frank's thoughts tugged away at the threads and knots of the mess in which he had become entangled. He had gambled a lie against time. He had another hour and half 's driving time and three-plus hours up to the mine, maybe more if he used the terrain to his advantage. Time was his ally. His mind was calm now, as if he were watching himself. He considered the possibilities. If Eddie had turned himself in, then Fish and Game would be alerted. If he slipped up and told them about Frank knowing he was the poacher, Meecham would be very angry at Frank for not reporting the information. But they wouldn't be looking for Smith the poacher in Ballarat until Sunday morning, tomorrow, and tomorrow would too late.

On the other hand, Frank knew they might be looking for him, wondering why he'd missed his walk and talk, but after the caboose, where would they look? It would be a search by phone, and he'd left his personal cell phone in the caboose. He'd planned to check into work this afternoon. Then there was Linda. After five o'clock, Linda would be annoyed, then angry, then worried. She would look for him, too. There would be an angry Linda and an angry and disappointed

Dave Meecham, but would they raise the alarm, especially on a weekend? Not right away, probably not in time, but there was always the possibility Linda would contact Meecham, or vice versa. Both Linda and Meecham were persistent and thorough, people who paid attention to things, remembered the details. Both of them knew how much he wanted to catch the sheep killer, and Linda knew about Eddie. He could only hope they'd think about Surprise Canyon, but he couldn't count on it. And by his own reckoning, he had maybe five hours to continue being Eddie Laguna before the Millers dispensed with his services.

The .45 under the seat—he'd have to find a way to get his hands on it before they started for the mine. And then there was maybe an ace in the hole. If their little hunting party made it all the way to the Silver Queen, Sorensen's precious Weatherby Magnum would be somewhere in the mine, maybe with a few rounds in the magazine. If he could come across it first, the odds might even out a bit. Of one thing he was becoming increasingly sure: Roy Miller wasn't intending to let Eddie Laguna make a round-trip.

●

Frank pulled the truck off the dirt track, leaving just barely enough room for another vehicle. The van pulled up behind him, effectively blocking the road. Roy craned his head around, frowning back at Hickey and the other Miller. Roy opened the door and got out, leaving the passenger door standing wide open. Frank waited for him to shut the door and walk back to the van, which would give him a chance to reach the .45, but Roy just stood there. Frank let his hand drop toward the floor of the truck.

"Pull off the fucking road." Miller waved at the van's driver, his voice taut with impatience. He eased himself back into the truck. "Pull off up there." He eyed Frank, who fought to stay calm. "Jesus, wake the fuck up. Pull farther up." He pointed to a narrow clearing to the right of the track, where the berm had been broken down by ATVs and four-wheel vehicles using the narrow arroyo as a short-cut to the ghost town of Ballarat.

Frank eased the truck off the track and onto the floor of the sandy wash. "Hope we don't get stuck in the sand."

"Don't worry about it, ace." Again, Roy opened the door, standing half in and half out. Frank dropped his hand once more. He'd have to retrieve the .45 and draw the slide before Miller was on him. Miscalculating meant dying. Frank watched as Roy stood with one arm resting on the open door, looking around. Roy waved Hickey and the other one to come on. Frank watched as they trudged up the wash carrying their gear. Hickey bore a small pack, probably full of candy bars, which seemed to be his principal form of sustenance. The redheaded Miller carried the canteens and a heavy barreled rifle. He noticed that Hickey had what looked like a Glock thrust into the front of his pants.

As they drew nearer, he gave the rifle a careful inspection. It was a .458 Winchester Magnum equipped with a scope. Scoping very heavy caliber guns violated standard practice. Guns like the .458 and the .600 Nitro Express were meant for killing elephants, lions, tigers, so what the hell were they doing with a scoped shoulder cannon? It was hard to find a moving target in a scope, especially a charging target running at you at forty miles an hour, so hunters of very big game had to stand their ground, use iron sights and get off their shot before what they were shooting at found them; at least that was the Hemingway tradition. No time for fooling around trying to locate in the scope what you had to hit. Roy Miller didn't appear to be carrying a weapon. His weapon consisted of the seemingly absolute control he exercised over the soft-brain and the psychopath ever trailing in his wake.

Frank sized up their expedition. Three one-quart canteens and Frank's half-gallon one—not enough water. That could work in his favor. Tired and thirsty crooks lacked efficiency, weren't up to snuff, or up to snuffing folks out. At least he hoped so. Hickey handed Roy a sort of kepi, like a legionnaire's hat with a neckerchief. Despite the dread sitting in the pit of his stomach, Frank smiled inwardly. He found his band of adventurers more than a bit strange: an albino in a legionnaire's cap, a woolly red troll armed with a shoulder cannon, and a dreamy-eyed sociopath with a gray ponytail; and then there was him, Frank Flynn, a one-man tribe, the last of the Meximicks.

•

The climb up the canyon lifted Frank's spirit, each breath, each step a tonic. He felt good. His companions had not fared so well in the heat of the afternoon. The hike sapped their strength, except for the redheaded creature. He didn't seem fatigued. His short legs worked like tireless pistons, churning through the sandy bottom of the wash, hopping with agility from rock to rock. Now and again, he would stop and swivel his head from side to side, making clicking sounds, then look furtively at Roy, as if waiting for a reproof.

Hickey seemed to suffer the most. Despite being thin and wiry, he stopped frequently, gasping to catch his breath. Clearly, he didn't do much in the way of hiking, or much of anything else physical. Frank enjoyed his discomfort. Hickey had been the first to run out of water. Less than halfway there, he had emptied his canteen. Then he had stumbled over to Frank, relieved him of his water, drank deeply, and walked away, tossing Frank's canteen on the ground. It was okay, though. Frank had drunk more than half the water, stocking up, anticipating that his water would be the property of whoever ran out first. So he popped a smooth round pebble in his mouth and led them up the rock slide to the jump where the huge granite monolith had split in two. He was pretty sure the red one's legs were too short to propel him across the gap. He'd soon see.

The four of them stood on the flat top of the monolith, the reflected glare of the afternoon sun causing them to squint behind their sunglasses. Roy Miller and Hickey wore dark Ray·Bans, stylish thugs. Frank's glasses were lightly tinted, enough to block out the ultraviolet rays, but not enough to darken the landscape. He didn't like the distortion of the light. It made him feel somehow out of touch with his surroundings, especially in the desert.

Roy surveyed their situation again, looking over the chasm, then at each of them, his gaze lingering on the redhead's truncated legs. "You know, Eddie, I don't think Jason here can make the jump. Can you make the jump, Jace?"

Jason nodded slowly up and down in silent assent.

"Yeah, right." Roy looked at the gap between the rocks, thinking about it. "I don't think so." He turned his bleached face toward Frank. "See, he's not squeaking or clicking, which means that his attention is focused. You know what I think focused his attention?" Roy pointed at the gap between the rocks. "That."

"Hey, it's not that bad. I'll go first, show you the way."

"No, I don't think I want you on that rock over there and us way over here, Eddie. It'd make me feel deserted like. Nope, what I think is that we'll go back and go up the other way, the long way, the route you didn't want to use. You know why? Because this isn't like you described it, Eddie. Why is that? Why isn't it like you said it'd be, 'a piece of cake'?"

"I wasn't thinking about his short legs." Frank gestured toward Jason with his head. "Hell, I've seen women jump it."

Roy backhanded Frank across the mouth, knocking him off balance. He stepped forward and drove a short, hard left into Frank's stomach. The first blow took Frank by surprise, but he tightened his stomach muscles in time to keep from having his breath knocked out of him, but not in time to keep from going down, scraping his right elbow through his shirt.

"Don't be a smart-ass, Eddie. I don't like wandering around out in the sun. I don't like people who lie to me. This is a lie, Eddie." He gestured toward the gap between the rocks. "Not a piece of cake."

Frank led them back down among the broken boulders. It was more difficult going down than it had been coming up, feeling for footholds, slipping on the steeper faces, the granite slopes sandpapering their skin. By the time they had reached the trail that wound its way up the left side of the canyon, they were scraped and bruised, and it was past five o'clock. Frank hoped the Meecham/Reyes team would be in motion. Maybe not a team yet, but definitely wondering where the hell he was. By now, Fish and Game would have Eddie. Now if only his boss and Linda connected. Somehow he had to make it down from this mountain.

The trail ran steeply up the left side of the canyon. By the time they passed the midpoint, they were parched with thirst. Had it been midsummer, dehydration would have been almost a certainty. As it was, Hickey looked wobbly and exhausted. Jason still seemed relatively undaunted. No noises now, but the short piston legs seemed to pump with steadfast regularity, propelling his thick torso up the trail, kicking up dust into the still late-afternoon air.

Roy paused to rest, looking back at Frank. "Water up there, right, Eddie? Lots of water, a pool, you said. You better hope to fuck you're right, or we're gonna have to call you Deadhawk. Maybe give you a new Indian name, Takes a Long Time to Die."

They crested the trail as the sun disappeared behind the back wall of the Sierras, throwing the canyon into a pale yellow light. From midmorning till its retreat behind the mountains, it had washed the land in a relentless glare that blurred the form of things. Now shades of color returned to the land, separating ridge from valley, and the shapes of things reemerged. Soon the yellows would turn to orange and pink and deepen into the blues and purples of the late-evening sky. Frank stood looking back at the mountain skyline, his heart lifting with the beauty.

"What's holding you up there, Deadhawk? Praying to the great spirit for water?" Hickey's voice was raspy with thirst.

"Right over there, tough guy." Frank pointed to the dark green line of vegetation that followed the spring through the tiny meadow. "Nickel a gallon. I own the water rights."

"Hey, that's it, Roy." Hickey flung up his hand, pointing wildly as he walked unsteadily across the dried grass that covered the floor of Surprise Canyon in a brown shroud.

# 23

•

Eddie was definitely going to keep his word to Frank and turn himself in to Fish and Game. Only not right away. There was no point in passing up fifteen thousand dollars. Besides, he'd gone to a lot of trouble hiking back up the canyon, lugging out the head and Smith's precious rifle. And then he had spent the best part of a week making a perfect mount, the head turned slightly away and up, as if sniffing the breeze, the great horns curling back, easier to see from an angle. Not one of those straight-ahead deer-caught-in-the-headlights looks. It was a great piece of work, and he was hoping Smith, whoever he was, might toss in an additional bonus. After all, hadn't he been the guide, done the work, gone back for the head and the rifle and thus saved the day? It was worth every penny he'd collect and more.

He pulled over to the side of the highway just south of Big Pine and got out, stretching his legs and arms. A couple of hours of driving, and it was time to unlimber. It was thirsty time, too. Time to add oil. The old flathead V-8 had just about run out of rings. Clouds of blue smoke puffed out the rusted tailpipe, choking the drivers in his immediate wake. He enjoyed clogging up the air-conditioning of the rich and white in their sleek trouble-free cars. It was especially good on the long grades leading up into the Sierras, with cars lined up behind him five or six deep. Cough! Cough! Cough! Welcome to Indian Country. He tilted in a can of fifty-weight Friction-Free Oil, recycled stuff, and very cheap. He traveled with a case in the truck bed. He was getting about a hundred miles to the can. A traveling case was about right, a drink for the truck, and now a drink for the driver.

He pulled a tall Bud from a Styrofoam ice chest, popped open the top, and took a long, deep swallow. Nothing like the first cold beer of the day. Better. Ready for Mr. Big Shot. It was perfect. Take his money and then turn him in. What an asshole. "Don't touch the rifle." Acting like Eddie was going to contaminate his precious rifle. And then putting his hand over his nose and breathing out in little puffs. "Your breath's rancid." There was nothing he could do about that until he got his teeth fixed. So thanks for paying for fixing my teeth, asshole. Now we can do lunch, golf it up.

He stopped again at the bottom of Walker Pass to put in some more oil for the climb out of the Owens Valley. Eddie was going to meet the man at six o'clock all right, but six o'clock Saturday evening in Jawbone Canyon, not six o'clock Sunday morning in Ballarat. Frank would be pissed, but when he had his money and the poacher had the head, then he'd call Frank, and he could pick up the poacher with the head and the rifle. Special delivery for Frank Flynn. Frank'd have to put in a good word after a bust like that. He frowned for a moment, thinking about the waste of the good job he'd done on the head. Then again, Fish and Game might donate it to a museum or something, maybe even with his name on it. He opened beer number three and propped the bottle between his legs.

A big semi ground up the pass on the right. A sign read PASSING LANE 1/4 MILE AHEAD. SLOWER TRAFFIC KEEP RIGHT. As the road widened to accommodate two lanes of uphill traffic, Eddie pulled out to go around the truck, which was going about twenty. Eddie had his pickup up to thirty, struggling in third, clouds of smoke choking the drivers lined up behind him, but he was losing ground, so he downshifted, deftly double-clutching into second. The synchromesh was on its way out. Now he was just barely going faster than the semi. The line of cars behind him zigged and zagged back and forth in futile frustration. He could hear someone leaning on his horn, music to his ears. As Eddie and the semi approached the end of the passing zone, he just managed to squeeze by, leaving the lineup behind him stuck behind the truck. He grinned. Things were really working out.

He'd left in plenty of time, and taking this road, he'd still be there well before six o'clock. He'd be able to see if the big-shot hunter was up to something. Watch him for a bit. Eddie didn't entirely trust Mr. Big Shot. Eddie's spirit voice told him to take heed, whispered in his ear. When he didn't pay attention to his voice, he was sorry. Being small, except for his mouth, had taught him to listen to his voice. When he listened, he could tell who was going to take a crack at him before it happened, and this gave him an edge, an opportunity to get away or hit someone with a board, or rock, or whatever was handy, a chance to even things up. When he didn't listen, he got the shit beat out of him.

Now this Smith guy definitely set Eddie's voice to whispering. He wasn't sure what the voice was saying, only that it was warning him about Smith, like a radio message with static. That's why he had decided to take the back way into Jawbone Canyon, bringing his father's old pistol, a single-action .44 long, Sam Colt's equalizer. The steel on the muzzle, around the cylinder, and on the trigger guard was worn down to bright metal where the bluing had been rubbed away. The walnut grips gave off a deep luster. Eddie rubbed the wood against the crease of his nose, rubbing in the oil from his skin as his father had showed him. He kept it in perfect working order, lightly oiled, resting in the holster he had made for it, a soft doeskin sewn to a stiff cowhide cup. Eddie could draw it out with great speed, and up to a point, he could shoot pretty well. At least he could hit a beer can at twenty-five feet or so—that is, if he took careful aim. He hadn't mastered the drawing and shooting part, but he had the drawing part down pat. Just having this weapon would be enough to discourage any funny stuff. It was a big gun, a discouragement in itself.

He stopped again to add oil just before the road dropped down into Kelso Valley, where the blacktop turned into graded gravel. It was a beautiful valley. To the north and west, the foothills leading up to the high country were covered with piñons. A narrow dirt road, Garringer Grade, led up a series of steep switchbacks to French Meadow, intermittent grasslands surrounded by ponderosa. To the south, the land rose from the valley floor into hills covered with juniper and Joshua trees. Kelso Valley was a place where the desert met the mountains. The valley floor was green with the last alfalfa crop of the year. White-face range cattle dotted the hills. A Paiute owned this bottom land and the cattle. Eddie wondered what it would be like to own land and cattle. He would like to meet this man, but Eddie was Shoshone. Still, it would be good to know an Indian with land that was his own, not reservation land, and cattle, too. Someday he would meet him, but for now he had to take the dirt road that led up past the Joshua trees to the series of ridges that the graded gravel road followed before it dropped down to meet the Jawbone Canyon road near the junction to Dove Springs. He would pick a place well above the junction and wait to see what Smith would do.

•

Dr. Michael Sorensen had rented a shiny new Range Rover—lots of room, and the air-conditioning could make ice cubes. Satisfactory for the purpose at hand. The smelly chatterbox guide had saved him a lot of trouble by getting his trophy head before it rotted in the mine, and he had remembered to bring out the rifle, as well; the Weatherby was his favorite. But the man was particularly filthy and had breath like an outhouse.

Now, with the change in plans, it would make it difficult to arrange another accident. It had been remarkably easy the first time—actually, almost an accident in and of itself. In a fit of anger at the destruction of the first ram's horns, and, to be perfectly frank, because of his fear of being caught, he had decided to put as much distance between himself and the dead bighorns as possible, leaving the incompetent guide to his just deserts. He'd made the foul-mouthed cretin hand over his shoes, canteen, and rifle, promising to leave them just down the canyon. And he had, too, with the exception of the boots. Those he had tossed away. He'd drunk the water, of course. The canteen was empty. There was plenty of water at the spring. The idiot should have waited by the spring. Obviously, the man had made a very bad decision. For a person who claimed an intimate knowledge of the desert, he hadn't done so well. There it was, natural selection working its immutable laws. Survival of the fittest was a fact of existence. The unfit perished, and the intelligent prevailed. The rest was bullshit.

He'd have to pay this smelly little creature some sort of fee. God, what teeth, what breath. He'd give him a thousand. That should do it. More money than someone like him had ever seen at one time. He ought to be grateful. If he gave the Indian cash, he'd be strapped for money on the way back. He liked to carry a couple of thousand in hundred-dollar bills. You never knew what might turn up, but he had his checkbook, and he always had plastic. After all, it was unlikely that someone like Redhawk, if that was his name, would complain about breach of contract. Considering his line of work, it was unlikely he had dealings with the police, or with lawyers, for that matter. Evidently, he didn't have a pot to piss in. Sorensen smiled to himself. Still, it would be good if the desert did its work. It would, after all, remove any possibility of a connection to him. He planned to get there early, find a nice little side canyon in which they could transact their business without interruption, then head back over Angeles Crest Highway to Pasadena as fast as possible. Done. Done. Done.

Sorensen anticipated the look of suppressed envy that was bound to cross his brother-in-law's face when he next came to visit and saw the magnificent horns. The doctor had been rehearsing the story of the hunt as he drove up. All the elements fit, the difficulty with the guide not wanting to walk around the ridge to remain upwind, refusing to continue the hunt. Then, of course, being unwilling to pass up the chance of taking such a magnificent animal, he had gone ahead on his own. His efforts to scale an impossibly steep ridge, and finally the shot, taken at six hundred—no, seven hundred yards, using a specially loaded 210-grain bullet. "Took the beast just behind the shoulder. I was lucky enough," he'd say to Dennis, "that he presented a broadside for a moment. He dropped with the one shot. The most difficult part was controlling my breathing after the climb—pulse had to have been one-forty or more—and, of course, packing out the head. But God, it was worth it." His oh-so-superior brother-in-law would be hunting one hell of a long time before he'd touch a trophy head of this size. Sorensen expected it to be in the top ten. A head with horns of this scale hadn't been taken since the fifties. The condescending Dennis didn't have anything in the top one hundred. So kiss my ass, Dennis, old sport. Perhaps I could write down a few hunting tips for you.

●

Eddie watched the big Range Rover work its way up the narrow road that clung to the side of the canyon. Frequently, it would disappear in a cloud of dust as the road turned back on itself. It was a remarkably windless afternoon, and the dust of the lumbering vehicle lay like a brown contrail across the land. He sipped beer number five. It was barely cool. The ice had melted, and the last two beers sloshed around in the tepid water at the bottom of the ice chest. Eddie decided to drink *numero cinco* before it got completely warm. Of course, he'd drunk a helluva lot of warm beer, but cool was better.

The Range Rover stopped near the mouth of a small side canyon. He watched as it backed up and then maneuvered around, going up the wash in reverse for about a hundred feet. It would be impossible for vehicles going up or down the road to see it until they were directly opposite the mouth of the wash. But Eddie could see it just fine. He wasn't going up or down the road. He was watching the vehicle and its occupant through navy-surplus spotting binoculars from the opposite ridge. He smiled to himself. Okay, voice, I see him. I see the way he tries to hide. I wonder why. Perhaps because he doesn't want to be out on the road, but I wonder why. He walked back to his truck, which he had parked just below the ridgeline. I think I'll take a walk down the road and talk to this Mr. Smith. See how much he wants his head. Eddie slung a soft canteen across his shoulder, picked up the holstered pistol, and slid it onto his belt, threading it through the stiffer cowhide, which made it easier to draw. It looked good there, the fringe hanging down, the polished walnut grips picking up the light. Then he slung the rifle over his shoulder and walked down the road in the early-evening light. He wasn't nervous a bit. Hey, *cinco cervezas* were good. And he had the equalizer.

# 24

•

Eddie worked his way along the ridge at the head of the canyon. Sorensen was sitting inside the Range Rover, so Eddie couldn't see him. He made his way down the narrow wash until he was about fifty feet behind the vehicle. The engine was running, the metallic tang of exhaust from the catalytic converter smothering the smells of the creosote and the dampness from the recent rain. The quiet thrum of the big V-8 intruded into the desert silence. Smith was running the air conditioner. All the comforts of home. Eddie picked up a handful of loose pebbles and tossed them at the shiny red vehicle. After a moment, the driver's window slid smoothly down. Eddie waited, scrunching down, out of sight. Smith stuck his head out and craned around, searching for the source of the gravel pelting down on the vehicle. Eddie tossed another handful of pebbles, five small rocks about three-quarters of an inch in diameter, big enough to make a racket. They struck the top of the car with a definite clatter and bounced onto the hood. The driver's door flew open, and Smith stepped out, pistol in hand. It looked like a 9-mm Browning, an expensive handgun. Figures, Eddie thought. It went with the package— rich white guy, rich white guy's car, rich white guy's rifle, rich white guy's pistol.

Eddie slowly raised himself to a standing position back of the rear right side of the vehicle. "Hey, don't be shooting up your guide." He grinned his best crazy Indian grin, exposing the blackened stumps and jagged remainders of his teeth. Eddie's grin turned genuine as he saw Smith's expression transform from that of disbelief to disgust and then to anger. "How're you doin', Mr. Smith? You missed the turnoff by a quarter mile, but I guess you know that."

"You scratched the paint. That will cost money."

"Naw, they'll be able to rub it right out. Besides, what's a few bucks to a rich dude like you?"

"They're not your bucks, little man. They're *my* bucks." He inspected Eddie with returning calm. "I see you're carrying a sidearm"—his eyes moved appraisingly to the rifle slung over Eddie's shoulder—"and my Weatherby, but I don't see my ram's head."

"That's because it's still in my truck. The rifle here is part of a good-faith agreement." He liked that "good-faith agreement" talk. Let Smith know he wasn't the only one with smarts. "Now how about a little good-faith cash."

Smith smirked. "Well, well, a legally trained mind. If the rifle's not damaged, a 'good-faith' five hundred might be appropriate."

Eddie unslung the rifle from his shoulder and handed it over to Smith. "Here you go."

Smith took the rifle and pulled back the bolt. Eddie knew the magazine was empty. He'd taken out the last three rounds himself. Smith closed the bolt and dry-fired. The mechanism made a distinct click, metal on metal. Eddie saw a small frown flit across the calm facade of Smith's face. Smith reached into the top pocket of his safari shirt and produced a money clip, from which he took five crisp one-hundred-dollar bills. Then he handed them to Eddie. Things were looking up. He rarely saw hundred-dollar bills, especially crisp new ones. He folded them in half and stuffed them into his pants pocket. Then he deftly produced the .44. It fairly flew into his hand. "Whadda ya think of my big ol' forty-four, Smith?" He flipped it around to hand it to Sorensen butt-first for his inspection. As Smith reached for it, Eddie did the border shuffle, flipping it back around, the muzzle pointed at Smith's torso. Smith's empty hand waved uncertainly in the air as he found himself looking down at the large-caliber gun pointed at his midsection. "Never seen the old border shuffle, Smith?" Eddie was enjoying the equality bestowed on him by Sam Colt's patented step stool for little guys. No more Mr. Big Shot, no more Mr. Smith, just plain old Smith, equalized.

For a moment, the hunter's easy assurance peeled away like paint bubbling in the sun, but then the habitual arrogance of a lifetime reasserted itself. "I hope you know you're fooling around with a loaded weapon."

Eddie smiled. "Hope you know it, too." He slipped the .44 back in its holster. "Just wanted to make sure we understand each other."

Smith eyed Eddie with some care, a new appraisal. Not quite the clown he had taken him for. "I didn't drive to this shit hole to stand around and watch a trick show. Let's get on with it. Where's your truck?"

"Where I left it." Eddie looked smug. "Here's what we're going to do." He cocked his hip out, letting his hand dangle over the butt of the pistol. "You're going to wait here. After a little while, you'll see me pull up on the road. You walk down to my truck. I give you the head, and you give me fifteen thousand dollars. Right?" Smith nodded in sullen agreement. Eddie could see he didn't like being told what to do, not calling the shots. Just too damn bad. No more crap from the big man. Hey, they'd been equalized.

Eddie pulled the battered Ford up at the mouth of the ravine, where he could see Smith standing beside the Range Rover. As Smith approached the truck, Eddie slipped out of the passenger's side and stood by the truck, resting his forearms against the side of the bed. He was very glad he had listened to his voice. He didn't trust this Smith at all. The mounted head lay in the back of the truck, covered with a plastic tarp. Smith was going to be really surprised.

Eddie watched the tall figure clad in clean khakis and straw hat cross the road with purposefully confident strides and lean against the opposite side of the truck bed as casually as if he were stepping up to a bar.

"Well?" Smith cocked a trimmed eyebrow.

Eddie reached over with a pocketknife and cut the cord holding the plastic tarp in place, then lifted it back, exposing the mounted head. Smith's face lost its blandness. His eyes widened with excitement. "That's good. That's really good." He looked back up at Eddie. "You didn't say that you had mounted the head. Damn good, too." He nodded to himself, his gaze on the ram's head, unable to take his eyes off the prize.

Eddie grinned with pleasure. Score one for the Indians—no, two. The big man had lost his cool, practically drooled, and he had complimented Eddie's work. The compliment should be worth a few bucks. "So how about the dough?" He looked up and down the road, furrowing his face in a furtive grimace. This would be a bad time for a car to come by.

Smith encompassed Eddie with his open and frank expression, the one he used to engender complete confidence. "I don't have the cash with me. I'd be foolish to carry that sort of money around." Eddie's good mood evaporated. He was gonna get fucked—again. He started to protest, but Smith raised his hand. "But I do have my checkbook."

"Come on, asshole. I take the check. You stop payment. No way."

"Wait a minute, Eddie, think it through," Smith said, his reasonable voice smoothing the ruffles. "If I did that, you'd still have the check—the check that connects me with the hunting incident. I think we are at what's called a standoff. I can't afford not to pay you. You have me at a disadvantage, Eddie. I have to trust you. Besides, as you said yourself, what's a few bucks to a rich dude like me?"

Eddie looked thoughtful. "How much cash you got in that money clip?" He gestured toward Smith's pocket.

"Not much, Eddie, maybe another twelve hundred."

Twelve hundred, better than a poke in the eye with a sharp stick. That was for sure. "So give me a check and the cash. Look at the work, man." He pointed at the mounted head staring awkwardly skyward over his shoulder. "Mounting the head wasn't part of the deal. That's extra."

Smith sighed in resignation. "As I said, it's beautiful work, Eddie. Okay, it's a deal." He reached across the bed of the truck and took Eddie's hard little brown hand in his soft white one. Eddie was grinning like the cat that had swallowed the canary. He didn't hear the voice.

The light was fading fast. The sun had dropped behind the western escarpment and the still, clear air was beginning to chill. Eddie poured another can of oil in the truck. Man this had been easy. Maybe too easy, the voice said. He glanced up and watched Smith hurry back to the climate-controlled interior of the Range Rover. They were both anxious to get out of there.

•

As Smith opened the rear door of the Range Rover, he heard Eddie's truck sputter into life. He'd have to hurry. He pulled the leather shooting case to him and let the hinged top and front down, revealing boxes of ammunition: 9-mm, .30-caliber carbine, .357 Magnum, and .300 Magnum. He pulled five .300 Magnums from the box, the brass casings gleaming in the half-light, and pushed them into the Weatherby's magazine. He slammed the rear hatch shut and hurried to the driver's side, shoved the rifle into the front passenger's seat, and started the Rover. He'd have just enough time for the right shot. He pulled out after Eddie's truck. He was at least a quarter mile behind him, but Eddie had to slow for the wash, and the wash was directly below a bend in the road that he would reach before Eddie reached the wash. It would be a downhill shot, maybe 250 yards. Really not that difficult.

He pulled over on the shoulder, stepped out into the dusk, and listened. He heard the truck coughing down the canyon at a snail's pace, coming closer, but still a bit too far away. He began to wonder if he was wasting his time. The truck would probably break down and the little shit would die of exposure, or asphyxiate from his own breath.

Then again, it was time to put Eddie out of his misery. As the truck came within range, he steadied the rifle against the hood and located the battered cab in the sight, shifting around in the crosshairs. Despite the waning light, it was going slowly enough to follow in the scope. He waited as the truck slowed to approach the drop into the wash. It was creeping along, almost stopped. He fixed the crosshairs on Eddie's head, just in front of his left ear, took up the slack, and squeezed. There was a metallic click, metal on metal. He yanked open the bolt and ejected a live round, then slammed the bolt forward, chambering another round. He found Eddie's head again and squeezed. Click, metal on metal. He removed the bolt and felt the bolt face. No firing pin was protruding. Someone had blunted the firing pin, damaged his rifle.

He could hear the truck grunting and chugging its way across the wash. The little shit was getting away. The goddamn Indian had his check. He'd have to catch him. Make sure Eddie didn't have a chance to expose him, make absolutely sure he didn't leave Jawbone Canyon alive. If he hurried, and he would hurry, he could catch him before he reached the highway.

## 25

•

"I don't go in caves." Roy peered into the darker reaches of the mine tunnel. They had drunk their fill of water at the spring, so much so that climbing up the talus slope and then around the mine tailings had been difficult. They felt heavy, full of water, but still thirsty, the onset of dehydration. The seemingly indestructible troll had slipped and fallen on a sharp rock, cutting his shin, crying out with pain. Blood seeped through the front of his pant leg, staining the faded denim a purplish blue. Now they stood in the waning heat, staring into the darkness of a mine tunnel, as if the looking itself would make something appear.

Frank wondered why Roy didn't go into caves. Was it because he was claustrophobic like himself, or was it because he was afraid of cave-ins, spiders, snakes, bugs? So far, Roy hadn't shown much concern about dangers, remaining calm, deliberate, almost laconic. Frank filed it away: Doesn't go into caves.

"So where is it, Eddie?"

"Hey, it's in there. He said he put it back in the tunnel to keep it away from animals and stuff. It's in there."

"How're you going to find it in the dark?" Hickey sat cross-legged in the tiny patch of shade cast by the western shoulder of the mine entrance. He produced a joint from his shirt pocket and lit it with a wooden match. "Goin' to light matches, light a candle in the dark?" He laughed softly.

Frank gave a triumphant grin, as Eddy might. "I'll use this." He held up a small flashlight about two and a half inches long and three-quarters of an inch thick. It was attached to his key chain. "It's got a special battery." He twisted the head of the flashlight and a tiny bulb came on. "It'll work great in the mine. Besides, I've been in there before. *No problema.*"

"Let's hope not, Eddie. Let's hope it's a 'piece of cake.'" The sandy voice was barely audible in the breeze. "You can show Hickey where it is. That way, you both come out."

Jason stood near the mouth of the tunnel, mute and still, eyes squeezed shut. Roy touched Jason's arm. Jason squeezed his eyes more tightly. Roy guided him, turning him around to face away from the tunnel and walking him over to the edge of the clearing, where the tailings sloped steeply away. "Sit down here, Jace, and just turn around and don't look. Watch for the animals and things. You're not going in the cave, Jace."

The bright little eyes came open. "Hickey goes in."

"And Hickey comes out. Caves don't hurt Hickey." Frank had been following the exchange, shifting his gaze from the pale face to the red one. There was real terror on Jason's face and a sort of crooked tenderness on the whitened flesh of Roy Miller. They'd experienced something together, something that unnerved them.

"What the fuck you staring at?" Roy glared at Frank.

"Nothing, man. Only wondering what shook Jason there."

"Don't worry about it, Eddie." The calm had returned. "You've got your own problems. You haven't completed your mission yet, finding the head. See Eddie, it's simple logic, right? If the head's there, then Dr. Sorensen's going to be here, too, just like you said. If there's no head, then you lied to us, Eddie. And liars burn in hell"—he paused, fixing his pale face on Frank's—"and other places, too. So you go on back in the tunnel and show Hickey you've been telling the truth. Then we'll wait for the doctor to show up, making his rounds. You follow?"

Frank nodded, glancing over at Hickey, who was taking a deep toke on the joint. He grinned up at Frank. "A little grass and you can see in the dark, man."

Roy bent over Jason's leg, looking at the blood oozing from the purple welt on his shin. The thick, curly red hair made the bruise appear less an injury than a tufted growth, except for the blood.

Clearly, it was painful. Jason had struggled the last hundred yards, complaining in a childlike voice, "My leg hurts, Roy." Then after a few minutes, he'd announced it again, as if it were a new discovery. "My leg hurts. It really hurts, Roy." Roy Miller seemed surprisingly patient, helping Jason over the difficult places. It never ceased to puzzle Frank, what made people tick. If Miller was capable of such tenderness, was he, Frank Flynn, capable of deliberate violence? Perhaps. Perhaps they all were. And, these people were monstrous, like a disease laying waste to all they touched.

•

"You first, man." Hickey stood at the mouth of the tunnel, the breeze blowing the graying ponytail across the side of his face. Frank stepped into the twilight of the tunnel, letting his eyes adjust. Soon it would be dark, then so black, the darkness would be complete. He hadn't been in the mine since he and Jimmy Tecopa explored its tunnels and shafts when they were kids, oblivious of the danger. That was before he got stuck in the chute, all those years ago. Now the tunnel seemed low and cramped and not nearly so big. They had come to the first turn much too soon. He remembered it as being a long way, but it couldn't have been more than fifty feet from the entrance. Without the light behind them, the darkness closed in. Frank turned on the flashlight. Its beam illuminated a circle of light about eighteen inches in diameter if he kept it pointed close to the ground, and that's where he kept it, following the narrow rails laid along the tunnel. There was a shaft after the turn, but first there was an ore car.

"Slow down, man. I can't see where I'm putting my feet."

"Just stay behind me. You'll be all right."

"I said slow down."

Frank waited for Hickey to catch up, shining the light backward so he could see the floor of the tunnel. "What's the deal with being afraid to go into tunnels?"

Hickey stumbled in the darkness. "Who's afraid? You see me here tripping around in the dark, right?"

"Not you, man, those other guys. I thought the short guy, Jason, was going to cry." Frank shined the light forward along the narrow tracks as Hickey shuffled forward, his footsteps muffled by the dust.

"Shine the light back here, asshole."

He came up near Frank, breathing in shallow gasps. Frank could smell the sweet, acrid odor of pot from Hickey's breath, mixed with the tangy smell of unwashed flesh.

"Not that it's any of your fucking business, but they were locked in a cellar when they were kids, so they don't like dark places. And in case you think Roy ain't up to coming in here if he has to, forget it, 'cause Roy ain't afraid of a fucking thing."

Frank started down the tunnel, moving the flashlight beam from side to side. He stepped up the pace, pulling away from Hickey's tentative stumbling. He had to stay far enough ahead of Hickey to see the rifle first. He'd grab it and cut the light. Then there would be two men in the darkness with guns, and things would even out. He'd have a chance.

So far, he'd seen no sign of the head or the rifle, but clearly someone had been in the tunnel. There were occasional tracks in the soft dust, going both ways, in and out. The flashlight beam illuminated the back of a small ore car resting on the tracks. It was as he remembered it, an inverted pyramid with a flat bottom, only smaller. He and Jimmy had tried to push it along the track years ago, but it had been too heavy for a couple of kids. If someone used the mine as a hiding place, it was clearly the best place to stash something. His heart began to pound. Hickey would see him stop and be on him in a few steps. He'd have to be quick.

He kept the flashlight low until he was almost on the ore car; then he swung the beam into the interior—rock and gravel, nothing more. He searched the ore car again. There was nothing—no head, no rifle. That damned Eddie had lied to him, and now he was one of the walking dead.

"What's that, man?"

He and Jimmy had gone beyond the ore car, sidling along the

narrow bit of floor to the left of the shaft. They had tossed rocks into the dark to see if it was bottomless. It wasn't. They could hear the rocks hit, a long way down. Even the planks that had been laid down alongside the shaft to provide the footing from giving way at each step were crumbling into dust.

"Hey, man, what's that?"

Frank cut the light. The darkness was total, suffocating. He began edging himself along the side of the tunnel, keeping close to wall. Bits of dirt trickled down the side and hit the floor.

"I can hear you moving around, man. This isn't going to do you no fucking good."

Frank held himself motionless. He hoped Hickey's sense of direction was disoriented by the absence of light. Hickey had the Glock.

"Turn the light back on, asshole. You ain't going nowhere."

"It just went out. Hang on a minute. I'm trying to fix it." Frank eased farther along the ledge. He placed his hands against the side of the tunnel for balance and bent his right leg, feeling out into the darkness with his left—nothing. A moment of giddiness rushed through him. The shaft was directly behind him.

"Turn on the goddamned light, Eddie. If I come out of here by myself, you can forget about seeing daylight again." The easy confidence had eroded. "Eddie?"

"Yeah, yeah, I'm trying. It's stuck. Just hang in there." He'd moved along the ledge another couple of feet. Again he steadied himself and reached behind him with the searching foot. The toe of his boot hit something. There it was again, the floor of the tunnel. He was beyond the shaft. He stepped carefully back, breathing with relief. "I think I've got it. Just a minute. He turned the flashlight on again, pointing it down the tunnel, away from the ore car and Hickey. "Hey, here it is, the head, right here."

"Give me some fucking light."

Frank stood across from Hickey, the shaft between them, invisible in the darkness. He turned back, holding the light up at face level. "This way, man."

"I can't see shit. Lower the light."

Frank lowered the light to thigh level, the small beam swallowed in the darkness. "Just go along the side of the ore car. Walk toward the light."

"Shit." Hickey's voice rasped in the dark.

Frank heard the crumbling sound, the sound of earth slipping as Hickey fell. He went silently. Frank imagined his arms flailing uselessly as he fell into darkness. He heard earth being dislodged and a grunt of pain as Hickey's body encountered an uneven protrusion of rock before striking the bottom with a soft thud.

He waited, his ears straining for sound. "Hickey?" he whispered into the enveloping blackness. "Hickey, you all right?" You all right? That was ludicrous. He was either dead or badly broken up. He shined the light down the shaft, the tiny beam throwing an ineffectual ray into the darkness. Hickey was in that darkness now, and for the moment, Frank was safe, but he felt removed and distant, as if he had fallen into the shaft with Hickey and lay smothered in a place where there was no light.

Frank worked feverishly in the dark, lifting the larger chunks of rock from the ore car. He was careful not to let any debris fall into the shaft. The idea of the rocks hitting Hickey's body sickened him. If he was going to have a chance to get away, the ore car might give him an advantage, but first he needed to be able to move it. He shined the light into the interior of the car. It was mostly empty now, just some dirt and gravel. He went to the front of the car and tugged. It didn't budge. He couldn't go to the rear of the car and push without the danger of falling into the shaft. Why wouldn't it move? The tunnel angled down and out. There was a gentle downgrade leading to the opening so that the filled ore cars would be easier to push. He shined his light on the front wheels. They were rusty, but they didn't look like they were rusted solid. The dry air and the shelter of the tunnel had slowed the process of erosion. The wheels were more dirty than frozen. He looked at the back wheels—same thing. Then he noticed a small piece of wood protruding from between the track and the wheel. They were chocked. Of course, they were chocked against the grade for loading.

He shined the light around, looking for something to block the front wheels after he freed the ones in the rear. He selected a wedge-shaped piece of ore and placed it on the track, where he could push it under the wheel with the back of his foot. Then he placed his back against the ore car and shoved. It went back surprisingly easy. Too easy. He was in danger of shoving it into the shaft. He stood up and grabbed the rock in the dark, pushing it forward until it hit the wheel, catching the car before it could roll forward. He shined the light on the rear wheels and then on the track, where a compressed sliver of wood no more than half an inch thick lay where it had been placed by a hand of someone now long dead. He reached forward and brushed it aside, making sure the track was clear except for the rock he had placed in front.

Time to take a look outside.

As he came to the bend in the tunnel, the waning light etched the rectangular entrance against the dark. He switched off the light and let his eyes adjust. He could see out, but they couldn't seen in, not as long as he kept the flashlight off. He wondered if they knew they could be seen from within. He moved with care, placing his feet in the powdery dust, avoiding rocks and rubble, silent in his approach. Jason sat with his back to the tunnel, where he could look down into the canyon. He rocked gently back and forth, humming a wordless lullaby in a rhythmic monotone. The bush of red hair was wreathed in a golden halo as the last of the sunlight touched the canyon walls. Frank was momentarily moved to go to him, to assure him that everything was okay. Then he remembered the empty bits of bright blue that glittered from the bearded face. Damaged and broken beyond repair.

There was no sign of Roy Miller. Frank approached the opening, scanning the surroundings. Jason held the .458 Winchester across his lap. Apparently, he was alone. Hickey's pack lay where he had tossed it, but the canteens were missing. He searched as much of the terrain as he could see. Where was Roy Miller? He must have gone to refill the canteens at the spring. It would take him at least half an hour. How long had he been gone? If he tried to sneak by, sooner or later Jason would see him and begin shooting. He would be an open target, completely exposed on the rocks and unable to run without fear of falling down the slope. The rocky ground meant slow going. Even a poor shot would eventually hit him. He thought about what Hickey had said and the look of fear on Jason's face. Perhaps he could scare him. Get him to drop the rifle. It was his best chance. Either that or hide in the mine until they came for him, a live man waiting to join a dead one.

He hurried back into the tunnel, nearly falling, cursing under his breath. He found the ore car, kicked loose the rock he'd jammed under the front wheel, and tugged. At first, the car didn't want to move. Then it gave, inching forward, a yard, ten feet, moving slowly down the track. He stepped to the back of the car and shoved. It picked up speed, gathering momentum. By the time he reached the bend, he had it going at a trot. Then he began to bellow.

The last thing Frank remembered seeing was the figure of Jason raising the rifle, eyes bright, the small mouth pursed in a circle of fear. Then he dove for the floor of the tunnel, letting go of the ore car. The smashing thunderclap from the .458 and his headlong dive into the ground interrupted his sense of time. The throbbing pain from his left elbow wrenched him back into reality. Apparently, he had banged his arm on one of the steel rails as he hit the ground. He drew himself to his knees and peered out of the tunnel mouth. The ore car had stopped about six or seven feet outside the entrance, where the rails disappeared into dirt and debris. Jason was gone, but where? He rose to his feet and came out into the open, keeping the ore car in front of him. It had a round hole about half an inch in diameter punched into the forward wall; the back wall had a ragged gash torn in the metal, an area nearly as big as the palm of his hand. It was definitely a dead monster. Jason must have just pointed and pulled the trigger. The scope would have been useless, in the way. He was very, very glad he hadn't done something foolish and tried to rush Jason, counting on his inability to find a target in the scope at close quarters. Holes like that would have been in what was left of his body.

The stillness was complete, as if the rifle shot and his yelling had never occurred. The hoarse cry of a raven pierced the silence. A pair of them were at eye level, swooping toward the rock face on the far side of the canyon. Headed for home. He breathed deeply and forced himself to think about what to do. Stepping from behind the ore car, he approached the edge of the level ground where he had last seen the redheaded Jason and looked down the steep face of the tailings. Jason lay near the base of the tailings, his body at an odd angle, like a broken Raggedy Andy. There was still a faint haze of dust in the air where he had tumbled down the rock-strewn slope. Frank realized he must have been propelled backward by the tremendous recoil of the .458.

Roy Miller stood next to the broken body, his white face looking like an erasure mark against the landscape. Frank stared in fascination as the tiny figure began to emit a moan. It started deep and low, filling the canyon with anguish and rage. The rifle lay halfway down the slope, maybe in working order, maybe not, certainly not the scope. The Glock lay in the mine shaft with Hickey. Frank was sure he hadn't seen Miller with a gun, but now didn't seem like the time to pat him down.

As he watched, Miller began scrambling up the slope toward the rifle. There was no way Frank could reach it before he did. Miller probably figured he had him trapped, and it was true, *if* Frank used the trail that skirted up and over the tumbled boulders at the far edge of the canyon. It was the long way. Frank knew another way. He set out across the talus slope, angling downward and across the uneven ground to intersect with the canyon near the ancient rock blind. He would have to beat Miller down the canyon and get to his truck before Miller got to him.

## 26

•

Dr. Michael Sorensen wasn't used to being bested, and the fact that he had been outwitted by an unwashed semiderelict did little to alleviate his rising sense of frustration and rage. But all was not lost. With any luck at all, he should overtake the slick little shit well before he reached the highway, settle up—so to speak—retrieve his check and money, and be on his way. There would be absolutely nothing to connect him to the Indian, nothing to connect him to decapitated bighorn sheep, and no one to take pleasure in his having been humiliated by a third-rate criminal with bad breath. Blunting the firing pin did indeed signal some forethought on the Indian's part, perhaps genetic craftiness, but then again, it was stupid to assume that he would get away before Sorensen figured out what had happened. He would make this absolutely clear.

He wheeled the Range Rover easily down the dirt road, going at least twenty miles an hour faster than the so-called Redhawk's pathetic junker. Eddie Laguna, the man to whom he had made out the check, couldn't be very far ahead of him. He strained for a glimpse of the battered truck in the twilight and almost drove over the embankment. He stamped on the brake pedal just in time to keep from dropping into the sand wash. This was the way Laguna had come all right. This is where the Indian's thick skull had appeared in the crosshairs. He studied the wash in the dim light, looking at where the track followed the sandy bottom and disappeared. It looked like slow going. On his left, he could just make out a faint dirt track that skirted the wash, following the top of the embankment. It appeared to be on solid ground and therefore faster. He eased the Range Rover onto the track near some sort of wooden sign on which was a cartoon figure of a smirking crow smoking a pipe. Primitive bullshit.

He punched the gas. The Range Rover's all-wheel-drive feature kept the vehicle in a straight path, chewing its way through the crust to the softer earth below. Another sign: MEET YOUR FATE. Wonderful! No doubt hapless hippies caught up in crystals and extraterrestrial crap had posted their pathetic ruminations to be read by little green men. He squinted ahead. He must be gaining on the Indian and his rust bucket. Voilà! There it was. A single red taillight winked in the deep gray of evening. A dim cone of yellow bobbed along ahead of the silhouette that was Eddie Laguna's truck. Not so slick after all, Redhawk. Pull up alongside, wave him to a friendly stop. Bang, bang—another good Indian.

The Range Rover began pulling sharply to the right, toward the wash. He wrestled the wheel away from the edge just in time. He realized he must have hit a patch of sand. The heavy vehicle plowed ahead, laboring as if it were down in the sandy bottom, although it wasn't. Up on the embankment, the ground was reasonably firm. He gave it more gas, but the response was sluggish at best. He was no longer gaining on Laguna's truck; it was still at least four or five hundred yards ahead. Despite his best efforts to keep the Rover on the track, it wallowed from side to side like a crippled beast. Finally, it could do no more than creep. He had the wheel turned away from the wash, but the Rover could only lunge ahead in labored increments, chewing away at the soft soil. He cursed under his breath, let up on the gas, and the Rover settled to a heavy stop. He got out and walked around the blocky body, which gleamed in the faint light. Shit. He had a flat. The right front tire was punctured. Damn his luck, damn the Indian. The right rear was flat, as well. He felt the blood pounding at his temples, his heart thumping in his chest. He watched in rising frustration as the Indian's taillight disappeared in the distance.

Sorensen closed his eyes and breathed deeply. The situation had changed. He always made it a point to deal with the realities confronting him. Keeping his eye on hard facts had been the key to his success. Now he needed to see if he could get out of here. That was first. The rest would follow. He could catch up with the Indian later, definitely before the man tried to cash the check. At the very least, he could stop payment Monday morning. There was no way he was going to let himself be cheated out of fifteen thousand dollars by an ignorant little shit.

If he could get the spare on the front wheel, he was sure that the Rover would have enough traction to move out with one flat tire. He switched on the interior light and began reading the manual to discover just where they had hidden the jack. He thumbed through the manual until he discovered a drawing of the jack's location. The handle was located under the backseat. The fucking spare was located under the vehicle. What's more, he didn't have a flashlight. He hadn't planned on driving around the damned desert at night.

Fumbling around in the dark, it took close to half an hour to take out the jack and handle and get it lined up under the vehicle. At first, it exerted pressure on the vehicle, taking up weight from the right side of the Rover, but then it stopped lifting and began burying itself in the ground. He released the pressure and the Rover settled its weight back on the flattened tires. He began frantically searching for something to put under the jack. Next to an outcropping, he found a flat rock that seemed perfect. It was at least eight or nine inches wide and a couple of feet long. It had broken away from the larger rock upthrust and lay on the ground in a darkened oval. A large scorpion skittered toward him as he lifted up the edge of the rock. He stomped on it repeatedly, his heart pounding with repugnance, fear, and pent-up anger.

From the exertion spent killing the scorpion, carrying the rock back to the vehicle, and then clearing away enough dirt to get rock and jack under the Range Rover, he had worked up a sweat despite the coolness of the night air. His soft cotton shirt felt clammy and cold.

He began turning the jack handle. At last, the front tire was clear. Placing the lug wrench over one of the bolts holding the wheel, he pushed down as hard as he could, leaning his weight into it. The handle remained rigid, the bolt secure. He needed more leverage. He stood up and put his foot on the wrench handle and bounced up and down, trying to loosen the bolt. Cursing with frustration, he placed his hands on the hood for balance and jumped with his full weight against the jack handle. The Land Rover shuddered and slipped toward him, crashing back onto the desert floor and throwing him backward into a clump of creosote bush. He lay there, conscious only of feeling helpless. The silence was unnerving. He strained to listen, hoping for the sound of an engine. Nothing, nothing but an occasional skittering in the brush. According to the map, it was about twenty-six miles to highway 395. And it was getting cold. He decided it was too far and too dark to take a chance on getting lost. Being near the vehicle felt safe. After all, somebody might come along and give him a ride, although that wasn't likely at night. He should stick with the vehicle. He shivered against the cold. How could it be so damn hot during the day and so cold at night? He'd try to get some sleep, wait until morning, and then head for the highway. Somebody was bound to come along.

He slept half-sitting up in the front seat, dozing off and on. He tried stretching out in back, but somehow it felt too vulnerable lying where he couldn't see out.

He woke again for the umpteenth time and looked into the night. A dark silhouette of skyline rimmed the paler sky, signaling the dawn. He pushed open the door, stood and stretched, and thought about coffee and orange juice. Orange juice would be good. Then he realized he was thirsty. He had drunk a couple of diet Cokes yesterday afternoon. The empties lay where he had tossed them on the floor. But there were no full ones and only two water bottles. He'd been limited to a tiny ice chest, but at the time it had seemed okay; besides, he hated drinking warm soft drinks, warm beer, or warm water, for that matter, warm anything but coffee. He kept his liquor of choice, Absolut vodka, in the freezer, and when he poured it into an iced crystal tumbler, it flowed like syrup, smooth and soft. Enough of that. He'd just have to get going. Twenty-six miles should take him no more than seven or eight hours, at the worst. He was sure to see somebody long before that. The dirt road had been recently graded, the soil pushed up into berms on either side. So that meant there had to be some traffic.

He started off down the upper track along the embankment at a leisurely pace, waiting to warm up before kicking into gear. The warm breeze returned, pushing into his face. The exercise and the balmy breeze felt invigorating. He picked up the pace. He knew he could walk close to four miles an hour for an extended time. He spent five or six hours a week on the treadmill, doing 4.3 miles an hour. This was simply another obstacle to overcome, a task to be performed, something with which he was completely comfortable.

In three hours of strenuous walking, he had failed to cover enough ground. He realized the situation needed reassessment, although he didn't think of it in quite that way. For one thing, the uneven surface prevented him from maintaining a pace of four miles an hour. The ground was either too rocky and hard, which hurt his feet, or it was soft and sandy, which made for slow going. His pace was more like three miles an hour, and it was work. His initial optimism had evaporated. It would have been okay if he hadn't had to make time. But he had to make time, because it was getting very warm. The morning breeze had turned into a hot blast of air blowing steadily from the south, directly in his face. It occurred to him that he probably should have tried to walk out at night while it was cool, rather than fight the heat, but that was looking back, and he never looked back. Regrets simply dragged people down.

He took refuge next to a large creosote bush, seeking some shelter from the heat and the relentless wind. The thin, pliable branches tipped with their tiny dark leaves tossed wildly about, tracing nervous shadow patterns on the desert floor. Sorensen felt a wave of panic. What if no one used the road? It had become clear that the highway was much too far away to reach on foot in this everlasting wind. He needed help, needed someone to come along and give him a ride and a drink of water. He was terribly thirsty.

By the time Sorensen reached the section of the road that climbed up to the ridgeline that overlooked Jawbone Canyon, he found himself staggering with increasing frequency. His legs felt weak and heavy. Every time he stopped, it became more difficult to get moving again. He was having difficulty concentrating. The only thing that he seemed to be able to think about was water—well, not water so much as drinking something liquid, alleviating his thirst. Anything wet. He was dimly aware that soon it would be impossible to keep going, but somehow that didn't seem as important as finding something to drink.

His eyes fell on a barrel cactus, and he felt a rush of relief. All he had to do was cut off the top and there would be water. He knelt and tried to cut away the top with his pocketknife, but he was too unsteady, and the cactus spines kept hooking into his skin. He sat down heavily in front of the cactus. That was better. He had more leverage. He began to saw the blade through the tough skin. His hands bled from the wounds, but soon there would be liquid, something with which to quench his all-consuming thirst. He made a circular cut like taking the top off a pumpkin, but there was no stem for a handle. He plunged the blade in at an angle and lifted. The flesh of the cactus refused to let go. The blade popped out from the pressure he was exerting, his hand flying up and the knife nearly stabbing him in the face.

He cut more deeply into the firm flesh and once more angled the knife blade in and lifted. It wouldn't budge. He cut frantically away at the hole, enlarging it, making it big enough to get his hand in so that he could get to the juice. The ground around him was littered with bits of cactus, its green skin and creamy flesh turning leathery in the sun and hot wind. He managed to get his hand in the hole, but there was no water, just tough cactus flesh. There was supposed to be water. Where was it? It was a lie. Anger lent him the strength to struggle to his feet. His hat fell to the ground, but he was too exhausted to retrieve it. He managed to stagger back to the graded road before he fell. It was the first time. The second time came fifty yards farther up the road. He actually made it to the uphill grade, almost another hundred yards, before going down the third time. He struggled to his feet and tottered a few steps before falling onto the sunbaked berm where the grade had been cut into the hillside. Even yet, he hoped for a Good Samaritan to come along and bring an end to his suffering.

## 27

•

Frank slipped along the left side of the canyon, keeping in the shade as much as possible. When he reached the broken boulders that formed the western edge of the small meadow, he headed out across the first of the table rocks without looking back. He felt amazingly calm. Either he would make it or he wouldn't. His other option was the chute, and for him, the choice had been made two decades ago, when he had become wedged in the narrow rock passage. He headed for the drop. Once there, he would gain precious time and distance. Only this time, he'd take time to slow down and hit the sandy bottom with a degree of caution. The alternative was unthinkable. He imagined lying injured on the ground, waiting for Roy Miller to find him. He'd rather take his chances on a bullet in the back.

He came to a stop near the edge of the drop. The floor of the narrow defile was invisible in the shadowed grays of twilight. He lowered himself to a sitting position, took a measured breath, and pushed himself away from his perch. He landed without incident, rolling with the fall as soon as his feet touched the ground. He'd saved at least a half an hour over following the trail along the canyon wall. Even if Miller had seen him disappear, Frank doubted that he would chance a drop into the dark without knowing what lay in wait, or how to get out.

Now the thing to do was pace himself on the hike out, move quickly and avoid accident. He was without a canteen, but the evening cool had supplanted the heat of day, and he knew where to look for water. He worked his way back into the narrowing canyon walls toward the upstream end, where the arroyo ran fast with runoff from the thunderstorms that swept up the western face of the Panamints. He knelt down and, digging into the soft sand a few inches, felt the dampness that he had hoped would be there. After going down about a foot, his fingers were wet. Another few inches and water puddled into the hole. He took the kerchief from around his neck and soaked it. Then he squeezed it into his mouth. He was glad he couldn't see exactly what he was doing, because he knew that the water seeping into the hole would be brown and muddy. He could taste the damp earthiness of it. No matter. The picture of Miller's upturned face flashed through his mind, urging him to hurry, but he forced himself to stick with the process until he took in enough moisture to see him through to the bottom of the canyon, where he'd find his truck and would be able to really satisfy his thirst from one of the plastic jugs he kept behind the seat.

For a moment, Frank stood quietly in the dark arroyo, thinking of the walk down the canyon, then thinking of Linda and his caboose, the soft yellow light from the cupola brushing the piñon and juniper. He filled his lungs with the evening air, taking slow, deep breaths, preparing himself. A deep rose light flushed the sky for a moment, and just as quickly the land plunged into night. A soft breeze pulled at his clothing in small gusts. By morning, the wind would rise, a hot wind that would funnel through the canyon in a keening voice, a wind that came from the mouths of spirits long gone, singing wordless songs. He pushed thoughts of Roy Miller and the dead men in the canyon from his mind and concentrated on reaching his truck.

He set off at a moderate pace, moving down the canyon almost without noise or noticeable effort, slipping silently through the night shadows, taking pleasure in the rhythm of his movement. Would Linda have called Meecham? He didn't think so. It would have been too late, well past five o'clock before she was sure he wasn't coming. He wondered how long she stood waiting in the sun, her annoyance bubbling into anger. He smiled. How much he wanted to see her. To let her know that he was all right.

Damn that Eddie, and damn me for a fool's fool for expecting him to be straight up, he thought. How many times did he have to relearn that people acted according to their own lights? Counting on people like Eddie Laguna was nothing more than wishful thinking. But Eddie shouldn't have lied. The lie had nearly cost Frank his life, and he wasn't out of it yet.

Throwing stones in a glass house, his mother's voice whispered in his head. He hadn't exactly lied to Dave Meecham, but he had withheld bits and pieces of truth. He knew it had been a deceitful act, worse because he'd understood the nature of his intent, and Dave Meecham was a friend. He would have to call Dave as soon as he could get to a phone. He sighed. That would be some conversation, explaining all this, explaining the two dead men, only this time he hadn't just been a corpse finder; he'd been a corpse maker.

•

The sight of his truck filled him with a wave of relief. There it was, waiting for him, just as he'd left it, familiar and reassuring. The van Hickey had been driving loomed behind the truck. He'd have to do something about that, but first the .45. He unlocked the cab, felt around under the seat until he touched the rough-checked grip. Holding the .45 in his hand produced a surge of power. He shook his head. Frank Flynn, gun nut. He thought about Hickey's death and the relief that swept over him when Hickey had fallen into the darkness, body thumping against the rocks. Relief? Oh, more than that. Now he wanted to kill Roy Miller, and he knew he might relish it. He could think of killing Miller as stamping out evil, but he knew better, for the evil had touched him, and he yearned to embrace it.

He tucked the pistol inside his belt with the clip-on holster and then removed a jug of water from behind the seat. He tipped it up to drink, glad that the water was warm; he could drink as much of it as he liked without the shock of the cold. He would maroon Miller here until others could come and take him. He wanted to find Linda and go home. Go to the creek and sit in the icy water, and let it wash him clean.

But for now, he had to disable the van and make tracks; that was the plan. He remembered Roy going back to make sure that Hickey had locked it up, carefully checking each door. Roy Miller was careful and methodical, as well as observant.

Frank found a fist-size rock and heaved it at the driver's window. The safety glass shattered, forming a concave pocket, the starburst pattern catching bits of light. Frank picked up the rock from where it had fallen next to the door and hurled it again with greater force. This time, it smashed through, making a sufficiently large hole for him to reach in and unlock the door.

He shined his tiny flashlight around as he moved into the van's interior. There was a large toolbox bolted against the right side of the open compartment. Bungee cords held spare motorcycle tires, belts, and an assortment of parts and tools against the wall. A clear plastic box lay on the floor next to the toolbox. It contained stacks of small drawers filled with miscellaneous nuts, bolts, screws, cotter pins, and other bits and pieces necessary for motorcycle road repairs. This was the party van, the mother ship, with tools, parts, and booze. It made long road trips possible for the Millers' little social club. At the rear of the compartment, there were three twin-size mattresses. A cheap, grubby sleeping bag lay on the mattress along the right-hand side of the van. A foam-rubber pillow without a pillowcase protruded from the opening. The mattress on the opposite side was covered with a blanket that must have been pinned from underneath, neat and clean. The sleeping bag lay carefully folded on top. The center bed reflected the same neat hand, a couple of wool blankets folded with matching corners, topped by a smaller tattered cover, a child's blanket made of flammable material no longer legal. He picked it up, the soft folds of cheap blue synthetic cloth worn so thin that the blanket felt almost weightless. He refolded it and placed it back where he had found it, wondering why he was taking the trouble, since the owner now lay among the rocks in Surprise Canyon.

He went through the toolbox and found a pair of pliers and a large screwdriver and took down a battery strap hanging from the opposite wall. He had things to do. He flipped the hood release and went to work. It took about ten minutes to remove the battery and put it in the back of his truck. Miller wouldn't be using the van for a while. Now it was time to leave. He turned the key in his truck and listened to the comforting purr and clatter of the engine. He eased the truck forward and then brought it to a stop. He lifted a half-full jug of water from behind the seat and carried it to the van, leaving it on the driver's seat. Marooned was one thing, thirsty another.

•

Roy couldn't understand what had happened to Eddie Laguna. One minute, the Indian had been there staring down at him, and then he had crossed over the rock slide, keeping next to the jumble of huge boulders that marked the end of the meadow as he headed toward the bottom of the canyon. Getting the rifle hadn't taken Roy more than five minutes, but by that time Laguna had disappeared into the rocks. Roy took the trail they had come by, up and around the wall of boulders, then down into the canyon below, planning to cut the Indian off. Eventually, Laguna would have to come down the same way for his truck, and there was no way he'd be able to get past Roy. The canyon was too narrow. Shooting him would be a last resort. It wasn't part of his plan. He had very special plans for Eddie Laguna, or whoever he was. He wondered about that. It was like the Indian had two personalities, mostly bullshit artist, but now and then there was something quick and sharp about him that didn't fit with the rest. He'd find out in time, because he planned on having a long, slow conversation with Eddie Laguna, give him that new name.

Roy felt confident about heading off the Indian. He was making time, jogging in the flat sandy stretches, stepping along with sure-footed care over the rocky spots. Now and then he stopped and drank deeply, emptying the smaller canteen and tossing it aside after less than half an hour of walking. Going down the canyon in the evening cool was much easier than climbing up had been, but he was still thirsty from the heat and exertion. It seemed like his body couldn't get enough water, which wasn't a problem, since he had Eddie's soft half-gallon canteen. He smiled to himself. The Indian would be getting pretty thirsty.

It came as a surprise to Roy when he rounded the last bend and saw the dark shape of the van pulled over at the side of the wash. It had taken less than half the time making his way down the canyon than it had going up in the afternoon heat. Something didn't seem right, and then he realized that the Indian's truck wasn't there. How the hell could that be? How could Laguna have gotten past him? He couldn't. Not unless he could fucking fly. Roy broke into a jog. Something was definitely wrong.

When he saw the smashed window, he cursed under his breath. Someone had stolen the Indian's truck and made a try at his. He opened the driver's door. A white plastic gallon jug rested on the seat, which was covered with bits of broken glass. He set the jug on the floor and brushed the glass from the seat. Then he put his key in the ignition and turned. Nothing. No strain of a dead battery, no metallic clicking, nothing. He pulled at the hood release and found it slack. Jumping from the van, he hurried around to the front and lifted the unlatched hood. It was too dark to see. He rummaged through the glove compartment until he found a book of matches. The feeble light from the match revealed all he needed to know. Only the battery straps remained dangling in the empty compartment.

Somehow, the Indian had been here first. In a few hours, there might be cops. He didn't plan on waiting around. He retrieved the rifle from where he had left it resting against the side of the van. It would only be in his way. And it was sure to frighten off any offers of help. He stuffed it into Hickey's grimy sleeping bag. Maybe he could get it later, maybe not. The thing was to move on. He refilled the soft canteen and drank from the plastic jug. Why had the Indian left the water?

It wasn't that far to Ballarat, about eleven miles. He'd been paying attention to the odometer and the route down the wash to the dirt road that followed the power lines. When they'd come through the cluster of wooden shacks that was Ballarat, he'd seen other vehicles tucked up near some of the structures that still looked habitable. Now he took the handle from a socket wrench set and slipped it into the cargo pocket of his pants, in case he was called upon to perform roadside repairs. You never knew. He headed down the dirt track toward the intersection with the road. Not that far. Even in the dark he could make out huge support towers marching across the floor of the Panamint Valley.

# 28

•

The growl of an engine reverberated in the silence of the desert night. Roy stopped and listened, trying to discern its direction, his figure a dark silhouette, head thrust forward in concentration. He turned, homing in on the sound, his body still and motionless. There it was, coming up the valley. He could see lights lifting into the night sky, only to disappear again as the vehicle followed the rise and fall of the road tracing the contours of the land.

Roy waited for the approaching car or truck—he didn't care which. By the sound of the engine, it was probably a truck. It was moving right along, kicking up a plume of dust and leaving a swirl of shadow. Roy tossed aside his canteen before the vehicle reached him, then stood in the road, waving both arms above his head, a man in distress. He knew he would stop for a stranded stranger, but then again, predators were curious and intelligent by nature. He waved his arms some more, assuming the role of supplicant. The truck came to a halt some fifty feet before reaching the point where Roy waited, a dark stick figure caught in the headlights, his shadow funneling away behind him in a grotesque parody of human form.

A raspy voice strained over the engine noise. "Whatcha want?"

"My car got stuck in a wash. I've been walking for hours. Can you give me a ride to town—or wherever you're going. I need a drink of water and to get to a phone. You don't happen to have any water with you, do you?"

"Wait a minute." The truck eased its way forward until the driver's window was alongside where Roy stood with head down and shoulders hunched, arms dangling at his sides as if heavy with the weight of exhaustion.

"Come on around the other side and get in." The driver spoke around a cigarette hanging from the corner of his mouth.

The blocky vehicle was a much-used and much-abused International Travelall. The rear bench seat had been removed to make room for more important stuff than occasional passengers. From what Roy could see, it was full of junk—a pick, different-size shovels, and some sort of contraption he didn't recognize, something with an engine. The front seat barely contained the broken springs, which pushed against the remains of a saddle blanket that served as a seat cover.

"Just shove that stuff on the floor." The driver gestured to a pile of old magazines and newspapers scattered about on the passenger side and the floor of the cab.

"Man, am I glad to see you. I was about done in."

The truck jerked its way forward, the dash lights and the glow of the driver's cigarette dancing in the dark.

"I'm going to Ballarat. It's as far as I go." The raspy voice was thick with phlegm.

Roy found the sound disgusting, and the smell; the cab reeked of stale tobacco and whiskey fumes.

"Hey, that's great, man. Say, you got any water?"

"Reach back of the seat and grab one a them plastic bottles."

As Roy felt around in the dark, he heard the man mumbling something. "Say again? Couldn't hear you."

"I was jus' wondering how someone could be so dumb."

"How do you mean?"

"How someone could be so dumb he'd be walking around in the Panamint Valley without any water." The driver turned his head. "Don't you carry water in your car, bub?"

"Yeah." Roy nodded in the dark. "Oh yeah, but I drank it all. Wasn't figuring on getting stuck."

The driver sighed and made a sort of sucking sound of disapproval for all the fools in the world who didn't know enough to carry extra water. Roy was thinking the guy had bad manners. He watched as the driver reached between his legs and tipped a pint bottle up to his mouth, taking a couple of deep swallows. Light reflecting back from the dim headlights as they passed over a cutbank in the road temporarily illuminated the cab, revealing the driver's creased face, grim and lifeless in the pale light. He held the bottle up to the windshield, measuring the remainder against the light. "Well, shit, not enough left to be passing around." He tipped back his head, emptying the bottle, and then lifted it above his mouth, shaking out the last few drops. The truck lurched up the berm on Roy's right and scraped against a large clump of catclaw. Roy had been riding with his arm resting on the window ledge and the sharp spines lacerated his skin and tore at the sleeve of his shirt.

"Shit, watch what the fuck you're doing."

The driver grabbed the wheel, yanking the Travelall back on the graded road. "No harm done there, fella. We're doin' jus' fine."

Dark splotches of blood seeped through Roy's tattered shirtsleeve. His arm was bleeding. Flickers of light touched the outer perimeter of Roy's vision. "Hey, that was some driving there, man. Say what's you're name, mister?" Roy thrust his arm out in the dark of the cab. "Mine's Leroy Miller."

"Leeeeeroy. Whoeee." The man guffawed. The raucous laughter fueled Roy's revulsion. The stench of cheap whiskey issued from the driver's mouth in gusts of bad breath. "LeeeRoy, that's okay. Knew a Leroy in the army. He was from Florida, dumber than dog shit. Couldn't find bright objects on the ground, but he was okay." The final phrase, he mumbled to himself. Then he boomed, "Well, my name's Randall Clark, but most folks call me Randy. And they're right, too." He broke into a falsetto cackle at his own joke. "I always hated being called Randall, but Randy's okay." He reached around, fumbling for Roy's hand.

Roy took the outstretched hand firmly in his own. "Well, listen up, Randy, because I really want to thank you for all this consideration, you know. And here's a little something to show my appreciation." Roy jerked on Clark's hand, pulling him to one side, and at the same time, he drove the point of his left elbow into Clark's Adam's apple. Clark attempted to speak, but it turned into a strangled gasping for air. He clutched at his neck, trying desperately to breathe. Roy turned his attention to stopping the Travelall, stepping on the brake with his left foot and turning the ignition key with his left hand. The sudden quiet that followed the silencing of the engine was broken only by the strangling sounds of Clark's agonized effort to breathe.

"Man, that's disgusting." Roy shook his head. "Can't listen to that shit and drive. Sounds like a toilet flushing. Guess you're gonna hafta walk." He opened the passenger door and dragged the hapless Clark out of the truck, the man's head bouncing on the door frame. "Bad manners, man. You brought all this shit on yourself." He looked down at the prostrate Clark and felt better. "Gotta be going." He got back into the truck and started the engine. Leaning over to shut the passenger door, he raised his voice in a cheery farewell. "You take care now, hear."

He reached the Panamint Valley Road and swung north toward the junction with 190. He figured the Indian had about a two- or three-hour head start on him. Doubtful if he'd call in the cops, but you never knew. He had to get another vehicle. If the Indian didn't go to the police, someone would discover old Randy's body come morning, and the truck would be hot. The rest stop near Lone Pine on 395 seemed like the best bet.

Roy thought about Hickey and Jace, both gone. Truth to be told, he didn't much care about Hickey. He'd begun to be a liability anyway, always doped up or chasing squack. Knock! Knock! Who's there? Hickey. Hickey who? There it was in a nutshell, Hickey who? Nobody home most of the time. Jace had always been a liability and a trial. But he was blood, and Roy had been looking out for him, for Jace and Donnie, as far back as he could remember, and man, it hadn't been easy. Between the two of them, they could fuck up a wet dream. It was a funny feeling, both of them gone, and he felt suddenly exhilarated, freer than he ever had. Hell, he didn't have to worry about one of them doing some dumb fucking thing that would bring the law down on them. If it hadn't been for him, they both would have been in the joint anyhow. Roy was through running with guys who couldn't tie their shoelaces. He'd take care of this business and then put his skills to use around the retirement communities—love those duffers. But right now, he had to make it back to the trailer, get his stuff—especially his bike and the rest of the money. He had a couple thousand stashed, and he could make that stretch for a long time.

Maybe it was time to go back to the valley, San Bernardino or Pomona, hide out among nine million people and let things cool off. Time was on his side. After a while, people'd get careless, forget about old Roy and the Sidewinders—well, shit, Sidewinder, just one snake in his pants now. His silent laugh breathed into the night.

●

The rest stop was divided into two areas, one for cars and the other for trucks, trailers, and motor homes. Roy pulled the Travelall into the section for trucks and trailers. A motor home would do just fine. Cops never looked at motor homes. They were full of families or old people with money. Rich old farts drove motor homes with stickers that said cute things like I'M DRIVING MY KID'S INHERITANCE. They belonged to the Good Sam Club, dedicated to helping one another out. It made him want to puke.

He chose a spot under a light and raised the hood. The flashlight he found in the glove compartment made it easy for him to take off the air filter. He set it up on the curb, where it was sure to be noticed, a man with a car problem, an irresistible invitation to the Good Sams of this world, God bless 'em. He took apart the flashlight and bent back the contact so it didn't work, then draped himself under the hood. Now all he needed to do was wait for one of the good old Sams—Sam, Sam the traveling man. And it was a short wait. There were two motor homes already there, one a cheap C class, the bed over the cab of the truck, the other one a big diesel pusher. Its own-er, returning from the rest room, stopped just short of where Roy leaned over the truck's fender.

"What's the problem?" The speaker wore chinos, dress shirt, and a navy windbreaker. Kind of natty, Roy thought, trim and fit. Sort of broke the mold, not all that dufferlike, guy still had some juice.

Roy extracted himself from under the hood. "Not sure. Doesn't seem to be getting gas."

The man stood on the sidewalk, away from the truck, looking thoughtful. Roy could see that he wanted to help, but he was hesitant. The truck was thick with dust, and Roy realized he hadn't washed up since early that morning.

"Hell of a time for it to quit on me." He shook his head in disgust. "I've got a claim over in the Panamints, trying to get to a friend's wedding in L.A. tomorrow. Should've allowed more time. Supposed to meet him tonight and get cleaned up." Roy smiled. "Can't go to a wedding looking like a desert rat."

The man stepped off the curb. "What do you mine for?"

Roy grinned. "Gold." He held up his hand. "It's not the mother lode, but it's a living. And my boss don't drive me too hard."

"No kidding. Didn't know there was still gold around here."

Good old gold. Lights people's eyes right up. "Oh yeah, lots of it. You driving north or south?"

"North. Heading up to Reno."

"Well then, you went through Randsburg, one of the biggest gold-mining operations in the state." Roy thumped the flashlight into the palm of his hand and shook it. "Damn flashlight went out on me."

"Let's take it over to my rig." The man gestured toward the large, sleek motor home, one of the expensive ones built on a bus chassis. Things were looking up, looking like cash money.

"I've got a flashlight I can let you have if we can't fix yours. Tell you what. I'll pull the motor home in next to your truck. That way, I can run a light with an extension cord. Take a look and see if we can figure it out."

"Hey, that'd be great."

Roy watched the man trot back to the motor home and disappear through a side door. The huge vehicle lumbered back into the drive-around, and then the driver expertly slid it alongside the truck. The side door opened again and the man waved Roy over. "Come on in."

Roy stepped into the posh surroundings of a small living

room—thick blue carpeting, matching overstuffed couch and chairs, and a large-screen TV. Definitely big bucks. A small blond woman at least twenty years younger than her companion turned away from the television to look at them. Her features were sharp and her eyes probing. She regarded Roy with obvious distaste.

"This is my wife, Cynthia, and I'm Ken Robertson." He held out his hand.

Roy smiled and took the outthrust hand, just like shaking with old Randy. "Pleased to meet you both. I'm Roy Miller, and I sure do appreciate your help."

# 29

•

Frank huddled in the shelter of the old-fashioned phone booth, one of the three amenities in Olancha, the other two being a gas station and a restaurant. With the door shut against the wind, he could make himself heard. Dave Meecham seemed unable to grasp the facts as Frank had presented them.

"You sure they're dead, Frank? Both of them?"

"As sure as I can be."

"What about the other guy, the redheaded one?"

"Jason. Yes, I think he was killed by the fall. Roy Miller was there. When he saw Jason, he came after me. If Jason had been alive, I think he would've stayed to help him." A blast of wind rocked the phone booth, blowing dust and grit under the door. Frank stood there, bathed in the purplish glare of the station's pole light. "He's still up there. I disabled his truck."

"Disabled his truck? That's a bad place to be stranded, Frank."

"I left a jug of water, but that's not the point. The point is that he's a killer. He was out to kill me. He kills people."

"Listen, Frank, I want you to meet me at the office at eight o'clock tomorrow morning. In the meantime, go home." Meecham paused. Frank thought he knew what was coming. "And Frank, consider yourself suspended with pay until we clear all this up." He hurried on, not giving Frank a chance to respond. "I'll get a hold of Bob Dewey over at the Sheriff's Department." Frank winced. Lieutenant Dewey considered the law-enforcement part of the BLM a joke, and he let it show.

"They'll wait for daylight before heading out," Meecham said.

"How will they know where to go?"

"I'll send Sierra and Wilson along to help out. They know the area. They'll be fine."

"Dave . . ."

"No, Frank, there's no way you're going. The Inyo Sheriff's Department thinks you're a loose cannon and maybe a guy with a grudge against poachers." Meecham dropped his voice. "Sometimes you step over the line, Frank. Since you and Deputy Harris picked up Donald Miller's body—he's the other brother, right?"

"Right."

"Since that little expedition, Harris has been having a field day making fun of BLM detective work. Sorry, Frank, but over there, you're Inspector Butt Print, and we're the other assholes."

"Well they can stuff it, Dave." Anger flooded through him in a hot flush. "Fat-ass squad-car cop couldn't wipe himself in the dark. Harris can put it where the sun doesn't shine—that is, if he can find it." The words gushed out, washing the flash of rage away in a torrent of invective.

"Got that off your chest now?"

"Yeah, okay. You're right. I'm hollering at the wrong guy." He sighed into the phone. "It's been a long day."

"Yeah, I can imagine." The concern in Meecham's voice was genuine. "Now listen to me carefully, Frank. I'm talking to you as your friend, not your boss. Harris and some of the others think you're a bit strange, overhyped on protecting the sheep, overhyped about killers wandering the desert. What I'm saying is, they could start looking at you, looking at you for taking out these guys because you think they're bad guys."

"Come on, Dave." He felt a sinking in his stomach. He'd been here before. He didn't quite fit, and there was always a price to be paid for not fitting. A wave of exhaustion passed over him. He felt bone-weary and discouraged. What did it take? Did someone need a picture of the Millers setting something on fire, beating someone to death?

"Frank, I know it's bullshit, but I want to be sure there's no way we can be seen as covering up, so Sierra and Wilson go." Frank heard

Meecham's voice coming from the phone, sounding like it was a million miles away. "And Frank"—Meecham gave a short chuckle—"this time, Sierra and Wilson are on the corpse detail. Think about it."

Frank thought about it. Sierra was uncommonly squeamish, didn't like to look at dead animals, much less touch them. Just the sight of blood made him queasy. And Wilson hated physical labor. He was more than just lazy, never rinsed out his cup, couldn't be bothered to pick up trash. Mainly, he liked chatting up the tourists. Mr. Charm. The corners of Frank's mouth turned down in a thin smile. "Thanks, Dave." Meecham was okay. "Oh, another thing. I was supposed to give a walk and talk—"

"I took it, Frank. They were hanging around the lawn waiting for you to show up. So I gave you a half hour, and then we went down to the kilns."

"I owe you one."

"You owe me more than one, amigo. By the way, you turning prima donna on me? Got your own little fan club, huh? That Rockford woman, the one from the college, she starts in bitching 'cause you're not leading the talk. Wants to know where you are. Oh, and you'd better get in touch with that Reyes—uh, that Linda Reyes—she sounded worried, like she might start a search party of her own."

"You talked to Linda?"

"I called her this afternoon, looking for you. She asked a lot of questions about where you might be. Smart lady. But I could hear the worry."

"My next phone call. And thanks again, Dave."

"*Por nada.* And don't go off getting into anything. Tomorrow morning, we'll sort this out."

"Miller's van is at the mouth of the canyon. There was bedding in the van, and I left a half-full gallon jug of water, so Miller should be nearby. And Dave, tell Sierra and Wilson to be very careful. Roy Miller kills people."

●

Linda didn't pick up his cell phone at the caboose. He figured she must have gone directly home or gone home after checking his place. Meecham said he'd called her that afternoon, trying to find out why the hell he hadn't shown up for his walk and talk. He dialed the number of the Joshua Tree Athletic Club, and she picked up on the first ring, her voice tense and hurried.

"It's me, Frank." He sounded oddly mechanical.

"Oh my God, are you okay? Where the hell have you been? I've been worried sick."

More worry than anger, that's good, he thought. "It's a long story, but I'm okay." He could hear her muffled voice telling some-one, "It's him. He's okay." Then he heard her breathing through the phone, waiting for him to go on, tell her what had happened. Habits of a good reporter—regaining control, ready to listen.

"I spent the day with Roy Miller, sort of by accident—he, uh, thought I was Eddie Laguna. So we went up in the canyon to wait for Dr. Sorensen, the poacher—only he didn't show up."

"Jesus Frank, what the hell happened?"

"I had to kill somebody." He felt his voice stick in his throat. "Left him at the bottom of a mine shaft. Not even sure he was dead."

He could hear voices in the background. He waited, listening to the wind and the faraway sounds in the Joshua Tree Athletic Club.

"Come to the club. I'm taking care of the bar, Frank. Dad and his friends are getting ready to—never mind that stuff. We'll talk and grill some steaks. Tonight's grill your own. There're some filets left and mushrooms and onions. Jan's been here since six o'clock, and Jimmy Tecopa. They've been waiting here in case you called. You better get here before everyone gets drunk."

He swallowed against the wave of emotion that choked off his voice.

"Frank, are you there? Can you hear me?"

"Yes."

"Well, are you going to be able to come? Say yes, Frank."

"Yes," he said. He could manage that much.

●

Frank pulled his beloved truck up near Linda's cabin, hoping people wouldn't hear his arrival. He hated being at the center of things, and he knew they were all waiting for him to show up and tell his story. He stepped out and carefully pushed the door closed to avoid the telltale thump.

"Hiya there, Flynnman." Linda stood silhouetted in the light coming from the side door to the club's kitchen.

"How'd you know I was here?" He looked past her and checked around the building for well-meaning friends lurking in the shadows.

"I was watching through the kitchen window. Sort of figured you'd go for a soft landing." She started across the gravel, closing the distance between them.

"God, it's good to hear your voice." He took her into his arms. "And smell your hair." They stood holding each other in silence.

Then she said, "You could've heard my voice sooner if you'd carry your cell phone." She pushed back from him. "How does Dave Meecham deal with that?"

"It's a long story." He grinned. "The thing is, I'm here now. And . . ." He held up his hand. "I've got a couple of cans and some string, so we can always be in contact."

"Not funny, Frank. I tried to call you—a bunch of times." She dropped her voice. "Mitch and Shawna were burned to death in their trailer. It was no accident. It was them."

"*What?* When did this happen?"

"They think it was sometime yesterday." Her voice was muted.

He shook his head slowly. "God, what a shame." His face creased in a thoughtful frown. "I can't figure out what makes him tick." He spoke softly. "Something's missing inside." He looked up. "But two of them are gone, and they should have Roy Miller soon. I fixed his van so it wouldn't run."

"Oh Frank, I've been so worried. It could've been you." She paused, her voice hardening. "Damn it, carry your phone, okay!"

He pulled her to him again. "I will. You're right. I wasn't thinking about other folks." He rocked her gently. "Being alone all the time, you forget about others." He tipped up her face. "I won't forget." He kissed her softly. "You can count on it." A slow grin spread across his face. "Besides, I know better than to come between a reporter and her story. Hell hath no fury like a reporter scooped."

She punched him none too gently in his abdomen. "That's the truth, Flynnman. Don't ever forget it."

"Hey, there you are—and there's Frank." Jack turned and shouted back through the open door. "Just hang on a moment. They're both out here."

"Looks like we gotta go to the party," she said, loudly enough to be heard.

"Yup." He leaned down. "But for now, I'm telling them that things worked out. Everything's okay. That's it."

"Don't worry. I'll run some interference." She dropped her voice. "Besides, tonight I want you to myself." She squeezed his arm.

"Sounds good." He felt himself blushing and was grateful for the dark. "And tomorrow's going to be tough."

"How come?"

"Guess I'll have to explain this all over again to the people at Inyo County Sheriff's Department." He paused. "And Dave's sorta pissed off."

"Why?"

"No cell phone."

"I'm with him."

•

"Why didn't you identify yourself?" Clearly, it was more an accusation than a question. Lt. Robert W. Dewey didn't bother to hide his skepticism. He'd listened to Frank's story without interruption, his long, angular frame upright in the wooden office chair, hands on his knees, his hazel eyes never leaving Frank's face.

It was the question Frank would have asked himself. "It wasn't a completely conscious decision. They took me for Eddie Laguna. At the time, it seemed like a good idea to play along. I had an idea who they were. I was off duty. My weapon was in the truck. I believed them to be dangerous. I think I was—am—correct in this assessment. So I played along, hoping to get clear as soon as I could. As it turned out, the opportunity didn't present itself."

"What made you think they were anything more than punk bikers?" Dewey's expression hardened. Frank could read the barely concealed contempt. He told himself that no matter what, he knew the truth because he'd been there. Or did he? Why *had* he gone along? He knew part of it was because he'd thought he might learn something, because he'd figured he could beat them out in the desert. And he had. Only he'd never thought it would cost two lives. In fact, he hadn't thought about it much at all. Full of himself catching the bad guys. He'd played it by ear, trusting to luck, or whoever watched over drunks and fools.

"They were more than punk bikers, Lieutenant. The one who called himself Hickey was armed with a Glock. At the Joshua Tree Athletic Club, they put a man in the hospital simply because they felt like it."

"Yeah, and the lady bartender scared the shit out of them with a shotgun. Real badasses."

Frank felt his face burning. People believed what they wanted, especially cops who were sure that they were trained and impartial observers, readers of human character, able spot a phony, a slime-ball, or a liar. Self-assurance hardened their prejudices. Well, to hell with them. Maybe his motives hadn't been pure, but Roy Miller and his companions were very bad people.

Frank looked around the room. There was Lieutenant Dewey from the Inyo County Sheriff's Department, Jack Mitchell from Fish and Game, and Dave Meecham. Even Meecham's face registered pained skepticism.

"I did what I thought was necessary at the time. It became clear to me that I wasn't going to make a round-trip. Miller all but told me I was a done deal. I believed him. When Hickey and I went into the mine, I did what I had to be sure I didn't stay there. Jason's death was an accident. He fell over backward from the recoil of a .458 Winchester, which he fired at me. I made my way down the canyon, disabled their van, left water, and called my superior, Chief Ranger Meecham. That's it."

"That's it, huh?" Dewey stared at Frank. "Let's see what my boys say, Flynn. And it still doesn't explain why you were at Laguna's in the first place. Feeding his cat? Pretty damn lame."

"I'd like to know that myself, Frank." Mitchell leaned forward, his tanned young face serious. He and Frank had become friendly over the last year, ever since Mitchell became the local Fish and Game agent. Frank had shown him some of the back country, the bighorns. He knew how Frank felt about poachers.

"I recognized Eddie Laguna's picture. I went to urge him to turn himself in voluntarily before his picture made the paper. I've known him for a long time. I figured it might go easier with him."

Mitchell and Meecham exchanged brief looks.

Dewey jumped in. "You like to poke your nose into other jurisdictions, don't you, Flynn? What's the deal here? Stick to taking care of rocks and tourists." Dewey didn't bother to conceal his contempt. Frank watched Dave Meecham's face cloud over.

"You think that was a useful observation, Bob? Public relations isn't your long suit." Meecham held up his hand. "That's it. This isn't an official inquiry; it's a courtesy offered by one law-enforcement agency to another. And now it's over. You have anything else to take up with one of my people, go through channels."

"You can count on it." Dewey's voice was hard with anger. The charged silence filled the room. Dewey looked down at the backs of his large, bony hands, which were clamped on his knees. The creased khakis rode high on his legs, exposing a couple of inches of hairless white skin.

Dewey sighed and grimaced with the effort of apology. "Oh hell, Dave, no offense intended. He's your man. It's just that wannabes are a pain in the ass."

Meecham shook his head, laughing without humor. "Talk to you later, Bob." They all had risen, anxious to escape the tension. Meecham turned to the Fish and Game agent. "Stick around for a minute, would you, Mitchell? Some things to clear up."

The beeping of Dewey's phone sent hands reaching for cell phones, hoping it was their call, until Dewey flipped open his phone, turning away from the others.

"This is Dewey." The angular head nodded slowly up and down in unconscious acknowledgment. "Where?" Dewey's body tensed and his head stilled. "Okay. Have Harris wait there. I'll call the coroner and see if we can get an ME out there."

Dewey turned back to the group. He looked at Frank while he addressed the others. "They found the body of a Randall Clark on the power-line road. His windpipe was crushed. Looks like your Roy Miller's a killer after all."

Frank looked stricken. "Damn, this is my fault." They were staring at him.

"What the hell are you talking about, Flynn?" Dewey's face registered bafflement.

Meecham looked at Dewey. "He left him water, Bob. Didn't want the son of a bitch to die of thirst."

Dewey stretched to his full six-three. Frank could imagine the popping and clicking of sinews and joints. He looked at Frank as if seeing him for the first time. "Okay, Flynn. There's already an APB out on him. I figure we'll have him in the next twenty-four hours." The morning sun filtered through the cottonwoods, filling the office with pale yellow light gently tinged with green. "The water was the right thing. There's no way you could've known."

"Thanks." Frank held his gaze. "And Lieutenant, Miller's gone. You can count on it. He and his brothers, and the other man, Hickey, lived somewhere along the Mojave River in Oro Grande. At least that's what Mitch Cooper told me. He used to be one of them."

"Where can I find this Mitch Cooper?"

"Can't. He burned to death in the fire over at the Ophir mine near Randsburg. Somebody tied him and his girlfriend up and set fire to the trailer. It's in Kern County, just over the line."

Dewey shook his head. "We'll pull out all the stops, Flynn. There's just one of him."

"Yeah, he'll be traveling light."

# 30

•

Under the cottonwoods surrounding the Independence Court House, Frank sat at a picnic table warped and bleached from the desert sun. It didn't take long for man-made things to melt away into the grays and browns of the Mojave and the Owens River Valley.

He felt like a man emerging from a nightmare. People like the Millers lived in a world of careless violence, and somehow he had been caught up in it. He had killed deliberately and felt little remorse, at least not for the dead man, although maybe for himself, for having had to take a life. Two if you counted Jason Miller. Frank did; he had caused the fall. Everything had become cluttered. He needed time to sort things out, and time was running short.

Right now, catching the poacher didn't seem so very important. Of course, there was the picture Linda had taken of the arrogant bastard, rifle in hand, but the picture of the poacher standing near a downed bighorn wasn't the same thing as catching him with one in possession. He couldn't testify that he'd seen Sorensen shoot the ram, because he hadn't. Neither had Linda. So all they had was a solid accusation. Great. And that damned Eddie had evidently skipped out. He shook his head in acknowledgment of his fruitless efforts to make things come out right. So much for being a good guy.

The light was autumn soft, the air still and warm. Indian summer. He smiled unconsciously. A couple of ravens hopped across the scruffy lawn, looking for a handout. Their bright black eyes gleamed with intelligence. Frank fished around in his shirt pocket and found a peanut. He held it up for the birds to see. The bolder of the pair hopped up on the opposite end of the table, its bill partially open, head cocked to one side. They watched each other intently, man and bird.

Ravens possessed an uncanny awareness of things; more than clever, they were alert to their surroundings, to human beings and their actions. Biologists thought they hunted with wolves in symbiotic harmony, dipping down with folded wing and calling out when they spotted game, then feasting after the kill. Some of the older Paiute and Shoshone said they did the same in the days when the people of the desert depended on finding game to live, following hunting parties into the desert, acting as eyes for the hunters. Frank pushed the peanut to a position halfway between them. The bird took two quick steps toward it, its glossy black feathers reflecting bits of rainbow. It looked directly into Frank's face, then took the peanut in its beak and swept away from the table in a low glide, followed by its mate. He wished he had more peanuts.

The sound of his cell phone startled him from his reverie. Meecham had made it more than clear that he was never to be without it, off or on duty. Always available. Crap.

"Flynn."

"Hey, Frank. Great party. How's your hangover?"

It was Jimmy Tecopa. By the time Frank had reached the Joshua Tree Athletic Club after his sojourn in Surprise Canyon, everyone was half in the bag. He'd drunk too much himself, but not as much as the rest, surely not as much as Jan and Jimmy, who had been on watch since late that afternoon, when Linda began trying to locate him.

"Frank?"

"My head's fine. Better than yours, I'll bet. You should stay away from the firewater, Jimmy. Nobody likes a drunken Indian."

"The pot calling the kettle black, or brown, I guess. And my head's fine. Been drinking Alka-Seltzer and Coronas. And oh my God, Frank, that first beer."

"Yeah, almost worth the hangover." He paused. "So why're you calling? Not just to bullshit?"

"Talking to you is always a treat, Frank. On the other hand, thought you'd like to know that while we were celebrating your escape from the bad guys, old Eddie Laguna drops into the Paiute Palace and drops more than a thousand bucks playing poker."

"What?"

"More than a thousand. Susan tried to steer him in another direction, but he had a head of steam up."

"Yeah?"

"Aren't you going to ask where the money came from?"

"I think I have an idea."

"Oh." Jimmy sounded disappointed. "Well anyhow, he drops a bundle, then tries to cash a check for fifteen thousand dollars. Hell, we wouldn't cash a banknote for fifteen thousand. Truth is, we rarely have that much on hand. The Paiute Palace isn't Vegas. So Susan tells him she can't cash the check. He wants to know why not, and she explains it's a two-party check and that it's too big. She said he seemed kind of crestfallen, and maybe relieved, maybe glad he couldn't get his hands on the cash, I guess."

"He just can't get it right, Jimmy. I'm not even sure he knows how it goes wrong."

"Like the rest of us, Frank. Easier to see how others screw it up."

"For sure, *amigo*." It seemed like the conversation ought to be over, but something was hanging. "Say, do you know who the check was from?"

"Thought you'd never ask." Frank could hear the smile in Jimmy's voice. "I was beginning to worry that my tax dollars were being squandered on an incompetent."

"So do you know?"

"Yeah, matter of fact, I do."

"You gonna tell me, or do I have to go over there and beat on a drum until your head splits?"

"Okay, okay, don't go badge-heavy on me. Yeah, Susan got a look at the check, and being the smart girl she is, she wrote down the name. It was Michael Sorensen. Check indicated he was a doctor. Mean anything to you?"

"As a matter of fact, a whole lot. Thanks, Jimmy, and thank Susan for me."

"You're welcome, but I think Susan would appreciate hearing it from you in person."

"You're right. And thanks again. Next beer's on me."

"That sounds about right. Gotta go. I'm on at three. Need to clean up, eat, and take a nap."

●

Eddie's old Ford was parked next to the trailer, its nose pushed under the sagging roof cover, the bumper resting against the flaking green paint. Evidently, the driver had just sort of aimed toward the trailer and managed to stop before ramming the side. Frank sincerely hoped Eddie wasn't too hungover to talk, but if he was, Frank was prepared to perform a radical cure, give the good cop a holiday, be the bad cop.

He banged on the screen door, making it clatter against the aluminum frame. Nothing. He pulled the screen open and pounded on the door, which drifted open, revealing Eddie's hovel in renewed filth. The stench of vomit filled his nostrils, which didn't do much for his hangover. Eddie lay on the couch, naked from the waist down, his torso clad in a worn and grubby T-shirt, yellowed at the armpits with layers of dried sweat. Not exactly every young American girl's dream. Frank went into the kitchen and picked up a pot three-quarters full of greasy water, returned to the couch, and poured it over Eddie's face. Eddie's reaction was surprisingly instant. He sat bolt upright, thrashing his hands in front of him.

"Shit." Eddie wiped his dripping face with his hands, peering up at Frank. "Whatcha do that for, for Christ's sake?" He mopped at his face with his T-shirt. After poking through the heaped cigarette butts in the ashtray, he selected one that had some length and carefully straightened it out against his bare thigh. Frank couldn't believe it. Eddie seemed completely relaxed.

Eddie discarded several empty matchbooks until he found one with matches. The first match burned down and went out before he could nurse the flame. The second sputtered to life, and Eddie squinted away from the smoke as he lit the butt. He took a big drag, held it in his lungs, and blew the nearly transparent smoke over his shoulder, away from Frank's face.

"Man, that's better. Uh, sorry, Frank. I know you don't smoke."

"Jesus, what difference does it make? This place reeks of stale tobacco and puke."

Eddie looked unabashed. He absently scratched at his genitals. "Had a rough night." He grinned. "How about a beer?"

"Pass." Frank watched in some amazement as Eddie went to the refrigerator, the skin hanging in loose folds on his skinny butt, and withdrew a tall Bud Lite. The man didn't seem to care that he was clad only in a T-shirt, or that he had a lot of explaining to do. The fact that he was a liar and petty crook, and that he'd lied to Frank, the cop with a heart of gold, clearly didn't bother him at all. Frank felt his attempt at righteous anger dissipate. Hell, he felt some envy for Eddie's absence of shame. He'd never known that sort of freedom, wasn't likely to, either. Eddie returned to the couch and sat at the near end, grinning at Frank.

"So I figured you'd be pissed off, but after I tell you what happened, we'll do a dance."

"Not unless you put on some pants. Put some pants on, for Christ's sake."

Eddie looked down at himself, as if realizing for the first time he was without the necessary clothing. "Oh yeah, sure." He picked up a pair of soiled jeans and pulled them up, his penis sticking out of the fly. He tugged one pocket inside out. "Hey, Frank, ever see a one-eared elephant?"

"Jesus, Mary, and Joseph. You think you're back in high school?"

Eddie looked befuddled. "High school?"

"Forget it. Just put your pecker in your pants and sit down."

Eddie sat back down and began grubbing through the cigarette butts again.

"Damn it, Eddie, let that go. Why the hell are you here and not under arrest? And don't tell me they released you on your own recognizance or some such bullshit. I already took some heat for not turning you in. I tried to give you a break, Eddie, and now you've made a problem for me. I look like a dumb ass among my peers."

Eddie studied his feet. Finally, some shame. Maybe the little shit wasn't beyond redemption.

"Look, Frank, I had a chance to collect the money I had coming, set up Mr. Big Shot, and still keep my word to you—only that sort of got delayed. Sorry about that." He gave Frank a practiced sorrowful look.

Frank returned his best hard-cop look, but he knew it wasn't really there on his face, in his eyes.

"Eddie, you almost got me killed, you know that?"

"What?"

"It's a long story. Later. Right now, I want to know what the hell you were doing instead of meeting Sorensen in Surprise Canyon. I figure you met him, but sure as hell not in Surprise Canyon. So tell me the whole thing. And Eddie, not one zig or zag from the truth, not one. Just tell it the way it happened."

Eddie managed to light another cigarette butt, this one so short that he had to tip his face away to keep from burning his nose. He took a long swallow of beer and sighed with satisfaction. Frank thought he looked particularly smug.

"Yeah, I met him, the son of a bitch, only Saturday evening at six o'clock, not Sunday morning like I let you think."

"Like you told me. Like you told me the ram's head and the rifle were in the mine."

"Well, I already had the head and rifle, and I figured Mr. Big would pay me the money he owed me, but I also figured he'd try and cheat me. But I was ready for him." Eddie grinned.

Eddie recounted how he got the drop on Sorensen, seeming particularly pleased about backing him off with his fast draw. His eyes gleamed with pleasure. "You should've seen the look on his face when I whipped out the old equalizer. Didn't look so damn big then. And just in case the puke got up the nerve to take a shot at me, I filed the firing pin on his rifle."

"The rifle stashed in the mine?" Frank looked stricken.

"Yeah. Hell, I wasn't going to give him a way to take me out."

"Shit. Eddie, the firing pin matched the indentations on the spent shells." It didn't register. "Like fingerprints. It was evidence."

Then Frank pictured Eddie's beat-up truck disappearing into the night, Eddie in possession of Sorensen's money. He felt a grudging admiration. Not so dumb after all. Sorensen had been outclassed by a trailer-court Indian. Eddie'd been sorely tempted, a chance to win one for the Indians and make the big score. He wondered if Eddie would actually have shot Sorensen if he'd tried something. Frank came to the conclusion that he probably would have. There was a toughness at Eddie's core he'd overlooked.

"So the money you dropped at the Paiute Palace was what you got from Sorensen?"

"Yeah." Eddie looked suddenly woebegone. Then he brightened. "But I've got his check for fifteen thousand dollars."

Frank slowly shook his head. "Yup, you've got his check, but you'll never get the cash."

Eddie leaned forward, his expression earnest. "He won't stop payment, Frank. I've got the goods on him."

"Yes, he will, Eddie, 'cause he's got the goods on you."

"Like hell. I'm turning myself in."

"Right. That's right. And Sorensen goes down."

"Yeah, so?"

"So what's going to happen to the evidence, Eddie? The check is evidence. Even if you found somewhere to cash it, which I very much doubt, any money paid to you for illegal activities will be seized by the court."

Frank's words clicked into place. Eddie's face fell, as if he'd been gripped by a wave of nausea. The dawning of an inescapable truth: He'd never see the money. He sagged back into the couch.

"Shit—shit, shit, shit."

Despite the trouble this sad little man had brought down on him, Frank felt for Eddie, for his broken dream. That was the hard part, losing hope.

Suddenly, Eddie grinned, exposing the blackened stumps where teeth should have been. "Well, they can't get the twelve hundred back. Man, that's gone. Wish I'd cashed in when I was six hundred to the good. For a while, I was on a roll." He shook his head. "Hell of a game, Frank. That fat asshole with the bolo ties and Roy Rogers shirts dropped more than I did. Whatizname, Monty Sessions, thinks he's a high roller." Eddie blew on the end of the cigarette butt. "Guess being a high roller means you can afford to lose."

"Probably so." Frank nodded in agreement. If you lived near the bottom of the heap, what was there to lose? Guys like Eddie just grew. Frank had had his mother, his reckless but loving father, and Mrs. Funmaker. He wondered for a minute how Eddie had come up, but he pretty much knew—dirt-poor and ignorant. Somehow, though, he had made his way, learned a craft, and figured out he was being screwed. He shook his head. He couldn't think about it now.

"Look, Eddie, I want you to go see Jack Mitchell at Fish and Game as soon as you get cleaned up."

"Aw shit. Man, I hate jail."

"It could be worse. You're still a cooperating witness. I don't think I'll have to take Prowler home with me. Hey, where is Prowler?"

"He doesn't like the smell of puke."

"He's a smart cat. Maybe you ought to take a hint before he finds a new owner." Frank rose. It was time to get back to the caboose and talk with Linda. He'd only given her the short version. He needed to think about all this some more. The thing that sat in his stomach like a lead weight was the fact that Roy Miller could be anywhere, any damn place he chose.

•

"That's it, huh?" Linda sat next to Frank, her feet propped up on railing at the end of the caboose.

"Hell, he didn't know Miller was coming by. What was I supposed to do, punch him out?" He sounded irritated, a bit petulant. "Well?"

"That doesn't require an answer."

"Okay." She was missing the point.

"Look, intentions count for something. He was making things come out right; at least that's what he thought. When the hell does a guy like Eddie have a chance to make real money? He doesn't." He turned to face Linda. "He's never had a real job. Never had a bank account. When someone insists on writing him a check for his work, he has to take it over to the casino and get Susan to cash it, and if the casino won't cash it, it's just paper. The paycheck-cashing leeches in Ridgecrest don't take personal checks."

"He was a guide for poachers. They killed bighorns, your bighorns. Maybe you can forgive him for that, but I can't."

"So don't." His mouth tightened. "You know, 'You could cut him a little slack.' Hey, who said that? Now I remember. It was someone talking about her dad."

Linda sat forward, her feet hitting the metal decking. "We'll talk later."

As she rose, Frank laid his hand on her arm. "That was a cheap shot." Linda stood looking down at him, her face troubled. "I mean it. Your dad's got nothing to do with it."

She looked thoughtful. "Maybe he does, in a way." She squinted into the distance. Haze had blown up the valley from the Los Angeles basin, tingeing everything a drab beige. "If Eddie weren't Shoshone or Paiute, if he were some creep like Donnie Miller, would you have given him a break?"

Frank shook his head. "Nope, I'd've gone after him hard." He sat with his head bent, stroking the bridge of his nose. He turned toward her, looking up into her face. "The thing is, he's not some creep—not like one of the Millers, that's for sure."

Linda raised her eyebrows.

"Okay, so he cheats the law now and then. Lives on the fringe and looks out for number one. From his point of view, the law was written by white people, the same white people who stole the land and left his people broke. Far as he's concerned, it's got nothing to do with him. Just another goddamn impediment." He looked up into her face. "Hell, you know; you're a reporter. Unemployment's better than forty percent in the reservation, and if it hadn't been for the Paiute Palace providing a few jobs, it would be worse." He held up his hand. "Eddie lives in two worlds, neither of his making. It's not a good place to be."

Linda brushed his cheek with the back of her hand. "I guess you know about that."

"Yeah." He nodded. "But I've come to terms with it. Eddie

called me an apple because he sees me as a Paiute, but I'm no more Paiute than I'm Irish or Mexican." He frowned. "But he was right about one thing: It ain't easy not knowing the rules." He grinned. "The difference is, I had too many; he didn't have any at all. Like finding your way in the dark."

She ruffled his hair. "Yeah, we've had it sort of easy." She frowned. "But I wish to God he'd get his teeth fixed." They both laughed.

"He says that's the first thing he's going to do—after he fixes the truck." Frank frowned. "Goddamn it, I think he held back some cash."

"Hey, he's your Indian."

"Native American. We're Native Americans." He laughed. "Too bad we learned so late. If we'd had a few more like Eddie, maybe the westward movement would've stopped at Plymouth Rock."

"Like in your lecture."

"Yeah, like in my lecture."

## 31

"Nice shot." Bill Jerome's face revealed no joy.

Shaw nodded in acknowledgment and walked around to the far side of the table, where the six ball rested against the side rail, not quite halfway between the end and side pockets. He gestured to the side pocket with the tip of his cue. "Three cushions." The room stilled as the geezers in the high-backed observer chairs leaned forward to watch. A young couple chatting away at the end of the bar let their conversation trail off into the silence. Ben Shaw shook his graying head in wonderment at the lack of common pool room etiquette.

"Put on a good show, don't they?" Jack Collins said sotto voce.

Frank nodded ever so slightly.

Shaw leaned his cue against the wall, lifted himself into an observer's chair, and began packing his pipe.

Bill Jerome's voice cut through the quiet. "You givin' up, Ben?"

Shaw shook his head. "Nope, just waiting till the Blarney Stone over there finishes up." He looked up from his pipe packing. "I mean, we wouldn't want to interrupt a meaningful exchange of ideas for something so trivial as a life-and-death snooker match." He glared over at Collins, who peeled back a toothy grin.

"Well, go ahead now, Ben. All eyes are on you."

Shaw lit the pipe with a wooden match and puffed billowing clouds of smoke into the still air, then tamped down the ash. "Good, glad you're paying attention. Your game needs a bit of work." He retrieved his cue and chalked the tip, holding the blue chalk in his left hand and rolling the base of the cue against his foot with the other.

He tapped off the excess against the edge of the leather pocket and bent low over the cue, his beard tickling the shaft as he slid it back and forth, smoothing the stroke. He struck the cue ball medium hard. The six came away from the side rail into the end rail at a shallow angle and then into the far side rail at a forty-degree angle and away, rolled across the felt, and dropped neatly into the side pocket.

Shaw resumed his seat, trying to look matter-of-fact as he puffed on his pipe, his eyes fairly beaming with pleasure. "Heh, heh, heh." He grinned and lifted his empty glass toward Bill Jerome. "Heh, heh, heh."

Jerome shambled over to the bar. "Two Pacificos."

"Were you guys just playing for beers?" The young man's voice was incredulous.

Jerome paused to look at the couple, his dark eyes and thin mouth unsmiling. "That's right. We're too good to play for money." The geezers wheezed and guffawed. Then Jerome broke into a small smile. "Might as well bring a couple beers for these two, as well. But you guys"—he gestured to the wall of geezers—"can just forget it."

"Yeah, they do put on quite a show." Watching the game at the Joshua Tree Athletic Club had become one of Frank's favorite pastimes. These old reprobates managed to squeeze a lot of pleasure out of not very much. It was a gift, the way they amused one another. He hoped Collins could keep them out of mischief for a while, although he wondered about Collins. He glanced around the room. The place was full of local folks, if eight or nine people besides the Grumpy Wrench Gang constituted "full." It was pretty good for a Wednesday afternoon in Red Mountain. The boys had their audience, and he was among 'em. Good beer, good company. He glanced above the bar and failed to make eye contact with the jackalope. Maybe Collins had taken it down as a matter of caution.

"Say, Jack, where's the horned beast?" Frank pointed above the bar, where the jackalope had surveyed the goings-on.

"Oh, that. Well, Frank, m'lad, I sold him, but not to worry, there's another on its way."

"Is that right? Who'd you sell him to, Jack?"

"Just a fellow who thought the jackalope was something rare." Collins busied himself wiping down the bar.

"Tell me about it."

"Oh, it's a long story."

"I'll make time for it, Jack. Sounds terribly interesting, even enlightening." Frank leaned forward, placing both elbows on the bar and resting his chin on his hands.

"Well, since the paper in Victorville picked up Linda's story about the jackalope preserve and whatnot, there've been people in here asking about 'em, interested, so to speak. That's all. She's quite a writer, my daughter is."

"That's all?"

"Are you sure you want to know about all this?" Collins raised his eyebrows, a pained expression on his face.

Frank nodded, his solemn face sharing Collins's concern. "Go on, Jack, difficult as it might be."

Collins heaved a sigh. "Now here we are in the Mojave Desert, in the only drinking establishment in Red Mountain, and one of the beasties is hanging above the bar, so folks naturally assumed we were informed, sort of experts, you might say."

"Yeah, I'd say you were the jackalope experts."

"There you are." Collins shrugged. "This fellow wanted to know all about jackalopes, how they came about, breeding habits, that sort of thing. So naturally, Ben and Bill there"—he waved his thick arm in their general direction—"and myself, we filled him and the missus in."

"I'll bet you did."

"There's a lot of doubters, Frank. People lack the power to believe. We don't even talk to those folks, just pass the whole thing off as a joke. But every so often, a man of faith comes to pass, and it's a bond, a brotherhood." Collins's voice dropped a register on the brotherhood part.

"So when one of the brothers wants to have the last jackalope buck taken in Jawbone Canyon by the last of the Paiute, I'd be a cruel man to deny him his heart's desire."

"How much?"

"A hundred and fifty, and a bargain at the price, if such a thing can be measured by the filth of lucre." Collins sniffed.

"Where'd you get it?"

"From a catalog. There's another half dozen on the way." Collins spread his hands in a gesture of helplessness. "It's more interesting than a piece of the true cross or a bit of the robe. Think of it like this: If and when they discover it might not be the last of the breed, they have a wonderful conversation piece, a good story, and even a chance to make a bit of profit. So where's the harm?"

"Guess it's not such a harebrained scheme." Frank grinned.

"Oh there you go, having a bit of fun with me."

"And I appreciate it, too."

"What's that?"

"Having the fun." He looked down at the back of his hands in thought.

"You don't look all that happy about it, Frank." Collins waited. "You caught the poacher, with some unlooked-for help"—he nodded his head in the direction of Shaw and Jerome—"but you were the man of the hour."

"Sorensen almost died." Frank raised his hand. "I know. No great loss, but I don't think you'd want it on your conscience."

Collins's expression hardened.

"It could have been the old couple I'd rescued from the camper who found him stuck out there."

"Yeah." Collins's large face went bland. "You know that's not going to happen again, at least not from us." He waved his hand around the bar. "Hurtin' people wouldn't have been good." He brightened. "But the part about Sorensen being attacked by an Indian was too good to be true. All the boys here been talking about it, the Paiute's last stand. Now half of 'em claim to have had a run-in with a half-clothed renegade."

"Eddie's a Shoshone." Frank decided not to mention Eddie's attire at their last meeting.

"And a damn fine one. Like to meet him sometime."

"Couldn't afford it, Jack. Eddie likes beer. Having a tavern owner for a friend would be a lifelong commitment." Frank thought about Eddie added to the mix of the Grumpy Wrench Gang and shuddered inwardly.

"Well, your poacher's through."

"For now, Jack. A fine and community service doesn't stop assholes like Sorensen. Besides that, he left a man in the desert to die, only I can't prove it, and nobody wants to hear about it anymore." He shook his head. "There've been too many deaths." Frank studied the surface of the bar.

Collins rested a stubby hand on Frank's arm. "It's been almost five months. I think we're through with Miller."

Frank caught Collins's eyes and held them. "Don't say it for me, Jack. You think about it, too."

"It'll come right, Frank. It won't be easy for a man who looks like he does to hide forever."

"He's a smart son of a bitch, Jack. And evil. He rode around with the bodies of the people he murdered in their motor home for two days." Frank looked away. "He needs to be dead." The words came out softly. "Then it'd be over."

They sat in the silence of darkened thoughts.

Collins emptied his glass and sighed. "It's the way he wins, you know."

"What're you saying?"

"He gets you to be like him, to think murder. It won't do. If he comes, then it's another matter. Don't let him get inside you, Frank. Once upon a time, Ben almost lost himself. It's in all of us, Adam's bite of the apple.

"By and large, it's a good world, and there's still all this." He waved his arm at his domain. "And there's Linda, sweet lass that she is." The last was said in a broad brogue. He frowned, glancing from side to side and mugging a ludicrously furtive expression, then leaned forward. "Oh, and you don't have to mention the jackalope business to Linda. She's a softhearted one, you know."

"You mean she wouldn't approve of petty larceny."

"Unkind, Frank, very unkind." He looked over Frank's shoulder. "And here she is, just in time to give her old da a chance to take the shine off Ben's easy opinion of himself."

"Dad. Frank." Linda was unsmiling, her face drawn.

"Would you watch the bar for me for a bit, darlin', while I give Ben a lesson in humility?"

"Sure, Dad." She laid a copy of the *Los Angeles Times* on the bar and exchanged places with Collins. "Take a look at page three." Linda gestured at the paper. Frank opened it and scanned the headlines. About halfway down the second column, the headline read TWO DEAD IN BIZARRE MURDER. "Dr. Michael Sorensen, leading infertility specialist, and his brother-in-law, Dennis Winthrop, were found dead in their Linda Vista home Tuesday morning by Maria Gutierrez, the Sorensens' maid. Ms. Gutierrez let herself into the Linda Vista home about ten o'clock and discovered the decapitated bodies in the game room, where the noted hunter had trophies from around world. Neighbors heard her screaming and called the Pasadena police. The investigating officer, Lt. Warren Isham, refused to speculate on a motive for the killings. The victim's wife, Denise Sorensen, said that her husband had received several threats from animal rights people since his conviction for poaching Desert bighorn sheep last November. Both Winthrop and Sorensen were prominent in trophy-hunting circles."

"It's him." Linda's mouth trembled ever so slightly. "I called Wayne Marx. It's his byline. The *Times* doesn't go in for gory details. Sorensen had been tortured before he was killed. Wayne said the skin was torn up, probably with pliers. The killer duct-taped horns on Sorensen's head and left it on the mantelpiece. God, they've got to catch him, Frank."

"I'll call Dewey right away. He'll talk with the Pasadena PD." He reached across the bar and took her hand. "It'll be all right. They'll get him." But before he gets someone else? he wondered. A familiar sense of dread squatted in his stomach like a dead toad. He felt powerless, waiting in helpless frustration. The pale face floated before his inner eye and stared at him with dead pink-rimmed eyes.

•

Highway 395 widens into four lanes just below Pearsonville, striving to become an interstate. A nice drive ruined. Cars doing eighty,

eighty-five, and more flew by Frank's truck, in a hurry, making time. "Did L.A. to Bishop in under five hours," they'd brag later. What an achievement. Maybe a pneumatic tube was the answer. Pop a sleepy pill, climb into the tube, and—poof—wake up in Reno. Miss the whole boring mess.

Sixty, that's it, folks. Just go on around me. I'm doin' sixty. Frank's hostility was driving away the blues.

The cell phone's reedy ring trilled above the engine noise.

"Flynn."

"Flynn? And here I thought I was calling my old pal Eddie, 'Redhawk' Laguna. Man, you sound just like him." The sandy voice was clear and distinct, dropping the words into the ether. Frank glanced at the caller ID; the number was blocked, probably a pay phone.

"How you doin', Miller? You're the white one. Roy, isn't it?"

"'Roy, isn't it?' That's good. You got style, Francisco, my little brown buddy. I should've noticed that. Didn't quite fit with an Eddie, did it?" Miller paused, his breathing audible in Frank's ear. "Well, thanks for asking. I'm doing good, doing just fine. Had a few bumps. But life's full of ups and downs, right?"

Frank waited, let the silence take up the slack.

"Just called to catch up on things, you know. Let you know we're neighbors again out here in the wide-open spaces."

As Frank pulled the truck off to the side of the road, the air blast from a semi shook the cab.

"Just curious. How'd you come by my cell number?"

"Curiosity killed the cat, Frank. Brother Jason caught lots of the curious ones. Put a real dent in the gene pool. I guess that's gasoline under the bridge. As a matter of fact, you wrote the number on one of your cards, Mr. BLM Cop, but I rescued it from a terrible fire. Man, that was tragic, young Christian couple like that. Think God was listening, Francisco?"

"What's on your mind, Miller?"

"Now it's just 'Miller.' What happened to 'Roy'? Man, you blow hot and cold. Not like blood relations, Francisco; they stick by you."

"Yeah, that's true. Oh, by the way, give my regards to the family when you see them next. Oops, slipped my mind. You're out of relations now. Sorry for your losses, Miller, but a guy like you must make a lot of friends. Gotta go now, Roy, got things to do." He disconnected and dialed up Lieutenant Dewey.

"Dewey. It's Frank Flynn. I just had a call from Roy Miller."

"You get the number? What time did he call?"

"I just hung up this minute. He probably called from a pay phone; the number was blocked. I'm on Three Ninety-five, just above Pearsonville. Listen, he said we were neighbors again, meaning he's back in the Mojave. Trying to rattle my cage."

"Pay attention, Flynn. You're on the top of the guy's list. You know about Sorensen?"

"Yeah, I was going to give you a call."

"Read it in the *Los Angeles Times*. Already talked with Pasadena PD. The guy's a real sicko."

"That's not news to me, Lieutenant."

"Let me know if he contacts you again."

"You can count on it."

Linda was going to have to stay away for a while. A wave of relief swept over him. Linda would be okay. Miller was coming for him, the one who'd killed his brother Jason. His fear mixed with elation. The waiting would be over. He refused to think about what was in his heart.

# 32

•

Watching required patience. Roy had patience but probably not much time. Somewhere deep down, he was aware that things would catch up with him, so he was vigilant. He lay on the air mattress, chest against the rolled sleeping bag, arms propped on his elbows, the binoculars resting easily against his hands. This was day six of watching the Joshua Tree Athletic Club. So far, only the woman kept regular hours, on the road by 7:00 A.M., usually back by 5:45. Once, she hadn't returned, probably doing the nasty with Francisco Flynn, the BLM cop.

The old farts were unpredictable, in and out, in and out, different times. Sometimes one or two of them would leave for a few hours, banging onto the highway in an ancient International pickup truck, back on the dirt parking lot before dark. But this morning, he'd hit pay dirt. He'd almost missed it, too. The truck pulled out at sunrise, carrying all three of them, just as he was setting up for the day. Three hours later and the woman's Honda was still parked by her cabin, and it was close to 9:00 A.M.

Once, Roy had followed the woman up on Sage Flat and lost her. Had to hang back too far, but it was just a matter of patience. Couldn't be very many people living up there in that rock garden.

He felt some respect for the cop. The cop had the way of the warrior, like in Castaneda's book. Lived alone. Unpredictable. Kept his cool. That was what made him dangerous—he didn't freeze up with fear the way most people did, just collapsing, hoping that begging would keep them alive. Man, it was all he could do to hold back when they started all that whining. But dead guys couldn't tell you much, and information was important. Knowing stuff was power. After he cut the first guy, Sorensen couldn't wait to tell him all about the cop and the reporter, how they were an item. He thought he was buying time. He had that hopeful look on his face until just before he died.

Roy searched the grounds for signs of activity. No smoke rose from the wood-frame house behind the Joshua Tree Athletic Club, where the old guys lived, or from the stone chimney poking above the tin roof of the tavern. Time to take a closer look. He pulled the stopper from the air mattress, rolled it into a compact bundle, and tied it and the sleeping bag to the rack behind the dirt bike. He coasted down the back of the hill before starting the engine. No point in waking folks up, being inconsiderate. He hated it when people were rude and inconsiderate.

Roy cut along the dirt tracks that skirted the mining district. There'd been three towns during the heyday of the gold boom, all within a mile of each other, vying for top spot: Randsburg, Johannesburg, and Red Mountain. Randsburg and Johannesburg were respectable, had homes where the miners lived with their families. Red Mountain became the center of sin—dance halls, bars, and whorehouses. When the gold played out, Red Mountain and Randsburg had become ghost towns. Now Randsburg was being partially resuscitated by tourist dollars. Red Mountain had the Joshua Tree Athletic Club and fond memories of past times. Randsburg had TV. Roy pulled the motorcycle up behind the van, where he had left it near some dilapidated cabins sporting TV dishes.

Roy's latest choice of transportation, a television-repair van he'd picked up in San Bernardino, allowed him to hide in plain sight. Watching the tube and listening to the wind were the main events out here in Nowheresville, so the van functioned as a social ambulance, saving citizens from drinking too much and doing one another harm. The gray coveralls he wore bore the same name that was on the van:

278

He pushed the light dirt bike up the narrow ramp of the van and rested it against the sidewall on the left. Not having Jace and Hickey around made it easier for him to move around and talk to people, no clicking and head bobbing, no cackling and pot. Regular folks seemed almost comfortable around him. They commented on the catchy sign, and Roy made up stories about Muriel, what a smart lady she was, how much he liked working for her. Yeah, he liked the van and the way people reacted. Hell, maybe he'd take up TV repair after finishing up with old Francisco and Linda, the lady bartender with the shotgun.

But sometimes he got funny looks. His dyed hair lay against his scalp like dirty straw, light brown wisps peeking out from under his cap. A small matador's knot tied off with a rubber band bobbed about at the back of his neck. The flat brown color lent his pale skin a chalky pallor that didn't look quite right, a lifeless dead-guy look, and the dye job made the pink-rimmed eyes look like animated marbles. The wraparound shades helped a lot, hid the pink-rimmed paleness that made people look away. All in all, he was pleased with the effect. The disguise achieved the required metamorphosis from albino biker to Mr. Television Repairman. Besides, the world was full of weird people, and hey, this was California, land of half-breeds.

●

Linda sat at her iMac; she liked its simplicity and ease of use and the way it handled photos and text. Perfect for a reporter. Working at home, she could get twice as much done as she could at her desk at work. No Marston hanging around doing Bogey imitations, trying for Clark Kent to her Lois Lane, no Lucky Rogers, the eager-to-please sidekick, just uninterrupted quiet, especially with her dad and his buddies off on one of their expeditions. Of course, there was Hobbes wanting to go in or out, or staring at her in feline concentration until she got up from the computer and put dry food in his dish. But now that she had the quiet time, the words wouldn't come, at least not with any fluidity. Her copy was stilted, no flow.

She glanced out the window. The early-spring sky was bright blue, crisp with the cold. Bits of cloud raced shadows across the face of Red Mountain. Spring in the Mojave could be cold and blustery. She wondered why the television-repair van was in the parking lot next to the club. Her dad hadn't said anything about the dish antenna not working or problems with reception. She shrugged, pushing it from her mind. She shifted her gaze back to the van. So why the TV repairman?

A tall figure in coveralls and cap came around from the driver's side of the van, hand on his hat, the wind whipping at his clothing. He leaned against the gusts and disappeared behind the front of the club. Well, it was locked, and she wasn't going to open it up. He'd find out for himself and go away. She returned to the computer screen, staring at the cursor blinking away where she had stopped typing. She closed her eyes, trying to concentrate on how to make earthquakes, magma activity, and the Richter scale intelligible and interesting to the *Courier*'s readership.

The Mammoth Lakes area was alive with volcanic activity. The eastern slope of the Sierras crawled with geologists, who poked their instruments into the ground, hopping around the country after each earthquake in perverse delight. She glanced back out the window, her eyes absently searching for the repairman. An unnamed anxiety began rising in her chest. Then it struck her with the force of a blow. It was him. Something about the way he moved. She looked out the window. Bits of wind-driven brush scooted along the ground. The cabin creaked in protest against the heavy gusts that pounded against it. She was suddenly aware of each wrenching sound, as if the walls would be ripped away and she would tumble endlessly across the desert floor.

She pushed the power switch on the computer, obliterating a couple hours of work, and eased herself away from the desk and window. The trapdoor to the tunnel was attached to the small utility table next to the stove, its hinges hidden against the outer legs and under the linoleum flooring. It wasn't invisible, but because people weren't usually looking for a secret tunnel, it went unnoticed. Even if a person spied the thin lines of separation in the flooring, it was unlikely someone would think the table concealed a trapdoor, but it did. The connecting tunnel was a remnant from the days when the club was a center of sin. Ladies of the evening negotiated with their customers in San Bernardino County and led them into Kern County through the tunnels that connected the Joshua Tree Athletic Club to crib houses. Linda's little cabin was a leftover from those days that had persisted into the fifties, defying prostitution ordinances in both jurisdictions.

Linda flipped a light switch next to the stove and lifted the table away from the wall, resting it on its side. Hobbes immediately ran to the opening, peering over the edge. She climbed partway into the opening, then picked up Hobbes with one hand. Grasping the handle on the bottom of the door, she pulled the table back into place and climbed to the bottom of steep wooden stairs. She squatted next to the ladder, her breaths coming in little gasps, pulling in the cool, musty odors under the house. Hobbes struggled under her arm, eager to be free to explore the forbidden tunnel. She held her breath, straining to hear. Above the pummeling of the wind, there was thumping, regular and rhythmic. Something was knocking at the door, not the wind. Had she locked the door? No, the cat had been in and out since early morning. It probably didn't make any difference. The ancient lock was the original. The skeleton key hung from a cord next to the door frame.

She waited, unable to hear anything but the cabin groaning in the wind. Now and then, intermittent lulls brought a whispery quiet, as if the wind were gathering itself for a renewed assault. She heard footsteps at the front of the cabin, slow and deliberate. Hobbes struggled, mewing in protest at being held against his will. Linda placed him on the floor, and he immediately darted down the tunnel into the gloom. She stood next to the ladder, her head above a few inches below the floor. There it was again. Careful footsteps, over near her desk now. The cabin consisted of a single room with divided living spaces: a living room/bedroom combination near the door, her desk in a corner, where it caught the light from two windows; the kitchen area—stove, refrigerator, and sink—occupying a corner toward the back; the toilet and tub tucked away in the opposite corner, behind a curtain that afforded a semblance of privacy from the rest of the room.

The footsteps came across the floor into the kitchen area, stopping next to the table almost directly above her. She covered her mouth and breathed into her hand. He couldn't possibly hear breathing. He'd hear her heart pounding first. Hobbes came skittering back and rubbed on her ankles, then flopped on his back, begging for a tummy scratch. A plaintive meow would be next. Linda crouched down and softly rubbed the cat's stomach. The steps moved nearer the stove and stopped. What was he doing? She backed away from the ladder and scurried along the narrow passageway. If she could get to the tavern and the shotgun and block the trapdoor, she'd be safe.

Her watch said 9:47. She knew she couldn't have been down in the tunnel for more than five minutes. She was never, never going to be caught anywhere alone again, not until he was captured or dead. Why hadn't someone stopped him by now? At the other end of the tunnel, she was more than a hundred feet from her cabin. Hobbes came racing out of the gloom. She was glad someone was having a good time. Bracing her feet against the wooden rungs of the homemade steps, she shoved up against the trapdoor. Something was blocking it. The door gave a fraction of an inch, just enough to reveal momentarily a crack of dim light; a heavy weight pressed it closed against her straining arms. She changed positions, placing her back against the bottom of the door and bracing her weight against the wall opposite the stairs. Linda shoved with her legs, using all of her strength. The door lifted a couple of inches. Her legs trembled with the effort; then the wooden step cracked and gave way, dumping her at the bottom of the entry, her leg scratched and bleeding. Someone, probably her dad, must have pushed the large cook's table that occupied the center of the kitchen over against the wall to mop the floor and hadn't put it back.

Linda took deep, centering breaths, fighting the panic. He wasn't going to find her. She waited, staring down the passageway. She wanted to be as far away as possible, but at this end of the tunnel, she didn't know where he was. The tunnel was an earthen corridor shored and timbered every four or five feet. Her dad and the boys had nailed up a plywood ceiling and provided a one-by-twelve plank walkway. There probably wasn't more than a couple of feet of earth separating the tunnel roof from the surface of the ground, but it was enough to dampen all sound. It was always cool. Quiet and musty with time. She had disappointed her dad and his pals because she never used it. She found being in the tunnel cramped and even a bit suffocating. She could sympathize with Frank's claustrophobia as she started into the gloom. As she neared the cabin stairs, she was plunged into darkness. In a minute, the lights came on again, then flicked off and on several times. He'd discovered the light switch. She held her breath, her heart pounding so hard, she was afraid it would somehow give her away.

His footsteps moved around the room again, this time more rapidly, like he was doing a once-over. Then she heard the door close. Silence. She looked at her watch; it had been no more than a half hour from the time she'd first seen the repair van. She'd wait. Her dad and the boys had said they were headed over to Ridgecrest to the Lowe's, a four- or five-hour expedition. She put her ear near one of the hinges on the door. Nothing except an occasional shudder from the wind.

She waited for another half an hour. She needed to pee. Returning to the steps, her head no more than a few inches from the floor, she heard the sounds of the wind buffeting the cabin, nothing more. She raised the table a couple of inches, trying to see out, but the door's edge was against the wall, limiting her view to a small portion of the kitchen area. During a momentary lull, she listened intently; the stillness was complete. Her heart pounded in her chest as she pushed the table back and scrambled quickly to her feet. Everything was just as she'd left it. Feeling suddenly giddy with relief, she crossed back to her desk and looked out the window. The heaviness of dread lumped in her chest. The van was still there.

Then she heard the sound of plastic rings scraping on the iron rod that supported the privacy curtain. "So there you are, Ms. Reyes. How ya doin'?" Roy pushed the curtain aside with one hand. In his other hand, he held a large automatic pistol. "Long time no see. Didn't expect to see you come up from the floor. Now I know why the light switch doesn't work. You're full of surprises." The pale forehead creased into a frown. "Say, where's that big old double-barrel shotgun? Back under the counter at the bar, huh?" He nodded to himself. "Didn't want to take any unnecessary chances, though. Better safe than sorry." He slipped the gun inside his jacket and smiled. "Guess we can have that interview now. Get to know each other. I'm kind of an interesting guy once you get to know me."

●

Someone was groaning. The sound vibrated in her ears and throat. Then she realized it was coming from her.

"Back among the living, are we? Had to whack you a couple a times to quiet you down."

From where she lay trussed up on the floor, she could see the mountains sliding by the driver's window of the van. They had to be heading north on 395. She slid forward as he hit the brakes and rolled against the wall on the turn.

"Ranger Frank lives somewhere up here along Sage Flat Road, right, Linda? Back on a first-name basis, if that's okay with you." He glanced back at her over his shoulder. "So where do I turn?"

"Find it yourself, Roy. Okay if I call you Roy?"

He shook his head. She felt the van slow and pull to a stop. Miller turned, removed his sunglasses, and slowly turned his head from side to side in disbelief. She recognized the pale face, but the lusterless brown hair gave him the appearance of an animated mannequin. He continued to move his head slowly back and forth, weary with the burden of inner truth.

"Linda, you think you can afford to be a smart-mouth without the shotgun? You think you still have the drop on ol' Roy?" His pale eyes were flat and lightless. She looked away. He got out of the truck and opened the rear doors. "There you go. Nice bright day." He stepped into the rear of the van and turned to close the doors. "On the other hand, we don't want to be distracted, especially you. You want to pay close attention, get in touch with reality."

He stepped over her and slid out a seat from the workbench attached to a metal arm that locked it in place. "The thing for you to think about is how soon you'll decide to cooperate. He pulled out a tool drawer and took out a pair of pruning shears. "See, if I have to do a little gardening, prune off a toe here, a finger there . . ." He let his voice trail off.

She tried to control the fear, but it enveloped her like a thick blanket.

His voice droned on. "Here a nip, there a nipple. So fucking noisy, all that screaming and hollering. Then after all that, the next thing you know, you'll be begging me to draw a map to his place. And messy. Mess up my clean truck, my best coveralls. You like the logo?" He turned around, revealing the name Muriel's Eyes on the Skies. "Pretty catchy, huh?" He drummed his fingers on the workbench. "For a reporter girl, you're not too bright." He reached down and rolled her over on her stomach. Grabbing one thumb, he twisted it up away from her hand. "Now here's a twig that needs to come off."

"It's the dirt road next to the abandoned railroad tracks." The voice she heard coming from herself sounded distant, as if she were only bearing witness to what was happening.

# 33

•

Frank dreaded the opening day of trout season, people marching up and down the creek, leaving behind empty Styrofoam worm containers and beer cans winking in the water. The wind had been whipping down the back wall of the Sierras in fits and gusts since daybreak. He glanced up at the tops of the cottonwoods bouncing about in all directions in a prolonged sigh, as if gasping for air. The high water in Sage Creek would make fishing next to impossible, sending the trout into deep recesses and turning the creek into a torrent of snags, but the fisherfolk would come anyway, pouring up from Southern California, five hours to the south, rods in their hands, hope in their hearts.

For now, Frank had Sage Creek almost to himself. He pulled the truck into the campground. One motor home stood there, the people tucked safely inside away from the wind. They were missing out. The sky was blue enamel, the air so clear that you could see the pine-serrated edges on the distant peaks. Soon the campground would be full, and there would be a campground host seven days a week until the season closed in September.

The lidded garbage cans by the faucet were full from the weekend, brimming over with trash. A couple of green garbage bags lay propped against the metal cans, their contents spilling onto the ground, scattering bits of paper and plastic into the wind. He shrugged. Squirrels and ravens had torn into the sacks. Ever the opportunists, ravens had followed Paiute hunting parties into the desert for leftovers. Now they followed campers. As much as Frank found the clever thieves fascinating, he rarely fed them, never out in the desert or near his place. They had long memories for places and people. Once he'd shared a crust from a sandwich with a raven hanging around a campground on Taboose Creek. It followed him around the rest of the day, croaking for more.

He lifted the broken trash bags into the back of his pickup and gathered up as much of the trash as he could chase down, planning to take it to the dump on his next trip to town. Since Miller's phone call, trips to the campground had become a regular part of his daily routine. He carefully avoided driving directly home and stuck to using the trail from the campground that followed the creek back to the caboose. It would be difficult to follow someone up the long climb from the desert floor without being seen, but it would be easy to stay at a distance and follow someone's progress with binoculars. Not so easy to follow him along the creek bed cut deep into the alluvial debris.

Frank was sure Miller would seek him out. The flash of Miller's white face staring up at him from the broken body of his brother was indelibly etched in his mind. There was no point in being foolhardy. Thinking about Miller made him involuntarily brush his hand against the butt of the .45 resting in the holster clipped to his belt. A loose T-shirt could conceal the whole thing if someone wasn't looking for it.

Frank chased down a couple more paper plates and some rib bones left over from a barbecue and tossed them in the bed of the truck. The bones were immediately seized upon by a cluster of feuding ravens. They normally traveled in mated pairs. Flocking up was unusual, but it was becoming more common as open food sources became available. He set off down the trail, the sounds of the quarreling birds drowned out in the roar of the swollen creek.

•

Roy left Linda gagged and alone in the back of the van while he went to check up on Frank's caboose.

"Got to do a little recon. You know, find the lay of the land." He pointed his finger at her pistol-fashion, grinning at his little joke.

"See how things stand," he added, glancing down at his crotch with a look of mock surprise. "Wouldn't want to walk into a problem and ruin our plans, would we?" His mouth gaped open in a silent laugh. "Don't go getting your hopes up now. Best way to get through all this stress is to go with the flow."

He looked down at Linda, who was lying on her side, hands and feet tied together behind her back. She was glad she did yoga. Maybe her muscles wouldn't cramp. "Not to worry." He patted her on the rump and closed one pale eye with mechanical slowness. "I'll be back." He paused, his face serious. "Remember the way my brother did that 'I'll be back'? Just like old Swartznigger. You remember Jace, right?" He raised his eyebrows in inquiry. "Naw, maybe not." He reached down behind the seat and lifted up a military-issue M1 carbine. The short clip protruded from the forearm. "See ya." He waved casually before shutting the door and disappearing from sight.

Linda's mind churned. Where would Frank be? If he was at home, he might be sitting up in the cupola, looking out over the valley, "woolgathering," as he called it. Then he'd see Miller coming. But it was a weekday, and most likely he was out, gone on some BLM business, or visiting some special place, checking out the campgrounds before opening day.

He hadn't talked much about his job lately. He'd mentioned that Dave Meecham had been particularly tickled that Frank and the BLM had been vindicated, but Frank hadn't seemed so pleased about it. When she had reminded him that Bob Dewey and the Inyo Sheriff's Department treated him with new respect, he'd shrugged, remarking, "A day late and a dollar short." After the call from Roy Miller, he withdrew, pulling into himself, waiting for events to unfold, so she'd waited with him, pushing thoughts of Miller aside, burying herself in work.

But now she had to think about him. Giving up was the first step toward despair and death. She needed to find a way to buy time. The pat on her bottom had been the first sign that Miller noticed her as a woman, that he might be distracted. She had shuddered at his touch, and now she shuddered at the thought of him touching her again. The sound of the driver's door opening made her jump. She rolled back over where she could see.

He shook his head. "All that wiggling around won't help, just a waste of energy. Save it for the sing-along." He chatted away, being affable. "Nobody home at the red caboose. That gives us time to plan our surprise. Sounds pretty good, huh? I bet you give the little brown feller surprises all the time."

Roy pulled the repair van up around behind an outcropping of rock some fifty yards beyond the caboose, where it would be concealed from someone approaching along the dirt road. After untying her ankles, he removed the gag. "Now don't start with the screaming and hollering, or I'll have to gag you again. Besides, who's to hear?" His smile conveyed an obscene intimacy.

"Now we're going to walk on back to that caboose. You know, I thought it was bullshit, living in a caboose, but it looks okay. Think I might give it a try. Don't think Ranger Frank will be needing it much longer." He frowned in thought. "What do you think? Roy's TV Repair. Call the loose caboose."

She looked away.

"Got nothing to say? Good. Saves time. Let's move along now." She walked ahead of him. He carried a red plastic gas can. When they reached the caboose, Linda made a dash for the creek, knowing that it was probably futile, but some chance was better than no chance at all, so she ran. He caught her before she reached the narrowing of the trail through the rocks, clubbing her across the shoulders with his fist.

"Now you've pissed me off, Ms. Reyes." He kicked her in the stomach. "That was dumb." He jerked her to her feet and pushed her ahead of him. She stumbled forward, gasping for air. "Do that again and you won't have any toes to run on." He shoved her from behind. "Understand?"

"Yes, I understand." She seemed to be outside herself again, watching as in a dream, one Linda calmly observing the plight of the other.

He thrust her on the ground. "Don't fucking move." She watched as he unsnapped the bungee cord holding the folding chairs to the rear of the platform.

"Here you go, a place to sit." He gestured politely with an empty hand as a waiter might usher someone to a seat.

He'd placed the chair away from the caboose, where it wouldn't be immediately visible from the dirt track. She felt his sinewy hands tying her ankles to the metal legs. He pulled the cord up and tied her arms down so that she was as one with the light aluminum frame. "Pretty good." He exposed the enamel of his teeth and the red gums. "You look like someone waiting for the man to throw the switch."

He squatted next to her. "So help me out with something here. You think knowing someone is going to die is worse than watching them die? Having time to worry about it?" He watched her face, waiting for it to register. "Well, I can tell you firsthand. Watching gets the nod." He nodded his own head, affirming his observation. "Yup, old Mitch and Shawna got to watch each other go out in a burst of flame. Sharing a final family moment."

"Go to hell, Miller." She glared at him, summoning her strength. "If you're waiting for me to break down, maybe I will, but not because of your sick talk."

He rose, the movement quick and fluid, then stood looking down at her, his face registering curiosity. "More balls than most, I'll say that for you." His face remained solemn. "Just a figure of speech, not being rude." The sandy voice was barely audible.

His pale blue eyes traveled over her body, as if seeing it for the first time, and came to rest on her face.

She met his gaze. "Why're you doing this? What for?"

His mouth hardened. "People like you wouldn't know." He waved his arm in a slow arc. "See all this? Looks pretty, doesn't it, all the plants and animals and nature. Springtime, right? But you know what it really is?"

She shook her head.

"It's eating itself. It feeds, the big stuff on the small stuff, the strong on the weak. Man, it just eats. You remember that fat ass that went all to Jell-O in the bar, the one called himself Art Schopenhauer?"

She nodded, unable to take her eyes away from him.

"The real one, the philosopher, he had it right. The only thing that's real is the 'will,' and the 'will' consumes without thought, just eats. There's God for you"—he waved his arm around—"out there eating. Fuck it, lady. I'm one of the eaters."

He grabbed her hair, jerking her head back, and stuffed a rag in her mouth and then wrapped her mouth tightly with nylon cord. "Can't stand the squawking." He lifted the gas can and poured it on her clothes, being careful not to splash it on her face. "He shouldn't have killed Jace; you know it. Look what a mess he got you in."

She could hear the sandy voice coming from behind her. "Now we'll 'set a spell,' as these hicks like to say, and wait for ol' Francisco, and then we'll see if he can keep his cool. You know, I'm guessing he'll come apart." His words, little bits of distinct sound, disappeared in the wind.

Out of the corner of her eye, Linda saw a raven glide across the sky from the direction of Sage Creek.

•

Frank walked below the cutbank, using it as a shelter from the wind. It always filled him with a sense of wonder, the way the wind would gust about, leaving little pockets of stillness, soft back eddies peeling away from whistling blasts strong enough to topple trees. He could almost visualize it swirling about like the currents in a river.

A pair of ravens followed him from the campground, their hoarse cries for food the only sound besides the rushing of wind and water. They'd seen him toss the rib bones in the back of his truck, and now they considered him a food source. Well, they were going to have a long wait. He planned on having lunch alone.

Frank paused before crossing the creek, his glance drawn to the bright green of the leaves tossing against the deep blue of the sky. One of the ravens winged across the ragged opening in the trees, croaking into the wind. Frank felt suddenly anxious to get home. The ravens had followed the course of his walk, flying ahead, then taking off at his approach and gliding down the streambed to wait for him, claws clasping on the next outcropping or dead snag, their eyes glittering, feathers ruffled in the wind. He watched them sail ahead, hovering in the wind, as he made his way along the creek. Occasionally a gust would blow them downstream. Then they would dip down, slipping through the air to the next perch.

As Frank approached the path to the caboose, the forward bird lifted above the cottonwoods, catching the sun, then folded one wing and dipped down, giving a sharp call of alarm. Its mate circled above, echoing its companion. They came to rest on the boulders that guarded the trail from the pool to the caboose and stalked about in obvious agitation, emitting hoarse cries. Frank stopped and held his breath, his senses heightened by their calls of alarm.

He moved to the narrow path between the rocks and eased forward until he could view the clearing behind the caboose. Linda sat stiffly in one of the cheap folding patio chairs, her back to the trail. Roy Miller sprawled next to her, long legs stretched out in front of him, the M1 carbine resting across his lap. Despite the brown hair pulled into a knot at the back of his head, there was no mistaking Miller's casual menace. The chairs had been placed in such a way that they would be unseen by someone approaching from the dirt track until they were almost at the caboose. If he'd been coming that way, he wouldn't have seen them until it was too late.

Frank watched Roy's head move about in conversation, his words carried away by the wind. He strained to catch what Roy was saying, but he could only make out scattered sound. The sight of the red plastic gas can lying on its side a few feet from Linda flooded his senses with a rush of adrenaline. He wanted to run forward and smash Miller, pummel him with his hands. He breathed deeply, concentrating on regaining rational thought. He estimated the distance at close to two hundred feet. Too far for a sure shot and too far to run without being caught in the open. He needed to be closer. The ground was rough but bare. Rounded pebbles near the stream trailed away into sand and broken bits of rock. His boots would make crunching sounds in the gravel. He leaned against one of the rocks and pulled them off. If he walked carefully, waiting for the wind to cover the sound of his movements, he could get close enough to make sure his first shot would count.

He stood in his stocking feet, feeling the ground and the damp coolness of the gravel coming through his socks. Drawing in his breath, he stepped away from the rocks and moved toward the sitting figures. It felt as if he were moving in a dream, colors vivid and intense, sounds distinct and separate, and the coppery taste of fear in his mouth.

A sudden gust of wind swept leaves and clouds of dust across the clearing, rocking Miller and Linda in their chairs and tumbling the gas container along the ground. Miller turned his head. For a terrible moment, Frank thought Miller was going to go after the gas can, but he watched the can as it skidded across the ground and lodged against the caboose. Instead, he turned his head back toward Linda, the knot of brown hair bobbing in time to words Frank couldn't hear. The wind died away into silence, the leaves still. Frank stood motionless, the sun warm on his back and neck. He forced himself to look past Miller's exposed back at the plastic can so that Miller wouldn't feel his eyes painting patterns of alarm. Frank caught the murmur of his sandy voice, the deliberate rhythm of sounds, but not the words themselves. The treetops stirred again and Frank eased forward. He shifted his weight as a sharp rock dug into the bottom of his foot. The wind raced along the ground, whipping at his trousers. Miller's hand shot up just in time to catch his hat from lifting away. Stay on his head, hat. Frank's lips formed the unspoken words.

A sudden shift in the wind blew back Miller's words as clearly as if he were speaking in Frank's ear. "Don't you hate the way the fucking wind blows stuff around. Pardon the language . . . but blowing sand everywhere . . . trouble with living in the desert. Not a bad place to die, though. Most of the stuff has a head start, right? All that dying goin' on out there, and no one to see it. Makes you stop and think, don't it?" He turned toward Linda, his head almost in profile. "Ol' Frank should be showing up pretty soon, huh?" Miller raised an arm and glanced at his wristwatch. "Sort of a homebody, far as I can tell. Doesn't party much. And here we are to say hello when he comes home." One of the ravens strutted along the roof of the caboose, making a sharp, staccato rattling sound.

Miller glanced over at the bird. "I hate those damn crows." Linda shook her head. Why the hell was she shaking her head? He was still trying to puzzle it out when the trill of his cell phone suffused the stillness. Miller reacted sooner than Frank, immediately throwing himself to one side, then rising to one knee to steady the M1. Frank had less to do; the .45 was already in his hand. His shot caught Miller high on the right side of his chest, tossing him backward with the impact, the carbine still clutched in one hand.

The phone trilled again, insistent and absurd.

Frank tried to step forward, but his left leg collapsed. He was conscious of the warmth of his own blood running down his leg, soaking into his sock. He watched as Miller managed to raise himself on one arm. The empty face turned away as Miller brought the carbine around in a slow arc, bringing it to bear on Linda. Frank fired from the ground, raised up on his left elbow. His second shot flipped Miller sideways onto his back. He waited, the .45 pointed at Miller's head.

A dull ache throbbed in the wounded leg. Very soon, it would become worse. He pulled the uninjured right leg up and managed to stand long enough to hop over the ground to where Miller lay, arms flung up, as if in greeting. He tried to kneel and lost his balance, falling across Miller's body. The acrid smell of blood and sweat filled his nostrils. He pressed the .45 into Miller's neck with one hand and patted him down with the other, twisting his torso from side to side so he could check the front pockets. He found a 9-mm Baretta in the right-hand front pocket and flung it over his shoulder. Then he grasped the M1 by the sling and sent it to join the Baretta. Miller gave a soft groan. Frank looked at the .45 pressed against Roy Miller's neck. He felt his hand tighten on the grip disabling the automatic safely. Just a small squeeze and the evil would be eradicated, gone. He could make up for his mistake. It would be so simple. He felt as if he were tumbling into a void. Linda's muffled cries seemed to be coming from a far-off place, from down in the dark mine shaft where Hickey lay.

He reached up and tore the sunglasses away from Miller's bleached face, exposing the pink-rimmed paleness. "Why Mitch and

Shawna? The couple in the motor home, the Robertsons, why them?"
Miller's pale eyes crinkled with the ghost of a smile. Frank could
barely hear his voice, rustling softly, like dead leaves blowing in the
wind. "It's a puzzle, isn't it?" The pale blue eyes dimmed, flat as plastic
buttons. Stretched out in death, Miller's lanky body seemed diminished, shorn of menace, the animus of evil dissipated in the wind.

Frank turned away from the empty face, dragging himself toward Linda. He needed to get the gag out of her mouth. He hated it,
the idea of the gag, stopping her breath. He pulled himself high
enough to remove the gag and untied her arms. "Why were you
shaking your head?"

She rubbed at her face where the cords had left red welts. Her
mouth creased into a crooked grin. "They're ravens, not crows. The
dumb bastard."

"Give Meecham a call, okay?" He fumbled in his pocket for
the cell phone. Just before he passed out, he remembered saying
something about the damned thing finally being useful.

# 34

•

"I'm not sure this is such a good idea." Frank watched Eddie's old Ford come to a sliding stop behind Jan's Gremlin, a dust cloud wafting ahead in the early-summer heat of late afternoon.

"Sure it is." Linda squeezed Frank's hand.

He shook his head in self-reproach, frowning at the small figure emerging from the truck.

"Come on, Frank. He wants to make it up to you. How else is he going to come even, look you in the eye and feel like an *hombre*?"

How does she know the way men think? he wondered. Being raised mostly by her dad and her adopted uncles had seeped into her thinking. She knew. He wished he knew more about women, but maybe not. He liked their mystery.

Jimmy Tecopa's shiny new Cherokee slipped past Eddie's truck and came to a stop well away from the other cars. He popped out of the Cherokee and ran around to open the passenger door for Susan Funmaker.

"Hey, Frank." Eddie waved up to where Frank and Linda sat at the end of the caboose, Frank with his bottom cradled in soft pillows carefully placed on a folding chair. "Ms. Reyes," he offered in tones unusually subdued for Eddie.

"Just Linda will do fine." She rose and came down the narrow steps and gave Eddie a hug. "We're glad you could come." He stood straight as a pole, his eyes wandering about, as if searching for help.

Frank laughed. "She'll let go in a minute. Just bear up, Redhawk." Eddie exposed his bad teeth in genuine relief.

Jimmy and Susan came up to stand next to them. "You can hug me anytime." Jimmy's hundred-watt smile flashed in the waning afternoon sunlight.

"You don't need a hug, but if it's okay with Susan, I'm hugging you, too. This is a good time for hugging." She threw her arms around Jimmy's neck and gave him a light kiss on the cheek. "I admire your taste in women, too," she whispered close to his ear.

Jan came out on the platform. "So here's the rest of the gang."

Frank rose to his feet, listing slightly to his right. "Jan, you already know Jimmy. This is Susan Funmaker, and this is Eddie Laguna."

Jan's mouth opened and then closed. "Eddie Laguna. Aren't you the tribal spokesman for the Nopah Shoshone?"

Eddie beamed. "That's right. How come you know that?"

"Jan's an anthropology instructor at Arroyo Seco College, Eddie. She knows lots of stuff about our people." Jimmy explained.

"Frank's told me many good things about you, Susan, and your mother, about growing up in the valley." She turned to Eddie. "Maybe one day you'd both come and speak to one of my classes, and perhaps Mr. Laguna could come and speak about some of the problems Native Americans are still experiencing. Would that be possible?"

Eddie shuffled his feet back and forth, grinning with pleasure. "Sure, just name the time, ma'am."

Frank thought Eddie would give some answers that Jan hadn't counted on. "Why don't you folks go on into the yard. Linda and I will be right there."

The aging International crew-cab truck belonging to Jack Collins came bounding down the dirt road and pulled up near the end of the caboose. Bill Jerome unfolded himself from the front seat and Ben Shaw lurched out from the back, cursing the cramped quarters.

"If you were trying to cripple me up back there, Jack, you succeeded. You aim for the bumps, or is it just that you're an incompetent?"

Jack waved at the growing group. "Howdy folks, the Joshua

Tree Athletic Club West is upon you." He turned back to his companions. "Come on, let's get the bar set up."

They untied a couple of folding sawhorses and two two-by-twelves. "Over here by the table okay?"

Linda preceded Frank down the steps of the caboose and waited as Frank carefully placed his feet, taking care not to jar his weight onto his injured left leg. She handed him a stout stick, and he made his way to the end of the near bench and sat carefully, leaning on his right buttock.

"How about the pillows?"

Frank winced. "Yeah, okay, maybe I better sit on the chair."

The shot from Miller's carbine had entered Frank's leg about six inches above the knee, traveled up the femur, and exited out his left gluteus maximus. No major arteries cut, minimum nerve damage, but a lot of muscle tissue had been damaged. His doctor kept telling him that he was a lucky man. He'd suffered no more than what was referred to as a "flesh wound" in the movies, a rare occurrence in the real world of gunshot wounds. In any Western, he'd've just tied a bandanna around his leg and ridden into the sunset. Real life was different. Just sitting upright was damned uncomfortable and something he'd been able to do for only a few hours at a time. The doctor had told him it would be a long time before the tenderness disappeared.

Other than short visits from friends, this was the first time he and Linda had had company since the shooting. His personal time had been taken up by BLM officials, Sheriff's Department investigators, county officials, and officials and investigators from various law-enforcement agencies around the state. The *San Bernardino Mercury* had dubbed the departed trio of thugs the "Miller Gang," lending a sort of ersatz glamour to their activities, and now lots of unsolved crimes were being laid to rest with Roy Miller's death. Frank pondered on the neat conveniences of death. Dead men didn't talk, but they seemed to be vulnerable to postmortem confession, sort of like the criminals' Congressional Medal, awarded posthumously.

He glanced over at the place on the ground where Miller's blood had drained the life from his body. Linda was right about one thing: He couldn't seem to go out in his yard without thinking about it, without the image of Miller lying on his back, the light going out of the pale eyes and the black exultation that had gripped his heart at their dimming.

●

Jimmy lifted a large Dutch oven from the fire and carefully removed the lid. The smell of tamale pie wafted into the evening air.

Linda and Jimmy had rented a large propane two-burner cooker, which Susan was busy using to cook fry bread. She gripped a huge blackened frying pan full of hot lard, into which she dropped bread dough. Tiny globules of crackling fat spat up and winked into flame. She flipped the dough with tongs, let it bubble for a few minutes, and lifted it out to drain in a large wire basket before setting it inside a stainless-steel pot.

The popping of beer tops came with greater frequency as the boys warmed to their task, handing out cold bottles of Mojave Red and Sierra Nevada from a galvanized tub filled with ice. Frank turned his head at the sound of another vehicle crunching its way up the dirt road.

"You didn't say anything about Dave Meecham coming."

"He wanted to come. He's been worried about you."

Jesus, the whole damned valley seemed to be worried about him. He gave Linda a dark look.

"Nothing I said. Frank, you don't say two words to people. Your butt's healing, but the rest of you isn't doing too well."

He glared at her and turned away.

Meecham came across the yard, nodding to Jimmy. "Dr. Rockford. How're things at the college?"

"About like they are at the BLM—here a problem, there a win." She came around from behind the table, where she was helping to set things up, and shook his hand. Meecham ambled over to Frank, who was sitting canted to one side on a patio chair. He looked down at his fellow ranger, a slight smile on his face. "How's it going, podner?"

"Good, Dave. I guess you could say I got the ass, but other than that, fine." He forced a crooked grin. "I don't know whether you know everyone. That's Eddie Laguna over there by the ice chest with Jimmy."

"We've met couple of times."

"Oh yeah, that's right, the inquiry."

Meecham stood looking around, not quite knowing what to do next.

"Sit down, Dave. We're about to eat some good food." Frank gestured with his hand toward the table, where Linda and Jan were making preparations.

"Thanks, Frank. You sure everyone's going to be comfortable with me here?"

"It's my place, Dave. Anyhow, I'm glad you're here. I'm not much into this healing-ceremony stuff." Frank lowered his voice. "Eddie's a good guy, means well, but hell, dancing and singing ain't going to make my butt feel better."

Meecham grinned. "You know, Frank, I was thinking about the nature of your wound. It looks like you were right all along."

Frank raised his eyebrows. "Yeah? How do you mean?"

"Well hell, now you have a distinctive butt print, looks like a whole new method of criminal identification is in the making."

"Thanks, Dave, thanks a lot." A rueful smile played across his face. "Like I said, it's the way to identify the real assholes."

"What's Laguna going to do?"

"After we eat, he's going to perform a healing ceremony. He says that Miller's spirit is still hanging around because he died here." Frank gestured to the place where Miller had died. "He thinks Miller's still trying to get me, give me ghost sickness."

"Can't do it very easily. His remains, as they say, are in a county plot with an aluminum number tag. I haven't seen those guys walking around much."

Frank grinned. "Naw, having a number is a disadvantage." He thrust his arms in front of him in the traditional zombie pose. "Beware Inyo County four three eight seven. Doesn't sound very scary." He laughed a bit too loudly. He was suddenly glad he didn't know Miller's plot number.

"Anyhow, stick around, Dave," he said. "Another rational mind is needed. They all seem to be into it one way or another. Linda says it can't hurt. Jan says cultural anthropologists have learned to be less skeptical about the 'efficacy of curing rituals.' That's the way she puts it. Jimmy and Susan don't comment, just give knowing looks. And hell, Eddie's a full-fledged nut. So stick around. It should be interesting. Who knows, maybe I'll throw down my stick and start dancing."

Linda came up and gave Meecham her hand. "Welcome, Dave. And by the way, Eddie's not trying to heal Frank's leg, just the butt hook that it's attached to."

Frank shrugged. "Guess my voice carried a bit too far," but inside he felt ashamed.

After a few beers, Eddie shed his earlier shyness like an old coat, at least when it came to the eating and drinking part. Frank watched as he squatted near the empty Dutch oven, wiping out the last of the tamale pie with the remaining piece of fry bread. It was a good thing they had used the twelve-quart oven. How could such a skinny little guy eat so much food? On the other hand, real food must have tasted pretty good to a person who lived on bologna sandwiches, Vienna sausages, and soda crackers. He smiled to himself. He was feeling better than he had in a long time. The talk, even if he wasn't taking much part in it, warmed him like an open fire.

For a while, the dull ache from his leg and buttock receded from his consciousness. Linda had been right about having friends. He just wished that he wasn't at the center of this healing ceremony. He wondered what Eddie had in mind for him. When he thought about it, he wanted to disappear into the caboose and watch from the cupola. That would be just fine.

He turned his head at the sound of a vehicle door slamming, and pretty soon Eddie emerged into the ring of lantern light coming from the kerosene lamps placed on the table and hanging nearby from Coleman sky hooks. Frank noticed that Eddie had dressed up in moccasins, clean jeans, and a faded denim shirt pressed for the occasion.

"Uh, Frank, can I use your place to get ready?"

"Sure Eddie, go on in.

"Thanks, Frank." Eddie nodded. The shadows from the fire and the lanterns made his face seem chiseled and grave. He headed for the caboose, calling over his shoulder, "Jimmy, throw some wood on the fire, okay? No lamplight." He disappeared into the caboose.

Giving Jimmy Tecopa orders? Frank couldn't believe it. But Jimmy rose obediently from the table and began throwing wood on the fire. Then he went around and cut all the lamps but the one on the table. The smell of burning juniper and piñons perfumed the evening air. The laughing and conversation died away and people murmured in lowered voices, awaiting Eddie's entrance. Frank sat outside the ring of firelight, his chair in the shadows.

Eddie emerged from the caboose wearing only jeans and moccasins. Streaks of dark paint that suggested feathers covered his torso and arms. His face was covered in black paint, with a white stripe running down the middle, tracing the contour of his nose to its base. He wore a cloth headband decorated with black feathers. The feathers hung loosely about his ears and the back of his head. A line of smaller feathers stretched in a crest from the front of the headdress to the back. They waved back and forth in unison as he walked. Everyone waited in hushed expectation, watching the slight figure made large by the firelight.

Eddie bent down to examine the ground in front of the fire. "Is this the place?" His face was shadowed, his eyes directed on Frank.

"Yeah, that's where he fell."

Eddie squatted closer to the ground. Grasping a handful of dirt, he brought it near his face, sniffing carefully. Then he let the dirt slip from his hand. He produced a small rattle from his front pocket and shook it at the ground, the dry sound of the rattle and the crackle of the fire filling the sudden silence. He rose and backed away, his body cupped inward, arms thrust forward.

Then he turned away from the place where Roy Miller had died and began to circle the spot slowly. His feet moved in a rhythmic step, toe-heel, toe-heel, one-two, one-two. He stretched his arms upward, the feathers on his head keeping time with his movements, the sound of the soft rattle distinct in the stillness. In the flickering light, his sharp features and the white streak down his nose gave him the appearance of a bird, a hawk or a raven. Frank felt a momentary thrill at the transformation, from Eddie to Redhawk, con man to medicine man. Maybe they were the same.

There was only the crackle of the fire and the dry voice of the rattle. Eddie began a soft chant, his voice rising up in measured tones. Frank didn't understand the words, but he knew they must be Shoshone. The soft guttural sounds flew into the night. And then he could understand the words, for Eddie had shifted seamlessly into English.

> *I call on my brother the coyote.*
> *My brother coyote who sees in the night, come eat of this.*
> *My mother is sick with this on her skin.*
> *My brother must come.*

Eddie reached down to the ground and flung handfuls of dirt into air. He leaped upward into the night, his figure casting moving shadows across the ground, the pace of his dancing matched in the flames of the fire. The rattle's voice filled the night sky with its sandy sound, and Frank's stomach knotted with dread. He knew that voice and it filled his ears. Eddie's voice rang into the night.

> *Bring the black sky watchers.*
> *They will eat of this flesh.*
> *It will not harm them.*

Eddie danced forward, his thin arms and body silhouetted against the fire. Frank watched as he approached. It was as if one of the dancing stick figures on the rocks had leaped into life and come for him.

"Come, my brother." Eddie reached down and took Frank's hands, pulling him to his feet. "We will finish driving away this bad thing." Frank hobbled with Eddie into the firelight. Eddie raised his arms and face to the night sky and intoned,

> *Sky and earth last forever.*
> *Men must die.*

*Hot winds bring evil.*
*All things change and die.*

Eddie grasped Frank's hand. "Raise your hands," he said, his voice barely audible. "Say these words with me."
Eddie sang out.

*My song reaches the sky,*

Frank repeated, hearing the words issuing from his mouth.

*My song reaches the sky,*

Eddie's voice lifted into the night.

*I shall vanish and be no more.*
*The land over which I wander shall remain.*
*And change not.*

Frank echoed.

*And change not.*

His voice seemed not to be his, and yet it was, strange and familiar to him as the desert itself, and he was standing there with this man, being and watching, a part of it all. They stood in the firelight, tiny sparks lifting into the night sky. Letting out a long breath, Eddie dropped his arms to his sides.
Frank leaned close to Eddie. "Are we finished?"
"Just one thing left." He whispered in Frank's ear, "Turn your back to them."
"Why? What the hell are you doing?" Eddie was fumbling with his pants.
"We're going to wash away this evil from your land." Eddie was already urinating on the spot where Miller's body had fallen.
"Jesus, Eddie, there are women here."

"That's why I told you to turn your back."

"Let me help out." Jimmy stood next to Eddie, his stream arcing into the night.

Dave Meecham came to stand next to Frank. "Always glad to lend a hand—so to speak."

Frank was suddenly aware of the fullness of his bladder. He shook his head, looking down at the streams of urine making a muddy puddle in the place where Miller had lain, and made it a foursome. Little rivulets of urine trickled toward the fire, tendrils of steam rising into the night air. Eddie grinned and began kicking dirt over the growing pond.

Jan's voice rose over the cluster of males. "Communal pissing seems to be a universal trait among the more unevolved male, *Cervesacum northamericus*. Never could understand it." Jimmy started laughing, and the laughter ignited like dry grass in the wind. Frank had to hobble back to his chair to keep from falling. Their voices sounded like coyotes howling in the night.

●

That evening, Linda and Frank sat with the chairs pulled up near the last of the glowing coals, a soft red in the pool of darkness at their feet. The moon slipped behind the mountains, casting the jagged escarpment of the Sierras into sharp relief. The stars brightened in the dimming of the moon's light. Linda's hair played about her forehead in the gentle breeze, her skin ivory pale in the starlight.

"It was okay, wasn't it?" She squeezed Frank's arm.

"It was more than okay; it was good."

"Well, see there. Eddie's a healer."

"My butt still aches."

"Sure, but when you look at that place on the ground, what're you going to think about?

Frank gave a low laugh. "Eddie says we should plant a fruit tree." He turned to Linda. "Why not? But it'd have to be an apple tree. I want to try fresh apple pie in the Dutch oven."

# EPILOGUE

●

Telescope Peak was still capped in gleaming white and there were springs running almost to the valley floor. The little meadow in Surprise Canyon flourished. Near the small stream that fed the meadow, the grass was still green, and flowers thrust up hopeful blossoms late into the summer.

"Good for the sheep. They'll be fat for the winter." Frank surveyed the slopes for any sign, but he and Linda were alone. Tiny blue butterflies were fluttering above the grasses that stretched away from the rivulet of clear water that brought life to the meadow. The hike up the canyon had been tough. He was out of shape, but not as much as he had anticipated. And his leg had held up—no weakness, no shooting pain. Of course, there hadn't been any leaping across the table rocks or scrambling about on the talus slopes. He and Linda had taken the longer, less strenuous trail that skirted the tumble of boulders guarding the canyon mouth. Nevertheless, he felt almost a hundred percent recovered, except that now and then, if he sat wrong, a sharp pain knifed through his buttock like an electric shock. The walking part was actually easier than sitting on hard surfaces.

"Let's see if we can watch by the waterfall." Linda pulled on his arm.

He didn't want to return to the rock blind just yet, not for a while. "We'll have to sit still. No wiggling around. That's tough for women."

She punched his arm. "Sure, sure, Mr. Macho. I don't think I'd go there if I were you. You're going to have to spend less time around cops and more time around reporters if you want to learn something about being patient."

"I like spending time around reporters." He cupped her face in his hands. "I like it very much."

"Come on." She headed across the canyon, away from the spring, the swish of her feet in the dry grass sending locusts buzzing into the air and launching clouds of tiny gnats. "Let's get there before the sheep."

Frank followed, the smell of the dry grass sharp in his nostrils. Linda's T-shirt clung to her back and against her spine, her soft hair damp against her neck.

"If we sit back here against the rock, the fall should give us cover." Frank knelt and explored the smooth sand for hidden rocks. If he was going to sit there practically motionless, he didn't want to be in pain.

After a few minutes, they felt almost cold despite waves of heat shimmering off the meadow. The damp from the sand and the clouds of spray that blew in their direction from time to time made them shiver. Occasional rainbows appeared as the mist lifted into the sunlight and scattered in the wind. They waited, watching puffy white clouds trail across the sky. Frank found himself dozing, his head slipping forward in easy drowsiness.

"It's been more than an hour. I'm getting hungry. Want a sandwich?" Linda nudged him with her elbow.

Frank frowned. "Have patience, Lois Lane, or you'll miss the story."

"Well, I'm hungry anyhow." She rummaged carefully in her pack and produced a chicken sandwich, layered with Swab's High Sierra Chileno Indian-style peppers and fresh tomatoes from the vegetable garden they had planted in Frank's yard. Now he had a yard, with a fence around just the garden part. He wasn't so sure about that, but he liked the fresh tomatoes and zucchini and melons.

"Shussh!" Frank put his finger to his lips and pointed with the other hand.

An old ewe made her way down the talus slope, leading a group of four in single file behind her. Rocks came spilling ahead of them, tumbling down the steep canyon walls, starting small avalanches of rocky debris. The new lambs raced across the face of the slope, dislodging rocks at each bound.

Linda gripped his arm. "It's a wonder they don't fall."

"Sometimes they do."

The lambs seemed to be suspended in air, bounding with effortless joy as the earth slipped from under their feet.

And on this day, none of them fell.